WORLD OF WARCRAFT
SYLVANAS

SYLVANAS

CHRISTIE GOLDEN

NEW YORK

Published in the United States by Del Rey, an imprint of Random House, a division of Penguin Random House LLC, New York.

DEL REY and the CIRCLE colophon are registered trademarks of Penguin Random House LLC.

Hardback ISBN 978-0-399-59418-2
Ebook ISBN 978-0-399-59419-9

Printed in the United States of America on acid-free paper

randomhousebooks.com

2 4 6 8 9 7 5 3 1

ScoutAutomatedPrintCode

First Edition

Book design by Jo Anne Metsch

This is, at its heart, a book about family,

be it our first family, or found ones.

I therefore dedicate it to my own:

My late father, James R. Golden, and

my mother, Elizabeth C. Golden,

and to my sister and brother,

Lizann and James R. Golden Jr. ("Chip" to us).

I love you all.

WORLD OF WARCRAFT
SYLVANAS

PROLOGUE

S ylvanas Windrunner stood at the top of the steps for a moment. She was not sure if the young king, pacing within the runic circle below, would become future prey—or future partner. It was all up to him . . . and her.

You will not succeed, the young lion had once said defiantly as he knelt before her. It was a ludicrous statement. Anduin Wrynn was held fast by chains woven of dark magic. He had received the worst pain the Mawsworn were capable of bestowing, yet had not broken—even managing to summon the Light in this place of cold, shattered misery. Through everything he had endured, Anduin retained a desire to help and heal, even if it meant his own suffering. And that display had intrigued the Jailer, he who ruled this realm of torment; he with whom Sylvanas had allied.

The Jailer wanted to use this shiny new weapon immediately. But something had stirred within the Banshee Queen. Something she couldn't quite explain. Was it hubris that compelled this desire, to see her greatest enemy swayed to her side?

You've seen what he can do when he believes in the cause.

Their first encounter had not gone well. She hoped this one would yield *better results. The Jailer had granted her the "measure of patience," she requested, but he would not wait forever.*

Anduin heard her steps and ceased pacing. He turned to face her, his blue eyes regarding her emotionless face, then he dropped his gaze to the tray she carried.

"I find myself wondering what that is, and where you obtained it."

"Do you think you're the only mortal in the Shadowlands?"

His eyes widened slightly. "So. My friends are still here. You're slipping, Sylvanas."

Sylvanas continued down the stairs. "Not at all. I told you before. No more secrets, no more lies."

"I do try to think the best of people. But I lost hope in you even before the war."

That surprised her, but she did not show it. "This is not a place for hope, Little Lion. But it is a place for reason. Overly gentle and trusting you may be, but I do not think you a fool."

"I see. You're going to attempt to convince me that I should help the Jailer destroy the cycle of life and death." He laughed softly, shaking his head. "No. I am certainly not the fool here."

Sylvanas had reached the invisible border of Anduin's prison. She could enter and exit as she wished, and the tray of food and water passed easily through the barrier.

She knew he had not had water for a day; had been denied food even longer. Yet Anduin simply glanced at the food, then back at her with narrowed eyes.

Sylvanas pushed down her irritation and bit back a sharp retort. Then, to his visible surprise, she sat on the stone floor and cocked an eyebrow at him. "Eat. I do not need to resort to poison. Any harm I wished to do, you would not be able to prevent."

"No."

So this was how it was to be. It was fine with her. He was quite literally a captive audience, and she had come to say much.

"I told you before, we wish you to join us willingly. I know you have empathy and compassion. That has been a weakness for you—but also a strength. So I will tell you how it was that I came to be the Jailer's part-

ner . . . and why I think you should be, too. I will share with you things I have shared with no one before." It cost her nothing; Anduin would serve, or he would be used. Either way, any words spoken within these dark halls would never be shared with another mortal soul. Not when her victory was so close at hand.

Anduin cocked his head and looked at her searchingly.

As if mocking her he sat, somehow graceful, if clanking, in his armor. He reached for the water, toasted her, and drank.

"Go on then, Sylvanas Windrunner. Tell me these truths you have never shared. It would seem I have nothing but time."

PART
I

With love, and courage.

—VERATH WINDRUNNER

CHAPTER ONE

"Let me see, let me see!" Vereesa begged. The balcony walls, white and curving as the throat of a swan, were too tall for her to peer over, and Sylvanas sighed. She cast a final longing look at the crowd milling below, then darted back into their chambers for a stool. As Vereesa happily clambered atop it, Sylvanas returned her attention to the scene.

Their parents did host some gatherings—Father said it was "prudent" to do so from time to time—but they were usually small affairs. While Lord Verath Windrunner was one of King Anasterian's most trusted advisers and his wife, Lireesa, was the ranger-general of Silvermoon, lesser nobles like the ostentatious Lord Saltheril threw much more lavish celebrations. But Lireesa had little patience with pretense and politics, and their quietly brilliant father's idea of a fine evening was a glass of wine, a good book, and candles to read by.

But today, everything was different. Some of those gathered at the base of the spire were nobility like the Windrunners. Others would have once been considered commoners, but their athleticism, agility, and almost uncanny skills in marksmanship and tracking had elevated them to another sort of nobility. Certainly Sylvanas and her sisters had been raised with respect for and almost awe of the Farstriders, and thus far Sylvanas had seen nothing to disabuse her of the notion that they were worthier of respect than someone who'd simply been born with a title.

She had seen many of the Farstriders already for one reason or another, but they had usually come at the ranger-general's request and interacted little with the rest of the family. Sylvanas was most familiar with Lor'themar Theron. Perhaps because of his white hair, he was one of the few elves who looked older than they were, and he bore himself with the same quiet, elegant dignity that Sylvanas saw in her father. Another Sylvanas had met was a relative newcomer, Halduron Brightwing. He had a cheerful grin and unruly dark blond hair, and he always greeted her and Vereesa if they were present. Like Halduron, the petite Jirri was also a relative newcomer, and clearly quite young if her obvious excitement and wonder at the spire was any indication. The blue-black color of Ranger Vor'athil's hair made him stand out in a sea that was overwhelmingly gold and silver. Beyond the crowd, Lieutenant Helios spoke quietly to Rangers Lethvalin and Salissa while Ranger Tomathren waited, impatiently, for Helios's attention.

Talthressar, Rellian, Auric Sunchaser, Alleria's friend Verana—so many of them. Sylvanas's heart was racing; she was so excited for what was to transpire that she might as well be the one undergoing the test, not her big sister, Alleria, who stood beside her mother in silence.

Ordinarily, the resemblance between mother and eldest daughter was uncanny. They had the same lean frame, though Alleria was still somewhat gawky on coltish long legs; hair that flowed like melted gold down their backs; the same curve of the mouth when they smiled. But now Lireesa's belly was round and full, the child growing within due to make its happy appearance sometime in the next few weeks. In this moment, neither woman smiled. What was about to happen was far too serious.

Sylvanas watched Lireesa turn to Alleria and nod. As the two stepped forward, the Farstriders spread out into a circle, with mother and daughter in the center.

The ranger-general's voice was strong and clear, used to uttering commands in the heat of battle and to having them be obeyed. It carried easily as she addressed the elite unit of the finest rangers in the entire kingdom.

"When I was a young woman, my mother, Alleria, trained me, the eldest child, to become ranger-general, as her mother had before her. Now my daughter, whom I have named after she who bore me, wishes to prove her worthiness and begin formal training. So that all may know that both Alleria and I understand the duty and importance of the position of ranger-general, I have set her a challenge."

Lireesa turned to her daughter. There was no softening of the older woman's mien as she spoke.

"Alleria Windrunner. Are you willing to do what is necessary to lead the Farstriders in times of both peace and war?"

"I am." Alleria's voice, unusually deep for one so young, betrayed no emotion.

"Then this is your challenge. Listen well. A springpaw lynx has been identified and tagged as your target. Its known territory ranges from Goldenmist Village to Farstrider Enclave. You must find it, slay it with a single arrow, field-dress it, and bring the pelt to me before the last ray of light fades. If you fail any of these charges, you fail the test."

The ranger-general presented a single arrow to Alleria. "Here is your arrow. May it fly true."

It was one of Lireesa's own: uniquely fletched in the colors of green, representing the Farstriders, gold, one of the Windrunner colors, and a natural-hued gold-and-brown feather obtained in one of Lireesa's legendary battles. Alleria hesitated just an instant before accepting it.

Most wouldn't have noticed it. But Sylvanas knew her big sister well and frowned slightly. Alleria was a quietly confident young woman, a superlative shot, and an untiring tracker when need be. This should be easy. Springpaws were dangerous to the inexperienced, yes, but all the Windrunner daughters had begun training the instant they were strong enough to pull back the string on a child's bow.

So why was Alleria worried? Perhaps it was simple nervousness. This wasn't an ordinary hunt. To fail before not just the ranger-general but the entire unit of Farstriders would be humiliating.

Alleria placed the arrow in her empty quiver. Sylvanas thought it looked lonely, with none of its fellows surrounding it.

Now Lireesa offered Alleria a knife. It was beautiful; its blade, broad and sharp, as long as Alleria's hand. The hilt was leather wrapped with golden threads.

"This is your skinning knife," Lireesa said. "Use it *only* for its task. Do not use it to attack your quarry. I will examine the pelt afterward, and I will know if you do."

Alleria nodded, accepting the knife and slipping it into its sheath. Finally, Lireesa placed a small sack in her daughter's hands.

"Water, bread, and dried meat," she said. "Enough for a single meal. If you grow hungry, you are permitted to gather food."

Alleria fastened the pouch securely to her belt.

A small, warm hand, slightly sticky with melon juice, slipped into Sylvanas's. Still not eye-to-eye with her sister even on a stool, Vereesa asked with a furrowed brow, "Is Lady Sun going to be all right?"

"Of course," Sylvanas replied, squeezing her hand. "Alleria is going to be just fine. It's only a springpaw. I bet even you could bring down one of those."

Her eyes lit up. "You think so?"

"Well . . . maybe not right this minute, but very soon."

Beaming, Vereesa returned her attention to the crowd below them. Lireesa placed her hands on her eldest daughter's shoulders, though the gesture was not affectionate, but firm.

"If you succeed, we will begin the training."

Alleria squared her shoulders. "Springpaw, I name you prey." It was a formal phrase, the Farstrider equivalent of a vow.

Lireesa stepped back and brought a fisted hand to her heart in the Farstrider salute. Immediately, all the others did so as well, with such perfect coordination that Sylvanas heard but one single thump as hands met chests. Alleria flipped the hood over the shining gold of her hair, turned to the forest, and strode forward. The circle of hunters opened to release her, and there was silence until her slender form was swallowed by the trees.

Vereesa leaped from the stool toward Sylvanas with perfect trust that her sister would catch her. Sylvanas did so, hugging her tight and then setting her down gently while mussing her soft, silvery hair.

A thought crossed the older girl's mind, and she could not hide a mischievous smile. "Come, let us talk to the Farstriders while we wait for Alleria."

They descended the ramp as fast as Vereesa's little legs could manage, Sylvanas still holding her hand. The perfect circle of Farstriders had now dissolved into smaller clusters of individuals. Some were partaking of the fare arranged on small tables, others talking among themselves. Verath had been standing beneath the balcony, keeping courteously out of the way while watching his daughter's ceremony. Now he moved forward, hands outstretched to claim his wife's. He squeezed them reassuringly. Lireesa squeezed back, then let out a sigh and released them. Sylvanas had observed that it was only when she was with her husband that the ranger-general allowed herself to relax.

Vereesa scurried over to their parents, and Verath bent to scoop her up. Sylvanas, though, was far more interested in the Farstriders than her family. She had left her bow at the base of the ramp. Now she picked it up, slung it over her shoulder with feigned nonchalance, and headed straight for Halduron, Lor'themar, and Jirri. They turned at her approach.

"Lady Sylvanas," Lor'themar said, and inclined his head. His brows rose in impressed surprise. "You have traded bows since the last time I saw you—and traded quite well."

It was true. The last time Lor'themar had come to the spire, Sylvanas was still training with a child's bow. She had been presented this one on her most recent birthday and learned that Lireesa had arranged for one of the famed bowyers of Quel'Thalas to craft it. It had been carved from dark wood, polished till it gleamed, and inlaid with swirls of gold that spelled out her name.

"It is beautiful, yes," she said, trying to sound casual. "But what's more important is that the draw is smooth as silk and the valley nice and comfortable. Care to see me shoot?"

"Not at the moment, no," Lor'themar said. "I am sure you're quite good. You know, it is said your mother showed promise from a young age as well. Many here were present at the Battle of Seven Arrows, and they still speak with wonder at her skill on that day." It wasn't quite hero worship in his eyes; Lor'themar was much too grounded, but he regarded Lireesa with the deepest respect for a moment, then turned back to Sylvanas. "You have her steady hand," he said, smiling slightly, "and I imagine you'll be just as fine an archer."

The Battle of Seven Arrows was a wonderful story, all the better for being true, but Sylvanas had heard it brought up so often it was all but meaningless to her now.

"Well," she replied, hiding her disappointment, "I bet you will be telling stories about *me* when I join the Farstriders."

Lor'themar inclined his head courteously, but Halduron smothered a smile. "That seems a way off."

"Not that far," Sylvanas shot back. "You're hardly ancient."

Vor'athil tried to cover his smirk. "She has you there," Lor'themar said. "Sylvanas, we are all waiting for Alleria right now. No one wants to leave until she returns."

Why not? Sylvanas wondered. Alleria had a lengthy list of tasks to accomplish that would surely take several hours—track the animal, dispatch it with an arrow, skin it, and return. Nevertheless, she had seen her father's diplomacy in action enough to know when not to press a point. Besides, if Lor'themar was correct, none of the Farstriders would be leaving anytime soon—which meant she could talk to all of them.

They were the kingdom's main military force; few citizens were more respected than they. She wished that she could at least see *them* shooting, but she would likely learn a great deal just by talking and listening to them.

The hours passed. By the time the midday meal was served, Sylvanas had spoken with every single one of her heroes. She was now hungry and growing bored with the whole thing. Why did Alleria's trial have to be so lengthy?

Lireesa was now seated, rubbing her enormous belly absently as she gazed where Alleria had gone. Sylvanas approached her father, who was sitting on the grass with Vereesa's head in his lap. He put a finger to his lips and Sylvanas nodded. Vereesa, she knew, had been up all night, refusing to sleep out of sheer excitement. Sylvanas, too, had not slept though she was less obvious about it. She pushed away any drowsiness, and chewed on a slice of bread and cheese as she sank down next to Verath.

"How long do you think this will go on?" Sylvanas whispered.

"Your mother was generous with her requirements," Verath said. "Alleria will need the whole day." His gaze, like his wife's, was where Alleria had last been seen.

Sylvanas made a face. "So, what am I supposed to do?"

"Wait," he said, simply. "Or whatever else you wish, my dear. You are not a Farstrider, you may come and go as you please."

"I just might, then," Sylvanas replied. She followed her father's gaze. "You . . . you *do* think Alleria will succeed?"

"She excels at all she has been asked to do," Verath said.

"That's not an answer."

"No, it is not," her father said.

"I like you better as a father than a diplomat," Sylvanas said. She had learned long ago there was no point in pressing him when he "put on his adviser robes," as Alleria called it.

"It is fortunate for you that I am both," he replied with a grin and a wink. This was true—many times Sylvanas had seen him smoothly interject himself into conversations between Lireesa and others when things began to grow heated. Because she knew she wouldn't get anything more from him, Sylvanas grunted in exasperation and rose, polishing off the light meal and reaching for a delicate spun-glass chalice of fruit nectar to wash it down.

She went to the family armory and grabbed a quiver and a hand-ful of arrows. She was itching to move, to jump from bough to bough of the beautiful golden-leafed, white-barked trees; to test her own skill at moving silently and shooting cleanly while her sister was doing the same.

Sylvanas made certain her departure wasn't noticed, and once she was out of sight of the gathered Farstriders, she veered back toward the direction Alleria had been heading. Something was going on, and Sylvanas wanted to know what. She'd felt the tension in the group, tamped down but present. Lor'themar's words were curious, and her father's evasiveness had only increased her suspicions. Even Lireesa seemed anxious, and that was highly unusual.

Sylvanas, just like her sister, had no idea which specific springpaw had been selected as Alleria's quarry. How would Alleria go about finding it? That task alone seemed impossible and doomed to failure. The practical thing would be to start with the pride that was closest to Windrunner Spire. Her mother would not have selected a beast as far away as, say, the West Sanctum. Not if Lireesa wanted her daughter to succeed, and Sylvanas was well aware the ranger-general was determined that Alleria would fulfill her birthright. So the closest, then.

Though the day was clear, it had rained last night. The forest smelled of damp, clean earth, and Sylvanas, knowing exactly what to look for, found traces of Alleria's passing. "You're easy to track, Lady Sun," she murmured, but there was no reason for Alleria to waste precious time attempting to hide her path. Sylvanas continued to follow Alleria's trail, then froze. The boot prints began to be spaced farther apart, and only the toes were now visible. Alleria had been running—and Sylvanas's heart contracted when she saw why.

The largest springpaw prints she had ever seen began to appear alongside Alleria's. Her sister was no longer predator, but prey—and the beast who hunted her was enormous.

Sylvanas began to run.

The words pounded in her brain: *Everyone is waiting for Alleria to return.*

She excels at all she has been asked to do.

And her response: *That's not an answer.*

Except it had been, hadn't it? Her father had known. *Everyone* had known, except for her and Vereesa. A sudden burst of anger lent her speed.

Her ears caught the sound of something crashing through the underbrush. An unmistakable snarling roar joined the noise. Something large and angry was barreling toward her.

Distance. I need distance.

Sylvanas leaped up, caught an overhanging branch, and pulled herself up, climbing high enough so that the springpaw couldn't pull her down if she missed. Her heart thumped in her chest and her breathing was quick as she swiftly pulled an arrow from her quiver and nocked her bow.

When the animal burst into view, Sylvanas gasped.

The outsized prints had told her it would be large, but to see it— this had to be the one they called Mauler. The one rumored to have developed a taste for elven flesh. She could well believe it. For an instant, panic almost overwhelmed her, but then a sudden calm descended. Precise. Detached. Cold.

She noticed so many things in the space of a heartbeat: Its size. Its speed. Its yellow teeth and claws that tore the earth as it ran.

The lone arrow in its side, too far from the heart to have killed it. The blood dripping down its golden flanks from the arrow and numerous cuts that looked to have been made by a hunting knife.

That it was chasing prey not fleeing on the ground—but in a tree—and Alleria was in the branches. Her face was flushed with exertion, and she clung to the branches for dear life.

Sylvanas realized with horror her sister had made a dreadful miscalculation. Alleria wasn't high enough to escape the sort of leap a springpaw the size of Mauler could make, *was making*—

Sylvanas's arrow pierced the lynx's right eye, emerging, clotted with blood, at the base of its skull. He dropped, his paws churning as his body spasmed, then lay motionless.

After the cacophony of the chase, the forest seemed unnaturally still. Birds were silent, too afraid to resume their songs. Even the wind did not dare to rustle the leaves.

Sylvanas's mouth was dry from panting, her body trembling from the release of tension as tight as any bowstring. She took a breath, steadied herself, and jumped from the tree.

Alleria climbed down as well. In silence, the two sisters stared down at the beast.

Finally, Sylvanas spoke. "Did you know it was this one?"

Alleria shook her golden head. She couldn't tear her eyes from the corpse. One hand clutched her bow; the other, the gore-covered knife. It was only then that Sylvanas realized that Alleria's leg was bleeding.

"You're hurt!" Sylvanas exclaimed, trying to tear off her sleeve for a bandage as she moved toward her sister. The Mauler had missed the major artery.

To her confusion, Alleria drew back. Her eyes bored angrily into her sister's. "Don't touch me!" she snapped.

Sylvanas blinked. "You're wounded, you—"

"Haven't you done enough?"

"What I've done is save your *life*, Alleria!" Bewilderment and hurt turned to hot anger. "A thank-you would be nice."

"I'll take care of it myself." Alleria wrenched off her cloak, tossing it down to the forest floor angrily and stabbing at it with her dagger.

As she had tried to do to the Mauler . . . after her single arrow did nothing but enrage the beast.

Sylvanas gasped lightly, comprehension dawning. She had intervened, and now Alleria had failed her test.

But she failed before I even shot, Sylvanas thought. Alleria hadn't killed him with one arrow.

"Alleria," she began, more calmly this time, "even before I—"

"Be quiet!" Alleria was shouting now, and tore furiously at the cloak, ripping off a strip of dark green fabric, venting her anger and shame on the inanimate object as she wrapped it tightly around her wounded leg.

Sylvanas stood by, silent, less obeying Alleria's request than being too frustrated and hurt to speak.

Alleria tentatively put weight on the injured leg and winced, hissing. Again Sylvanas moved to help, again Alleria halted her. Alleria took her bow, her beautiful bow that had been given to her only a few hours ago, and used it for a cane as they moved slowly toward home.

"What. Happened."

Lireesa's face appeared to be composed. Only her children could see the banked fire of anger in their mother's eyes.

"I missed the kill," Alleria said quietly, trying and failing to keep her face as expressionless as her mother's.

"Obviously, as I see no unmarred pelt before me."

Alleria's face twitched slightly.

"The Mauler is at least dead, I hope."

"He is," Alleria replied. Sylvanas remained quiet. Let their mother assume Alleria had put the beast down. It would go easier on both of them.

The older girl's gaze darted to Sylvanas for a moment, then flickered back to Lireesa. "But I cannot claim the kill. I was treed, and it was Sylvanas who shot him."

Sylvanas's eyes grew wide. What had Alleria just done?

Now their mother's simmering fury was turned on Sylvanas. "Is this true?"

Sylvanas wanted badly to lie. All Alleria had needed to do to avoid the worst of the storm was remain silent, but she had volunteered unrequested information and now made them both clear targets of their mother's displeasure. Lying would only make things worse.

The younger Windrunner straightened and met her mother's eyes evenly. "It is. Alleria's life was in danger. I took the shot when I had it."

"I see," Lireesa said. "So you took even *that* away from her."

Sylvanas felt her face grow hot. "That monster was—"

"You do not know what would have happened." Lireesa's statement cut off Sylvanas's protest with brutal sharpness. "Alleria did indeed fail, as she did not kill the beast with one arrow. But she might have killed it regardless. She might have returned and requested another opportunity to prove herself against a uniquely dangerous creature. There are subtleties in these things, Sylvanas, that you do not appreciate. Perhaps you did save her life. We will never know. But all here *do* know you robbed Alleria of any opportunity to handle the situation by herself, cheated her out of her victory, and shamed her before the people she was born to lead."

Sylvanas bit her lip hard to keep from bursting into tears. Not because she was hurt—though she was—but because she was so terribly *angry*. Angry that her sister had unknowingly been tasked with doing something so dangerous. Angry that Alleria had resented her for trying to help. Angry that no one here seemed to understand that Lireesa might well be planning funeral rites for her eldest daughter instead of publicly embarrassing her. She opened her mouth to shout *It's not fair!* when a calm voice spoke.

"Ranger-General," Verath said, speaking with the greatest respect to his wife, "as you say, there are things Sylvanas is too young yet to fully understand. If you had instructed her to stay here, I am certain she would have obeyed."

Sylvanas was not at all certain, but she was wise enough to stay silent.

"I will take her and Vereesa out for some air while you resolve the situation with your Farstriders. And I will put this event in the proper context for her."

Lireesa visibly calmed at her husband's words. She said nothing, but nodded, and the angry furrow of her brow relaxed ever so slightly.

It was not the first time their father had gracefully inserted himself between his daughters and their mother, and it would likely not be the last. Lireesa had a quick temper and a sharp tongue, but she was also fast to forgive and forget . . . usually. Sylvanas suspected that this time it would take more than the duration of a jaunt to Silvermoon for her mother and Alleria to sort things out.

And perhaps even more time for the air to clear between the ranger-general and her middle daughter. Sylvanas could not suppress a glower as she prepared her hawkstrider, while her father hoisted a giggling Vereesa atop his quel'dorei steed as the head groom Talvas held the reins and smiled benevolently at the littlest Wind-runner. His horse, with its coat of gleaming white, black mane and tail, and distinctive single, curved horn, was bestowed by King Anas-terian only upon those of high rank or exceptional distinction. Each of her parents had one: Verath, the stallion Parley, and Lireesa the mare Arrowflight. Before Vereesa was born, it had been Sylvanas who perched in front of Verath as they rode, Parley sensing the need for gentleness and bearing the children of his master without falter-ing. Now that was Vereesa's place. Sylvanas loved her hawkstrider, whom she had named Snap, and been proud of herself the day she finally rode solo. But sometimes, she missed the warm comfort of her father literally at her back. Today was one of those times.

Snap's long, taloned legs moved swiftly, and Verath slowed Par-ley's gait to a gentle canter so as not to outpace the large avian. Syl-vanas fumed quietly, and her father did not press her. They had passed Windrunner Village and the Sanctum of the Moon and were well into Tranquillien when Sylvanas finally spoke.

"What Mother did wasn't fair."

"Which part of what she did?" her father asked.

"*Any* of it. Letting Alleria think she was supposed to kill an ordi-nary springpaw. Demanding one arrow and no knife marks. Not making sure someone was watching her. And," she said, saving the worst affront for last, "being angry at me for saving my sister's life."

Verath nodded but didn't reply at once. Then he said, "Your mother needs to be tough on Alleria. Do you know why?"

Because she likes to, Sylvanas thought. But even before the thought had truly formed, she knew it was too harsh a judgment. "I don't know," she said honestly.

"The position of ranger-general is crucial to the defense of our kingdom. It is the only hereditary position, other than the monarchy itself. It's always passed from the ranger-general to one of their chil-dren. And for the last few thousand years, the ranger-general of Sil-vermoon has always been the eldest child of a Windrunner."

"I know all this," Sylvanas said, sulking.

"Yes, but you are not using that knowledge to understand the situation."

Gentle as it was, it was still one of the sharpest rebukes Sylvanas had heard from her father, and her cheeks reddened.

"So," she said, anxious to do better, "if she wanted to, Mama could give Alleria the title even if Alleria is a bad hunter."

"She could. And what would happen if she did?"

"The Farstriders would be angry and accuse her of . . ." Sudden comprehension dawned. "Mama has to push Alleria hard so the Farstriders can see she was not only born to the position, but truly deserving of it. If Mama is soft on her, people would think she was playing favorites."

"Exactly right," her father replied. "And that is a burden Alleria should not have to carry. Simply leading the Farstriders well will be challenge enough.

"It was a measure of confidence in Alleria's success that your mother sent her after the Mauler," Verath continued. "It was less a test of those specific skills than to see how Alleria would behave in the face of something genuinely dangerous. It was never about passing or failing. Lireesa had faith Alleria would survive, and, regardless of what happened, Alleria's actions would expose both her strengths and her weaknesses. Knowing these, Lireesa could help her improve on the first and eliminate the second. An evaluation, if you like."

Sylvanas's heart, until this moment beating rapidly with anger and resentment, suddenly felt heavy in her chest as understanding dawned.

"So . . . missing the shot *didn't* mean Alleria failed."

"No, it did not," her father said, and his voice was gentle and filled with sympathy. She didn't look at him, but she felt his kind gaze on her.

"But when I shot Mauler, I ruined the test."

"Yes."

Sylvanas sat with this realization for a while, thinking her way through it, recalling every moment of the incident. Her mother's cutting words came back to her: *There are subtleties in these things, Sylvanas, which you do not appreciate.* Finally, she said, "Mother should have told me."

"I agree."

She looked at him, pleased and surprised. "You do?"

"You are a young woman now, Sylvanas, no longer a child. Lireesa should have told you the importance of the test and you would have understood, would you not?"

"I would," Sylvanas said, finally looking over at him. "But I still think that's a cruel thing to have done to Alleria. And I am *not* sorry I shot. You weren't there, Father. Springpaws can climb, and Alleria could not get high enough in time to escape him. I know I did the right thing."

He chuckled, his eyes bright. "Right and wrong, just like fair and unfair, are highly subjective. But in the end, there's only one thing that matters."

She cocked her head. "And that is?"

"You acted out of love, and with courage. Everyone there—including the ranger-general herself—understands that."

"I don't think so." *Not the way she looked at me.*

"If not now, then she will realize it soon. Just as I do."

Sylvanas's chest began to ease, and she smiled gratefully at her father. He understood her, even when she got into scrapes and trouble; even when she disobeyed or did something wrong. He knew her, knew her heart and her intentions, and always remembered these even when he was the one to dole out the reprimands.

Sylvanas turned her face up to the blue sky and took a deep breath of the clean, healing scent of the forest.

"I wish you hadn't told Mother we were going to Silvermoon." She was not overfond of the elven capital. It was too large, too bright, too oh-so-very crimson and gold. Statues were everywhere, and the cost of any given noble's outfit could have fed a small village. "I would much rather have gone exploring with you."

"Now is not the time to add an extra concern to your mother's plate."

Sylvanas scowled. He was correct. "Sometimes you're too stuffy," she muttered, and he laughed.

"I'll tell you what. We will go to Silvermoon, just as I promised your mother. But we can stop along the way."

Sylvanas turned in her saddle to look at him, her mood shifting almost at once. "Our favorite spot?"

"Our favorite spot."

"Can we stay until the fireflies come out?"

"Not today, dear one. But we can stay for a little while."

They exchanged grins, and Sylvanas felt as though a shadow passing in front of the sun had finally retreated.

The silence that fell was now companionable, and Sylvanas pushed back her hood to let the wind play with her pale yellow locks. Lady Moon, Alleria had dubbed her; Alleria herself was Lady Sun, and Vereesa, Little Moon. Sylvanas had pointed out that her hair was still technically blond, albeit pale, and Alleria had replied, "It's closer to white than gold, and besides, would you rather be Lady Moon or Little Sun?" Naturally, Sylvanas had opted for the former, thus saddling Vereesa with Little Moon.

Soon a new Windrunner would join the family. Idly, Sylvanas wondered what color the child's hair would be. White, like their father's and the moon? Gold, like Lireesa and the sun? Black, like the night sky? Red, like her hawkstrider?

The thought amused her. She gave her father a sly look, blurted, "Race you!" and signaled Snap to run full-out.

"Race! Race! Race!" shouted Vereesa happily, digging her fingers into Parley's mane. Verath, as always, gave Sylvanas a head start, but she expected him—as always—to win. *I'll never let you win, my daughter,* he had told her once. *You wouldn't like that.*

He was right. She would lose the race, but that wasn't the point of it.

The point of it was joy.

The "favorite spot" beloved by the Windrunner family would not look like anything special to the casual observer. But to them, it represented many happy memories, stretching all the way back to the days when a strong-willed, passionate woman had paid suit to the court's rising star, a youth with the tact and insight of one much older than his age, but who still had a lover's heart.

"I was always a child of the city," Verath had told Sylvanas the first time he and Lireesa had brought their three children to this small, grassy spot next to the river. Alleria was knee-deep in the cold, clean water, Sylvanas was in her father's lap, and their mother was nursing the infant Vereesa. "I fell in love with your mother and the forest at the same time. In a way, it was like falling in love with one single beautiful, vibrant thing."

Verath regarded his wife, who lifted her head, feeling his gaze, and smiled softly at him. Sylvanas had looked from one to the other, not quite understanding the unspoken words between them, but knowing them to be loving ones, and knowing as well that she was safe.

Today it was Sylvanas who was wading in the water, gasping at the bone-deep cold and laughing as small, silvery fish nibbled at her toes. Vereesa sat on a sun-warmed rock, attempting to make a flower crown, mangling it horribly, and not caring in the slightest. Verath had stretched his lanky legs on the grass and was watching the soft white clouds when he frowned and sat up, still staring skyward.

Sylvanas turned to look, too, craning her neck and shielding her eyes. There was a small speck—no, *two* specks—silhouetted in the sun that were drawing closer, their wings beating as they approached.

"Lord Verath!"

"Halduron!" her father called as Halduron, Jirri, and the dragonhawks approached. Although she was clearly trying to control her emotions, the normally smiling Jirri was pale and almost . . . frightened?

"My lord, you must return to the spire at once," Jirri said "Lady Lireesa has gone into labor!"

Sylvanas had never seen her father look so distressed. "But the child isn't due for several weeks—"

"Apparently, someone neglected to inform the child," Halduron retorted. His effort at lightening the mood was received with worried silence as Verath handed Vereesa to him. He settled the girl safely in front of him while Jirri slipped off her dragonhawk and Verath and Sylvanas climbed atop it.

Sylvanas was not particularly interested in children other than her younger sister; nor had she given much thought to having children of her own. Alleria was the only one who needed to produce the future ranger-general. She sat behind her father, arms around his waist, resting her cheek on his back. Verath's reaction had unsettled her, and she was doing her utmost not to worry. Her mother had doubtless summoned some of the finest healers in the land the moment it became apparent that the newest addition to the family was determined to join it ahead of schedule.

Sylvanas and her father leaped off the dragonhawks almost before the creatures were close enough to land. Halduron handed Vereesa back to her father, and Verath and Sylvanas raced up the stairs. A sensitive child, Vereesa had picked up on the tension and started crying the moment they departed, much to Halduron's consternation, and she now was sobbing at full tilt. There was no sound from above, of another child crying its first breath. Sylvanas did not think she had ever been truly afraid of anything in her life, but suddenly fear locked her in its cold grasp. She was clumsy as she ran.

Despite his weeping burden, Verath reached the room before Sylvanas, vanishing into the quarters he and his wife shared. Sylvanas stumbled in a second after, bracing for the worst.

She saw instead a sight so beautiful it could have been a painting hung in Sunfury Spire. Warm sunlight streamed in through the open casement window, bathing her mother and the bundle she bore in white-gold. The transom at the top was made of stained glass, casting its own rainbow hues. Verath cupped Lireesa's flushed face in his hands, and as Sylvanas stepped inside, relief making her weak, her parents kissed for a long, sweet moment, then pressed their foreheads together. Tears were on Verath's cheeks, yet Sylvanas had never seen him smile with such joy.

Alleria leaned against the wall, smiling herself, and another worry Sylvanas hadn't realized she'd been carrying fell away. The new arrival, it would seem, had already worked a minor miracle if Alleria's test was all but forgotten. Lireesa pulled back from her husband's embrace, her hand still on his cheek.

"Everything's fine," she reassured her children. "This little boy simply couldn't wait any longer."

A boy. A brother for the three sisters. Sylvanas realized she'd simply assumed the baby would be a girl, but she was glad he wasn't. Four girls would have been boring.

Vereesa had stopped crying and now wedged her way between the parents. "Let me see, let me see!" Had only half a day passed since she'd said that to Sylvanas, wanting to see Alleria? It seemed like a lifetime ago.

Sylvanas stepped from the doorway quietly to stand at the foot of the bed, wondering if this giddy elation filling the room would extend to her. Lireesa turned her eyes toward Sylvanas, and her smile was warm and genuine. "Would you like to hold him, Sylvanas?"

Sylvanas nodded. The lump in her throat stopped her from speaking. She reached down as Lireesa reached up, and gathered the small, warm bundle in her arms.

The infant fidgeted, turning his head and dislodging part of the blanket that had been tucked around him. Sylvanas took a swift breath as she finally beheld his face, her eyes wide and suddenly stinging with tears.

He was perfect. Wisps of gold hair, bright as newly minted coins, adorned his head. His cheeks were pink as roses, and his deep blue eyes were fixated on her.

Joy and fierceness flooded her in a sudden burst as the world narrowed to this moment, this small being, and Sylvanas did not think she had ever cared about anything more than this confoundingly tiny bundle. Carefully, she shifted him so she could touch his face, his skin so soft, so perfect.

"What's his name?" Her words came out in an awed, hushed whisper.

"Lirath," Lireesa said.

"Lirath," Sylvanas repeated, trying it out. As Vereesa's was, so was the baby's name an amalgam of his mother's and father's. It rolled pleasingly off the tongue, and though it was of course impossible, Lirath gurgled as if responding to it. "Lirath, one day, I'm going to show you our favorite spot. You can splash in the water, or dance with us, or just sit and watch the world like Father does. I can't wait to show you fireflies."

She leaned over and kissed his smooth forehead, unmarred as yet by sun or sorrow. As she drew back, the baby waved a chubby arm and tiny fingers grasped a few strands of her hair.

"He likes your hair, Lady Moon," Alleria said. Her voice was warm and soft. Everything, Sylvanas thought, was warm and soft right here, right now.

"Well," Sylvanas replied, her voice still low and tinged with wonder, watching the infant's fascination with a simple lock of hair, "he is golden-haired, like you, Lady Sun, so I think he should be Little Lord Sun."

"Two suns, two moons!" Vereesa crowed, bouncing slightly.

"Hold him carefully, Sylvanas," Lireesa said. "You don't want to hurt him."

Sylvanas recalled her father's words.

I will never hurt you. Ever. And no one else will, either. With love and courage, I will keep you safe.

CHAPTER TWO

Lord Saltheril sat, eyes wide, perfect physique nearly motionless, as Lirath performed. Music to dance to, music to move the spirit, music to make the heart ache: Saltheril listened with a focus even Sylvanas could grudgingly admire.

The entire Windrunner family had a deep appreciation for art. Their parents had instilled in them from a young age that a world without beauty was no world worth living in. Music, sculpture, poetry, and the tranquility and inspiration they brought was what Lireesa and the Farstriders fought to protect; what their father defended at court. Sylvanas thought magic was useful, yes—but no display Grand Magister Belo'vir had conjured could rival the simpler magic of artistic creation. And so the girls danced, and sang, as other children did. But Sylvanas's Little Lord Sun—not so little, not anymore—was a true prodigy, and everyone he played for was the better for hearing him.

Word of Lirath's uncanny gift for music and song had reached beyond Windrunner Village and neighboring areas, all the way to the ears of the elegant, polished, impeccably tailored Lord Saltheril. He was famous—or perhaps *infamous*—for his extravagant parties. He'd been skeptical as to whether the youth really was as good as rumor had it, and Saltheril had mentioned the boy to Verath. Lirath's father had invited the lord to come see for himself, and it was clear within moments that he, like all who heard Lirath perform, was captivated.

Sylvanas was proud of who Lirath was growing up to be, but she was a bit sad to see the child yielding way to the adult. She leaned up against a doorway, smiling wistfully as she watched him perform, as she had done at least a thousand times. And, as a thousand times before, Lirath astonished her.

Sylvanas had been the first to remark that, even before the baby could speak, Lirath was singing himself to sleep. "He is just making noises," Lireesa had said. "The three of you did the same thing."

"No, there's a melody," Sylvanas insisted. And there had been.

As Lirath grew, Windrunner Spire was often filled with his singing, and when he was introduced to instruments, he picked them up easily. A true Windrunner, he was driven to excel, practicing diligently. Once Sylvanas had noticed his lute strings were red. Lirath had played until his fingertips bled, but said not a word.

Under Lord Saltheril's rapt gaze, Lirath played the lute and the lyre, the pipes and the flute, the mandolin and the harp, all with equal skill and equal power to touch the spirit. Then he placed the harp to the side and stood quietly for a moment. He raised his head and used Sylvanas's favorite instrument—his voice.

> By the light
> By the light of the sun
> Children of the blood
> Our enemies are breaking through
> Children of the blood
> By the light
> Failing children of the blood
> They are breaking through
> O children of the blood
> By the light of the sun
> Failing children of the blood

They are breaking through
O children of the blood
By the light of the sun
The sun

"Lament of the Highborne," more than ten thousand years old, was revised after the Troll Wars and the breaking of the Amani Empire some three millennia ago. The quel'dorei had joined with the humans of Arathor, and owed them much. The event was honored kingdom-wide with a ceremony and celebration every year. But rather than being a rousing song of triumph, this song focused on the tremendous loss of life that had been necessary to earn that victory.

Sylvanas both loved and hated it when Lirath performed the piece solo. When the Windrunner children sang together, Sylvanas focused on the harmonies, holding emotions at bay. But when Lirath alone gave voice to the ancient song, his pure tenor soaring and then softening, it was as if he sang of a grief that had only just happened, of pain so fresh it still bled, and it always broke her, just a little bit.

Scowling at herself, Sylvanas palmed the tears from her eyes, looking up just in time to see the great Lord Saltheril, he of the jaded palate and cynical drawl, tucking away his handkerchief.

He composed his handsome features as he rose to his feet, applauding. "Well done, young fellow. Well done indeed." To Verath, he said, "I confess . . . I was doubtful the praise being heaped upon the boy's fair head was accurate. Usually, musicians of his caliber are much older and found only in Silvermoon. But I must say, Verath, your family does seem to have an inordinate number of talents and skills. You, of course, the ranger-general, Alleria, and now young Lirath."

Sylvanas and Vereesa exchanged annoyed glances. They might as well not have existed. Then again, Sylvanas had no need for, or indeed no interest in, Saltheril's favor.

"I would be delighted to host a salon at my little country haven as his debut," the noble was saying. "A few select, distinguished individuals. Small and private. Tasteful." He paused, then added, with a glance at Vereesa and Sylvanas, "Of course, the family is welcome to attend."

Three days later, Sylvanas found herself wearing a simple dress that Saltheril's latest ladylove, the heiress Elisara Sunstriker, had witheringly pronounced "charmingly rustic." Considering how many had complimented Sylvanas by the time Elisara gave her unsolicited opinion, Sylvanas allowed herself to enjoy the other woman's jealousy. Now she leaned idly against a tree at Saltheril's Haven as Lirath performed for the *select, distinguished individuals* the lord had mentioned. Normally Sylvanas was happy to surrender to the enchantment Lirath wove, but tonight she was observing the observers. It amused her how self-important they were, each one believing themselves unique when in reality they were all exactly alike: clad in sumptuous clothing, wearing arrogant expressions, making comments that were civil on the surface but sharp enough to wound. And yet Verath—commonsense, kind, and, Sylvanas had to admit, long-suffering—moved comfortably through the gathering. He stopped to congratulate one on the birth of a child, another on an award, still another for an elevation to a higher station, and others for their stunning wardrobes.

How does he do it? she wondered. Magisters had nothing on the kind of magic her father wielded. No wonder he had limitless patience with his lively brood.

Things moved quickly after the event, and Lirath was soon performing regularly at Saltheril's soirees. He became almost more of a draw than the parties themselves. Six months following Lirath's debut, he returned to Windrunner Spire from Saltheril's Haven looking both stunned and excited.

"There's my Lady Moon!" he called up to Sylvanas as she stood waving at him from one of the balconies.

"And there's my Little Lord Sun!" she called back.

"Come down, come down! I have something to tell you!"

Sylvanas hastened to meet him, a little worried at how flushed he was and how quickly he was breathing. "Are you well?" she asked.

"I have never been better. Oh, Lady Moon . . . Saltheril wants me to perform before *Prince Kael'thas*!"

Now it was Sylvanas's turn to be shocked and delighted. Kael'thas Sunstrider spent most of his time in Dalaran, the magi's city. Only rarely did he venture home. She flung her arms around her baby brother, noticing for the first time that he was now as tall as she, feeling his frame slim as a willow as she hugged him, both of them laughing.

"You are far and away the best of us, you know," Sylvanas said as she drew back and mussed his hair. Lirath flushed again.

"I don't think so at all. I am honored, and excited, but it's just music."

"Oh yes, oh my, and it's *just* Prince Kael'thas," she said, feigning boredom. "Even Father has to make an appointment to meet with the prince when he is in Silvermoon, and now he's coming to see *you* perform!"

The blood abruptly drained from his face. "Oh," he said. "Oh."

"What is it? What's wrong?"

"Sylvanas . . . what if I'm awful?"

"You won't be. You will captivate him just like you do everyone else."

"But—I have never—"

"Mother and Father will be there to cheer you on."

He relaxed a little but didn't look entirely reassured. "Oh good. Still, how can you be sure I won't mess it up?"

"Because," Sylvanas replied, "do you think that Saltheril would have invited Kael'thas, who is hardly ever here, to a performance if he thought you would embarrass him?"

He laughed at that, and the tension bled out of him. "I cannot argue with you—you always win anyway."

"Of course I do, Little Lord Sun. Always remember that."

"What do you mean, you're not going?"

Sylvanas's voice was sharp and angry. Lireesa frowned at the tone.

"Your father and I must always put duty before pleasure. Lirath is younger than you, and he understands."

"Of course I do, Mother," Lirath said. His voice was calm and pleasant as always, and he wore a smile. Sylvanas, though, knew him better than anyone, and she could see by the tense way he held himself that he was greatly disappointed.

Verath had been summoned by Anasterian a few hours ago for "urgent business," sending a courier shortly afterward to let the family know the king would likely have need of him well into the evening. Now, right before Lirath was to leave for Lord Saltheril's Haven, Halduron Brightwing had arrived to inform the ranger-general that there might be trouble brewing near troll territory.

"Then let Alleria go, at least," Sylvanas said. She was already distressed that she and Vereesa were deemed too young to attend unaccompanied. "*Someone* from the family should be there."

"Alleria is my heir," Lireesa said with exaggerated patience. "She will assume the mantle of ranger-general in my absence. She must remain here to rouse the rest of the Farstriders in case they are needed."

Lireesa spoke as if Alleria were not even present, even though all four of the children stood together at the base of Windrunner Spire. The eldest child had a neutral expression, her arms crossed in front of her chest; but her eyes were cold.

Sylvanas shot a glare at Halduron Brightwing, who gave a small, helpless shrug. It wasn't fair. Usually Lor'themar Theron stepped in for Lireesa unless a threat was imminent, but he had already left for Saltheril's party. Lirath was nervous, despite his brave face, and a family member in the crowd would have comforted him.

"My lady," Halduron said, "we should go."

"Of course." Lireesa swung onto her dragonhawk. She looked back at Lirath, and her expression softened. "I regret that the day has taken this turn. Your father and I both would be there otherwise."

"I know," Lirath said, but he didn't meet his mother's eyes. "Please be safe."

"Always," Lireesa said. Then she hesitated, and added, "I know you will do us proud, my son." Her normally hard face melted into a genuine smile. And then her dragonhawk sprang into the air, and she was gone.

Alleria sighed. "Come on," she said to her siblings. Sylvanas and Lirath remained where they stood, but Vereesa, looking anxiously from Alleria to the others, turned to accompany Alleria back to the spire. Sylvanas was silent, watching after her mother until she disappeared from view.

"I am so sorry, Little Lord Sun," she said, quietly.

"It's all right."

"You know there will be other opportunities, yes?" There would be, but who knew when next Kael'thas would even be in Quel'Thalas. It could be years. She turned to look at him. "You are certain to impress the prince. I have every faith that your next performance will be held with the whole royal court in attendance."

"No, really, Lady Moon, it's all right. Our parents have more important things to do than sit and watch me play." Lirath's voice was threaded with resigned pain, and Sylvanas felt her chest ache for his disappointment.

No, they don't, she thought, illogically but stubbornly.

"It is cruel of Mother to insist that Alleria remain here," she said. "If there's trouble, a messenger could just as easily go to the haven and notify the Farstriders there."

"You know that is not the real reason," Lirath replied. And Sylvanas did. Alleria and her mother had been quarreling recently about Alleria's training. Lireesa had ordered this to remind Alleria that the ranger-general was in charge, and Alleria must always obey. This was the third time Lireesa had ordered her daughter to remain behind "just in case."

It was cruel, and petty, and it also hurt Lirath, who hadn't deserved it.

"We love you and we couldn't be prouder of you," Sylvanas said.

"I do know that, truly. I just . . . well."

Sylvanas hugged him tightly, then let him go, watching him run lightly toward the stables and his saddled hawkstrider. Her heart hardened. This wasn't right. Little Lord Sun deserved better than this.

An idea occurred to her, brash and dangerous, and she started to smile.

All she needed to do now was convince Lady Sun.

"Absolutely not!" Alleria snapped, moments later. "One of these days your intrigues are going to get you into some real trouble."

"Now you sound just like Father. They don't ever really hurt anyone."

Alleria raised an eyebrow.

"That was *one* time, and no one is going to die from sugaring their meal instead of salting it."

Over the last few years, Sylvanas had entertained herself by sneaking into places she wasn't invited, and in a few instances even laying harmless traps for the unwary, claiming that she was "practicing her hunting skills." Her father calmly pointed out that an enemy would not be defeated by having a bucket of icy water abruptly poured on them.

"It would certainly catch them off guard," Sylvanas had responded.

Verath had sighed. "My darling girl, sometimes I fear the greatest threat to this nation is a clever, idle mind."

Sylvanas smiled at the memory, then continued, "Sister, you know as well as I do that you won't be summoned. You will stay here and shoot arrows with Vereesa until Mother returns home, just like always."

Despite her practiced stoicism, Alleria winced.

Now I'm *the one being cruel,* Sylvanas thought. She had a slight pang of regret, but the harsh words were necessary.

"I promise I won't get into trouble," she said. "I never attend Saltheril's stupid parties. No one there will recognize me." She hoped Alleria had forgotten that Lor'themar would be in attendance. "I'll slip in, watch him play for a little while, then slip back out and come straight home."

Vereesa, their sweet little peacemaker, stepped between her older sisters and slipped her hands into theirs. "All Lirath wants is someone in the audience who loves him," Vereesa said earnestly. "Wouldn't you want the same if you were performing in front of Prince Kael'thas?"

Alleria looked from her to Sylvanas, then sighed. "Yes. I would. Very well, Lady Moon, you win. I will keep your secret. Just don't be so . . ." She floundered for words. ". . . so *you*."

Sylvanas snorted with laughter. She knew exactly what her sister meant, and that troubled her not at all. "I will be the perfect lady, I promise. Now can you help me get into one of Mother's dresses?"

None of the Windrunner women cared much for dresses. People often told the sisters they were beautiful, and Sylvanas enjoyed the compliments, but in the end, flattery didn't mean much to any of them. Hardened leather armor that thwarted enemies was better than gleaming satin gowns, and well-crafted, balanced arrows were their accessories of choice. Even so, there were social functions they were required to attend from time to time, given the importance of their parents' roles. Lireesa had robes that were more opulent than anything Sylvanas would usually consent to wear, and Sylvanas wrinkled her nose in displeasure as she and Alleria struggled to fasten the inordinate number of buttons, hooks, and lacing.

"How does anyone *wear* these?" she muttered. "And *why*?"

"Your feet are bigger than Mother's," Vereesa observed. She sat on their parents' bed, observing the unusual sight and chewing on her lower lip.

"Yes, but Mother's taller, which means the gown will hide my shoes," Sylvanas replied.

"Then the hem will get dirty."

Sylvanas smiled. While the younger girl was obviously excited about the escapade, she was clearly also worried they'd get caught.

"I'll clean it," Sylvanas reassured her. She was anxious to get going. Who knew but Father's council session might end early, or Lireesa return with more troll ears as trophies. Alleria started to braid her hair, but Sylvanas was done. "This is good enough," she announced, grabbing a hat, clapping it atop her head, and stepping in front of the mirror to examine their handiwork.

She almost didn't recognize herself. Her hair was usually a mess, and she often wore breeches and tunics that bore grass and other stains on them. The young woman in the mirror looked elegant and graceful, poised and sophisticated in the long green dress and the sweeping hat atop pale gold tresses. Sylvanas smiled and curtsied toward the reflection. It did the same.

Her smile grew.

Perfect.

CHAPTER THREE

Sylvanas listened intently to the strains of lute music wafting from Saltheril's Haven, picking up her pace. Was Lirath already mid-performance? But no, another instrument was joining in. She sagged in relief. Other musicians provided atmosphere for the gossip and flirtations going on; her brother would be the center of attention when he performed.

She scanned the crowd quickly, trying to locate anyone she might recognize who could give her away. Her gaze traveled over the sea of bright-colored clothing, glossy locks, and garish hats, until it landed on a white head of hair.

"Lor'themar," Sylvanas murmured, and smoothly turned so she could put herself at the opposite side of the crowd.

"Good day, my lady," came a voice. She started, and turned to see a tall, robed figure made even taller by a ridiculous topknot. "I do not believe we've met. Allow me to introduce myself. I am Arcanist Sheynathren."

Sylvanas ducked her chin so that the hat's wide brim would cover more of her face. "A pleasure, sir. I am Lady Ranaria, perhaps you know my cousin, Lady Elana?"

She'd made up the names on the spot. It was safer than claiming to be anyone who actually existed. Sheynathren's brow furrowed, then smoothed out.

"Ah, yes," he said. "Lady Elana."

Sylvanas restrained herself from smirking. "It is a warm day, Lady Ranaria," her would-be suitor continued. "Might I get you a cool drink?"

"That would be lovely," Sylvanas said. He bowed and threaded his way through the crowd, topknot bobbing. The instant he turned his back, Sylvanas headed in the opposite direction. She was surprised at how many people had turned out, and was even more glad she had decided to sneak in. Lirath was brilliant, but he'd never performed before a crowd this large. He'd be so happy to—

"Sylvanas!"

She whirled at the sharp whisper, terrified someone had recognized her, only to see Lirath staring at her with wide blue eyes the color of the finest summer day.

"Shhh, keep your voice down."

"I—what are you doing here? And in Mother's gown? You look . . . strange."

"Never mind that. What do you think I'm doing, silly? I came here to see you!"

Lirath sighed, but his lips threatened to betray a smile. "You are going to get in so much trouble."

"I'll be fine. When do you go on?"

"In just a few minutes. I was going to get a cup of punch. My mouth is so dry!"

It was hard for Sylvanas not to hug him, but she refrained. "Go ahead. Don't worry."

He looked at her for a long moment, and Sylvanas thought she'd never seen him so happy. "Don't get so choked up that you cannot sing," she said, a bit harshly.

"You could leave right now, and I'll sing like the Thalassian red songbird," he replied. "It means a lot that you would risk this. You are my favorite sister."

"You say that to all of us."

"Well, yes. And it's true. It's just . . . truer with you."

Now it was Sylvanas who felt her throat tighten with emotion. "I will stay for a couple of songs, then go."

"Good. I'm glad. You will be safer that way."

He beamed at her, then made his way to the refreshment table. A loud snort of laughter drew her attention. A knot of four youths stood a few feet away, and one of them was smirking while the others laughed. All had ruddy, plump cheeks and soft hands, and were clad in the usual finery. One of them sneaked a sip from a flask, and they passed it around furtively till all had taken a swig. Judging from their red faces and slightly unsteady stances, the flask either was already low or had been refilled more than once. Two of them wore the colors of the house of Salonar.

"No, no, but look at him," the smirking boy said. Sylvanas recognized him now as Aravan, one of the younger nobles. He inclined his head toward the punch table, where Lirath was ladling a cup of melon juice punch. "If I tapped him on the shoulder he would probably fall over."

Sylvanas pressed her lips together, suppressing a retort, but her fists still clenched. She glanced at Lirath, who was moving back in her direction. He'd just had a growth spurt and now was taller than anyone except their father. He wasn't weak. His body just hadn't caught up with his height yet.

Aravan wasn't done. "I hear they tried to teach him how to fight, and he was terrible. Absolutely useless."

Lirath stopped in his tracks.

"But isn't his mother ranger-general?" another boy asked.

"Yes! That's what makes it worse. They have to be so embarrassed."

Quite deliberately, Lirath squared his shoulders and strode to the front area. Sylvanas's heart thudded almost audibly in her ears, and her body was taut as a bowstring.

"Oh, but he plays the flute," said Aravan's brother, Rendris. "I'm sure *that* will be handy in a duel."

"Now, brother, he does not *have* to fight! He can just sing a tragic song about the battle!"

The words stung so badly because they were true. Lirath *couldn't* learn to fight. The child who was so coordinated he could even dance while playing the flute became clumsy when musical instruments were replaced by instruments of war. Sylvanas felt Lirath's shame and hurt wash over and through her as keenly as if it were her own. Then came the anger, hot and dangerous, and then an icy coldness settled in her chest.

She took as deep a breath as she could manage with the tightly laced gown, glanced over at the laughing boys one more time to brand their images into her brain, then moved with the throng toward the pavilion.

She would make them pay for the hurt they'd caused her brother, but not now. Sylvanas would do nothing further to harm Lirath's composure. She only hoped that the hateful words spewed by the vermin spawn had not disheartened Little Lord Sun enough to ruin his royal debut.

With the skill of a tactician, she scanned her battlefield. Lor'themar smiling at a nobleman, her prey still drunkenly boasting, and, with a little chuckle, poor Sheynathren who was carrying two cups of punch and scanning the crowd to find her.

Sylvanas took a seat in the back, in as much shadow as she could find, an easy exit nearby. She had fully intended to leave after the first few songs, as she'd promised her brother.

But now she had work to do.

Suddenly a great cheer went up, and everyone was on their feet. "Prince Kael'thas! Prince Kael'thas!"

And there he was. Sylvanas found herself reluctantly impressed. She'd seen glimpses of him, golden hair gleaming in the sun, clad in red and gold, but never up close. Many of the nobles here were emphasizing their own importance, lifting their chins so that a disdainful glare was all the more effective. They moved gracefully, but like performers in a play, with bows too deep and arm gestures too broad. Kael'thas, son of Anasterian, heir to the throne of Quel'Thalas, did not need such tricks to command attention.

He bore himself with easy elegance, smiling and nodding to those he knew and acknowledging all gathered with a sweeping glance. No one took their seat until he did, settling regally into an opulently carved, gilded chair and waving a hand airily.

"My lords, my ladies," Saltheril said. "I hope you have enjoyed yourselves at one of my justly famous gatherings. As these parties are known for having only the finest food, drink, and *guests* . . ." He paused, smiling benevolently as the audience tittered. ". . . they are also renowned for the finest entertainment outside the palace. I have discovered a remarkable talent in the form of young Lirath Windrunner—yes, I see we all know the name. He is the youngest child of our beloved adviser and our ranger-general. Dancing is welcomed, smiles and applause encouraged, and I must warn you: You may discover you require a handkerchief."

Lirath stepped forward to enthusiastic applause. *He* is *thin,* Sylvanas thought. *And slight.* Knowing of the cruelty only a few moments old, Sylvanas thought Lirath looked alone and vulnerable onstage. He bowed gracefully, lifted the flute to his lips, and began to play.

After the first few hauntingly sweet notes, the crowd was his. They stopped their chitchat, their fan waving, and leaned forward, faces rapt. Even the boys who had said such cutting things were silent now.

Sylvanas allowed herself a slow smile. No one could do what Lirath did. It was good the youths were seeing the power her brother could wield.

But it wasn't going to save them.

After the first song, Sylvanas stepped back into the shadows. No one was paying her any attention. She lifted the cumbersome skirts and ran back to her hawkstrider, opening the saddlebag and hoping she hadn't removed the item she sought.

Her fingers closed around a small leather pouch. "This will teach them to beware what words leave their mouths," she said, and patted Snap.

By the time she returned, Lirath had paused for a break. Sylvanas was pleased to see that a not-inconsiderable crowd had gathered around him. She regarded him fondly, then turned to her mission.

There had been five of them. Five, who had pointed and laughed at someone they perceived as lesser just because he had more talent and brains than muscles. Five, who had assumed that just because he couldn't fight, her Little Lord Sun was worthless.

There were several areas where food and punch had been laid out. Sylvanas moved toward the least crowded one, checked to make sure she wasn't being observed, and began.

She moved quickly, filling five delicate glass cups with the light green beverage. Opening the small pouch, she dropped a pinch of powder in each one, then tucked the pouch back in her bodice. It would have been easier to ask a server to give the beverages to the youths, but Sylvanas relished the task too much to surrender it to another. Setting aside the cups she had prepared, Sylvanas picked up two of them and went to the boys.

They were flirting with two vapid-looking young women, who gave Sylvanas a glare as she approached. She ignored it, smiling at the pair. "I saw you all from over there and thought you might like something sweet."

"Thank you, milady," Aravan said.

"Why yes, we're parched."

Sylvanas smiled prettily, and then to their dismay returned to the table, threading her way through the crowd. She came to an abrupt halt, her eyes going wide.

Lord Saltheril and his Lady Elisara stood beside the table she'd come from. She'd only been gone a moment, but in their hands were two of the remaining three drinks.

Sylvanas opened her mouth to stop them. Pompous and arrogant as he was, Saltheril had been good to the family, especially Lirath, and that went a long way with Sylvanas. When Elisara frowned and touched a gloved hand to her mouth, Sylvanas realized it was already too late.

A wail went up behind her, followed by the sound of a cup crashing to the stone floor. Sylvanas whirled. Despite the direness of the situation, Sylvanas couldn't help but smile. The leader of the bullies looked like he was about to cry, or faint, or perhaps both. He was trying to speak, but spittle and drool sprayed from his mouth. His swollen tongue lolled.

You sharpen your tongue at my brother's expense, your speech will pay the price.

Sylvanas turned back for one last glance at Saltheril, and to her horror realized he was staring directly at her. He pointed an accusing finger and shouted a command in a furious tone. It was gibberish. Despite herself, Sylvanas snickered at how ridiculous he looked, desperately trying to utter actual words and producing only babbles.

Strong hands closed around her arms, and the music abruptly ceased. Sylvanas tried to wriggle free, but these were trained guards, not annoyed partygoers, and she lowered her head as she was dragged before Saltheril.

He had a hand to his mouth to hide his drooling and, with effort, got some slurred but intelligible words out. "Wha ha you done? You dishono be an Pince Kael'pas!"

Don't laugh. Don't laugh.

She laughed. Some other partygoers—those who had not drunk the concoction—began to laugh, too. Saltheril turned crimson all the way up to his long ears.

"It's my fault."

Still held firmly by a guard on either side, Sylvanas whipped her head around to see Lirath pushing his way through the crowd, pale but resolute.

"I begged her to come."

"My lord, that is not true," Sylvanas said. "Lirath had no idea I would be here. Please do not blame him for my offense. It's mine, and mine alone." She had only wanted to show her brother support, but her anger with the bullies had clouded her judgment.

The lord's face turned thunderous. He pointed at Lirath, Sylvanas, and the main party entrance. With effort, he said with only the slightest slurring, "Neveh come back!"

"My lord Saltheril!"

The voice belonged to Lor'themar Theron, who moved to stand beside Sylvanas. He didn't look at her.

"I want to assure you that everyone will be just fine within the hour. I believe that Lady Sylvanas put some woundwood into your beverage. While it's in very poor taste, it is harmless, and I ask that you be the better person and forgive her this childish prank. She is still very young, and Lirath had nothing to do with this. I am sure the adviser and the ranger-general would appreciate this kindness." His smooth voice subtly emphasized the titles, and it was not lost on Saltheril.

The comment stung, but Sylvanas bit her lip and remained silent. Of course Lor'themar recognized what she'd done. The rangers always kept woundwood on hand; it sometimes made the difference between life and death. The woundwood tree was so named because its leaves, when dried and mixed with liquid, formed a numbing paste. When it was applied as a poultice, the pain was deadened temporarily, and one had time to escape to safety.

Saltheril drew himself up to his full height and opened his mouth.

"I agree with Theron," came a clear, elegant voice. The crowd that had stymied Sylvanas's escape parted quickly to admit their prince. "The Windrunner family has served the Sunstriders for generations. Surely what was intended as a harmless prank by a high-spirited girl can be forgiven. And," Kael'thas added, with seeming lightness, "I should very much miss the boy's music. *Very* much."

For a moment, Sylvanas thought the lord might refuse the veiled order. Then he scowled. Turning to Lirath, he nodded. Lirath sighed in relief. Then Saltheril turned his cold gaze on Sylvanas.

"You," he said, already starting to regain control of his mouth, "*banished.*"

Sylvanas was escorted out. Her cheeks were red, and she was a jumble of emotions. Instead of going home, she tethered Snap to a tree and sat atop a boulder on the road back, waiting for hours until, at last, she saw Lirath approaching.

He reined in his hawkstrider, and they regarded each other.

"I ruined your debut for the prince," Sylvanas said. "That was the last thing I wanted to do."

Lirath's usually open face was closed and wary. "I know you mean that."

"Did—is everything all right now?"

"Yes," he said. "The prince was extraordinarily kind." At last, the smile Sylvanas so craved curved his lips, ever so slightly. "He wants me to play again."

"I'm so glad. And so sorry."

Lirath sighed and nodded. "Well," he said, lightly, "you got yourself banished. So we'll call it even."

Welcoming the shift in his tone, Sylvanas attemped a smile. "It's no real loss. I would never attend his parties anyway." She untethered Snap, climbed up, and they began heading down the road to home.

"I know Saltheril is a bit . . . full of himself," Lirath said diplomatically. "But why did you put the woundwood in his punch?"

"It wasn't meant for him. He picked up the cup by accident. I really *am* sorry about that. But it was funny."

"Who *was* it for, then?"

She didn't answer at once. The silence lingered, and then he said, "Oh."

Sylvanas nodded. "I couldn't let stand what they said about you," she said, renewed defiance creeping into her voice. "Especially since I know you heard it. That might have made you ruin your performance for the prince. It was worth getting banished to see them blubbering and drooling. They deserved that and more."

"You do realize they thought they had been poisoned?"

She whirled to stare at him, her shocked expression answer enough. It had never occurred to her, not until this moment when he said it out loud. In retrospect, mere banishment was almost a reward.

"I didn't think so," Lirath said, kindly. "But, Lady Moon, you are sometimes too single-minded. People will end up getting hurt."

He was right. She needed to be better about that. "I will do better," she promised him. "In the meantime, everything turned out fine. You will still get to perform, and I won't have to attend dull soirees."

Sylvanas had expected a chuckle, but Lirath fell silent.

Dusk was coming, and Lirath's face was growing harder to see. "Sylvanas," he said, and his voice sounded much older, and oddly compassionate. "Do you really think that was the first time I had heard that?"

Her eyes widened. "Oh, Lirath, no . . ."

"It happens every time I play. Someone always points out that I must be the disappointment of the family. That I am too weak to be worth anything. And . . ." He paused. "What if they're right?"

How could he think this? How could he not know how deeply his music affected people? How his family was in awe of his skill?

"Lirath, no, that's not true at all!"

"Maybe I should spend more time training. I should learn how to fight. To defend myself and others who can't. Become a ranger, just like the rest of you. Saving people is much more important than just entertaining them."

A shiver went through Sylvanas. The thought of Lirath fighting a troll, being chased by a beast as Alleria had been . . . injured, maybe dying—no. She couldn't bear that. He had gifts she couldn't comprehend, only marvel at. His warmth and kindness were always a balm to her, to the family—to everyone who heard him sing or play, or even simply saw him smile. Lirath had been given a gift at birth and had honed it with his own determination and passion, just as she had. His was music; hers was archery. Only now, when he had spoken the words, did Sylvanas realize how much she wanted, no, *needed* him to be safe and happy, sharing his gift in a peaceful place.

"Those boys are pampered fools who have nothing better to do with their time and gold than to eat, drink, and belittle others who have actual skill," she said, her voice sharp. "Pay no attention to them. Being a ranger in this household is nothing new. Being a musician and having Kael'thas himself rush to your defense—*that's* something special. Don't underestimate the value of what you do, Lirath. There is more than one way to save people. And one of those ways is giving them a respite from worry and fear by offering peace and beauty. We couldn't be prouder of you."

He nodded, reassured by her words. Sylvanas's tight chest eased.

Hopefully, this would be the only time rangering came up. That life was not suited to him—nor he to it.

She grinned at him. "We will still have plenty to do together even if I can't go to Saltheril's parties. We Windrunners make our own entertainment. I'd never trade dancing or swimming with the three of you, or all the games we make up, or just . . ." She shrugged. "Just being with you. But my Little Lord Sun, you must promise me one thing."

He was smiling now, too, and all was right with her world. "Name it."

"Don't get so important you don't want to play for me anymore."

He laughed, a sweet sound, a bright sound. "Never, Lady Moon. Never." Sylvanas felt the weight of the day's events lift, like a heavy pack dropped with a relieved sigh. She and Lirath were quiet as they walked up the ramp to the spire, but it was a warm, comfortable silence.

Until they heard sharp words, cracking like a whip, dispelling the stillness of the evening and the tranquility so recently restored. "You cannot be serious. It is your birthright, Alleria! The eldest Windrunner has always become ranger-general!"

"I don't want something given to me just because I happened to be born first. I want something I've earned!"

Alleria's voice rose. Sylvanas glanced at Lirath. After all they'd been through today, this was the last thing she wanted Lirath to endure. They moved quietly inside, intent on going to their rooms unnoticed by the arguing pair. Sylvanas glanced in that direction and saw a small figure sitting beside the cracked door.

Vereesa put a finger to her lips, then beckoned them over. Moving silently, the three children sat and listened as their mother and Alleria quarreled.

"Did you think I made your trial so difficult and dangerous because I hoped you would fail?"

"No, of course n—"

"Then why? I wanted you to feel you were worthy. I wanted everyone to know that."

Sylvanas felt her face turn red. She had hoped that her error, made years ago for the best of reasons, had been forgotten. Clearly not.

"It just doesn't feel right," Alleria said, her voice slightly quieter.

Lireesa sighed. "It can feel intimidating, at times. But do not doubt. You were born to do this; it will feel right once you step into the role. It did for me."

The three siblings looked at one another, confused. Did that mean that once, Lireesa had not wanted to be ranger-general?

"What you do is important, Mother. I know that. But there is a whole *world* out there, one you've never let us see. A world full of other people, other cultures, other ideas the quel'dorei would do well to know about! Our kingdom would have been overrun thousands of years ago if it had not been for human aid."

"We taught the humans magic as thanks for their help. I would think that would cancel out any debt. Do not forget, it would have gone ill for them, as well, had the trolls been victorious. Let your father and the other council members deal with the world out there. The only people who should matter are right here. And they need protection. That is your task, Alleria."

"Please don't make me feel guilty, Mother." Alleria's voice dropped lower, even softer, and Lirath, sitting between Sylvanas and Vereesa, winced.

Sylvanas realized she should have gone straight to her room, or at least made sure that Lirath went to his. He thrived on harmony; his gifts to others went deeper than making music. It made her feel almost sick to watch him growing angry and frustrated. Not that she could blame him.

Vereesa picked up on it almost instantly. *Our little peacemaker,* Sylvanas thought. It was as if the two older siblings received all the energy and sharpness of their mother, while the younger had inherited a love of balance and peace from their father. *At least it's an even number to balance it out,* Sylvanas thought.

"It will be all right, Lirath," Vereesa whispered. "They will figure out what is best. Come now. Let's go to bed."

Lirath allowed himself to be led away, but he gave Sylvanas a bleak look over his shoulder that cut deep. Today should have been *his* day, but it had ended up being all about everyone *but* him. His parents called away; Sylvanas almost ruining it. And now . . . now it was all about Mother and Alleria.

Sylvanas thought she should probably go to bed, too. She didn't want to encounter her mother in this state and give her the news that her daughter had gotten herself banished from Saltheril's parties. And yet she lingered, sitting with her back against the wall and her knees to her chest, clasping them with her arms.

Sylvanas didn't mind the occasional heated argument. She'd certainly participated in—or even started—her share of them. But something about this one felt different. This wasn't a minor squabble—it affected the paths of two women and, really, the whole family. Even the Farstriders—and maybe the kingdom itself. What would happen if Alleria refused to become ranger-general? Would their mother banish Alleria, as Saltheril had Sylvanas?

At last, the voices dropped to murmurs so soft Sylvanas had to strain to hear them. Both women sounded tired. They had worn themselves out. It was time for Sylvanas to withdraw before she was caught.

She took a deep breath and headed to her room. A few minutes later, with the covers pulled up to her chin, she lay on her side and looked out the window at the dark, blue-black sky with scattered, shining stars. She would make it up to Lirath tomorrow, she told herself. They'd go to their favorite spot, with a picnic, and stay till the fireflies came. A memory stirred: Lirath, four years old or so, piping a song as the fireflies drifted and blinked in the lavender twilight.

"Look, Lady Moon!" he had crowed. "Even the stars have come to dance!"

"If ever the stars would come to dance," Sylvanas whispered, "it would be for you, baby brother. Only for you."

CHAPTER FOUR

"Again," Verath said.

"Aeriah Sunfire was known for his firsthand account of the creation of the Sunwell—"

"No, he did not write about the Sunwell, he wrote the troll histories, volumes five through seven. His grandfather, Sunfire the Elder, wrote one through four, and—"

Sylvanas let out a sound of extreme exasperation. "I understand why you want me to study ancient battles," she said. "Strategy is important. And I know why I have to be familiar with the geography of our kingdom. But this Younger, Elder, First of Her Name, the Fifteenth, The One Wearing the Blue Cloak In That Portrait—how in the world do you keep them all straight? And even more important, why?"

"We have been over this," her father said, pouring a cup of wine for each of them and handing her a goblet. "Thalassians are extremely—"

"—proud of their ancestry," Sylvanas muttered.

"And therefore, understanding and appreciating those legacies—"

"—makes them more malleable to negotiations."

Sylvanas took a sip of the wine and rubbed her eyes with the heel of one hand. "This is just . . ." She groped for words. "Catering to egos."

"My dear girl," Verath said, his eyes twinkling over the rim of the goblet as he took a sip, "what do you think politics is? You cannot accomplish anything unless people come to the table."

"You can accomplish a great deal with a quiver of arrows and a bow," Sylvanas replied. "I am officially a Farstrider now. Why can't I just be that?"

"Because, as I have said before, an idle mind makes mischief," he answered with his customary kind honesty. "And Alleria will eventually become their ranger-general, despite her current uncertainty. You know I hold the Farstriders in the greatest esteem, Sylvanas, and I would gamble my life there are none who could surpass them in this whole world of ours at what they do. But you, my sweet child, are not a follower. You are a leader, and if you were to live solely as a Farstrider, you would chafe and languish, or else rebel."

Sylvanas frowned. What he said was true. "But," she said, hunting for words as she might hunt a wild creature, "my soul is in the forest." Flowery words for her, but they were true. She was never so alive as when she was on the chase; never so focused as when she took aim at her quarry. Beautiful as Windrunner Spire was, Eversong Forest was more so for her. The smell of trees and grass and blooming things, of life, tethered her to this world.

"We named you for the beautiful woods of our homeland, and you have proved that naming true. I am not asking you to leave the Farstriders." He held up his hands in mock horror, and she chuckled slightly. "But come with me from time to time, eh? Observe and learn." Verath patted her head, as he had done so often when she was a child. "Things . . . may be changing from the way they have always been."

"The portal?" Sylvanas asked. "You mean what the scouts are saying about green monsters coming out of a magical gate?"

"When you have lived as long as I have, you will know that every bit of information is worth investigating, no matter how preposterous it sounds. Skepticism, of course, is healthy. That sharp mind of yours, as long as it is an open one, would be useful to your kingdom. That sharp tongue, however," he added, his eyes twinkling, "must learn to appreciate the benefits of silence."

"Now I *know* I am not suited to this," Sylvanas returned, and he laughed.

"On the contrary," her father replied, "the king has many—*too many*—who are eager to tell him exactly what he wants to hear. Fortunately, Anasterian is wise, and treasures those bold enough to speak truth to him. This is why he is a fine king."

It was not Anasterian whom she minded, though. The king was old, but still quick witted and strong. He had seen much and from all she could tell he was a good and universally admired ruler. It was the court she despised: all frippery and frivolity, the sort perfectly embodied by Lord Saltheril.

Sylvanas sighed. "I will come to Anasterian's court," she said, "until *he* throws me out, too."

Sylvanas tried—she really did—to be the apt pupil her father so clearly wanted her to be. But she found herself missing some of the more exciting activities, stealing away for spur-of-the-moment scouting missions, hunts, and sometimes simple archery practice with her two favorite Farstriders who, along with her, were rapidly becoming known as the Trio. They were obedient to their ranger-general, courteous to the heir apparent, and yet somehow carved out their own unit. Their personalities complemented one another— Lor'themar the pensive one, Halduron the merry one, and Sylvanas the mischievous one.

She noticed that the future ranger-general was doing something similar. When she had the chance, Alleria and a handful of others— Verana, Rellian, Talthressar, and Auric, among others—slipped away on their own. Sylvanas had no idea what they were up to, but it was clear that a rift, subtle and courteous, was forming between those who followed Lireesa and those who gravitated toward Alleria.

The only thing that superseded hours spent with the Trio was when Lirath was available between practicing and performing. True to his promise to her, he always made time for her, even though he was kept very busy in Silvermoon. Kael'thas had insisted he move to the Artists' Quarters and begin a formal apprenticeship, and Sylvanas suspected the title of royal musician would be bestowed on her brother sooner rather than later.

Sometimes they went to the family's spot in Eversong; other times they visited the beach below the spire. If the weather was fair, they swam, if not, they walked and collected seashells.

One day, in the heat of the afternoon, they sought out the coolness of the ocean, shucking off their shoes and outer garments. It was low tide, and as he always did, Lirath made a point of checking to see if any stranded creature was stuck in a little tide pool. It seemed there was at least one today, and Lirath carefully bore the flailing little fish in cupped hands to the water.

She watched as he placed his latest rescue safely into the ocean, and followed it, walking, then running in the surf to dive straight through an oncoming wave.

We hunt creatures, Sylvanas thought. *And he saves them.* She took a quick dip herself in the cool, soothing sea, then stretched out on the sand to dry off.

She allowed her eyes to close and her mind to wander. In a few weeks' time, the Remembrance, the anniversary of the final battle in the Troll Wars, would be celebrated. Anasterian Sunstrider, wielding the powerful, magical blade Felo'melorn, had slaughtered so many trolls that it was said a tide of blood crested the walls of Zul'Aman.

Sylvanas always wondered what it would have been like to fight in those battles, had discussed the strategies with her father many an evening. Unfortunately, her only "battle" around the Remembrance would be getting fitted for a ball gown.

Her eyes fluttered open. Sylvanas peered in confusion at the glorious sunset, then realized her clothes were completely dry. She'd thought only to rest, not nap, and was annoyed that she had squandered her time with Lirath snoring on the beach.

She got to her feet and brushed off the sand, looking around for him. He was nowhere to be seen. Had he noticed her drowsing and returned to the spire alone? That didn't seem like him. A prickle of concern stirred, and Sylvanas padded barefoot to where the waves lapped at the shore, shading her eyes against the sun and peering at silvery blue water.

Nothing.

He really should have known better than to walk off without letting her know. She would give him a piece of her mind for making her worry. Sylvanas went to fetch her overdress and shoes, but stopped.

Lirath's shoes were still there.

Her mouth went abruptly dry. "Lirath?" she called, her voice cracking, sprinting back to the water, her feet barely touching the damp sand, praying to see an arm rise out of the waves to let her know he was fine—

Something was floating on the surface. Something not moving, bobbing with the waves; a form with bright blond hair spreading out like a flowing gold wave of its own.

Lirath!

Terror surged through Sylvanas, quickly quelled and harnessed into action. She launched herself into the water, using her fear to propel herself forward faster than she had ever swam before. Lirath was floating facedown, terrifyingly still. Time seemed to slow, but then there he was, and she flipped him faceup, and—

—Lirath's blue eyes opened.

"Thank you for the rescue, Lady Moon," he said, mirth in his voice.

Fear bled out of her, leaving her weak with relief for a heartbeat before anger rushed to take fear's place. Releasing him at once, she glared at him as he floated before her, laughing, completely safe, not at *all* drowned, and she punched his shoulder.

"Ow!" He was still laughing even as he rubbed the spot.

"I am so glad you're all right," Sylvanas said, "so that I can drown you myself. You scared me half to death, you wretch, how did you even *go* so long without breathing?"

"What do you think happens to lungs when you play wind instruments for hours a day?" he asked, treading water in front of her. "It's the perfect prank!"

"You are very bad at pranks, Little Lord Sun. Never pull one on me again."

Sylvanas tried to keep it light, but he, who knew her so well, could see he had truly upset her. "I'm sorry," he said, his voice and eyes kind. "I did not know it would distress you so much."

And just like that, the anger and the fear both receded, and Sylvanas reached out to hug him, resting her head for a moment on his shoulder, feeling ocean-chilled skin, hearing breath and heartbeats. He returned the embrace, whispering an apology again. Sylvanas thought back to when she had put the woundwood in the punch. The boys thought they had been poisoned. Suddenly, it didn't seem so funny.

She released him and took a deep breath. "You know," she said, "Maybe we should both stop playing pranks."

"Maybe we should," he agreed.

"Except, of course, on people who really deserve them."

"Of course," Lirath replied as they both began to strike out for the shore. "Except for them."

"The last time I wore a formal gown to a party, things did not go well," Sylvanas pointed out. She, her sisters, and her mother were in a carriage, a rare thing for them. Sylvanas had tried and failed to persuade them all to simply ride their dragonhawks or, in her mother's case, the exquisitely beautiful horse given to her by King Anasterian himself, but Lireesa had held firm. They would arrive together, with appropriate transport, and that would be the end of it.

"Do not remind me," Lireesa said. "Your father has asked us all to go, and go we shall. None of us enjoy this, but we are Windrunners, and we have a duty to the crown."

Out of her mother's view, Sylvanas rolled her eyes. Vereesa stifled a giggle. At least her mother had allowed her daughters to choose their preferred styles and colors of dress. Alleria had selected green, Vereesa red, and Sylvanas blue.

All were full length. Alleria's had an attached cloak, Vereesa's an embroidered bodice, while Sylvanas simply requested hers have no sleeves. If she couldn't wear her armor, then at least she would not have to deal with excessive fabric.

Lireesa didn't reprimand either Sylvanas or Vereesa. There was an odd look on her face; a sorrow, a softness, that Sylvanas had never seen there before. Vereesa, of course, picked up on it right away. "Is something wrong, Mother?"

"No, my sweet girl," Lireesa said.

Sylvanas blinked. She had a vague childhood memory of endearments, and she had seen how tender Lireesa had been with Lirath, but it had been a long time since their mother's face had worn anything save a stern expression. "But I am a little sad. All of you are adults now, even you, even Lirath. I still see you in my mind's eye as children, but you are such no longer."

Vereesa, sitting next to her, linked her arm around Lireesa's and laid her head on her mother's silk-covered shoulder. "That may be," Vereesa said, "but we are still here. We're not leaving you."

Sylvanas stayed silent, but her gaze flickered to Alleria. Their eyes met, then Alleria glanced out the window.

Neither of them said a word.

Their father greeted them at the stairs to the Court of the Sun. "Well," Verath said, surveying them with a smile, "I had almost forgotten what you four looked like underneath the dirt you seem to acquire. Turns out you are all quite beautiful."

They were, Sylvanas agreed. Alleria wore her hair long, letting the golden tresses flow over the green cape that swayed gracefully behind her. Vereesa looked every inch the noblewoman she was, her hair pale as moonlight and the gems on her bodice glittering like stars. Sylvanas was drawing looks because her arms were bare for all to see, and while her vanity was somewhat stoked by the attention, for the most part she could not have cared less.

"Can we see Lirath?" she asked.

"Not just yet," Lireesa replied.

Sylvanas straightened, smiling at her admirers, then followed her parents inside. There was the greeting line, of course, and although Sylvanas hated it—she already knew everyone—tonight was very important to her father, and she would not embarrass him. Anasterian, whose famous battle the evening celebrated, cut a commanding figure as always. Elegant and poised, long white hair flowing down his back, he was resplendent in his heavy, jeweled robe of deep crimson and bright gold. The sword of legend, Felo'melorn, was sheathed at his side.

Magi, of course, were always present in large numbers, given their importance to the people. Grandmagister Belo'vir of the powerful house of Salonar had a cluster of people around him nearly constantly, namely his trusted colleagues Rommath and Dar'Khan Drathir. Though Lor'themar was fond of Dar'Khan, something about him rubbed Sylvanas the wrong way. She did not like how he looked at her, eyes glowing, perfect features in shadow beneath the sweeping brim of his hat. It was one thing to be found attractive; it was another to be regarded as a meal to be devoured.

"You look stunning, Lady Sylvanas, as always," Dar'Khan said, his voice rich and smooth.

"And you, Magister, never change." The words sounded polite, and, self-focused as Dar'Khan was, he took them as the compliment they most definitely were not.

Rommath nodded at her. "Lady Sylvanas," he said.

"Magister Rommath," she replied, and then moved on. Rommath, while more pleasant than Dar'Khan, was too cold and serious for her liking. The line continued with various nobility and court members, and Sylvanas's mouth soon began to ache from the forced smiles.

She brightened at the chance to meet some of the court artists.

Most of them knew her primarily as Lirath's sister, which was unexpected and oddly charming. The musicians, of course, were currently busy performing, but Sylvanas hoped to meet some of them later. Once she was done with the line, Sylvanas was besieged by hopeful suitors and giggling ladies who sought to curry favor with the family, then finally, the myriad cousins of one variety or other of the Windrunners themselves. Out of all of them, other than the artists, the only person Sylvanas cared for at all was Priestess Liadrin, although sometimes the priestess's gentle demeanor tried her patience.

At one point, when going in search of beverages for Vereesa and Verath, Sylvanas found herself standing next to Lord Saltheril.

"My lord," she said, as sweetly as she could. Saltheril turned with a practiced, pleasant expression on his face, which shifted to utterly, genuinely annoyed.

"How pleasant to see you here," said Sylvanas.

Clearly Saltheril did not share the sentiment, and his frown deepened. He attempted to move past her. "Your pardon," he said.

But Sylvanas wasn't done. "Still throwing your famous parties?" she said, finishing her beverage. "I do hope so. We wouldn't know, of course, as Lirath hasn't been performing at them for some time, and the rest of us have been extremely busy with court matters."

"And yet," came a smooth tenor voice behind her, "somehow I have not encountered you. You have grown quite a bit since I last saw you, Lady Sylvanas."

Saltheril alternately paled and flushed. "Your Highness," he said, bowing deeply.

The prince of Quel'Thalas acknowledged the obeisance with a smile and nod, but his attention was on Sylvanas. As he plucked a cup of wine from a golden serving tray, he saluted her with it. A smile played around his mouth. "No woundwood in this goblet, I trust."

"Not this time," Sylvanas quipped, adding quickly, "Your Highness." She accepted two fresh cups and dropped a curtsy. "You will pardon me, but my father and sister are waiting."

"They can wait a moment longer," Kael'thas said. "Your parents are truly remarkable individuals. While everyone knows about the

Battle of the Seven Arrows, of course, few are as aware of the good your father has done the kingdom."

"Battling trolls is assuredly more noticeable than battling other politicians," Sylvanas replied. She refused to show her irritation at another reminder of her mother's nigh-legendary status.

"Ah, but sometimes, the battles in comfortable chambers over delicacies and beverages turn out to be the more important and long lasting. Quel'Thalas is very blessed indeed to have both of your parents. And," he said, inclining his golden head graciously, "they have borne equally remarkable children. I am grateful to be able to borrow your brother as often as I have. He is quite popular at court."

"Our family appreciates your patronage," Sylvanas said dutifully, adding, "Lirath is very good at what he does."

"As are all of you. Your father tells me you are a budding diplomat."

She laughed. "My father, I fear, lives in hope. I am not diplomatic at all."

Kael'thas missed—or chose to miss—the wordplay. "My own father seldom stirs from his kingdom without cause. I, on the other hand, enjoy encountering other races—humans, gnomes, dwarves—and am honored to serve alongside other magi in Dalaran. Our land is glorious, to be certain, and I love it dearly—but there is so much more to Azeroth. Beautiful, much of it, but also deadly, and to be fought against.

"You may yet flower into statecraft. I would imagine it requires similar skills to hunting: timing, preparation, patience."

Sylvanas smiled despite herself. In a completely genuine tone, she said, "Laying traps? Killing cleanly? Skinning?"

Her apparent sincerity baffled the prince, and for a long moment he was clearly struggling between laughing at the joke and trying to find a way to politely answer a possibly serious question. Sylvanas desperately wanted to find out which he would choose, but that famous hunter-diplomat skill called patience eluded her, as she had used up all of hers on Saltheril. A smile cracked her seemingly earnest expression and she laughed.

Kael'thas followed suit, still uncomfortable. "You are a most un-usual woman, even for a Windrunner," he said gamely.

"I will take that as a compliment, Your Highness. But I really must be getting back." Sylvanas curtsied again and moved to thread her way to the crowd that inevitably gathered whenever their prince was doing, well, anything.

Someone jostled Sylvanas. She stumbled and caught herself, but sacrificed some of the wine in one of the cups . . . on the robe of the prince of Quel'Thalas.

Her eyes widened and she glanced up. Kael'thas stared down at his saturated robe, not angry, but assuredly bemused. "Your Highness, I am so sorry," she said, and meant it. She should have stopped then, but the quip escaped her: "At least it matches the color of your robe!"

A chuckle, uncertain and ready to be shushed by a single glance from the prince, rippled through the crowd. It *did* match the robe, so accurately it might simply have been spilled water. Gold and red, those were the colors of the prince; Sylvanas often wondered if he wore anything but that and the purple robes of the Dalaran magi. Now, however, was definitely not the time to ask. She hurried away, hearing Saltheril's voice as the noble said, "Oh, my prince, how clumsy that Windrunner girl is! I swear, Lord Verath just lets his children run around like *wild beasts!*"

And with that barb, Sylvanas realized that it was likely well past time for her to leave the party. She returned to where she had left her father and Vereesa, looked around, and observed they had given up on her and were dancing. Sylvanas smiled a little. The two true diplomats of the family, both white-haired and kind-eyed.

A familiar voice caught her ear. "It's called Feeble Old Man," Halduron was saying. Sylvanas knew exactly what he was talking about and had to smile. He was chatting with Vor'athil and Jirri, who had been a brand-new recruit on the day Alleria had set out to hunt a springpaw. She still looked quite young and was clearly very inter-ested in the story.

"That hardly sounds threatening," Vor'athil said.

"That's the point!" Halduron exclaimed. "I dress in an old, tattered cloak, you see. My head's covered, I'm hunched over, I'm leaning on my spear as if it's a staff. The trolls think I am easy prey. And when they attack . . . half of them are full of arrows before they even reach me—"

"Oh, you have Farstriders hidden in the trees!" Jirri said.

"Yes!" Halduron said gleefully. "And I throw off the cape and impale the trolls with my spear."

Vor'athil had narrowed his eyes skeptically. "That seems a bit elaborate. How often does it work?"

Halduron grinned. "Let's just say . . . no troll has survived to tell his brethren of the trick."

"You must be parched after bragging so much, Halduron," Lor'themar teased. Sylvanas turned to smile at him as he stepped beside her. It turned into an annoyed scowl as her friend plucked both beverages from her hands and offered them to Jirri and Halduron.

Sylvanas sighed. "Well, that's what Father and Vereesa get for not being patient," she said, intercepting Halduron's goblet and taking a sip from it before handing it to her friend.

"Kael's new red stain is going to be all the rage in fashion soon," Lor'themar said with a perfectly straight face. Sylvanas winced, then smiled.

"I could not help but hear the latest gossip," Lor'themar said. "I discount it utterly."

"Oh, do tell," Sylvanas said wryly.

"It seems," he continued, "that all the nobles will be gathered for a royal wedding soon. None other than the union of two great houses will do for the gossips It seems our prince has set his sights on . . . Lady Sylvanas Windrunner."

"*What?*" After blurting out the single word, Sylvanas dropped her voice to a soft murmur. "That's ridiculous!"

"I don't know, *Queen Sylvanas* has a nice ring to it," Lor'themar deadpanned.

"And we know how much you love formal events, meaningless chitchat, and—"

"Please," Sylvanas groaned. "He is nice enough, I suppose, and has certainly been very good to our family, especially Lirath. I'll always be grateful for that. But I cannot think of a worse fate than being married to a prince. Leave my forest for stilted conversation over punch? Become an accessory, worn on the royal arm rather than pinned to the royal chest? Completely change who I am, dress in gaudy formal robes to match his, be paraded out to perform like a trained animal at stupid parties like—"

Sylvanas stopped abruptly. Neither ranger was looking at her, and both of them had gone noticeably paler.

Oh no.

"Fortunately for the both of us, Lady Sylvanas," came the smooth voice, "I pay little attention to gossip. Rest assured that I cannot imagine this fantastical event, either. Since you are clearly not having a pleasant time at this stupid party, please do feel free to excuse yourself. You've done quite enough for the crown this evening."

Sylvanas felt her cheeks grow hot. She dropped a curtsy, and turned to leave. Kael caught her arm for a moment, then said, softly, for her ears only, "Had I asked for your hand . . . the last thing I would wish would be to change who you are."

Then he was gone. Sylvanas had not thought it possible to feel worse. Before, she was red with simple embarrassment, but now she burned with shame. She felt dozens of eyes boring into her as her friends regarded her with awkward empathy. It wasn't really the prince himself she disliked—though truth be told, she didn't know him all that well—it was the falseness of court life, the posturing, the expectations, the pretense. But Sylvanas couldn't explain that. She couldn't do anything at all except murmur, "Excuse me," and leave.

CHAPTER FIVE

When she reached the spire, Sylvanas exchanged the lovely gown—how it had managed to escape the wine that had saturated the prince's robe, Sylvanas did not know—and shrugged into her more comfortable tunic, shirt, and leather armor. She sighed with relief, nodded at her reflection in the mirror, and joined two Farstriders, Cyndia and Lyana, at their twilight archery practice. She spent the next few hours in activities much more familiar, and in company much more pleasant, than the recent debacle at court. "Remembrance" indeed; Sylvanas wondered if she'd ever forget it.

She stayed out as late as she dared, trying to time it just right—she did not want to beat her parents home, nor did she want to arrive before they had headed to bed. Sylvanas was not at all looking forward to anything they might have to say to her, though, as always, she would be forgiven. Until the next time.

To her surprise, it was neither her father nor her mother who was waiting for her, but Lirath. He was pacing up and down when she called out to him and waved. Sylvanas sprinted the rest of the way up, concerned at his expression.

"What is wrong, my Little Lord Sun?" she queried.

His eyes narrowed. "Don't. Not right now."

She blinked. "All right," she said. "What's happened?"

Lirath laughed. Even his anger had a musical sound. "Of course. You have always been so focused on yourself, on *your* needs and wants and whims, you don't even know, do you?"

"If I did, I wouldn't be asking. Are . . . are you angry that I left?"

"Oh no. By the time you flounced off I was glad to see you go."

The words were cruel, meant to hurt, and they did. She blinked, as startled by the verbal attack as she would have been by a physical one. "Why would you say that?"

"You can't be this obtuse. You're supposed to be the clever one!"

Now he was starting to get underneath her skin, and her own ire rose. "Is this what you're learning at the palace? How to insult and hurt people?"

He closed the distance between them in two strides. "That. That right there. If I wanted to study insults and how to hurt someone, I'd come to you, because that is *exactly* what you did today. You stood there, a guest of the royal family, needling the heir to the throne of Quel'Thalas, insulting him behind his back, and then kiting off to whatever adventure you had waiting while leaving the rest of us to pick up the pieces. How do you think that reflects on the family? On me?"

His voice cracked on the last word, and Sylvanas realized that buried below the harshness of his anger was the vulnerability of his hurt. She softened.

"Little Lord—" she began.

"I said, don't! I'm not little anymore, Sylvanas, so stop treating me like I'm a child."

"Well," she said, "you're certainly behaving like a child throwing a tantrum." Now her words were the ones that cut.

Lirath visibly flinched. "His Highness has been nothing but good to the Windrunners, and especially to me. And he forgave you for your unspeakably reckless little stunt at Saltheril's party, or have you forgotten that?"

Kael'thas had indeed been good to their family, and it had been the prince who had gentled the punishment Saltheril had been set to deliver. Lirath was right. Her behavior tonight had been out of line. She had insulted—and hurt—someone. And because he was right, and because she was in the wrong and she despised it, she doubled down.

"I was trying to protect you!"

Lirath scoffed. "*Protect me?* If Aravan and Rendris had been truly set on ruining me, your prank would have made them double their attacks, not cease them. I don't need protecting, Sylvanas. I can fight my own battles."

Blood thundered in Sylvanas's ears as her outrage rose. She had taken a deep breath, ready to issue a blistering retort, when a voice shouted, "Enough!"

Both Sylvanas and Lirath turned, startled, to see Vereesa standing there. She was still in her elegant gown, her hair combed and adorned with a sparkling jewel, but somehow their younger sister managed to look disheveled. Her fists were clenched, her pretty face red as her gown and wet with tears. "Stop it! *Both* of you!"

The pair stood silent. Vereesa panted heavily, as if she'd been running. "I can't keep this up," she blurted, her voice thick. "Father is always away. Mother and Alleria can barely be in the same room with each other without shouting, and now the two of you are fighting. What is *wrong* with all of you? Don't you remember when everything was different? When we, we used to go to our spot, and, laugh and dance and play games, and, and . . ."

Sylvanas's face still burned, but this time with shame for the second time that night. Lirath's golden head was lowered, and though she could not see his face, his shoulders had relaxed. Without speaking, they both turned and went to their sister, wrapping their arms around her. Vereesa leaned her head against Sylvanas and sobbed for a moment, then pulled back from her siblings, wiping a hand across her face.

"I am sorry," she said.

"Don't be," Lirath said quickly, his voice its normal warm tone, concern on his face.

"Lirath is right. *We're* sorry. You have every right to be angry at us."

Vereesa had composed herself. "I don't even care who's *right* anymore," she murmured. "I just want all this to *stop*."

Sylvanas smoothed her white hair back. "It will. Eventually. Things will come to a head."

Vereesa laughed shakily. "That is my Sylvanas, she always has a comforting word."

Sylvanas smiled, too. "It will happen as it will. Nothing stays the same, Vereesa. Even—especially—if we want it to."

She could hear the sadness in her own voice as she spoke. The words were true, and she was only now realizing it; realizing what was really troubling her. Lirath was right, on many counts. He was no longer "little." She was a fully fledged adult and member of the Farstriders. Vereesa would be inducted soon. They all had destinies, directions . . . but were these the paths they wanted? It certainly seemed Alleria did not want her charted course. Vereesa appeared content enough—when her family wasn't squabbling—but maybe she was tired with always being saddled with peacekeeping. And as for herself—Sylvanas was still trying to figure that out.

At least Lirath had been born to do what he was doing.

"It's been a long day," Vereesa said. "I'm heading to bed."

"Me too," Lirath said quickly, as if anxious to put the day and all its challenges behind him. But Sylvanas was not going to leave this unfinished.

"Lirath, can we talk?"

Vereesa's lips tightened. "If you argue again, I'm going to pour a bucket of water on you both."

It was a feeble joke, but all three seized on it and chuckled. "Don't worry," Sylvanas said to both her sister and her brother. "Good night, Vereesa."

Sylvanas and Lirath were silent until Vereesa was out of earshot. Lirath turned to look at Sylvanas, the wariness that lingered in his eyes still visible even in the torchlight. Again, Sylvanas felt a stab, knowing that she had put that wariness there.

"Well?" he said, cautiously.

Sylvanas took a deep breath of the soft night air, redolent with the smells of the ocean, of woods and grass. It calmed her. Gesturing for him to follow, she headed down toward the beach, toward the constant rhythm of the ocean and away from the spire's current sense of discord. The last time Sylvanas had been here, it had been with him. How content they had been, playing in the surf, gathering seashells. And how terrified she had been when she thought he had drowned.

She had intended to choose her words well, with deliberation, but as they walked, the words came tumbling out like a wave crashing on the shore.

"I'm sorry," Sylvanas said, looking out over the ocean, black and silvered and blue in the moonslight. "I was rude to Kael'thas, and he didn't deserve it. It wasn't him I was angry with. It was what he represented, what . . . I-I'm being told to be . . . or not be. Sometimes I'm afraid I've gone too far down a path to turn back. Father wants one thing, Mother doesn't care, and I want something else entirely. But I don't know what." She felt him beside her but didn't look at him. If she looked at him, she might not have the courage to say the words.

"I do not know where I'm supposed to be, Lirath." Her voice, soft and forlorn, sounded small. "A diplomat? I understand strategy and politics, but I don't like them, and I don't have the patience. When I am with the Farstriders I feel free, but not challenged. I don't feel like I'm being asked to grow—and I should be. I should always strive to be something more. Something better."

Now Sylvanas did risk a look up at him. Gone was the frown and the tightness of his face. It was open, kind, and he was listening. As she knew he would.

"I don't know what's going to happen with Alleria and Mother," Sylvanas continued. "Vereesa is worn thin trying to keep the peace among us all. The only one of us—besides Father—who is stable, where they should be . . . is you. You have this gift, and you are able to pursue it, and, well, everybody loves you."

Sylvanas smiled through her sadness. "Me most of all. And you know exactly what you want to do, and exactly where you want to be."

Lirath's expression turned sober, and now it was he who looked away. "That is not true at all."

"*What?*"

Sylvanas almost gaped. Everything she had assumed to be true about the world centered on the fact that Lirath, at least, her beloved Little Lord Sun, was going to be safe and loved, even if everyone and everything around him spun out of control.

He shifted his weight uneasily. "I love performing. And music. And I do feel happy when I can sing and entertain people. Do you remember our conversation after the disaster at Saltheril's?"

The combination of his serious tone and his words of choice made her almost laugh despite herself. "It *was* a disaster," she agreed, smiling, then she, too, became somber. "And I do. I had thought you had forgotten about that."

"How could I possibly forget, when nearly everyone in my family is a Farstrider?" he replied. He spoke quietly, calmly, but there was a sorrow underlying the words. "Father's work is important to the kingdom as well. I just dance and sing pretty songs."

Sylvanas almost wept at the self-contempt in his voice. She took his hands in both of hers, remembering how she had been galvanized at once by the little bundle with pink cheeks and blue eyes. She thought of tiny fingers reaching out, grasping a lock of her hair, wondering at the newness of this world; saw in her mind's eye those same hands, fingertips bloody from practicing, from a determination to excel.

She looked up at him. "We both honor life, little brother. I'm training to protect people so you can help them find joy. I may keep them alive, but you . . . you give them reasons to *live*. And knowing that—that gives me a reason to stay strong. Because I am fighting *for* something."

Sylvanas didn't expect her voice to crack, or her eyes to fill with tears. She certainly didn't expect to see his own eyes shimmer suddenly brighter in the moonslight, or for him to throw his arms around her and hug her tight.

"We have *never* argued like this before in our lives," Lirath said. "I hate it."

"Me too," Sylvanas said, squeezing him back, as if she could make the embrace into a shield to protect him. When he was an infant, she had hated to hear him cry, and as he had grown, she hated to see him in any kind of pain. She still did.

Let me be the one at the edge of danger, she thought. *The one in the woods, the one with the sweat and blood and stenches and pain. Let him be the one safe beside the fire, where the only concern is which song to sing.* She wondered if this was a prayer and decided it didn't matter.

They pulled back, smiling at each other. Sylvanas was always ready for a battle of words, or even of blows if need be, but not with Lirath. Never with Lirath.

"It's late," Sylvanas said. "We should retire before our parents get home, or else we won't sleep for a decade."

"At least," Lirath said with perfect seriousness, then grinned.

Wordlessly, but in an easy camaraderie, they walked back to the spire, which stood silent and peaceful as it reached up toward a night sky crowded with stars.

CHAPTER SIX

Sylvanas managed to elude both her parents the following morning by sneaking out early, before the sun that meant so much to the quel'dorei had peeked its head over the horizon, and the world was dull gray and damp with dew.

Sleep had not provided much rest, so she welcomed the steely cold and raced through the dew-slick grass, leaping up as easily as one of the red squirrels into the boughs of the gold-leafed trees. She darted from branch to branch to branch, picking specific trees as targets and firing arrow after arrow into them. She returned about an hour after sunrise, flushed and panting, feeling that some measure of calmness had settled into her soul.

A shouted refusal chased even that tiny gift away.

"I will not do it!"

Sylvanas stopped.

So. The words were said, finally. Alleria had grown tired of explaining, of deferring, of prolonging what everyone, including Sylvanas, had thought was inevitable: taking on the mantle of ranger-general. Sylvanas licked dry lips, then moved steadily forward. The shouting grew louder.

"You do not dare to refuse this, Alleria! It is a solemn duty, and I will not allow it!"

Sylvanas felt her face go carefully blank and her body hum with tension as she drew closer.

"I will take my company and go," Alleria said, trying to bring down the heat of the conversation. "Only a few of us. You will still have the veterans. I don't want to command a kingdom's military, I simply want to contribute. To do something that helps people other than us, Mother. We are not the center of the world, and if we do not soon realize that, we will stagnate!"

The world around Sylvanas, so full of the sounds of nature and its creatures, had been chastened into silence. Her own footfalls sounded thunderous to her ears. She kept her pace steady.

"I don't want to step into footprints made by others hundreds of years ago. I want to make my own path," Alleria pleaded. "My own destiny."

"This is a terrible mistake."

"But it will at least be *mine* to make! You've never let me have a choice in anything. I have been nothing to you but an heir to a title. Even my name comes from your mother. I have never been *me.*"

"You have always been you. Do not wallow in self-pity."

Despite herself, Sylvanas flinched. This was different. Her mother and her older sister had argued often before, but this time, the verbal daggers bit deep, striking bone. Crippling.

"I don't belong." Alleria's voice had grown cold, as cold with resolve as her mother's was with contempt. "My soul feels *trapped,* Mother. I am not running away from what you taught me. I will remember everything, and I'll use it to help people, just like you do. I will just be helping different people."

"You would turn away from us?"

"I'm not turning away from anything." Sylvanas's brow furrowed. She had never heard that tone in Alleria's voice before. So steadfast. So certain.

So much like Father's.

"I am turning *toward* something. And I hope one day you will see that."

"All I see is a stubborn child, willing to run off to adventure while leaving her people defenseless."

"I'm not the only one of us who can shoot an arrow," Alleria said. "Sylvanas was already as good as I am years ago. Better. Better, maybe, than I will ever be."

Sylvanas stopped. The siblings loved each other and did not shy from affection. But she had never heard Alleria praise her. Alleria thought her the better archer?

What was even more stunning to Sylvanas was that her mother didn't disagree with Alleria's words. "It does not matter if she is the better shot. Sylvanas does not have the temperament for leadership. She is not dedicated enough. She has had countless opportunities to gain allies at court, and she has squandered every one of them through foolishness and mischief."

Heat flooded Sylvanas's cheeks. Her mother was obviously referring to last night.

"Now you grasp at straws. She has Halduron and Lor'themar on her side. Many of the Farstriders appreciate her distaste for formalities and pretense. And I cannot think of a single challenge Sylvanas has faced but not met. Let her turn her mind to leadership, and you will see her exceed your expectations. She is the ranger-general you are hoping for—not me."

Sylvanas heard quick footsteps, but she didn't draw back. Alleria, normally so focused, was so intent on escaping the argument the two almost bumped into each other. Alleria was flushed, but at the same time looked somehow calmer and more resolute than Sylvanas had ever seen her.

For a heartbeat, there was silence. Then Alleria said, "I meant what I said. About you."

Sylvanas took a quick, sharp breath. Alleria turned to go.

The future ranger-general, the epitome of stillness an instant before, shot out her hand and grasped that of Alleria. For a moment they stood, neither looking at the other, Sylvanas facing her mother, poised to move forward, and Alleria turning her back on her. Their fingers interlaced, and each woman held on tightly. There were volumes of unspoken words in the gesture; then Alleria gave a final squeeze, and released her sister's hand.

Sylvanas felt shaken, as though the earth had trembled beneath her, and in a way it had. The warm feel of her sister's hand lingered in her palm as she stepped forward to face her mother.

"I will forgive you, Alleria, but not now."

Lireesa's voice was harsher than Sylvanas had ever heard it. And yet it was somehow softened, shaped by grief and disappointment but not anger. She stood with her back to Sylvanas, her body rounded, drawing in on herself. Sylvanas closed her fingers around her palm, as if she could grasp the echo of Alleria's touch and hold it for an eternity. When she spoke, her voice was gentle.

"It's me, Mother."

Before her eyes, Lireesa changed. Her back stiffened, straightened. Became the posture of a soldier, not a mother, and when Lireesa turned around, Sylvanas saw on her ranger-general's face the dampness of tears, and the implacableness of resolution.

And suddenly the ghost of her sister's grasp dissolved as surely as nightmists in daylight, and all the warmth, love, and strength it had imparted vanished with it. When Sylvanas spoke, it was with a fierceness equal to her mother's, but without hint of the pain that drove its vitriol.

"I may be your second choice, Mother," Sylvanas Windrunner said, "but you will see that I am not second best."

The days passed, as unmoved by the turmoil in the Windrunner household as they had been by the family's joyful hours. Alleria selected her rangers. Vereesa was inducted into the Farstriders. Lireesa informed the Farstriders that Alleria had been given a new mission: Instead of becoming ranger-general, Lireesa had decided that it was time for the Farstriders to reclaim the meaning of their name, and to once again look to the world beyond their borders. Therefore, Sylvanas would become ranger-general in Alleria's stead. It clearly stung Lireesa that none of them seemed surprised, that in fact many seemed pleased. Sylvanas, her mother announced, would begin her training once Alleria and her group had departed. Lirath, always the ray of hope in the family, returned that same day from Silvermoon with the news that he was now officially a royal musician.

Verath, ever the diplomat, had accompanied his son back to the spire. He had with him several bottles of Suntouched Reserve wine, gifted to him by Anasterian himself. Verath claimed it had been cellared for so many years that "the dust made everyone sneeze when it was brought up." Sylvanas rolled her eyes, then looked at the vintage, and allowed that her father might not be exaggerating after all.

The party was the perfect diversion. In the afternoon, the spire would host a small group of friends and relatives, and at twilight the guests would depart, leaving the family to spend the rest of the evening alone together.

There seemed to be a slight thawing of the iciness that had existed between Alleria and their mother for the last, well, years, now. Pleased as she was to see it, Sylvanas could not help but wonder what acquiring the title of ranger-general might mean for her.

Vereesa veered between sorrow at seeing her sister go, and clear relief that a decision had been made and the arguments had finally stopped. Lirath seemed overjoyed with his new role, less because he was sought after than because it placed him in a position where he could train some of the promising newcomers—though Sylvanas still thought of their conversation on the shore, and what feelings were hidden beneath his smile.

And Sylvanas? Despite her mother's belief that she wasn't "dedicated enough," Sylvanas took the responsibility very seriously indeed. As she had told Lirath that same night on the beach, she hadn't felt challenged by simply being a Farstrider. She was confident that, if nothing else, her mother would make her training as grueling as possible, and odd as it might have seemed to others, she found herself looking forward to it.

Verath did not wear his robes of state that evening, but rather purple silk breeches, leather boots, and a white shirt open at the throat. Lireesa, too, was out of her normal "uniform" of light leather armor, wearing a simple sky-blue dress that suited her startlingly well. It made her seem softer, somehow; more than the armor, more than the formal gown.

How might they all be different, Sylvanas wondered, if Lireesa had not been so driven and bent on driving others? If their world had been gentler? If Lireesa had not inherited the role of ranger-general, might this smiling woman in the sky-blue dress have been the mother the Windrunner children loved?

But such reveries were foolish. The only one of them who had known true gentleness from their mother had been the last of them, Lirath, who had not taken the path his sisters had and so was not the recipient of Lireesa's sometimes too-intent focus.

Sylvanas was glad he had been the one to walk that path. Lirath might think he wanted to be a Farstrider, but it was obvious he had been born to be something different: a balm to others, not a defender of them. She could not bear to have seen Lirath grow up like his sisters, tempered by the harshness of Lireesa's forge of will.

Alleria was in full uniform, as were the handful of her friends who would be departing with her: Verana, Rellian, Auric, and Talthressar. The rest of the Farstriders had come as they wished, all casual, all friends. The focus was on Alleria and her unit, of course. Sylvanas smothered a grin as a few young women from Goldenmist Village came forward, professing how terribly brokenhearted they would be to see the eldest Windrunner child depart.

"What's so funny?" Halduron asked, slipping up beside her. Lor'themar, too, was approaching, to stand next to Sylvanas. She had been more relieved than she cared to admit that neither of them had been asked to accompany Alleria—or, if asked, had declined. They were still here, and the Trio would not be disbanded, and for that she was grateful.

"It's the Salonar girls," she said. "From their reaction, you would think *they* were the ones losing a sister. I don't think they've seen her in years." She wrinkled her nose. "Look at how they're carrying on!"

"Whereas the *actual* sister won't miss her at all."

"Ah, Lor'themar, you know that's not true."

"You'll miss her once your mother turns her attention to your training," Halduron said.

"How could I forget the Mauler?" she retorted. "Don't worry. I've had a lifetime to prepare."

At that moment, the weeping girls curtsied and left. Alleria sighed, turned her head, and noticed Sylvanas regarding her. Sylvanas rolled her eyes, forcing Alleria to stifle a laugh and look serious as the next heartbroken soul who wanted to look good in front of Lireesa and Verath Windrunner lamented their daughter's departure.

Sylvanas would make her farewells at a more private time, before Alleria left at dawn. Despite her nonchalance, she would miss her older sibling. Alleria was not as close to her as Lirath or Vereesa, but Sylvanas loved her, and there would be an emptiness where she used to be.

"Are you truly all right, Sylvanas?" It was Lor'themar, who was always attuned to the emotions of those around him.

She gave him a playful shove. "When am I not?" she quipped. Well aware of the lie, his eyes narrowed. "I will miss her, of course. But she will be back to visit. Mother will go hunt her down if she doesn't."

When dusk fell, the partygoers thanked their hosts and departed, some to continue celebrating in a rowdier fashion elsewhere, others to head home to familial obligations. Some, it was true, left more courteously than others, but Suntouched wine was aptly named, and few could be condemned for being a trifle the worse—or better—for its consumption.

When all but the Windrunners had departed, the celebration was moved from the base of the spire to the family's favorite place in Eversong Woods. They did not bring much with them: a bowl of fruit, a few more bottles of the Suntouched Reserve, Lirath's pipes, his lute, and a small handheld drum.

Sylvanas had worried that the tension of the last several months would spoil this small, intimate celebration. She need not have been concerned. Lirath's voice rose to the sparkling stars in the night sky along with the fragrant scent of woodsmoke as the three sisters stepped forward into the wild, flowing dances they had improvised since childhood. Hands readily clasped; smiles warmed faces; lithe bodies, honed from training and lives lived mostly under the sun and stars, moved with the grace of willows in an unspoken harmony. And at one point, Sylvanas saw Verath rise, bow deeply to their mother, and extend a hand.

Lireesa smiled, and for a moment Sylvanas had her first real glimpse of the girl Lireesa must have once been, before time and duties took their toll. She took her partner's hand, and they, too, began to dance on the soft grass, their moves familiar and effortless and their eyes only for each other.

Why did we stop doing this? Sylvanas wondered suddenly, with a pang. *Why has it taken Alleria's departure for us to come back here as a whole family?* Hard on the heels of that thought was, *Will we ever be a whole family again?* But Sylvanas fiercely banished it.

In that moment of perfect lavender dusk, the fireflies appeared. Her eyes immediately met Lirath's, and his face melted into a smile as bright as sunshine. "Look, Lady Moon," he said, "even the stars have come to dance."

She could not help but smile in return. After Lirath had finished playing, Verath insisted on refilling everyone's cups, as he had a toast. When all were ready, he lifted his goblet.

"I am proud to be part of this remarkable family," he stated. "My beloved wife is ranger-general, one who commands utmost respect from those she leads to victory after victory, and who has most certainly won my heart forever."

"The best battle I have ever fought," Lireesa said, her eyes warm and bright.

"The easiest, certainly," Verath said teasingly.

He turned to Alleria. "My eldest daughter is embarking on a journey that will bring the outside world to the gates of Silvermoon for the first time in perhaps too long. She is someone who remembers debts owed; who will forge new friendships while cherishing those she already has. I am proud you are blazing your own trail, my child, but I hope you will always know the way home."

Alleria stole a quick glance at Lireesa as Verath spoke, but Lireesa seemed at peace, now that the decision was final.

"My clever girl, my fierce girl, will follow in her mother's footsteps as the future ranger-general. Though you will no longer be at court quite so often, Sylvanas, do not think you have escaped me. I've come to rely on your instincts regarding strategy, if not your skill with diplomacy."

Sylvanas laughed at that, and he gave her a wink before turning to address his youngest children. "Vereesa, our loving mediator. I do not think you know how much we rely on you to keep the peace. We are all, shall we say, strong-minded individuals. It's you who reminds us that we are also a family. I have little doubt you will turn this skill toward uniting many hearts in our kingdom."

Vereesa beamed, her cheeks flush and her eyes shimmering with happy tears. "And Lirath. What can I say? You have been such a blessing to us all. Not only was our home—and now, the most honored and exclusive places in Quel'Thalas—uplifted daily by your music, but your spirit is as pure as your voice. True beauty cannot be purchased at the bazaar. It springs forth without fanfare in nature, and comes from those rare few who can grasp something the rest of us cannot, and it is they who bring it forth into the world. You are the youngest ever to be given the rank of royal musician. I cannot wait to see where your skill and kind heart take you as the years unfold."

Lirath looked almost overcome. He seemed to be searching for words, then finally said, simply, "Thank you, Father. I hope I make you proud."

They cheered, they toasted, the wine warmed them. But it seemed their mother had something to say, too, and Sylvanas braced herself.

"No one in my family, including me, cares much for formal garb, or lavish parties, or jewelry," Lireesa began. Sylvanas glanced at her siblings; they looked as confused as she felt. "And I know that we have had our share of disagreements." Her eyes flickered to Alleria's. Alleria bit her lip.

Please, Mother, Sylvanas implored silently, *do not ruin this night.*

Lireesa continued. "But there was a moment, in the not-too-distant past, when I was happy for all of it. For formal gowns, which meant we were at peace and could savor frivolity. For my family, who were all together. And especially for my children, who looked so beautiful on that night. I remember the gowns my girls wore, the formal robes chosen by my son as he performed before the royal court. So your father and I commissioned something, so that Alleria always will remember that night, and her family."

Verath gave Lireesa a pouch, and the ranger-general withdrew a necklace. It was a chain upon which hung three gemstones: a ruby, a sapphire, and an emerald. Lireesa walked toward Alleria, the child who should have been her heir.

"Three gems for my daughters," she said. "And for my son"—she smiled, her eyes shimmering in the faint light with what might have been tears—"the artful chain that holds them together. I give you this, Alleria, to remind you of your family, even when your heart takes you far from us."

Alleria smiled. "I will *always* remember you, no matter how distantly I might travel."

It was a beautiful moment, and an awkward one, growing more uncomfortable as it stretched on. Then, with no warning, Lirath launched into a bawdy and hilarious tavern tune about a serving girl with two suitors, a hunter and a soldier, and everyone started laughing the minute they heard the first few notes.

Even Lireesa clapped and chimed in at the call-and-response, but Sylvanas hung back, leaning against a tree, sipping from a goblet filled with the heady wine from a dusty bottle.

Verath stepped beside her, and they clinked goblets as they watched the family, smiling and laughing, painted in shades of orange and yellow by the fire.

"It feels like more than Alleria leaving," Sylvanas said, softly.

Sylvanas's eyes went to Lirath, laughing even as he sang. "He used to be my little shadow," Sylvanas said, unable to keep the wistfulness from her voice. "My Little Lord Sun. Now he plays for a king."

"Change is inevitable, my dear child."

"I know, but . . . I'm not sure I'm ready for things to change."

"The world does not care what we want. It is up to us to change as well. The only other choice is to be left behind and forever bitter."

He turned to her, smiling fondly. "We're all feeling it, but you, perhaps, more than most. This night . . . it is the end of something. Tomorrow, something else begins." He turned back to look at the dancing. "That's why I said what I did. Why we gave Alleria the necklace. We're old enough to know you must savor these moments because nothing lasts forever. And . . . that is all right."

"I suppose," Sylvanas said, with an exaggerated sigh, "it *would* be boring if everything stayed the same."

Verath laughed. "That's my girl."

INTERLUDE

Anduin had listened without interrupting. Sylvanas had not thought in detail about her childhood in years. She was surprised at how clear some of her memories were, even now. It stirred within her the old, familiar combination of pain and then anger. But somehow, now that a solution, a rectification of all that had gone so horribly, cruelly wrong in her life, was so close at hand, the memories did not hurt—or anger—her as much. She had let go of many things, walking this path, and perhaps this weight was some of it.

She fell silent, unwilling as of yet to revisit the moments where the tight-knit fabric of family, friends, and a future full of hope began to unravel, and the silence between them was long. Anduin broke it by moving the tray forward with a scraping sound, nudging it with one armored finger until it was partway out of the circle.

"Why do you tell me this?" he asked quietly.

"You did not know it," Sylvanas said.

"Did you hope to play on my sympathy? Did you think your story of a strong, loving, present family would move me somehow?"

Of course she had. She'd all but told him that was what she intended.

His face was hard, his expression flat, and she could hear his anger simmering beneath his words as he got to his feet.

"I'm certain your various spies have ferreted out all the details about my childhood, but let me remind you, just in case there are any gaps in your knowledge," Anduin said. "When I was an infant, my mother was killed by a bloodthirsty mob. People she was standing up for. I imagine you know what a stone, thrown with angry force, can do to a skull."

Sylvanas did. She remained silent.

"You remember how hard your mother drove you. I don't remember mine at all. My father saw it happen. It . . . broke him. He could barely stand to look at me as I grew up. I have no warm, wise conversations with him during my childhood to look back on. Then he vanished when I was ten, and I suddenly became the king of Stormwind. You?" he scoffed. "At that age, you still were using a child's bow."

He was calm, but also angry and he was hurt. Anduin was right. She had been fully informed of almost every moment of Anduin's brief life thus far, but it had always been comprised of cold facts. Sylvanas knew what else he would say, and abruptly wished he would not say it.

"Varian returned full of anger. It took us a long time to reconcile. But we did. We did," he repeated, more softly, as if to himself. "And then . . . the Broken Shore. But you know about that."

"I do," Sylvanas said, not rising to the bait.

"Your life," Anduin said, quietly, "was filled with riches. Riches I've never known. Your world was one of safety and certainty. Of harmless pranks and easy forgiveness. You knew both of your parents. You had sisters and a brother. Your youth was filled with grace and laughter, beauty and love and support, and friendship. And yes—I know that world is no more—for any of us. But at least, you had the chance to taste it before it was gone."

Sylvanas rose now, too. "Do not envy me, Little Lion. You have lost much, certainly. But it is nothing compared with what I have lost."

"Is it nothing compared with what the night elves lost? Or should I say, what you took from them?"

And there it was: the burning of Teldrassil. Sylvanas knew he would throw it at her but had not expected he would do so just yet. "I did what I did for a reason. For the greatest reason of all." Her voice rose before she could properly guard its cadence.

"*You became a* butcher, *Sylvanas, slaughtering innocents, all in the name of self-righteous lies!*"

It was not the petulant cry of a child, but the just fury of what the world would see as a good man. She could not rely on his empathy, not yet. She wondered if Anduin had chosen the word butcher *deliberately, but even now, after all that had been done to him, she did not think him that cruel.*

They stared at each other for a long minute. Sylvanas tamped down her anger. "I will speak of that in due time. But perhaps you will feel better when I tell you all that happened after Alleria left Quel'Thalas. You might not envy me quite as much then."

She sank down onto the stone again, indicating that he sit as well. He made no move to do so. "Stand if you must, then, but I will be here for a time, and . . ." Sylvanas couldn't resist a hint of smugness. "You do not appear to be going anywhere soon."

PART
II

Stay strong. Stay angry.

—SYLVANAS WINDRUNNER

CHAPTER SEVEN

"I can't believe she put you on patrol duty, like a trainee!" Halduron grumbled. "Whatever she thinks about you becoming ranger-general, you are far better than that."

"I wish I could say I'm surprised," Sylvanas replied as she packed what she would need for the day. "Actually . . . I *am* surprised. Surprised that it took her this long."

"We all knew she would be hard on you," Lor'themar said. "She cannot show favoritism."

"Of course," Sylvanas replied. "I expected to be treated like everyone else." Now that Alleria had flaunted tradition and stirred the pot, Sylvanas was *not* just anyone else, and Lireesa seemed determined to make her pay in one way or another. Every lesson was as much a trap as a test. Sylvanas wanted to say more, but she refused to sound like a whining child.

There had been a turn in Lireesa's demeanor following Alleria's departure. That fleeting glimpse of the woman who had danced lovingly with her husband, who had gifted Alleria with symbols of her family, seemed to depart with Alleria herself.

Lireesa had always been harsh, and Sylvanas understood why. But when Sylvanas's training began, it felt to her as if her mother was determined to drill the laughter out of her most challenging daughter. *And,* Sylvanas mused bitterly, *she is succeeding.*

So here she was, performing tasks like a fresh recruit. She finished packing—some fruit, dried meat, water, bandages—and would leave as soon as the previous cycle of scouts had returned.

"Have Anaryth and Rendevan returned yet?"

The other Farstriders, engaged in fletching arrows or stringing bows, only shook their heads.

Sylvanas shifted her weight from one foot to the other for a moment, then said, "I'm going ahead anyway." She needed to be somewhere other than here, enduring the looks of unwanted sympathy from her friends and fellow rangers.

"I am coming with you." Surprised, Sylvanas looked at Lor'themar. She had half expected Halduron to make the offer, but Lor'themar had beaten him to it.

"Your ranger-general said I was to go alone," she reminded him.

"*I* never heard her say that," he said, and picked up his bow.

While the Amani trolls to the east of Quel'Thalas were an ever-present threat, there had been little activity from them recently. Vereesa had yet to experience combat, and Sylvanas had only tasted it once. Scouts seldom had anything to report. Patrols were maintained as tradition, as a formality, and sometimes as reprimands.

She and Lor'themar trudged along in companionable silence, drawing closer to the marker.

"Do you think you will ever be tested, as Alleria was?" Lor'themar asked.

Sylvanas scowled. "I thought I would be. But at this point, I do not think that will happen." She hesitated, then, because this was Lor'themar, she added, "It feels as if she doesn't think me worth enough to be formally presented to the Farstriders as their future ranger-general."

And that hurt more than she had expected.

Lor'themar nodded. "The argument could be made that you have already been tapped to be ranger-general. Perhaps Lireesa does not feel you need such a test."

Sylvanas stopped in her tracks, regarded him, then spread her arms wide, indicating the menial task she had been set. "I think our current mission supports my original opinion."

Lor'themar chuckled sadly. "Perhaps you are right. Lireesa made no secret of her disappointment in Alleria's decision."

Sylvanas resumed walking. "It doesn't matter. Let her do what she feels she must. But if she wants me to step down, she will have to order me to do it. I will not do it on my own."

"I have no doubt of that."

They were approaching the first Amani marker. It was a large slab of stone, hung with ceremonial masks, a sort of shrine that served as a warning. From this point on, interlopers were in Amani territory. Candles were tended to as best wind permitted. Offerings were made, sometimes the skulls of their victims.

Sylvanas had passed by it more times than she could count. It had unnerved her the first time Lireesa brought her here when she was a small child. "These are the enemies, Sylvanas," her mother had said. "They are cruel and show no mercy. We defeated them long ago, but like all vermin, they are hard to eradicate. If you see them—run."

Sylvanas stared at the skulls. "But I want to fight them."

"You will," Lireesa said. "And you will be ready."

It was a good memory of her mother, and Sylvanas wished she had more of them. Her gaze flickered to the marker they were preparing to pass. Lor'themar saw it, too.

Rendevan sat cross-legged, his back against the tall, cold stone. His head was in his lap.

The two Farstriders acted as one, the only communication between them shared instincts and training. They both knew the various hand signals: arm extended, get to ground; palm up, hold position; hand on heart, prepare to fire. But there was no need—their bows were out and fitted with arrows in a fraction of an instant.

They stood, back-to-back, ears straining, eyes searching for any sign that the trolls who had slaughtered Rendevan and posed his body in such a sickening fashion were still about. The minutes stretched on, and finally Sylvanas lowered her right hand, fingers splayed—*stand down, do not fire*. She pointed at the body, held up two fingers, tapped near her eye, then made a circle in the air. *There were two Farstriders. Look for the second, and make a circuit.*

Lor'themar nodded and turned to obey. Sylvanas went to the marker, checked to make sure no hidden trap awaited her, and knelt down beside the fallen Farstrider. "You were both so new," she said, softly. "You deserved a chance to at least taste life before it was taken from you."

She visually examined the corpse, checking for any telltale smudges or smears that might be poison, then rose. Sorrow for the squandered life vied with anger, but neither could be indulged now. Sylvanas took a step toward Lor'themar, opening her mouth to speak as, out of habit, her gaze darted to the pile of skulls on the other side of the marker.

She froze. There was no need to continue looking for Anaryth. Her skull was the most recent one added to the horrific pile. The blood was still wet. Flies buzzed about.

We failed you.

"Lor'themar," she called, dragging her gaze away from Anaryth's wide, staring eyes, "Let's take them back and—"

A horrible cry rent the air, and the trolls charged. Sylvanas nocked her bow and fired, the arrow going right through one's throat. The troll fell, his scream turning to a choked, burbling sound. She heard a buzzing and leaped away just as a dart painted with poison whizzed past her ear. Landing lightly, Sylvanas drew and fired, drew and fired. Behind her were two more, quite dead. Lor'themar had been busy.

A troll shaman lay at the elf's feet as he struggled with one of the creatures. It had knocked Lor'themar's bow out of his hand with its crooked spear, and now, cackling, drew back for the kill.

An arrow suddenly seemed to sprout from its eye, and the troll dropped like a stone. Sylvanas whirled, another arrow already nocked, and gazed past it into the copse of trees.

"Don't shoot!" The voice was rough, and deep, and clearly not that of a troll.

Sylvanas did not move. "Drop the bow and come out where I can see you!"

A bow fell from the branches of the white-barked trees, followed by a male figure who put up his hands to show he had no weapons.

Sylvanas blinked.

"You . . . are a human," she said.

"Ah, what gave me away?"

He was not the first human Sylvanas had ever seen. On rare occasions, human couriers had approached the king, the prince, or, sometimes, even her father. They were uniform in their demeanor and tended to blend together in her mind. None of them had been remarkable enough for her to remember.

This one was tall, burly, and dressed in field garb. His quiver was strapped to his back. The hard leather of his jerkin was crisscrossed with scratches made by a variety of weapons, judging by their depth and shape. His boots were mud-spattered, and the hem of his cloak was dark with old stains. Sylvanas narrowed her eyes, regarding him. Old stains, yes . . . but new ones as well, dark and wet. Blood, perhaps?

He was also possibly the ugliest person she had ever seen. His face was lumpy, as if it had been punched many times, and the bones broken had poorly healed. Small dark eyes peered out from beneath bushy black eyebrows.

Still, Sylvanas did not lower her bow. "Lor'themar, did we get them all?" she called.

"It seems so," he responded. "It would appear I am in your debt, human."

The stranger shifted uncomfortably. "It was nothing," he said. His voice suited the rest of him perfectly: rough and raspy. "Just lucky I was there."

"Lucky, yes, but not a coincidence," said Sylvanas. "Were you spying on us?"

The man sighed. "Can I lower my hands?"

"Not yet. I asked you a question."

"Yes. I was spying. On *them*," he replied, nodding his head in the direction of a sprawled troll's body. "I was sent here to observe troll behavior and report back. Lordaeron wanted current information on them because we suspect they might be cooperating with the Horde or, at the very least, allowing a Horde presence here. *That* is the message I was bringing your king, when the troll ambush on you two Farstriders so rudely interrupted my travels. I'm Nathanos Marris, by the way."

"I am the woman with an arrow pointed at your heart."

"That did not escape my notice."

Their eyes met. Sylvanas waited a moment, then lowered her bow. She had heard from her father and sister that the human kingdoms had been discussing the problem, the green monsters from another world she'd heard threatening humans to the south. She knew Alleria had felt solidarity with their cause.

She looked around at the bodies scattered on the grass. Six had Farstrider arrows in them. Three had arrows fletched in green and brown.

Not only had Nathanos slain the troll that surely would have finished off Lor'themar, he'd taken out two others as well.

"Help us bring our friends home," she said, "and then I will take you to the king."

"We failed them," Sylvanas said quietly, her voice cold. Lor'themar and Nathanos had borne the fallen back to Farstrider Retreat while Sylvanas walked a few strides in front of them, turning her head, alert for another ambush. There had been none, and the two scouts had been laid gently onto the stone flooring. Several Farstriders had been present, and began their solemn work of cleaning and preparing the bodies.

"We needed to vary the routes and times. Our scouts' arrival was like clockwork." She thought for a moment, then nodded. "I will take the human to the court. He can deliver his message to the king, and

I will speak with the ranger-general about this. Stay here, Lor'themar. Tend them well."

Lor'themar nodded. To the human, she said, "Follow me."

Several dragonhawks undulated in the warm breeze just outside the retreat; tranquil, almost sleeping. Sylvanas paused in front of them. "Ever ridden one of these?" she asked Nathanos.

"No."

"Ever seen one?"

". . . No."

She raised an eyebrow. "Do you even know what it is?"

"It's a dragonhawk." The human's voice had an edge to it.

"At least they teach you something in Lordaeron. Hop on," Sylvanas said, swinging up onto the back of hers and gesturing to the second beast. To his credit, Nathanos didn't even pause. And the instant his rear met the saddle, the dragonhawk surged upward, flapping its membranous wings, its body bobbing as it hovered, awaiting direction.

Sylvanas knew that humans were accustomed to riding horseback, and maybe atop the occasional gryphon. But the half-lion, half-eagle creatures had a broader, flatter back, and a feathered neck to cling to if need be. Dragonhawk scales were smooth . . . and slippery. Few had the skill it took to ride one without a saddle. Sylvanas was one, and while she preferred it that way, the others Halduron had brought were both well equipped.

"Just follow me," she called from her own beast, shouting to be heard over the wind caused by its beating wings.

A short time later, Sylvanas and Nathanos dismounted outside the Court of the Sun. Sylvanas tried to be as discreet as possible, but Nathanos attracted attention the instant he dismounted. Children pointed. Adults paused to stare, some furtively, some openly. Only the palace guards seemed unmoved, their training drilled into them. Once inside, Sylvanas spoke quietly to their commander.

"I'll take you to the council room," he said promptly.

"I know the way," Sylvanas replied.

Nathanos did not bother to disguise his curiosity as they walked together. He looked at the rows of ancient tomes, the various statuary, the magnificent paintings and magically preserved historical documents that were framed and placed upon the walls.

"Silvermoon is quite an impressive city," Sylvanas said.

"Not the word I was thinking of, but yes, that works, too."

She found herself smiling ever so slightly. Dirty, smelly, and rude as this human was, it was a refreshing change from her usual experience at court.

Anasterian, Grand Magister Belo'vir, his apprentice Rommath, and her parents were seated at a table with a large map in front of them, already engaged in discussions when Sylvanas entered. Conversation stopped as all eyes turned to the newcomer.

"Your Majesty, Magisters, Ranger-General, and Chief Adviser—this is Nathanos Marris, a Ranger Captain from Lordaeron."

Nathanos bowed with surprising grace.

"He was sent to observe the activities of the Amani, as there is growing concern about a possible threat from the Horde," Sylvanas continued. "You should also know that he saved Lor'themar's life, and fought with us against a troll ambush."

"What of Anaryth and Rendevan? They were patrolling the area this morning."

Sylvanas shook her head darkly. She would speak with her mother later, and steps would be taken to send a message to the trolls.

"The Farstriders sacrifice much to keep the kingdom safe," King Anasterian said. "Sometimes everything." His voice and expression were solemn. "Quel'Thalas will remember."

Farstriders were protectors of the people. They understood they could die in the line of duty. Yet a loss was always felt. Even Anasterian, who had seen so much death in his long lifetime, never failed to acknowledge that loss, and it was one reason Sylvanas respected him so deeply.

The king turned his eyes to Nathanos, sharp despite the centuries upon his shoulders. "We were not told to expect you, Ranger Marris. We would have escorted you properly."

"With due respect, Your Majesty, concern regarding the visibility of such an escort was precisely why you were not alerted. I bring information, and I was ordered to gather more as I made my way to Silvermoon."

He patted a weatherworn leather pouch. "I have here all the information we humans have gathered on Amani activity, which we share in good faith. I also bring a warning. The Horde's activity appears to be increasing. There's a very real concern that they are attempting to recruit the Amani, which would place your kingdom in immediate jeopardy."

"That might explain their boldness in killing our scouts," Sylvanas said. "They've been quiet for some time, and this looks like they're trying to goad us into rash action—"

Lireesa cut her daughter off with a sharp look. "A tactician never leaps to a conclusion before gathering the facts."

Sylvanas had opened her mouth for a tart response when the king held up his hand, a flash of annoyance in those ancient eyes. "We will know more once we have read the missives," the king said. "Ranger Marris, you and the information you bear are welcome here, and we thank you for the service you have performed for the quel'dorei. Please, rest and take some refreshment. You are free to explore Silvermoon, as long as one of our Farstriders accompanies you."

"I will escort him around the city myself," Sylvanas said. As her mother's glare intensified, Sylvanas added, "Given the current situation, I feel it would be useful to learn more about how Lordaeron trains its rangers."

Anasterian inclined his head. "Very well. Do not wander far; we may have questions."

Sylvanas bowed, and Nathanos emulated her. With a nod to the rest of the king's council, Sylvanas took the grubby ranger by the arm and left the chamber.

Nathanos was silent until they had left the Court of the Sun.

"I know I'm irresistible, but this is a bit sudden, don't you think?"

Sylvanas halted in mid-stride. "My mistake," she said with false sweetness, sounding almost like a purring cat. "I'll find another Farstrider to show you around."

"I didn't say *that*," Nathanos replied. "But you might let go of my arm."

Sylvanas realized she'd been holding his wrist in a death grip ever since they'd left. "I would apologize," she said, releasing him, "but you lack the manners to appreciate it."

"I am many things," Nathanos said, "and unmannered is certainly one of them. I rescued one of your Farstriders, you rescued me from boredom. Let's call it even. I'll find an inn and enjoy your no-doubt excellent wine until I'm summoned."

"I am not about to disobey the king's order—nor are you," Sylvanas replied. "Besides, you are the first human I've met who wasn't a courier, and I would like to know what passes for archery among your military."

He smiled, slowly. "I believe I'll surprise you."

"Farstriders' Square is a short distance," Sylvanas said. They descended the long ramp, walking toward the beautiful fountain at its base.

Nathanos frowned. "Is *that* the famous Sunwell?" he scoffed. "I thought it would be much more impressive. Looks like a place you'd toss coins into rather than a legendary font of magic."

Sylvanas gaped. "I . . . how is it possible a rustic bumpkin like you is deemed worthy to be a spy? The Sunwell isn't even located—"

It was then that she saw the twinkle in his eyes that betrayed him, though the rest of his face was impassive. She let out a huff of embarrassment that she passed off as exasperation.

"The Sunwell is located on the Isle of Quel'Danas," Nathanos continued, in a conversational tone, as if he were the one leading the tour and not Sylvanas. "The ancestor of the very king I just chatted with managed to steal a vial of water from the Well of Eternity on his way out the door of exile. Funny, how stealing something can make you king, if the item in question is good enough."

"And yet, look what it has done." Sylvanas gestured to the beauty all around them. "We enjoy nearly perfect health. We have impenetrable magical borders that have protected our land for millennia. It—"

"—Made you shorter than the night elves you're descended from," Nathanos said.

Sylvanas stopped in her tracks. She was annoyed, but much more amused, though she did not let him see that. "Be silent," she warned, "or I will silence you myself."

"And how would you manage th—"

Before he could finish his thought, she had clapped her hand over his mouth. Nathanos held up his hands in mock surrender, and Sylvanas removed her hand.

They continued in oddly companionable silence after that as Sylvanas led them past the fountain and down winding steps into the square. Here Farstriders and others practiced their combat skills. There were training dummies and targets set up. Some trainers stood overlooking the area, keeping an eye on their students from above. Others were down at ground level, where they could easily step forward and correct a stance. Ranger Nalyss was instructing Lyana, one of the newer recruits, but snapped to attention at the sight of Sylvanas approaching. Everyone else present quickly followed.

Sylvanas let them stay so for a beat, enjoying how it must look to Nathanos, then said, "At ease."

Nalyss bowed. "Good day, Lady Sylvanas. What do you need from us?

"Only the use of a bow, some arrows, and a target," she replied. "And," she added, "a little space."

Nalyss signaled to the others, and they moved to oblige, giving Sylvanas and Nathanos plenty of room. They also started to move the gathering crowd away from the activity. To Nathanos, he said, "You may use my bow and quiver, if you wish."

Nathanos shook his head. "No thanks. I know this one best."

"An archer should be able to shoot true with any bow or arrow," Sylvanas said. "And the ones crafted in Quel'Thalas are exquisite."

"The prettiest bow and arrows with the most brightly colored feathers will not make a bad archer a good one."

Sylvanas cocked an eyebrow. "Are you telling me you're a bad archer?"

"You know," he began, "it's said in Lordaeron that high elves are the finest archers in the world."

"Oh, we are." Elves were made for the sport. Lithe, more slightly built, with superior eyesight and reflexes that could dodge a flash of lightning.

"It's also said in Lordaeron," he continued, rubbing his chin, "that they are the most stuck-up, arrogant, self-centered, and vain people in the world."

"Both descriptions are quite true. Do you want to try our weapons?"

"I already said no," Nathanos said. "I thought you elves would have exceptional hearing, what with your extremely long ears."

Sylvanas clucked her tongue and tucked a lock of hair behind one of said ears. "Don't be jealous. I'm sure yours are fine, for a human."

He sighed. "My tiny ears have heard you, my lady. I am ready to accept your challenge, using my clumsy, badly strung bow and my pathetic arrows."

A ghost of a smile touched her lips. "I'm pleased that you understand the situation so clearly," she said, and now he, too, fought to hide a smile.

I'm . . . enjoying this, she thought. How long had it been since she had been playful, had exchanged barbs that didn't wound but instead amused? Certainly not since Alleria had left. Her elder sister had taken more than a few Farstriders with her; she had taken her mother's dreams, and her sisters' joy.

Except . . . maybe she hadn't. Maybe Sylvanas's joy was her own, and others could take it only if she let them.

"So where would you like me to stand?"

"Follow me." He did so as she strode directly away from the target, all the way across the square, then turned around. At this distance, Sylvanas knew, a bear would appear the size of her thumbnail. The targets were much, much smaller.

"That's a long way," Nathanos said.

"You can concede now. I wouldn't hold it against you."

"Oh yes you would. Besides, I want to see the look on your face when I win."

"You'll be waiting quite a while." She waved a hand graciously in the direction of the target. "Please. Do go first."

He scowled, which served only to make his lumpy face even more unpleasing, regarded the target for a moment, and settled himself.

Then Nathanos began to fire, the smoothness of the motion riveting. Draw the arrow from the quiver, fit it to the bowstring, aim, and release. It took only a couple of seconds, and five arrows were protruding from the target.

Despite the distance, Nathanos's arrows were all tightly grouped within the center circle. Sylvanas struggled to keep her face impassive as they walked, silently, to the target.

When they reached it, Sylvanas saw that, not content with simply a tight grouping of arrows, he had placed one dead center in the target.

Lireesa, of course, was this skilled. Alleria almost as much so. Sylvanas herself could equal this display, and the Farstriders had the advantage of using the beautifully crafted, highly accurate elven bows and arrows. Nathanos had made do with a human one. She looked at him again. A good clean shot in battle, obviously, was in the end more valuable than a pretty display of mathematically perfect marksmanship. Nathanos excelled at both.

He wasn't even trying to hide his smirk. Everything she had assumed about him was now in question, given this remarkable—nigh impossible—performance.

Show-off.

"Not bad," Sylvanas said, with as much nonchalance as possible.

Nathanos scoffed. "Let's see you do better," he said, reaching to tug his arrows from the target.

Sylvanas placed a gloved hand on his arm. He turned to her, not drawing back, waiting to see what she would do.

"Leave them," she said.

His expression grew puzzled, but he nodded. "As the lady commands," he said, "though it will probably cost us both some arrows."

She and Nathanos strode back to their mark, and Sylvanas slung her quiver over her shoulder and picked up her own bow.

Taking aim, she drew back the string, chose her first target, and opened her fingers to let the missile fly.

It sang through the air, found one of Nathanos's arrows, and sank into the target not beside it but *through* it, with such force that the shattered pieces of his arrow fell to the ground.

Nathanos shrugged. "Lucky shot. It happens. You've cost me an arrow, though, and likely ruined your own."

"Ah, you are confusing luck and skill," Sylvanas said, deeply pleased with herself.

"Well, you will need more luck if you want to do it again. No one is that good."

Sylvanas quirked the side of her mouth in a smile. Four more times she aimed and released; four more arrows flew. When they reached the target, she and Nathanos could both see clear as day that three other arrows had been split as well. But rather than simply shatter the man's arrows, two of Sylvanas' arrows had embedded themselves into Nathanos's arrows, forming a pair of long double arrows that would have looked almost comical if it hadn't been so impressive.

Sylvanas and Nathanos were silent for a moment. Then Nathanos sniffed and rubbed his gloved hand on his nose, not looking at her.

"You missed one," he said mildly.

"I sought to spare your pride one indignity, at least," said Sylvanas. She reached for the double arrow and pulled them apart, handing Nathanos his, split open at the end by hers.

"Is that the best you can do?"

"No. Only a select few see me at my very best."

There was a long pause, but strangely enough, it wasn't awkward. Then he said, "I like a challenge."

"You seem like someone who would. But don't be too hard on yourself if you fail."

"Ah. Now, see . . . I *don't* like failing."

Sylvanas thought for a moment. "Do your people need you back immediately?"

"If they do, they'll send for me."

She smiled.

CHAPTER EIGHT

Sylvanas was running hard toward her home, her heart pounding and her mind racing. She had to hurry, or it would be too late.

She was about to charge up the ramp when she saw her sister. "Vereesa," she panted. "Has Lirath arrived yet?"

Vereesa regarded her with disapproval so fierce it approached anger. "Yes. He was here. The four of us enjoyed a lovely meal to celebrate. I made him a leather scroll case to carry his songs in."

Sylvanas cursed inwardly.

"Did he say anything? Where he might be going?"

"No." Vereesa was not going to give Sylvanas anything to ease her conscience about missing Lirath. She supposed she deserved it. How had she possibly forgotten her baby brother's name day, when the first moment she saw him had been emblazoned on her soul? Especially when the whole family had adjusted their schedules to spend it together?

She hurried down to the stables, grabbed the reins of a dragonhawk, and flew to Silvermoon. Guilt washed over her as the land passed beneath.

The guards nodded in recognition as she entered the palace.

While being a Windrunner did have its burdens, it also had advantages. Any of them could freely wander Sunfury Spire and even Magisters' Terrace—save for the private royal quarters—at any time.

She headed directly to the Artists' Quarters and heard his music long before she appeared at his door; the soft, lonely, wistful sounds of a flute playing a lament. It made her miserable.

She paused a moment at the door of his chamber, then knocked gently. The beautiful sound ceased.

"Yes?" he called.

"Lirath, it's me," Sylvanas said. She was met with silence. "Please open the door."

For a long moment, she feared he would not; then she heard soft footfalls approaching.

Lirath was poor at hiding his feelings, and the look of wariness and sadness on his fine-featured face made Sylvanas's heart crack even more.

"I'm so sorry," she said. "Can we talk?"

"We're talking now."

"Outside." Away from gossiping servants. Away from the stuffy formality of the royal court. Outside, where she could breathe.

Lirath looked down, then sighed. "Very well."

They did not go unnoticed. Everywhere they went, someone nodded, bowed. Some even tried to strike up conversations with misplaced bonhomie until Sylvanas shut them down with nothing more than a narrow-eyed gaze. *Maybe outside was not the better choice.*

At last they arrived in a secluded corner of the city. Lirath stopped, arms folded, looking down at her expectantly from his lanky adult height of half a head taller. For a moment, he seemed unrecognizable to her: lips pressed thin in anger, a frown creasing his forehead, hair so much longer than her own falling across broad shoulders in a cascade of liquid gold. Who was this stranger? Where was her brother, the laughing child, the gentle boy?

"Your hair is so long," Sylvanas blurted.

He looked at her askance. "What?"

"I just . . . hadn't noticed."

"You haven't noticed because you haven't seen me in well over a fortnight!" The words cracked like a whip, startling Sylvanas from her reverie into a cold present.

"You live at home," Lirath added. "I have to live here. You are all welcome to come visit me—used to visit me often—but you've stopped, Sylvanas. Even on my name day. And," he added bitterly, "I know exactly why."

Shame caused Sylvanas's cheeks to flush hotly. She knew, too. Sylvanas had never made any secret of her dislike of the city, or indeed of Prince Kael'thas. Though, if she was being honest, much of that discomfort came from their meeting some time ago now at the Remembrance celebration. She had made excuses left and right not to attend court gatherings or parties since then, longing instead for the comfort of the forests and the single-minded focus the hunt brought. Even home, once a happy place, was no sanctuary; not when her mother lived there, too.

There was also another reason. Nathanos's visit had stretched from days into months, and he continued to delight her with his quips and bluntness. They made a good team when hunting, and more and more, Sylvanas chose to spend time with him. He certainly suited her better than life at court did. Even, she realized with a twinge of shame, if Lirath was also at court.

"You're right," she said, quietly. "I *have* avoided coming into Silvermoon. That doesn't mean I don't want to see you."

"I'd like to believe that," he said, and his voice was his again; Lirath's voice, calm and kind, with that musicality in it that turned even his speaking voice to song. "But Mother and Father both remembered, and they are kept so busy they barely have time to breathe."

She wanted to lie. To make up a story about trolls or training or something, anything, to obscure the fact that she had simply forgotten about his name day—the first celebrated without Alleria. *And,* she mused bitterly, *without me.*

"You're starting to forget me," he said softly, sadly.

"No," Sylvanas replied, that word at least coming with honest surety. "I could *never* forget you, Lirath."

He spread his arms helplessly. "Yet here we are," he said. "You've left me behind, Sylvanas. You've all left me behind. I barely see you. Vereesa? Today was the first time I've seen her in months. She's seldom home when I come and she's yet to come see me. Father is the only one I see regularly, and even he has lost his smile of late."

"I'm a Farstrider," she snapped. "Do you think I would not have to devote time to the dangers that threaten our people?" There had been more and more rumblings of attacks here and there. Of this mysterious "Horde." Monstrous green creatures filled with the lust for slaughter.

"And don't you understand how hard Mother is on me?" she continued. "You know how hard she drove our sister. And trust me, baby brother, whatever she gave Alleria, she has doubled with me." *Because I'm not the one she wanted. Because she resents that I am here and Alleria is not.*

"Don't blame Mother for your choices," Lirath said, so coldly, so abruptly, it felt like a blade of ice had sliced through her heart.

Sylvanas desperately missed Vereesa in this moment. This would be when she would walk in, with calming words and pleading in her eyes. She would hug them both, and they would hug each other, and all would be well.

But there was no Vereesa to broker peace, no Father to deliver wise counsel. There was only she and Lirath, whom she loved more than anything in the world, and this anger and defensiveness between them. She wanted to tell him everything she was feeling, and had felt. That the day he was born, her life had changed so profoundly. That she made him a promise to keep him safe. That she would fight a thousand trolls single-handedly rather than see any harm come to him.

That there was no one she loved more.

But these were words that did not come easily even at her best, and she could not live if she bared her heart to him and he rejected her.

And so, rather than loose the words that would render her utterly vulnerable, or others that would pierce him like arrows fired from her bow, that would wound them both beyond repair, Sylvanas simply turned and ran.

"You're brooding," Nathanos said.

She did not share what had happened, but Nathanos picked up on it anyway. He had a knack for doing that, sometimes to her delight but more often to her annoyance.

"I am not."

"Actually," Halduron said, poking at the roast that turned on a spit over the fire, "you are, Sylvanas."

She scowled and didn't reply. She was indeed brooding, and nothing she did—even surrounding herself with good company—could shake it.

After the argument with Lirath, she had gone to the council room to speak with their father, but had been told by Verath's aide that there were long talks going on between Anasterian and his council, and her father, regretfully, could not be disturbed.

She went to the fountain and sat there for a while, absently tossing in pebbles. What would Verath say in this situation? That she should take more care in the future to think of others, and apologize, certainly, but she had gone to apologize, and it had been rebuffed.

So? her father would say. *Try again. When you are in the wrong, Sylvanas, excuses do not make your actions right. They make them understandable, and perhaps forgivable, if they are true.*

Sylvanas had done that. She was in the right.

Sometimes, my daughter, Verath would say, brushing a lock of pale gold hair out of her gray eyes, *it is better to be kind than right. Not just because that itself is the decent thing to do, but because one day, you may be grateful for some kindness from others in return.*

What a foolish quarrel this had been. Yes, Sylvanas was busy, but everyone was busy, and she had forgotten his name day. The things her brother had said—he was angry, and Sylvanas knew he didn't mean them. There wasn't a cruel bone in Lirath's body.

Even so, he would still be upset with her. This had been their worst argument to date, and, Sylvanas was forced to admit, with very good reason. They both needed some time to breathe, to think. Morning would be soon enough; they'd have to see each other again, anyway.

Their parents were leaving at dawn to speak with the Alliance.

Sylvanas knew that she should be excited. It would be the first time her mother had left her in charge; the first time Lireesa had demonstrated anything resembling trust in her supposed heir. Instead, she found herself envious.

The rumors surrounding the once mysterious "Horde" had not faded into obscurity. They had fought a war, destroyed a major city, and no matter how the Alliance seemed to beat them back, they always resurged stronger.

Sylvanas had seen more Alliance couriers in the past few months than she had in the whole of her lifetime. Her father often slept at the palace, as meetings lasted days. Despite the infrequency with which she visited court, Sylvanas had noticed that, more and more, the venerated King Anasterian struggled to make decisions. She had discreetly alluded to this in a conversation with her father, and he had confirmed her suspicions with equal discretion. Finally, after what Sylvanas assumed was pressure on her father's part to do so, the king had selected Verath to travel as an ambassador to Lordaeron's capital city, to learn more details about the recent attacks and the foe's true danger.

Lireesa had insisted on accompanying her husband, and had also tapped some of the older, more experienced Farstriders to go with them. All had some familiarity with the humans, their politics, and their leaders.

"We are hoping to help alleviate a crisis, not spark a new one," she had said to Sylvanas, without even attempting subtlety. Sylvanas was both annoyed and disappointed. Her growing—friendship? Flirtation? Romance? Sylvanas wasn't sure what to call it—with Nathanos Marris had kindled a curiosity about the humans, and she would have enjoyed a chance to explore one of their cities with him.

Nathanos, for his part, had grumbled something along the lines that even *he* didn't like human cities, preferring to spend time near his family farmstead located far outside them. But Sylvanas teased that one day she would drag him into one, if only so she could firmly agree with him.

She and Vereesa showed up in the cold, gray early hour before dawn, to watch Talvas and the groomsmen saddle the horses.

"They'll be happy for the exercise," said Talvas. "They so seldom travel outside our borders."

Lirath arrived soon after, flying his dragonhawk in from Silvermoon. When he alighted and made his way toward the gathered family, Sylvanas didn't meet his eyes.

Lireesa was still giving orders up to the last moment. Verath, meanwhile, was speaking personally and at length with each of the servants, shaking their hands, thanking them and asking them to take good care of the spire until they returned.

"How long will you be gone?" Lirath asked him.

"Not long, I hope," he replied. "But of course, we will stay as long as need be."

"Do you think you will get a chance to see Alleria?" Vereesa asked, hopefully.

"Perhaps. She may be out in the field, though. I will tell her you asked about her."

Their father looked at each of them in turn. "Anasterian is grateful for this family's service and has asked me to inform you that if you have need of anything in our absence, you have but to ask the court."

Sylvanas tried and failed not to wrinkle her nose in instinctive distaste. "Do not worry, Father," she said. "We will be fine on our own. Though, we will miss you." She didn't resist when he pulled her into his arms for a tight embrace. His cheek was slightly coarse against her soft one; he had not shaved that morning.

She pulled back. "Don't tell me you are going to grow a beard," she said.

His eyes bright with good humor, he rubbed his stubbly chin

with exaggerated thought. "Hmm. I had not planned to, but now that you mention it—"

"Your face is too handsome to hide behind a beard," Vereesa announced.

Lirath laughed.

"I do not know," Sylvanas mused. "Perhaps he *should* conceal his face. He is so handsome, he might intimidate the humans."

"No, he is not growing a beard," Lireesa said. "He will not present himself to the humans and speak for Anasterian looking scraggly and unkempt like your human pet."

Her *human pet*? Sylvanas felt an unwanted blush warm her cheeks and was grateful for the dim light. Nathanos was not *hers*, and she was most assuredly not *his*.

"If anyone is going to intimidate the humans, it will be you, my fierce wife," Verath teased, bringing a little smile to Lireesa's face and gracefully distracting the ranger-general's attention from her heir.

"We should go," Lireesa said. "Sylvanas—you are in charge now. I expect you to conduct yourself accordingly."

"Yes, Mother," Sylvanas said, keeping her sharp tongue under control.

"Vereesa, listen to Sylvanas if she gives you a direct order. She's more than your sister now, she's your commanding officer. And Lirath . . ." Lireesa softened as she always did, as all of them did, around the youngest Windrunner. He embraced her tightly and she returned it, patting his cheek gently. "We are all so proud of you. I cannot wait to hear what new compositions you have for us to listen to."

"I'm composing a limerick about the orcs," he quipped. "So many things rhyme with *green*."

They laughed, and Lireesa swung up into the horse's saddle. Their father followed suit, kissing his youngest daughter on the top of her head and telling her not to worry, embracing his son, who was now taller even than he, and returning to Sylvanas once more.

"This is your chance," he said quietly, for her ears alone. "Your mother is hard to impress, but if anyone can do it, you can. Believe in yourself, my dear girl, as I have always believed in you."

One final kiss on her forehead, warm and comforting as a blanket on a cold night, then he was astride the steed, and he, Lireesa, and several of the Farstriders were on the first leg of their journey.

The three children kept their gaze on the Thalassian Way, long after the images of their parents dwindled to specks and then were gone even from Sylvanas's sharp gaze.

"I miss them already," Vereesa said, stepping beside Lirath for comfort. She looked sad and worried.

"Me too," Lirath said in a melancholy voice.

The three stood in awkward silence, shivering in the chill.

"Mean," Sylvanas said.

Lirath turned to her in utter confusion. "What?"

"Mean," she repeated. "It rhymes with *green*."

His face softened and he smiled, and her heart lifted. He understood.

"So it does," he agreed, keeping one arm around Vereesa and opening the other to invite Sylvanas in for a hug. Wordlessly she accepted, resting her head on his shoulder and feeling the tension leave her.

I could never forget you, my Little Lord Sun.

"Clean," Vereesa said, then shook her head. "No, orcs are certainly not that, given all we've heard."

"Preen," Sylvanas said. "Bean. Spleen. Obscene."

They were all laughing by the time Lirath joined in, and Sylvanas was content.

CHAPTER NINE

Sylvanas, indeed, all the Windrunner siblings, had made do without their mother before. And on rare occasions, without their father. But the elder Windrunners had not left the confines of their kingdom for such an extended absence in their living memory. It was different for Lirath, who had already gotten used to living away from home, but Vereesa seemed uncomfortable. She was more content when the family was all together and safe.

Sylvanas felt free. She hadn't realized the extent to which she had inured herself to her mother's discipline. She still pushed herself hard, and woke at the same early hour, but there was an ease about her days now that she had never experienced before.

And there was another feeling she had not experienced before, one she had never had time or patience to pursue. Or, frankly, interest. But Nathanos Marris, the oft-scowling, sharp-witted, irreverent human, interested her greatly.

She did not shirk her duties, but she also allowed herself to indulge in something she hadn't for a long, long time. Sylvanas let herself *play*.

Nathanos was almost as often the object of her amusement as he was her interest, but his tongue was as sharp as hers and he had no hesitation in firing off a scathing retort.

It was delightful, and heady, and heart pounding, and Sylvanas loved it.

At one point, she had taken him on one of her favorite paths to see the Sanctum of the Sun, admire its turning orbs that represented the stars, and explore the less-traveled path behind it that led up to Sungraze Peak. The first part was easy, but the last required more than a little climbing.

"So," Nathanos said as he plopped down beneath an ancient tree, "what's my reward?" He took a swig from the waterskin and stretched out, arms beneath his head.

Sylvanas gestured at the breathtaking panorama unfolding below them. "This," she said. From here, they could see the Sanctum of the Sun to the south and just glimpse Tranquillien in the northwest. But there was also a beautiful view of the sunset and Windrunner Spire, and the calm stillness of a lake . . .

"I like being up here alone, with nobody needing or wanting anything from me. You're the first person I've taken here."

That seemed to take Nathanos by surprise, and he had no sly quip for her. Sylvanas sat beside him, hands clasped around her knees. The silence stretched out as a soft breeze tousled their hair, bearing the scent of flowers.

"Why me?" Nathanos asked, quietly. It was an honest question, with no pretense or wryness about it. "You could have your pick of anyone, and they would be guaranteed to be better company than me."

Sylvanas couldn't help but smile as she returned her gaze to the glorious sanctum and sighed.

"Look at what surrounds us; here, in Silvermoon . . . everywhere. Everything you see is beautiful. All our statues are polished, all our music is elegant, all our weapons are bright and gleaming and lovely. Everyone has eyes you can get lost in, regal noses, flawless skin. It's all so very pretty."

Sylvanas loved her people, but a thread of arrogant superiority was inextricably woven into the fabric of the quel'dorei tapestry. She took great delight in deflating swelled egos in her equals and superiors, and she had never liked bullies. But taking them down a peg was one thing. If need be, she would still give her life to protect any one of them.

Sylvanas turned back to Nathanos, whose dark gaze was fixed on her face. "But the world isn't perfect, Nathanos. And the only people who know that, who truly understand that, are the ones who have to go out and deal with that world. It's not pretty, when a troll is snarling a handspan from your face, or you've only wounded a springpaw and it's about to rip your belly to bloody shreds.

"I think . . . this is what sets the Farstriders apart more than anything else—because our eyes are truly open. Everyone else lives in their soft and safe version of the world. Those we protect, we protect them not just from the danger. We protect them from the true face of this world."

She sighed and turned to lay down, propping herself up on one elbow. "To me, beauty is commonplace. Perfection is dull. And—" Sylvanas brushed his mop of scruffy brown hair from his brow and laughed softly. "Nathanos Marris, you are the ugliest and least dull person I have ever met, and *that* . . ." she said, her voice falling to a whisper as she leaned down and brought her face closer to his, ". . . is why I like you."

Nathanos reached up, his callused fingers pleasantly rough on the smooth curve of her cheek. There was a startling gentleness in the gesture, and a sense of wonder in his eyes as he touched her that made Sylvanas's heart beat faster.

"My lady," he said in a rough whisper, "you are too smart to be so foolish."

She could not help but smile slightly as she recalled her words from the first day they met. "Be silent, or I will silence you myself."

His eyes lit up. He remembered that moment, too, and in a voice laced with humor replied, "And how would you manage th—"

And then he spoke nothing more as Sylvanas pressed her lips to his, one of his large, powerful hands cupping the back of her head as the other slipped around her waist. He held her tightly, and Sylvanas had the feeling he would never, ever let her go.

When a summons came from the court, Sylvanas and Vereesa were at the retreat, busily preparing a bear pelt. The courier blanched at the carnage spread out on the grass, then said, "Lady Vereesa, Lady Sylvanas—you are ordered to report to His Majesty, the king, at once."

The two sisters looked at each other.

"Something you did?" Vereesa asked—not as an accusation, but as a simple question.

Sylvanas wasn't angry; it was a reasonable assumption.

"Oddly enough, no," she said. She frowned. She was called to court now and then, but that was because she was the future ranger-general. Extending the invitation to Vereesa as well could only mean one thing—danger. Turning back to the courier, she asked, "Is this a Farstrider matter?"

"I regret that I have not been informed about the reason for the summons, only that I am to bring the two of you as quickly as possible."

Perhaps her parents had sent word of a pending attack. Maybe the orcs were at last turning their sights on Quel'thalas, and the time had come for war. Even as the thought crossed her mind, Sylvanas was running to the waiting dragonhawks, Vereesa hard on her heels.

Sylvanas had been prepared to enter a war council in progress, so she and her sister were confused when they were led to a smaller, more intimate antechamber and told the king would be with them shortly.

Neither of them sat in the offered chairs. Vereesa leaned against the wall, fidgeting with the sheathed blade at her hip as if she wished she could draw it and attack whatever emergency was about to be sprung on them. For her part, Sylvanas paced like a caged animal, her mind racing with the need to know and her skin fairly crawling with the need to act.

The door opened, and His Majesty, King Anasterian Sunstrider, entered the room. But neither of the Windrunner sisters focused attention on their liege, instead turning to the one who was with him.

Lirath.

In that awful heartbeat, they all knew.

This was not a Farstrider matter.

It was a family one.

No. It can't be that. It's something else.

Anasterian's face was etched with reserved, but genuine, sorrow, and he waved them all to sit. Sylvanas obeyed, feeling strangely stiff, as if her body were an unfamiliar thing she had forgotten how to move. She did not want to sit and listen. Because she knew what her king was going to say, and the second the words were uttered, it would be real, and everything would fall apart.

"I have received a report," the king said. "Know that my own heart is heavy with grief that I must inform you that your parents, and all who accompanied them . . . are dead."

Sylvanas's heart lurched and for a terrible moment she felt faint.

"Both?"

The single word contained such a world of pain, shock, and horror that the crack in Lirath's voice left a gaping feeling in Sylvanas's chest.

"Tragically, yes. It is a great loss not only to you, the children they were so proud of, but to everyone in this kingdom. They were much admired and, in many cases, beloved by all who knew them."

Both. Mother and Father, gone, just like that. It can't be. There must have been some mistake. Their parents were not old, not like the king. Elves lived long lives; the children should have had decades, probably *centuries* together. Earlier she had been taut and anxious, but now Sylvanas felt frozen. Lirath and Vereesa were so pale as to be almost bloodless.

Anasterian was speaking, but Sylvanas couldn't comprehend his words. They reached her, but in a slightly distorted way, so they were almost nonsensical.

Focus, Sylvanas, she told herself. *You have to be strong right now.*

She took a long, shaky breath, and forced herself to concentrate on Anasterian's words. "They were ambushed while making camp for the evening, but presently we are not yet certain by whom."

Sylvanas blinked. Surely she had misheard.

"*Ambushed?* No," she said, flatly. An accident, perhaps. A sudden storm, a fire—Nature itself, perhaps, could defeat even their indomitable mother. But not a living enemy. Lireesa was many things, but she would never let down her guard, not for an instant, particularly if their father's life—

"This information is wrong. My mother would *never* allow her party to be taken by surprise. This is *Lireesa Windrunner!*"

And abruptly, she remembered how much she had hated listening to all the stories about Lireesa's nigh-godlike achievements. Now Sylvanas would give anything to watch Lireesa sitting and laughing with friends, trying to dismiss the talk of her heroism, while her husband smiled and held her hand.

Anasterian looked at her sympathetically. "I share your disbelief. Never would I have thought . . ." He shook his head. "Inconceivable as it seems, all evidence, little though there was, points to this being the truth."

Sylvanas belatedly realized that with her mother's death, she was ranger-general now. She needed to act like it.

"Your Majesty." Speaking his title helped. It made him a king again in her eyes; a king grieving personally, yes, but one who had also lost his ranger-general and his chief adviser in a single, dreadful incident. "When you say *little evidence,* what do you mean, precisely?"

How cold and detached she sounded.

"Unfortunately for our investigation," Anasterian replied, "by the time the bodies were discovered, scavengers had already done their work."

Anasterian was trying to be as delicate as possible, but Sylvanas was from a long line of hunters. She was well acquainted with what scavengers did to corpses.

"Then you cannot be certain it was them." Vereesa said, her voice strained, as disbelieving as her sister had been. Lirath sat unspeaking, pale and still as a statue, in the moment.

Anasterian regarded her with kindness. "Lady Vereesa, the bodies were discovered by the Windrunner household."

Another hope, snuffed out like a candleflame. Like the lives of her parents, and the Farstriders who had died defending them. No one but the Windrunner children themselves would have been better able to identify the lord and lady of the house than the servants who had spent their lives beside them.

"Everyone in the party has been accounted for. The assailants took anything of value—including secret information meant for the Alliance leaders."

"Then this is no simple robbery," Sylvanas said. She was composed now, latching onto discipline and training like a lifeline. Her siblings looked at her, then at each other. They, too, did what they could to calm themselves. She was deeply proud of them, especially Lirath, who did not have the grim experience she and Vereesa had with death.

"No, it is not," Anasterian agreed. "We suspect the work of our old friends, the Amani. No doubt they would relish access to any information about our military movements."

"Does Alleria know?"

"I have sent a messenger, but the eldest Windrunner will be difficult to track down."

The eldest Windrunner. Alleria was, now, wasn't she?

They're gone. They're both gone.

"We must find out exactly what happened." Sylvanas's voice still sounded so strange, and strained, in her own ears. "I will go to the site."

"Others are already there," Anasterian said. "Including Theron."

But they aren't me! The thought screamed in her brain. *I'm the ranger-general. And they were* my *parents and* my *Farstriders. No one would do as thorough an investigation as I.*

As if reading her agonized, angry thoughts, the king added,

"Lor'themar has assured me that he will scour the area. He will be relentless and exhaustive in his investigation. Once that is done, their remains will be brought home with all the reverence they are due." He paused, then added, kindly, "I understand your desire for their deaths to have been due to something strange and unfamiliar. A great threat, like the Dark Eagle, not at the hands of simple trolls. But when we have had enemies at our door for millennia, it is not difficult to know who to blame. Let others handle this particularly cruel aspect of the tragedy now. Much of leadership is understanding when to delegate. Lireesa and Verath Windrunner will be brought home as soon as possible, with every care and respect given them. You know this."

"I will not shy away from my first duty as ranger-general—to discover who slew two vital court members and several Farstriders in such a cowardly fashion. My king, I ask you, please . . . let me lead this investigation. We three are Windrunners, and we will not shirk our duties. Not even the painful ones."

Sylvanas had learned most of her ranger's skills from her mother, but she had learned much from Verath, too. And one such lesson was that many times, the royal court was a more dangerous place than the wilderness.

Wild beasts were driven by simple things—hunger, or dominance. Trolls, by hatred, pure and simple.

The predators in the Sunstrider court were far worse. Greed, ego, fear, and pride drove them, and those were hungers that could never be sated.

Sylvanas was well aware that she was not popular, and that if she showed any sign of weakness now, she would be as doomed as an injured doe when the great cats struck. The one thing her mother had given her, albeit grudgingly, was to name Sylvanas as her heir. Sylvanas would not let *anyone* take that title—that honor—away from her, especially if they thought to use Lireesa's death as evidence of her daughter appearing unsuited to the role.

Anasterian was silent for a time, and Sylvanas wondered if she had pushed too hard. "Against my better judgment," he said at last,

"I will grant your request. The crown appreciates your devotion. But take care, Ranger-General, that your desire for justice does not blind you to what truths you uncover." He rose, and the children of Lireesa and Verath rose as well.

"Once again, I am truly sorry for your loss," the king said. "Ranger-General, you will depart on the morrow."

"My liege, with your permission, I will depart within the hour."

"Sister, it can wait," Vereesa said, even as Sylvanas looked up, meeting the gaze of their king.

"No. Justice . . . punishment cannot wait, sister," Sylvanas retorted.

A shadow of annoyance, quickly dispelled through centuries of practice, flickered across Anasterian's patrician visage. "As you wish. Make your farewells here, then, and meet me in the council chamber when you are ready. You will be given a full debriefing. Take your time," he added, and closed the door.

Vereesa's face crumpled. Lirath, still in a state of semi-shock, blinked and looked from one to the other. His face abruptly seemed to register what was going on.

"Lady Moon," he said, his voice shaking. "Don't leave. Not yet. *Please.*" He had never begged for anything, but he was begging now. Sylvanas's heart broke a little bit more.

"You know I must," she said. She wanted to be kinder, to hug him, the baby of the family, far too young to be an orphan. *All* of them were too young, and that thought made her angry. She found strength she badly needed in the emotion.

"We know," Vereesa said. "People will look to us as an example. They will be frightened and worried. We must comfort them by being strong."

Even now, Vereesa was the one to speak of comforting others. Sylvanas loved her fiercely.

"I know," Lirath said. "I'm just not ready to be alone, yet."

"You won't be," Vereesa hastened to assure him, giving him the embrace Sylvanas could not, would not.

Sylvanas bitterly wished she did not have to say what she was about to. "Vereesa," Sylvanas said, "most of the other high-ranking Farstriders were—were with our parents. The rest are likely at the murder site investigating. I will need you to represent the family properly among their number, here in Silvermoon till I return."

Vereesa's face fell, but she nodded. Lirath bit his lip but did not protest. Vereesa, then, would *not* be with him. They were Windrunners. They understood.

"Write them a lament, Lirath," Sylvanas said, suddenly.

Her brother stared at her. "I . . . I cannot . . ."

"Yes, you can. It would mean so much to them. And . . . to us," she added. *To me. I will know that someone is turning such terrible pain into beauty. And that will give me strength.* "You are the only one who can do them justice."

Sylvanas heard her voice crack on the last word. *Justice.* She would make sure her parents had it. She needed to leave, right now, or else would lose herself to grief. And so she nodded one more time at them, standing in front of her, holding each other's hands, as they had all done when they were younger, and the world was kinder.

Her first task was to attend a thorough debriefing.

Her second . . . was to find Nathanos Marris.

It was harder to tell him than Sylvanas had expected. She gave him the briefest of summaries, calling her parents "the ranger-general" and "the chief adviser," instead of using Mother or Father, or even their names. It was better that way. Keeping the emotions at arm's length would permit her to focus on finding the killers.

Nathanos had instinctively moved to embrace her, but Sylvanas stepped back.

Mother and the Farstriders could have handled trolls, she had told him. *I want you to come with me because I suspect Horde activity. You are more familiar with them than any of us here, and you grew up in the area. You may notice something we would miss.*

Of course, he had replied. *Good thinking. Let's go.*

The site was located in the Eastweald a few miles south of the

Alliance's Northwatch Tower. They flew in silence, each on a separate dragonhawk. Sylvanas's mind was whirling with a thousand thoughts, half of them helpful, half of them threatening to break her entirely.

She spotted the corpses before anything else. Eight of them there were, covered with cloth. Sylvanas could not blame the devastated household; their first instinct would be to show respect, but the loving gesture had been a mistake. Difficult as it would be to see the mutilated bodies of family and friends, Sylvanas knew that some clues, possibly vital ones, would have already been destroyed.

She tore her gaze away from the shapes on the earth and felt the tightness in her chest ease as she spotted Lor'themar and Halduron below, with a few other familiar, trusted Farstriders as well as some of the hunters from Quel'Lithien Lodge, including their leader, Ranger Lord Renthar Hawkspear. Someone in royal livery whom she did not recognize was there, too.

Sylvanas frowned. On one hand, it was natural that Anasterian would want to have someone who could report to him directly; to be his eyes here. On the other . . . that was what the Farstriders were supposed to do. She recalled how anxious the king had been for her to not examine the site herself. Sylvanas had no doubt that some of it—perhaps most of it—was genuine compassion.

But some of it wasn't, and the slim figure standing to the side, wearing the king's livery, was the proof.

As her dragonhawk began to descend, the familiar, but no less horrible scent of decomposition rose to meet them. She landed, slipped off her dragonhawk, and strode to her friends, nodding at Halduron and turning to Lor'themar. She did not even acknowledge the king's representative. He was there to observe, not to help. So let him observe.

"Report," she asked. "Assume I've been told nothing. What are your thoughts?"

Lor'themar glanced at Nathanos. Sylvanas did not have time to waste on long explanations, so she said bluntly, "The Eastweald is his home, and if this is Horde activity, he would know that better than us."

Lor'themar nodded, then, adopting her cool demeanor, filled her in.

Two days ago, one of the white horses ridden by Lireesa and Verath had shown up at the spire. It was unharmed, but agitated, and the household feared the worst—and they had been correct.

Because scavengers had fed on the corpses, it was not easy to ascertain time of death; but the Farstriders were used to even the subtlest clues of decay and placed the time at no more than a week, probably only three or four days.

Lor'themar led them around the site. Small markers had been placed near anything that might be useful to examine, so that no one would accidentally tread on them. It had been quite a bit too late for that, Sylvanas thought; much of what could have been useful had already been trod upon, and the recent rain had done nothing to help.

"There weren't many prints," Lor'themar said quietly. "But everything we saw does seem to point to the trolls." He pointed to the northeast. "Zul'Mashar might have recognized a good opportunity to strike."

"The Mossflayer numbers are not what they once were," Sylvanas said. "Such an audacious attack is more likely to have come from the Amani. But why would they travel so far from Quel'Thalas?"

"Perhaps the prize was worth the journey," came a voice. Renthar Hawkspear approached and bowed. Taller than most, and with a more muscled physique, he cut a commanding figure, his black hair up in a topknot and his face strong and sharp. "Ranger-General," he said. "I wish you were here on other business."

"So do we all," Sylvanas replied. "And yes. But the prize practically walked right past them as the group headed toward the gate. It would be terrible strategy to follow and attack so far away. And whatever they may be, the Amani do understand strategy."

Sylvanas shook her head. "No, Renthar, something is not adding up." She walked over to where one of the corpses lay.

"Sylvanas," Halduron said quickly, but the warning came too late. Sylvanas had already removed the cloth.

Terrible though the thought was, she had hoped she would reveal the still face of a Farstrider. Instead, Sylvanas found herself staring at the arrow-riddled body of their leader.

Lireesa Windrunner's face was pale, her body stiff. Sylvanas felt as if she had been struck, but then felt an emotion other than grief welling up inside her: pride. Her mother had died doing what she had vowed to do: defending others. Trying to keep her people—her family . . . safe. She died the hero she had been in life, even if this time her sacrifice seemed to be in vain.

I won't let it be, Sylvanas thought. *You'd want me to find who did this. I will, I promise.*

She clenched her jaw and forced herself to focus. So many arrows . . . She tugged one free, and saw the poison on the tip. Definitely troll.

Could Anasterian be right? Had her mother simply been taken unawares?

Her gaze roved over the body, silently asking her mother to reveal any clues that would help Sylvanas avenge her. She paused.

There were two other holes in the leather armor, made by an arrow that had been not merely removed—but *tugged* out.

Nathanos had stepped up beside her, silent, but present and steady. She straightened. "The ranger-general would never simply pull out an arrow, certainly not in the heat of battle. Someone wanted their arrows back."

"Is that not the way of archers?" the courtier put in. "Do you not recover them, so as not to waste ammunition?"

"Most times we do," Sylvanas said. "But then why were not all the arrows removed? Why leave some, but not others?"

"Because," Lor'themar said, stepping beside her, "they only wanted us to *notice* some, but not others."

Halduron had come over, too, now, and the Trio looked at one another. They, and Nathanos, all knew what was going on. But their shared instincts would not convince the king. They had to find proof. Sylvanas knelt again beside her mother's body. "Thank you, Mother," she whispered. "I will find them. I will protect our people from them. May you rest with ease. Your duty is done."

Her gaze fell on the quiver, caught under Lireesa's body as she fell. Three arrows yet remained. Sylvanas bit her lip, then reached out and pulled her mother's arrows from the slightly flattened quiver. She looked at them for a moment; at the colors of the Windrunners and the Farstriders, the distinctive brown-and-gold. Then she stood, slipping the arrows into her own quiver, accepting her legacy.

She was not formally ranger-general, not yet, but even so, all the Farstriders who had witnessed her action inclined their heads with respect.

Nathanos looked at her for a moment, his eyes searching hers, and said, "I have a hunch. Will you accompany me?"

"Yes," she said at once.

"I will come, too," Renthar said, and Lor'themar and Halduron nodded as well.

"No," Sylvanas said. "Stay here. Keep looking for clues. Look for cuts not made by weapons we know. Or . . . by weapons much larger than usual. We will return shortly."

All three of them looked disapprovingly at Nathanos, even Lor'themar, whose life he had saved. "Shall I close the investigation?" Lor'themar asked.

"Not yet."

"Your . . . parents, and those who died fighting alongside them, deserve proper treatment."

"My parents, and those who died fighting alongside them, deserve justice," Sylvanas said, more harshly than she had intended. "We will not be long."

They shared a single dragonhawk so their words would not be lost in the wind. Sylvanas clutched the saddle, unwilling to touch Nathanos for fear she might break down. "Where are we going?"

"In a happier time, my family's farmstead. It's south of here."

"I see . . . and what would we do there?" she said, a ghost of her old impish self peeking out, desperately seeking lightness in the darkness of the day's revelations.

"Why, I would introduce you to my little cousin, Stephon," Nathanos said in a deadpan voice. She smiled a little. He always knew what she needed.

"But today . . . we're scouting. I respect the Farstriders, but I do not think they looked past the immediate area for clues."

Silence stretched on between them.

"It was the Horde, wasn't it." It was a statement, not a question.

"I think so, yes. No one removes only a few arrows."

"They removed the ones that would betray them. Orcish arrows. They left the troll ones to trick us into thinking the trolls acted alone." Her voice was clipped, cold. They would pay.

"They cleaned their tracks as well, and the rain was their friend," Nathanos said. "I am hoping they grew careless farther south."

They flew on in silence. Sylvanas kept her eyes on the ground as Nathanos kept the dragonhawk close to the ground, so low its wings almost touched the earth on the downbeat.

"There," she said. "On your left."

Nathanos turned the beast's head and it veered to the west. "I see them," he said. "But the outline of the footprint is not clear. It could easily be a troll's print that widened with the rain."

"We know what happened," Sylvanas said. "Halduron, Renthar, Lor'themar—we all know."

Any Farstrider, or indeed anyone with any experience with arrows at all, knew better than to remove one on the battlefield. The resulting blood loss would be more dangerous than the arrow itself. If possible, the arrow would be cut in half and removed in two pieces to avoid pulling the barbs through the flesh.

"Yes," Nathanos said, grimly. "Horde arrows are fletched differently, and they are slightly larger."

"They are not fools, these orcs," Sylvanas muttered. "They collaborated with the trolls, as was feared. The orcs waited until the group was far enough from any defense, then attacked while the trolls closed in behind. The king was right about that. It was an ambush."

Nathanos was silent, then he said in a soft voice that few other than Sylvanas had ever heard, "You would not have saved them."

She closed her eyes in pain. "We will never know. I could have tried."

"I am glad you did not."

They continued to fly over the area, until any tracks that might have been of use merged with those of ordinary citizens who trod the roads. Nothing. Not a corpse, or overly large wagon marks, or even a footprint.

"We should return," she said at last. "We have nothing to prove their murderers were anyone other than the old enemy."

"I'm sorry. And no, you did not fail them. Sometimes, the enemies win. Today was one such day. But we will not hear the end of it, not for a long time, and we can change the ultimate outcome of what's to come."

"We will," she said, and then was silent.

When they returned, Sylvanas spoke with Lor'themar, Renthar, and Halduron. "I believe this was done by the Horde," she said. "I have fought trolls. I have seen what is left after a battle. And there are things here that are simply wrong. But without any hard evidence to take to our king . . ." She paused, then swallowed hard. "I have no choice but to say the investigation is closed."

Lor'themar and Halduron looked at her with sympathy. Renthar scowled. "That does not sit well with me, nor you, I see."

"No. And if anything else is discovered, I trust Quel'Lithien Lodge will report to me at once."

"With all speed possible," he assured her.

"I must agree with you—" Then Lor'themar hesitated. "How should we address you now? Ranger-General? Ranger Lord?"

The question hurt as if she herself had been impaled by a Horde arrow. "I am neither. For now . . . you may call me Sylvanas." She squared her shoulders. "I must pay my respects to the fallen. Then please arrange for the bodies to be brought home with all due care, as they deserve."

"It shall be done," Halduron said.

She walked through the site once more, pausing at every covered form on the ground. The Farstriders had all been much older, some with literal centuries of experience. How many Horde had it taken to bring them down? Sylvanas wondered. How many corpses of their own had the monsters had to move?

Now that she knew to look for it, she could see where nearly every one of them had an arrow removed. And there were two Farstriders with deep cuts from weapons far heavier than any troll would wield.

Sylvanas knew it would not be enough to change anything.

Finally, she paused in front of the last body. That of her father. *Father*. This should not have been his fate. He should have lived to see generations of descendants, have been able to spend his time in later life with a good book and a glass of wine. She was not yet ready to let him go.

She hesitated. If she saw the body, it would make everything real. She would have lost not only her fiery, exacting, heroic mother, but her gentle, wise, humorous father, who was in his own way as strong as his wife.

Before she knew it, she had dropped to her knees beside him. Tears burned in her eyes but she refused to let them fall. She tried and failed to control the shaking of her hand as she pulled back the cloth and looked at the beloved face, whose skin was now as white as his hair. She noted that he had shaved the stubble they had teased him about the last time she had seen him. Strange, what odd and seemingly trivial details the mind clung to.

You always loved me, no matter what I did. Your punishments were reasoned and fair, and you taught me to think. Mother's duty to the crown always put her in danger. I never thought yours would.

"I will fight for both of you," she whispered. "For the Quel'Thalas you always loved."

Her friends gave her space and time to grieve, and when she returned to them, she was resolute. "I will take word to the king myself," she said. "And I will stop by Windrunner Spire on the way, to thank them, and offer what comfort I can."

————

The household had been rocked to its core. Many of them had served the Windrunners all their lives. A few were even here carrying on an ancestral tradition—the honor of aiding one of the land's most famous families.

She did what she could, Nathanos waiting outside for her. When at last she emerged, she said, "There is one more stop. You can come with me if you like."

Nathanos was known and, if not welcomed, always treated respectfully by those who tended the household's mounts. Sylvanas felt another pang, one of so very many today, when she caught sight of Arrowflight. The mare whickered in recognition and butted her head against Sylvanas, who stroked her soft white mane.

"My lady!" exclaimed Talvas, the head groomsman. "'Tis a miracle!"

What a strange, cruel thing to say in such a dark moment, Sylvanas thought, and then realized what he meant. "It is," she agreed. "At least we still have Arrowflight. You have always taken such good care of—"

"Nay, my lady! Her too, yes, but come see!"

She and Nathanos followed him out and her heart jumped. Behind the stables was another white horse.

Parley!

Her joy was short-lived as she saw the blood that dripped down his right flank. Before she could say anything, Talvas reassured her, "He will be fine, my lady. There was no poison, and we removed the arrow with all care. We are now cleansing the wound, but it's a bit painful."

Sylvanas fumbled in her pouch. "Here," she said. "Woundwood."

Talvas knew exactly what to do. "Thank you! He will be glad of it."

Slowly Sylvanas walked toward the horse. Nathanos followed Talvas, talking to him quietly. Parley's nostrils flared, and he lowered his head so she could pet his soft muzzle, his trembling slowly ceasing at the touch of a familiar hand.

Both of them. Somehow both steeds had survived and found

their way home, although their masters had not. It was, indeed, a miracle.

She thought of the many days she had ridden Parley, her father's warmth at her back, the stallion careful of his burden, the sun on her face.

"Sylvanas."

She turned to see Nathanos standing there. She looked at his face, then at the object he held in his hand.

The arrow was not of a troll's making. Sylvanas took a quick breath. There had been no poison . . .

"Is it . . . ?"

"Yes. It's a Horde arrow."

Sylvanas flung her arms around Parley's neck. She was not superstitious, but somehow she knew that wherever her parents were, they were at peace.

Thank you, Father. You've given me one final gift. I will keep my promise to you.

It would take courage, to challenge a king. Anasterian might punish her if he did not agree with her conclusion. He might even remove her from the Farstriders.

Her cheek pressed against the warmth of the horse's neck, she could almost hear her father's voice, one final time:

Believe in yourself, my dear girl, as I have always believed in you.

Sylvanas was received warmly enough. Upon her arrival, she was escorted to a room she had never seen before, a side chamber that was much more intimate and cozier than any of the larger ones. Thick rugs covered the stone floor, and while there were portraits and statuary, the scale was much smaller. Instead of a vast table capable of seating up to twenty, there was only a small one with two comfortable-looking chairs, a decanter of wine, and two glasses. A fire burned cheerily, and between its flames and the flicker of candles, it was altogether a welcoming place. If her heart hadn't been so wounded and her mission so urgent, Sylvanas would have enjoyed it. As it was, when Anasterian waved her to a seat, she replied, "Thank you, Your Majesty, if it please you, I prefer to stand."

"It would please me if you sat," he said. "Your task has been a painful one."

Sylvanas knew an order when she heard one, no matter how pleasant the words or tone, so she obeyed. The king poured a glass of wine for himself. "Will you have a glass as well? If you prefer, I can have some tea or juice brought in."

"Nothing for me, thank you," she said.

"To business, then," the king said. "Tell me your report, and your conclusion."

Sylvanas did so. He maintained a pleasant, interested expression as she told him about the search for clues, the evidence that seemed to point to troll activity—and the evidence that didn't.

"I was prepared to agree with your assertion, Your Majesty," she said. "Until my father's horse returned . . . with this in his side."

She placed a white cloth on the table between them, and unwrapped it.

For a long moment, the king stared at the arrow. Then he rose, and stood by the fire, waving at her to stay seated, then turned his back to her as he gazed into the embers. "Your father always spoke well of you. Difficult as this situation must be, you have displayed resolve and dedication to your duty. Your parents died as they lived, serving the crown, protecting the kingdom, and doing what was best for their people."

He turned to her then. "I believe you will do the same."

"I trust that is so, my liege."

The king nodded and indicated the arrow. "May I?" At her nod, he carefully picked it up. The dried blood of her father's steed was still painted on it.

"Your investigation was thorough. And this does seem to confirm your suspicion that the Horde, not simply the trolls, was behind the slaughter. But . . . it is of no use to us. Not if we both want to do what is best for the people."

Anasterian let the arrow fall from his hands into the fire.

Without thinking, Sylvanas leaped from her seat and lunged toward the hearth, trying to retrieve at least something of the arrow that told the truth. Anasterian's hand grabbed her wrist.

"What are you *doing*?" she cried. "That was the only way we could prove what happened!"

He chose to ignore her outburst, speaking calmly. "I have seen war, Sylvanas. So have your parents. It is a horrible thing. The troll attacks already cost us, in lives, and in the faith of our people that we will keep them safe. This is not our war."

"It is now!"

"It is only if we choose to make it so."

She stared at him disbelieving. Recklessly she said, "My father once told me you were wise to treasure those bold enough to speak truth to you. Did he lie?"

Displeasure flickered across his face. She knew she was pushing too hard, but she couldn't seem to stop.

"He did not lie. I do treasure you for what you have uncovered. But I must also speak truth to you. Stoking fears of invasion and mysterious monsters can only bring harm to this kingdom. We are safe, Sylvanas. They will never take our land. We have the Sunwell to protect us, and I have every faith in your Farstriders to defend us should the need arise. Your parents always did what was best for our people, even if they disagreed. Will you carry that legacy forward? Or will you defy your king?"

It was so terribly unfair. And it was wrong.

The worst part was, she understood Anasterian's decision. The kingdom was indeed well protected. There were ways to gather information and prepare without risk. Her heart protested, but Sylvanas knew that her king knew much more of politics and war than she did. And besides . . . she knew that her parents would have seen this, too, and have obeyed their king.

As she had to.

"Will you at least allow me to double our patrols? Send us extra arms and supplies? We know the danger is out there, the Farstriders must be ready to meet it."

"I cannot see the need for such measures," Anasterian said. "Your parents journeyed beyond the Sunwell's protection, and for their fate I am deeply sorry, but I must have your word, Ranger-General. You must not speak of this to anyone. I cannot be looking over my shoulder, uncertain of your loyalty."

She bowed her head. "I understand your reasoning, my liege, and I will do as my parents have. I remain a loyal subject to my king."

He relaxed. "I value this more than you know. Comfort yourself with the knowledge that in this choice, you are truly serving your people."

Sylvanas bowed and left. She would keep the vows she just made. But she had chosen her words carefully. She would not speak of this openly. But that did not mean she could not pursue her own search for justice or prepare her troops for the coming storm.

The next several days were a merciful blur.

The ceremony to honor the fallen ranger-general and ambassador and councilor was all it should have been—reverent, poignant, full of meaning. The bodies were encased in mortcloths woven in the Windrunner colors; their names carefully embroidered with gold thread. Flowers of every hue were placed on the bodies and the bier that supported them. Verath and Lireesa Windrunner would lie in state for a full day, so that those they had served so well in life could pay their respects.

Sylvanas, Vereesa, and Lirath stood beside the wrapped forms, clad in mourning clothes and wearing the family tabard.

Alleria did not attend.

Sylvanas had not spoken to Lirath since that day when Anasterian had called the Windrunner children together to inform them of the devastating news. Her bother looked terrible, the dark clothing only serving to emphasize his pallor. He was so young, so poor at hiding his emotions, that it was clear every minute here was torture. After about an hour, he seemed to make some kind of decision, leaving his position and walking up to Sylvanas.

His cheekbones, always high and elegant, appeared to jut through his skin. His eyes glittered from the hollows of their sockets. He even held himself differently, slightly hunched instead of tall and broad, as if he could curl in on himself far enough to disappear entirely.

Sylvanas regarded him with what sympathy she could spare, ready to comfort, to make amends, but his words surprised her.

"Train me."

The same thing he had always seemed to ask her, over the years. Except this time, it wasn't a child's plea, or a youth's insecurity. It was a demand, spoken by someone suddenly forced to become an adult in the cruelest way possible.

She took him gently by the arm and steered him away from the crowd of mourners still gathering.

"We will talk about this later," she said.

"No. We will talk about it *now*."

She blinked. There was a hardness to him she'd never seen before. "I know you're in shock," she said. "But we've discussed this before."

"Everything has changed now," he said harshly. "When I asked before, it was in a world of softness, of privilege, of wine and song and laughter and *family*. That world's gone now. And it's never coming back. You and Alleria and Vereesa—you at least get to strike at the monsters who took them from us!"

He was right about that, at least. But he was wrong, too. Because even in her own grief, Sylvanas knew that the world of softness and music would not be gone forever. Things had changed, yes. But the quel'dorei survived. Lirath would adapt.

They all would. Sylvanas wanted more for him than for her sisters, though. Lireesa and Verath's daughters had already known the world could be punishing and violent.

The three stood between that darkness, that hard truth, and their people, so the people could recover, and laugh, and sing again. And Sylvanas was determined that Lirath would never taste that bitter draught.

"Everything feels so empty, now. Frivolous. Mother and Father are dead, and I am wasting my life. That *cannot* be what they would have wanted!"

Sylvanas was worn thin, and she almost snapped at him. Instead, she took a deep breath. "Lirath," she said, as kindly and quietly as she could manage. "Do you know how hard it was on them that all their daughters followed Mother's path? A path of danger, of violence, where we could die at any minute? Don't you think they sighed with relief knowing that at least *one* of their children might be safe? Don't you think Alleria and Vereesa and I do?"

His face crumpled and he looked away. But his jaw was still clenched.

"It's hard enough having to bury Mother and Father, to mourn them. Do you think I want to bury you? Mourn you? I don't. I won't. And that is why I refuse to teach you."

There was a long pause, then Lirath squared his shoulders and looked back at his sister.

"Of all of us, I thought *you* would believe in me. But you don't."

He started to say something else, paused, then gave a short nod, cold and curt. It was frightening, as if something in him had abruptly broken.

"You don't," he said again, almost to himself. He turned without another word, making his way through the crowd, his back to her. Sylvanas wanted to run after him, but she couldn't.

Let him be angry. Let him live to hate me for the rest of his long, full, safe life.

Vereesa moved to her sister, looking after Lirath. "Vereesa . . . go after him. He shouldn't be alone right now. You need to be there for him, as I cannot."

He needs you, not me. He doesn't want me. I'm sorry, Little Lord Sun, but I made you a promise you don't even remember. With love and courage, I will keep you safe.

Vereesa searched her eyes, seeing how much it hurt her sister to send Vereesa when Sylvanas so clearly yearned to go, but the elder sister's position would not permit her. "Of course," Vereesa said quietly. She turned and followed their brother.

Sylvanas locked her legs into position and endured, through the growing heat of the day, the welcome cool in the evening, and well into nightfall as the flood of mourners thinned to a stream, and finally a trickle that petered out when the moons and stars took dominion in the sky.

"Sylvanas."

The voice was gruff and sounded annoyed. Sylvanas, however, knew the speaker well enough to recognize concern in the tone.

Nathanos stepped beside her, looking uncomfortable. He carried a cloth-covered plate.

"What is it?" Sylvanas asked, eyeing the dish.

"It's a troll head," he said, irritated. "What do you think it is? Food. I'll wager you've not eaten a bite since yesterday. I don't think you want to fall flat on your face in front of the world tomorrow when you're formally named ranger-general."

If anything could have made her smile, his words would have. He was right. She had been standing all day and not touched a bit of food or even drunk water. She hesitated. It felt disrespectful, somehow, when her parents could never again enjoy such simple things.

Nathanos looked at her searchingly, then, as always, he understood. Gently, he placed a hand on her back and steered Sylvanas away from the bier. Now, away from the image of cloth-clad bodies being bathed in moonslight, she accepted the plate, opening her mouth to say she was thirsty, but Nathanos was already holding a waterskin.

Sylvanas nodded her head in thanks, and drank. The water was cold and clean, as if he had scooped it from the river Elrendar, reminding Sylvanas that despite all evidence to the contrary, she was alive and could stave off physical needs no longer.

"Let me take you home," Nathanos offered.

Sylvanas shook her head. The thought of returning to Windrunner Spire was unbearable, knowing that she would never hear her father's warm laughter or even her mother's barbed scolding, that there would no longer be dancing in their favorite hollow while Lirath played and sang, that her parents would now whirl together in each other's arms, eyes locked, faces soft with love, only as ghosts, if indeed spirits they had become.

She wondered if they had died quickly. How many enemies Lireesa had taken with her. If her father suffered. Which of them had watched the other die first.

Suddenly, Sylvanas did not want to eat, or drink, or do anything except stand beside her fallen family until her body collapsed from sheer exhaustion. And yet—she did not want that, either. She did not want to sleep, because when she woke, her eyes would flutter open on another new day of a world without her parents in it.

She wanted to do nothing to enable that cruel dawn to approach more quickly.

"You need food and rest," Nathanos said.

"I'm fine."

"You're too smart to say that," he said. "Do I have to pin you down and force-feed you? Because I will."

When Nathanos didn't even get a hint of a smile or a challenge from her, his face furrowed into deep grooves. "No one else is coming now, it's just us," he said, more quietly. "Sit. Eat."

Sylvanas did so, feeling a start of pain as limbs and joints locked so long into position were allowed to move again. Awkward and heavy with grief, she let Nathanos ease her down and accepted the bread, cheese, and water he offered. The bread was dry and tasteless, and she almost couldn't swallow the cheese, but she forced herself to do so.

At one point, Sylvanas sagged, so depleted, so alone, even though she still had family, the Farstriders, the Trio, and Nathanos. She leaned her head against Nathanos's shoulder.

Just for a moment, I will close my eyes.

The last several days had been the most devastating of her life. Tomorrow promised to be little easier. And the days after that? They would unfold as they would. But they would not get the better of her.

Despite herself, sleep finally won the battle. Blessedly, she had no dreams.

CHAPTER TEN

S ylvanas woke in her own bed. For a moment, she drifted in
that half-asleep, half-awake stage, feeling something nudging
at the back of her mind.

Memory descended like a hammer strike. She flinched, trying to
curl herself into a ball, to shut out the world, but sternly she forbade
herself. She owed it to her parents—especially to Lireesa—to be
stronger than ever. Sylvanas Windrunner refused to go down in history as a weak ranger-general.

Someone had laid out her clothes. Servants? She could not see
how Nathanos would allow anyone near her right now; it had to
have been him. Besides, he would be the only one who would know
what armor she would need today.

She arrived at Farstrider Retreat with her head high, and if her
face was still pale, it revealed no trace of vulnerability. Nathanos did
not accompany her as he was not a Farstrider. Sylvanas took some
comfort in seeing Vereesa, also clad in her armor. Sorrow somehow
made her features even more beautiful. Sylvanas wondered what her
own grief had done to hers, but she did not care. This was a part of
them now. There had been a recall of all the Farstriders possible on
such short notice; Alleria, still, was not among them. So be it.

As the highest-ranking Farstrider other than Sylvanas herself, Lor'themar would be swearing her in. He gave her a reassuring smile. A few more stragglers entered, and then all were assembled who would be coming.

Lor'themar stepped forward. "There is always sorrow, when naming a new ranger-general," he said. "It means that we have lost one, even as we stand poised to gain another. So before we continue, I would like to take a moment to speak of Lireesa Windrunner. Many of you have served your whole lives under her. She was brave, clearheaded, stalwart, and bold. When we received the news, perhaps you, like me, simply could not believe such a fierce spirit was gone.

"There are many stories about her valor and skill. But there is one that exceeds all the others, because it tells us not only of Lireesa's battle prowess, but also of how deeply she cared about the Farstriders she led. Who here was present at that battle's beginning?"

Four hands were raised. Sylvanas suddenly wished she had asked her mother to tell her own story; Lireesa was too modest. Now she would only ever hear about it as a legend.

"Let us tell the story, then. Vor'athil, will you begin?"

Vor'athil nodded. "It will be an honor. The Amani had been quiet for some time. Then, completely unexpectedly, they launched an incursion. No simple raid, but a well-planned and -executed attack. Not only were all their finest warriors in the vanguard—but so was a terrifying creature. The tortured thing had been an eagle, once. But the trolls had cruelly warped it with their dark magic, twisting it into a true monster."

He paused. Rellian took up the tale. "Lireesa's unit, which had been out hunting in the area, was the only one close enough to respond. Four of us still live who were with her then. We numbered only seven, and we had lost a few of our arrows in the hunt. We stood our ground a league away from our mark, and many troll warriors fell. But these arrows, we could not retrieve, and too soon our ammunition was low. We were prepared to use all we had, then fight hand-to-hand and die protecting our people. But Lireesa would not hear of it."

Sylvanas knew the story by heart, but had never heard it re-counted solely by veterans, nor in such heartfelt tones. Emotions rose in her: grief, admiration, love, and concern that she might not lead this group as well as her mother had. *I don't want to let you down.*

Salissa, standing beside him, spoke next. "Lireesa had one arrow remaining. She asked each of us to give her one of ours. Then she gave the order to fall back and defend the village, and turned, alone, to face the enemy. We thought she was sacrificing herself to allow our escape, and we were devastated. But . . . this was Lireesa. I suppose we should not have doubted."

Auric Sunchaser cleared his throat. "We barely had time to put up some defenses and prepare the villagers to fight for their lives when we saw the trolls approaching—without the monstrous Dark Eagle they had created. And outpacing them was Lireesa Windrun-ner. It is . . . impossible to tell you how morale surged. I have never seen its like, before or since. By the time the trolls arrived a few moments later, they were fought off by such vigor and passion that those who survived fled. Not a single elven life was lost. After our victory, Lireesa took us to the battlefield. There lay the dreadful Dark Eagle, enormous, hideous . . . dead. It had an arrow in each eye, one in its throat, and four tightly clustered in its heart. I could not help myself. I exclaimed, 'You have slain this monster on your own.'"

He lifted his gaze and smiled at Sylvanas. "'No,' Lireesa said, and she pointed to the seven arrows, six of which we had given her, em-bedded in the monster's corpse. 'I succeeded, because you lent me your strength.'"

There was a respectful pause, then Lor'themar broke it. "Lireesa will never be replaced. But we are lucky that she will be succeeded by her daughter, continuing a very long line of Windrunner ranger-generals." He turned again to the assembled rangers who had formed a circle with Sylvanas and Lor'themar in the center. "We honor tra-dition, but we also are free-willed. We serve our people, but we are not servants. As was done in millennia past, I will ask, and you will answer, if you will follow Lady Sylvanas Windrunner, supporting and obeying her as you did her mother."

Lor'themar nodded to Halduron, and the young ranger replied with a resounding "Yes!" The yeses followed around the circle quickly, automatically, until Helios did not respond.

Lor'themar frowned. "Helios, what is your answer?"

Helios looked at Sylvanas steadily as he replied, "You speak of tradition. And that we have been led by a Windrunner for centuries. But we have also traditionally pledged ourselves to the ranger-general's eldest child. Which tradition is the true one? Many of us still believe that Alleria should be given the title."

Sylvanas was stunned. She knew she was not universally beloved at court, but among the Farstriders, she thought she had a second family . . . Helios was not citing tradition because he valued it. It was because he did not want *her*.

Her fists clenched. Anger, bright and hot, flared in her belly, welcomed after the bleak lethargy and pain of the previous day. She opened her mouth to defend herself, but another, calmer voice than her own spoke first.

"*I* believe," said Lor'themar Theron, "that would be a mistake."

Halduron stepped up beside Lor'themar. "I agree," said Halduron. "I would gladly have followed Alleria Windrunner, had she wished to inherit the title. But she did not and made no secret of it. It was a source of friction that, in the end, splintered the Farstriders. Lady Sylvanas accepted the title, although it should never have been her responsibility, and she has not wavered."

"Which of you is unaware that, within an hour of learning about her parents, Sylvanas was on her way to conduct an investigation into their deaths?" said Lor'themar. "We grieve the late ranger-general and councilor deeply. How must she have felt? Yet she pushed aside her emotions and set herself to learning about the threat—as much to protect us as to bring closure to her family. Alleria and those she left with have still not responded to the summons sent to her."

Sylvanas was trembling, and tears threatened to fill her eyes. She had thought the family had kept the rift between Alleria and Lireesa secret, but now she realized how impossible it would be to keep secrets from those trained to listen and observe. Friendship did not demand the statements Halduron and Lor'themar were making now, in front of court, the public, and their fellow Farstriders. The two spoke for her because they believed what they said. They had watched her struggle, and seen her determination, and they wanted to make sure others saw it, too.

"As you say, Lady Alleria has not yet replied," Helios said, unruffled. "We should give her the chance to decline. It is her inheritance."

"Which she already abdicated, years ago," Lor'themar reminded him.

"She might not have wished the title at the time, but now? No. Everything is different now. We should delay until she can be reached."

Lor'themar frowned. "I submit to you that in Lady Sylvanas, we have the skill and temperament of her mother, and the wisdom of her father. Alleria chose the wider world. It is an admirable decision, but it does reflect her loyalties. Sylvanas"—he turned to look at her—"chose *us*."

"I *did* choose the wider world," came a familiar voice. "And Sylvanas did choose you."

Sylvanas's heart seemed to stop for a moment. Murmurs rippled through the room as every head turned to see Alleria Windrunner, her armor stained, her face sweaty. Dark rings made her eyes seem hollow, but even so they blazed fiercely.

"And it was the right decision. For the two of us, for the Farstriders, and for Quel'Thalas."

She entered the retreat, striding boldly up to stand shoulder-to-shoulder with Sylvanas. Vereesa said nothing, but it was impossible for her to hide her smile.

"I came as soon as I could," Alleria whispered, for Sylvanas's ears alone. "I should have been there for all of you. I'm sorry."

All at once, the cold knot of anger and resentment in Sylvanas's chest dissolved. Grief and pain would take time to recede, and likely would never disappear altogether. But at least this wound of Alleria's absence would no longer torment her.

"You're here now," Sylvanas said, and tears, blinked away an instant later, filled Alleria's eyes.

The eldest Windrunner turned to address the gathered Farstriders. "I came here thinking to see the Farstriders uniting behind the leader our mother chose for you. Instead, you squabble like children, using my absence as an excuse to nurse your private grievances. That is not who we are." Helios pressed his lips together in silent disapproval. Alleria did not miss it, and said, "You wished to delay the vote until I responded? Here I am, Helios, and I tell you with my whole heart that I am where I am supposed to be to best help our home . . . and so is my sister. I am so glad she is here protecting Quel'thalas . . . just as I was glad many years ago, when she protected me, and saved my life."

Sylvanas could not believe it. In front of everyone, including many who had been present that day, Alleria Windrunner thanked her sister for breaking the rules, for spoiling her test. But perhaps in the dawning of this new era, Sylvanas could see that moment in a different light. That moment had set Alleria on a different path, one that she was always destined to walk.

"Does anyone else request a formal vote?" Alleria demanded. "If so, let me cast the first yea, in favor of my sister."

Not a single hand was raised. Sylvanas noted with satisfaction that many of the Farstriders who had sided with Helios looked embarrassed.

She squared her shoulders and turned to Lor'themar. "I am ready."

It was custom that, after a ranger-general was sworn in, they would symbolically "take care" of the Farstriders by preparing a simple meal of small items—cubed cheese, cut fruit, slices of bread—and offering the tray to every member they would lead into battle one day. Vereesa, thoughtful as always, had prepared the meal for her sister, but the tone in the room was hardly one of camaraderie after Helios's divisive suggestion and Alleria's abrupt arrival. And, as always, the other two members of the Trio stepped in smoothly to offer to distribute the food while the three sisters took the rare chance to speak with each other as they walked to where the dragonhawks were teth- ered. "I would have been there had I known," Alleria said. "I am so sorry I didn't. Are you both all right?"

Sylvanas gave a bitter chuckle. "Of course we are. We're Wind- runners, we have to be."

Vereesa said, "It's good to see you, Alleria. Even if only for a few moments. Are you sure you cannot stay longer?"

"I have to report to the king, and then return immediately to Lordaeron. But I will make time to visit the Artists' Quarters and see our brother. Hopefully, His Majesty will listen to what I have to tell him."

"I am not at all sure he will," Sylvanas said. She stopped, and they did as well, both looking at her curiously. Anasterian had instructed her to tell no one. But these were her sisters—one of whom had al- most become ranger-general. Sylvanas trusted them with her life, and her secrets. In a quiet voice, she informed them of the investiga- tion, her conclusion—and Anasterian's rejection of it. "He believes he is helping our people by not causing fear when nothing is yet certain. Trolls, we understand. The Horde . . . we do not."

"Yet," Alleria said. "This news disappoints me. I thought better of him. Still, I must try."

"You didn't tell me, Sylvanas," Vereesa said, quietly.

"I have not had a moment alone with you since learning of it," Sylvanas said, a touch sharply. "Lor'themar and a few others were at the site. They knew even without evidence that it was the Horde. Only Nathanos was with me when I found proof. I promised the king that I remain loyal to him. But I am also loyal to you, my sisters, and would have you at least know the truth."

Alleria looked somber. "We feared the worst, when we heard the news."

"Your friends have few allies here in Quel'Thalas, Alleria. I hope that one day soon, you will have more."

"But . . . what about Lirath?" Vereesa asked. "Will you tell him, too?"

Sylvanas glanced down. "One day, yes. But not now. I fear it will only damage him further, or make him take up arms and try to kill the whole Horde by himself."

Alleria looked at her searchingly. "Are you sure?" she said. "They were his parents, not just ours. He deserves to know. And if he wants to fight, why not train him?"

"You asked me to stay with him, after the funeral," Vereesa said. "He misses them, just as we do, but we have one another and the Farstriders. We have a chance to strike back. He doesn't."

Sylvanas smiled a little. "Brave words from one who has yet to make her first kill."

Vereesa reddened. "Lirath wants to belong," she said. "He wants to believe he still has a family. Alleria, you are gone now. You walk another path. Sylvanas and I see each other all the time. He is alone in Silvermoon."

A pang of guilt struck Sylvanas. "He will be glad to see you, Alleria. And I will visit him as well. We both will, Vereesa. But do not tell him about Mother and Father."

"I still think you should train him," Alleria said. "He is smart and dexterous—he will learn quickly, now that he is a bit older."

They did not know Lirath like she did. They did not know just how fully he had filled her heart the day he was born. They had not heard her whispered promise. Tell him a terrible new threat to Azeroth had ambushed and butchered their parents? Put a sword into a hand that had known only fifes and harps? The thought of her sisters' pain upon seeing their murdered parents stiffening on the earth made her sad. The thought of Lirath seeing them— intolerable.

"No," she said, flatly. "He has suffered enough."

Alleria sighed. "He is an adult, old enough to make his own choices. But train him or not, as you will. In the meantime, I will not tell him about the attack. It should come from you, Sylvanas. Consider it—and think on training him, too."

"I will," she said, to keep the peace, to not bring tension between them now, when the world was turning upside down. She had already given the idea all the attention it was due. Lirath would never need to defend himself. That was her task.

They embraced, then, the three of them. Sylvanas thought back to the days when they would dance barefoot in the sunlight while their parents made them feel safe and Lirath's songs made them feel that the world was full of grace and magic and mystery.

Then Alleria swung herself atop her dragonhawk and was gone, heading toward a city that denied even what was in front of them, to a king who thought ignorance was protection.

"You want to do *what?*"

Lor'themar seldom raised his voice. Even rarer was the note of utter bafflement in his tone.

"I intend to offer Nathanos a position in the Farstriders." Sylvanas's voice was calm.

"You . . ." Halduron laughed, slightly nervous. "You cannot possibly be serious."

"Oh, I am. Deadly."

"But . . . he is *human*," Lor'themar said, still lost in the perceived illogic of it all.

"There is nothing in the code of the organization that says one must be quel'dorei to be a Farstrider. He is as good a shot and tracker as either of you, and that is saying a great deal. He also brings an entirely different range of information, skill, and experience that can only serve us. Which," she added, "you have both just witnessed. Anasterian may not wish to frighten the populace, but that does not mean we cannot learn more about these orcs who so—" She stopped herself and took a deep breath, releasing the hand she had unknowingly clenched tight. "Who struck at the heart of the things we hold dear—at civilized diplomacy, and just defense and protection of the populace."

"Fine, then let him teach us what he knows—or better yet, go back to Lordaeron and send someone else in his place," Lor'themar said, finally seeming to shake himself out of his shock. "He is a braggart, and a bully, and he has remained among us far too long already."

"He saved your *life*," Sylvanas corrected. "And you would repay him by sneering?"

"I have expressed my gratitude," Lor'themar replied. "Many times. But truly, saving a life should not warrant such exceptional treatment. Looking out for one's comrades should not be considered remarkable behavior."

"Sylvanas," Halduron said, in a more placating tone than Lor'themar had used, "no matter what title or position you squander on him—Nathanos will never be accepted. Not because he is a human, but because he is this particular one. You do not stand on the most stable ground as it is, as has recently been brought home to you. There are others than Helios who would smile to see you fail."

"They will not be smiling if I do fail. I am the one who stands between them and death."

"*We,* Sylvanas. *We* stand between them," said Halduron. He was growing angry. It was a rare sight, and Sylvanas had never before seen its heat directed at her. "The Farstriders have had enough of strife. Please, do not bring anything unnecessary—"

"Any *thing*? Unnecessary?" The rage Sylvanas had attempted to redirect now threatened to boil over. "Nathanos is not a *thing*, Halduron. And he is very necessary to us right now."

To me. He is necessary to me. I will not relinquish him to the Alliance. Halduron and Lor'themar were not there on the cold gray dawning of that first day without—

"Neither the king nor the prince will support this," Lor'themar cautioned. "You have had a history of butting heads with them. They will forbid it."

"Kael'thas spends more time with humans than he does with his own people. I imagine he will think differently." In truth, she did not, but she was not about to let her friends know that. She would deal with the Sunstriders later. Somehow.

"People . . . will talk," Lor'themar said, choosing his words with the same deliberateness her father had displayed on so many occasions.

Sylvanas was done. "Let them," she said. "I will still do this. We need every weapon we can find." She would do everything in her power so that no other family had to grieve as hers had. And she needed Nathanos, ugly, blunt, sarcastic Nathanos, who somehow understood her better than anyone, even Lirath. The human knew much of pain and anger and cruelty, things she was becoming more acquainted with by the hour.

"Nathanos stays, and he will be a Farstrider. And that," Sylvanas snapped, forestalling any more argument, "is an order."

"I didn't ask you to make me a Farstrider," Nathanos said when she told him the news a few days later. They were walking hand in hand around Lake Elrendar, their footsteps so light from practice they barely disturbed the local fauna.

"I know. *I* wanted to make you a Farstrider. Maybe even a ranger lord."

"*What?* Why?"

"You're very good. We need you," Sylvanas said.

"Not buying that."

"It's as you wish," she said.

"I think," Nathanos mused, "that you somehow thought I'd leave if you didn't. That belief insults both my superior intelligence and my excellent vision."

Sylvanas smiled at that, relieved at the certainty of knowing that he was willing to become a Farstrider, that someone she cared for, at least, wouldn't abandon her through death or disinterest. The latter, he had always made clear. And the former . . . deny it as they might, but Nathanos was the equal of Halduron and Lor'themar. He would not fall in battle.

Since the attack, Sylvanas had found reasons to avoid anything that reminded her too intensely of the life they had all lived before. She had assigned Vereesa duties that kept them separate and, despite her words to Alleria during her older sister's unexpected and timely visit, was not ready to reach out to Lirath. She could not risk collapsing under the weight of his pain; both of them would fall, then.

Sylvanas took comfort in knowing he had friends who cared about him at court, among them the prince himself, and Vereesa was spending more of her free time with him as well. For now, that would be enough.

The wind shifted, bearing the subtle trace of an unwelcome scent: smoke. Nathanos smelled it, too. "Fire," he said, and even as he spoke, they both heard the long, low sound of a warning horn.

By this point Sylvanas was sprinting back to the enclave. He followed, and she saw that several Farstriders were already borne aloft by dragonhawks and heading the same direction.

Her mind was racing. While the Sunwell protected Quel'Thalas and bathed it in magic, it could not prevent every mishap. Campfires sometimes burned out of control. The odd lightning strike made a lethal torch out of a simple tree. But Sylvanas knew in her heart this fire was not caused by one of those rare events. It came too close on the heels of her sister's warning.

She saw as she flew south that it was not one fire, but four, all to the south of the river Elrendar. Plumes of thick black smoke curled upward. These fires had been deliberately set.

Sylvanas was not a stranger to battle. She and Alleria had both followed their mother's orders in the occasional skirmish with the old enemy. Now it was Sylvanas who needed to lead, so very much earlier than anyone had ever expected.

Part of her quailed from the responsibility. The rest of her faced it squarely.

I may be your second choice, Mother, but you will see that I am not second best.

Such a prideful statement. That conversation seemed so long ago, but now it was time to prove the words true—if not to her mother, who was past hearing them, then to herself.

"We are under attack!" Sylvanas called, bringing the dragonhawk down. "Four fires, one due south, two southwest, one northeast near Suncrown Village. Evacuating citizens is the top priority. I'll wager that you'll find not just the fires but those who set it lurking in the edges of the forest, so do some cleanup of that mess as well."

"Halduron, Lor'themar—tackle the two to the west. Take the spear unit. Helios—head south. Keep your eyes open. I do not think the trolls are acting alone."

"You think it's the Horde?" Helios asked. Sylvanas noticed that he, and her friends as well, all glanced over at Nathanos. It was a faint comfort in a dark time to see that even if they would not accept him, they would still listen to him.

But she was their ranger-general, and so she was the one to respond. "It is too bold for a typical troll attack," Sylvanas said. "Nathanos—go with Helios. Hurry." He nodded once, curtly, and he, Helios, Halduron, and Lor'themar hastened off. Sylvanas Windrunner watched them go for just a heartbeat, then steeled herself to face the monsters who had slain her parents.

The moment she dreaded and yearned for was not long in arriving.

She had taken her own advice, and led a group of rangers not toward the fires, but away from them. The Horde had set them to draw the elves, knowing they would come to protect their forests. But the green things and their troll allies did not give the quel'dorei the credit they were due, and she would see to it that this would cost them.

She heard them before anyone else, and made a quick gesture. The Farstriders leaped into the trees so deftly the leaves barely quivered, and the orcs approached. They were loud, and laughing, and she could not help but imagine them coming for her parents.

Mother could not even stand against them. What chance do I have? I have no Battle of Seven Arrows to give me strength. But hard on the heels of that debilitating thought was another. *I have her training. Her blood. And by the Sunwell, her* will.

She gave a signal that passed swiftly through those gathered, silent, shielded by golden leaves: *Pick your target.*

Sylvanas found hers at once. It was the biggest, the ugliest, the one that strode with confidence and pride in destroying beauty with fire and hope with slaughter. She imagined it was this one—short yellow tusks, tiny cruel eyes—whose arrow had killed her mother.

She took aim, then shot the arrow neatly into one of those cruel eyes. Sylvanas found a second orc, who had, like the others, abruptly shifted into a defensive posture, a sword as big as she in each over-sized fist.

This one is for my father.

A few moments and an eternity later, every member of the Horde unit was dead or dying. Two of her own had been casualties. One Farstrider had lost her grip and toppled to the earth. She fell to an axe blade, but Sylvanas saw to it that her body was covered with that of her killer, his thick green skin peppered with arrows. The other was wounded, but would survive. Despite his protests, Sylvanas ordered him removed from the battle.

The next several hours were filled with blood and flame as more fires sprang up. Of course the Horde would not be content with battle. This menace would destroy whatever it touched; anything of beauty needed to be violated. It had not been so very long since she had said to Nathanos, *Those we protect, we protect them not just from the danger. We protect them from the true face of this world.* Well, the true face of another world had shown itself in the worst way possible, right at her very doorstep. And that face was more hideous than any nightmare, with an even darker heart.

Sylvanas pushed ever southward, doing what she could to drive the Horde back, through the gates, out of her glorious homeland. The Farstriders in other units were doing the same at her command, and though the air was thick and dark and hard to breathe, no one faltered. If the orcs got past them, they knew what was at stake . . .

Sylvanas thought of the small villages, filled with friends and relatives. Of her family's own home, still being tended by those who had wept bitterly when learning the fates of Lireesa and Verath. And she thought of the old song that Lirath often sang, his sweet voice devastating in its heartbreak, the lament for lives lost thousands of years ago. Had he written one for their parents? She did not know. Sylvanas resolved that, when this was over and the quel'dorei were once again victorious, she would seek her brother out and embrace him. Elves were capable of living for centuries. That did not mean they would, and this dark day was brutal proof.

Sylvanas's emphasis on evacuating the civilians saved lives, and for that she was glad. But so many graceful buildings were lost, as well as huge swaths of the forest south of the river. Fortunately, for Goldenmist Village, there was a natural firebreak in the form of the Elrendar, which also proved to be a challenge for the trolls and orcs who would cross it.

Sylvanas ordered her unit to stand on the river's banks, spread along as much of its length as possible, and pick off any Horde foolish enough to attempt a crossing. There was a ray of hope in that it seemed likely they could save the northern half of their land, but the southern part of the forest would take years to recover. And that broke Sylvanas's heart.

There was motion on the other side, and Sylvanas was instantly alert. Two elven figures were running as fast as they could to the river. Behind them, the golden leaves of the trees shook as monsters concealed in the branches leaped from bough to bough, emitting horrible, cackling laughter.

Sylvanas blinked. She knew the runners. They were Vereesa—and Alleria.

Unwilling to see their prey escape into the water, the trolls moved down to the ground. Sylvanas dropped her clenched fist, and at the signal her entire unit began to fire. She joined them, taking satisfaction in seeing the large, ugly bodies at last lying still.

Sylvanas held up her bow in greeting. "Welcome home, Alleria!" she called. "Now what is this trouble you've brought us?"

"I did not bring it, Sylvanas," Alleria called back. "I had hoped to outrun it. But I do bring possible salvation. I must speak to the council."

Sylvanas shook her head and repeated the warning she had given her sister the last time she had arrived unexpectedly in the forests of their homeland. "I do not know if they will listen."

"They will listen," Alleria said, and Sylvanas heard the banked anger of the righteous in her voice. "I will give them no choice. I have something to show them." She lifted a sack that contained something round and heavy. The bottom of the sack was soaked with blood. Sylvanas knew what it must be.

"Orc?" she asked, hopefully.

"Troll," Alleria replied. "But that will be enough. And I did not come alone. Alliance troops, commanded by a paladin named Turalyon, followed the Horde here, and are eager to catch them."

Paladin? Nathanos had said something about them. They were warrior priests who used both the powers of the Light and a solid hammer or sword. Sylvanas approved of the combination.

"Where are they now?"

"In the southwest," Alleria replied.

"My unit will join them," Sylvanas replied. "We will get you a dragonhawk. Good luck. You will need it."

Lor'themar and Halduron were already at the meeting site with their units, and to Sylvanas's surprise, so were the warriors Alleria had requested from Anasterian. Sylvanas felt a sharp, angry pang. It wasn't so long ago that Anasterian had looked her in the eye and promised that this very battle could never happen, that the Horde would never dare threaten the borders of Quel'thalas, that the justice her parents deserved was worth less than the price of peace. In the time since, she had—despite his initial refusal—asked his council for supplemental aid, for more patrols, and received nothing from the court but a faint warning that further protest would not be acceptable. Alleria, who had left them all behind, had returned now, and the old king lent her his ear . . . and his troops.

But Sylvanas quickly banished the thought. By now, the populace had been disabused of any notion that their kingdom was safe. And if Anasterian had been with his council when Alleria met him, it would have been folly to refuse to fight the enemy on their doorstep.

The ranger-general took a quick assessment of the battlefield, and began to fire. The young paladin, Sir Turalyon, proved to know his strategy; in short order, they developed a rhythm, the archers raining arrows on tight clusters of orcs, the spear units coming after them to finish the job and defend the Alliance soldiers in their midst as they hacked away with their swords. It was carnage, and it was deserved, and Sylvanas rejoiced.

Shadows fell, then vanished, and Sylvanas looked up. Silhouetted against the sky were gryphons, ridden by dwarves. One of them swooped low as the dwarf hurled his hammer. It connected with an orc's skull in a most satisfactory manner, then returned to its thrower.

It appeared the tide was turning.

Then, to Sylvanas's shock, she saw that Alleria had raised her bow into the air, holding it in the position that meant retreat.

For a moment, Sylvanas was confused, but then another shadow fell over those fighting at the edge of the forest. Sylvanas again looked up and gasped.

It was silhouetted against the sun for a long moment, a gigantic shape with mighty wings like those of a bat, and a long neck and tail. She had seen this creature before, but only in paintings, or occasionally gracing the pages of an otherwise ordinary tome. As it soared, the sunlight glinted on a body covered in red scales.

It was beautiful, and utterly terrifying, and Sylvanas simply stood, struck to her core.

A red dragon.

Then the beast broke the spell, shook its head, then arched its long sinuous neck. Sylvanas realized what was about to happen, had happened . . .

"Fall back, fall back!" she cried.

There was a mad scramble as the Alliance ran full-tilt to escape immolation from above. The dragon wheeled, returning for more passes. The sky filled with smoke, and the trees were gone, simply *gone*; not burned, but turned to ash. No wonder the fires had done so much damage. No wonder they seemed to spring up from nowhere.

During one pass from the great creature, Sylvanas could make out a tiny shape perched atop the beast's back.

The mighty dragon, breathing fire hot enough to turn metal to liquid, a being so powerful that it inspired awe at even the mere mention of its name—seemed to be obeying the commands of a single, simple orc.

I do not know what to name these things that crawled from the portal, Sylvanas thought bleakly. *Monster is too kind a word.*

Sylvanas shook off the daze, the shock of seeing two impossible things in as many minutes. She ran toward the gathering of warriors, paladins, and Farstriders, seeking out Alleria and Turalyon. Sylvanas searched the crowd until she spotted the paladin on his horse. Her sisters and Lor'themar fell into step with her as she approached them.

"They are already retreating," said Turalyon. "They know they cannot breach Silvermoon. So they have done what they came to do: demoralize and sow fear."

But they had done something else, too. They had ignited in all three of the Windrunner sisters a hatred hot as any dragonflame.

"If Quel'Thalas is not safe from incursion, what is?" asked the ranger-general of Silvermoon.

No one had an answer.

It took every ounce of restraint from Sylvanas to allow the Horde to retreat, but there was nothing they could do. Their numbers were too diminished, and the forces that remained were needed to assess the damage and control the fires threatening the villages and woods.

Turalyon suspected the Horde was finally ready to march on Lordaeron's capital city. There was no rest for the weary, and Sylvanas watched as Alliance soldiers stayed still only for bandaging, then began to move back toward the road that led from Quel'Thalas to the Eastweald.

"You go ahead," Alleria said to Turalyon. "I'll catch up."

"Of course." The paladin inclined his golden head toward Sylvanas. "The Alliance, and I, are very grateful for your aid this day."

Sylvanas watched him go, noting the look he threw Alleria, and the hint of a smile on her face. She was concerned for her sister's heart, but had no grounds to condemn her. After all she, too, was involved with a human, one far less popular than Turalyon.

"I suppose this means you cannot stay," Vereesa said.

Alleria shook her head regretfully. "It seems whenever my path leads me here, it leads me away just as quickly. Our family has experienced the cruelty of the Horde, but we must not allow others to suffer that fate if at all possible. There is no time to linger if Lordaeron is to have any warning at all."

Sylvanas understood. She was the only one of them who had seen Lireesa and Verath where they had fallen. Her younger siblings had only seen the corpses after they had been cleaned, their limbs arranged peacefully, the sight of the grievous wounds concealed by formal robes, and perhaps a touch of illusion magic to soften the blow further. No. She would not wish what she had endured on anyone.

"We must follow the Horde before they elude us again and have a chance to regroup," Alleria said.

"Go swiftly then, sister," Sylvanas said, and the two embraced. Vereesa next hugged her eldest sister tightly, unwilling to let go, and Alleria had to gently disengage herself. She nodded, as if to confirm something, and smiled slightly before turning to retreat with the young paladin.

Sylvanas knew that this was the first time Vereesa had seen bloodshed in battle. Her little sister should not be dwelling on it. There was time for her to work through her feelings later. Right now Vereesa needed to feel useful; that she had purpose.

"Find some of your fellows," Sylvanas said. "Send them off in small groups to help extinguish fires in the places that need aid."

The youngest sister nodded as Sylvanas had expected, grateful to have helpful work to ward off brooding on what had transpired. "I will make a sweep along the shoreline."

"Vereesa?"

The younger woman turned. "You did well today. Mother would have been proud of you. I am."

Vereesa smiled that sweet smile of hers. "She would have been proud of all of us. I wish she could have seen us fight together."

"The Windrunner sisters are a force to be reckoned with," Sylvanas agreed. It was a pity the eldest had given her bow to the Alliance—and perhaps her heart to the young paladin.

Sylvanas was tired, but also still alert, still tense from the battle. None of the sisters had mentioned it, but it was highly likely that both Windrunner Village and the spire had come under attack—from trolls, or orcs, or red dragonfire. Lireesa had drilled the household on evacuation practices, so Sylvanas was hopeful she would find it at least empty, if not intact, but she was deeply concerned about the village.

The final conflict had been enacted closer to her family home than she would have liked, so the walk was not far. It was hard to see in the still-smoky air. Ash lay thick on the earth, muffling sound like snow.

Sylvanas slowed as she approached, expecting to be challenged by the scouts positioned farthest from the village. She scanned the woods, but her sharp eyes saw and heard nothing. Sylvanas brought the horn to her lips and blew a long, mournful note. The echoes died; no one responded.

Perhaps they had already heard the good news and were busy helping quell the fires that still raged throughout their land. But something was not right. The feeling prickled at the back of her neck, and she again went into high alert.

Her eye was drawn by the strange, odd lumps marring the green sweep of the hills. Sun glinted off metal, and she saw glimpses of a green that was not the good, natural hue of grass and growing things.

Orcs.

A sudden fear buffeted her with the force of a massive wave, and for no good reason she could determine Sylvanas began to run as fast as her legs could bear her, her heart racing, trying to deny the awful terror that hammered in her brain.

Ten, twenty, more of them were revealed to her with each step she ran, flying over the grass so swiftly she barely felt her feet touch the earth. And then, as Sylvanas had hoped she would not, she saw other bodies.

Slim figures. One clad in Farstrider armor—Jadia. Other corpses wore bits and pieces of armor, doubtless grabbed at the last moment in a valiant but doomed effort to ward off the invaders. Closer she came to the village that her family had protected for so many centuries, and now she was seeing brightly colored clothing: civilians, patrons of the arts, or politicians climbing the ladder to power. They would hear no more music, paint no more art; decide no one's fate, not even their own.

Movement caught her eye and she whirled. A woman in a long, wine-red dress—

Please let there be some survivors—

She sprinted, hope flooding her and giving her speed, but as Sylvanas dropped to her knees beside the woman, the ranger-general realized at once she had been mistaken. The movement had been nothing but wind in long, unbound hair. The dark red fabric, silk that had once rustled as its owner danced and drank and laughed the night away, had merely hidden the more crimson stain of far too much of her lifeblood.

Sylvanas rocked back on her heels, looking around in dazed, grieving horror. It would seem she had not heeded the lesson her parents had lost their lives for her to learn: The Horde was more intelligent and better prepared than anyone had expected. How many signs of their presence had she missed? Enough to understand how horribly well they had scouted the landscape. It was the only way she could fathom how enough of the monsters had slipped past their watch.

Sylvanas got to her feet and began to search for survivors among the carnage, and in that grim task, discovered many she had known: Belaria Salonar, who had come with her sister to say an effusive goodbye to Alleria. Aravan and Rendris, the youths into whose cups she had sprinkled woundwood at a party that seemed so long ago now.

One limp form, sprawled facedown, had been tall and lean in life, with long gold hair that—

Lirath?

Sylvanas exhaled in relief, shaking as the sudden spurt of adrenaline faded. Of course it was not him. The male figure was clad in archer's leathers, not the long, colorful robes of a royal musician. An orcish throwing axe, short and ugly, was embedded in his back. The blood glistened in the sunlight; still wet. The elf had lived for some time until the wound finally claimed his life.

The hue of his hair . . . gold as a newly minted coin . . .

Her legs quivered as she walked, unsteadily, over to the body. Kneeling beside it, Sylvanas paused.

She did not lack courage, she knew. Or will. Some said she was recklessly brave, but she did not feel brave now. She felt small, and afraid, and lost.

Sylvanas simply could not bring herself to look at him. She thought of pulling the coverings off the bodies of her mother, then her father. She had thought her heart would never hurt more than it did at those moments.

How pathetically wrong she had been, and how fate must have laughed, knowing what it held in store for her.

Gently, Sylvanas touched him with the same care she had shown him in the first hour of his life, easing him onto his back, dreading what death might have done to him already. Lirath's face was relaxed in death, but the shredded hands and the blood trail behind him told the story of how he had tried to crawl to safety as his life ebbed. Sylvanas reached to touch that still face, brushing away the dirt and grass. She gathered him, so still, so cold, into her arms, cradling his golden head on her lap, one arm around him. Holding him, as she had when he was a baby, when his blue eyes had fixed on hers and she had made a deep vow.

I will never hurt you. Ever. And no one else will, either. With love, and courage, I will keep you safe.

Sylvanas had broken that vow twice. She had been the one to wound him with words, even before this terrible day. She had failed not only her promise, not only her brother, but also the people of Windrunner Village. Her first true battle, and she had let it take away the brightest beacon of hope and peace she had ever known.

And because she had so failed, there would be no chance for reconciliation, no warm laugh or embrace. Lirath was forever silent; forever still.

Sylvanas reached for one of the damaged hands, still pliable enough for her to entwine hers with his. She looked at the torn nails, the dirt, the blood, and saw only slim fingers flying across the holes of a flute or pressed against the strings of a lute; she closed her eyes, and heard in the breeze the sweetest voice she would ever hear.

My Little Lord Sun.

Sylvanas had striven so hard to keep the world's harshness away from him, and in that striving had only driven him toward it. She would have gladly given her life to save his, and yet Sylvanas had not even had the grace to admit she was wrong.

It was not true. It could not be. Lirath was so vibrant, so quick, so *alive.* Surely, somehow, this was a trick, a prank, like the one he had played on her when she thought him drowned. But the world went on, and he remained still and silent.

Sylvanas could not weep. She could not move, not just yet. So she sat in the bright afternoon sunshine, gently rocking in her arms the one she had loved best in the world, and did the only thing she could for him.

She took a deep, shaky breath.

> "By the light
> By the light of the sun
> Children of the blood
> Our enemies are breaking through
> Children of the blood
> By the light
> Failing children of the blood
> They are breaking through . . ."

CHAPTER ELEVEN

What saved Sylvanas was sealing herself up tight, closing her mind and heart.

She had cleaned her brother's body as best she could. The image of her parents, their bodies partially consumed by scavengers, was emblazoned on her mind's eye, so she did everything she could to keep the body safe. She then went to the enclave. One look at her, her armor stained with Lirath's blood and her face ashen and impassive, made it cruelly clear to all those Farstriders who had returned there from the battlefield that something was very wrong.

Where is Vereesa? Sylvanas wondered. She should tell Little Moon first. But no. Others had died in the battle as well, and each deserved as much care as her brother. Perhaps it was best after all if she could speak privately with her sister later.

Sylvanas told the Farstriders what had happened as matter-of-factly as if she were speaking of strangers: that the enemy had come around them and slaughtered most of Windrunner Village. She was able to identify many of the bodies, but not all, and informed them that the fallen would need to be removed, tended to, claimed, and properly buried.

"That should not be difficult," Halduron said, his voice heavy. "Among us, we have all lost someone."

They were somber as they walked slowly among the bodies near Windrunner Village. Though they had faced death and loss in the past and would in the future, like her, they all seemed stunned that there were so many dead.

"Sylvanas," said Nathanos, appearing at her elbow without her noticing, "Come with me. There . . . there is—"

"I know," she said quietly. "Who do you think covered him?"

Nathanos had never been at a loss for words the entire time Sylvanas had known him, but now he seemed to be rendered mute. She thought back to the day of Alleria's test, when Halduron came to their favorite spot to bring Verath, Vereesa, and Sylvanas herself back to the spire—No. She would not think of that.

"He was being trained," Sylvanas said, the words almost devoid of emotion. "He was wearing archer's armor. It fit him well and was not new—but not damaged."

Not until a wave of monsters had descended, accompanied by the old familiar, hated enemy, the trolls. Not until it was too late for his half-completed training to do anything but give him a false sense of confidence.

The words of her sisters floated back to her unbidden, unwanted.

If he wants to fight, why not train him?

We have one another and the Farstriders. We have a chance to strike back. He doesn't.

But he had seized that chance, when it came. As Sylvanas would have.

He will learn quickly, now that he is a bit older. "Just . . . not quickly enough," she whispered only for her ears, only for his, if her brother's spirit lingered here.

Had she trained him from youth, Lirath would have been better able to fight properly, or at least to know when he was outmatched. He might even have survived. Had he continued untaught, he would have been safe inside Silvermoon. She closed her eyes, opened them again.

"Had someone not indulged Lirath's fantasy of being a warrior, my brother would be alive," Sylvanas said, her words sharp and cruel and hard as daggers. "Whoever did this is as responsible as the creatures who buried the axe in his back."

There was a sharp, sobbing gasp behind her, and Sylvanas whirled.

Her younger sister stood, eyes wide, staring at the covered body. At this moment, Vereesa's pale face and white hair reminded Sylvanas of a delicate ceramic statue their mother had once had, beautiful and fragile. The statue had been broken during one of the endless rambunctious playtimes of the Windrunner children. She'd forgotten about it now, but the memory rushed back, as clear as when it had happened years ago.

We are Windrunners.

We are not fragile. We will not shatter.

"Vereesa. Look at me." Her sister did, her eyes shiny with tears.

"Sylvanas," Vereesa whispered, her trembling voice so faint as to be barely audible, "please. Please tell me it is not . . . it's not . . ."

"It is Lirath." There was no reason to gentle the blow. There was time to mourn their brother later. Now, though, they needed to find the one who had filled Lirath's head with foolish, fatal dreams.

Vereesa swayed. Sylvanas caught her, her hand digging into Vereesa's upper arm, and shook the other woman, roughly. "Don't you dare," Sylvanas hissed. "Stay strong. Stay angry."

Their gazes locked. Tears filled Vereesa's eyes and slipped down her cheeks. "Little Lord Sun," she whispered.

"No," Sylvanas snapped, her own voice quivering, threatening to betray her. "Not now. Do you hear me?"

Sylvanas could bury a body. She could even bury Lirath. But if she allowed herself to think on their childhood, on the moment she had held him and given him that name, Sylvanas knew she would not be able to do what she needed to—find and punish not only the orcs who had done this, but also the one who had given Lirath the idea that he ever stood a chance on the battlefield.

Vereesa nodded and swallowed hard, trying to imitate Sylvanas's detachment, unaware of how desperately Sylvanas wrestled with such composure.

"Vereesa, listen to me. Our brother must have justice. We must find the one who trained him. Do you agree?"

Vereesa stopped trembling and blinked back the tears, pressing her lips together in a thin, hard line. "I do," she said, and her voice was clear and strong.

And then, to Sylvanas's utter confusion, Vereesa knelt before her. Or, rather, crumpled.

"His blood is on my hands."

For a blessed second, Sylvanas could not comprehend what Vereesa was saying. Of course she felt responsible. So did Sylvanas. Both, either of them, should have—

But then she looked into Vereesa's eyes, and saw the truth there, and she understood.

"You-"

"I trained him, Sylvanas. It is my fault he is dead."

Vereesa. Lirath's own sister. And before Sylvanas knew quite what had happened, Nathanos had her wrist in a powerful grip, squeezing painfully. Lor'themar had seized Vereesa and pulled her out of striking range, and now he stared at her in pain and empathy and anger.

"This is not a place for rage," Nathanos said quietly.

"Oh yes it is," Sylvanas snarled. How was it her heart could break so many times? Why did it keep beating, keep her here for the torment of so much loss?

"Look me in the eye and tell me what your brother would say," Nathanos whispered.

"How *dare* you!" Sylvanas cried, but it was too late. The image had been seeded in her brain, and she could not unsee Lirath's face, could not unhear his unspoken words urging her to stop, to think, to remember that they were all family, and that Vereesa had acted out of love and with courage, just as Sylvanas had. And for one mad instant, she hated Lirath for that.

Lor'themar was guiding a shaking Vereesa away, looking back over his shoulder at Sylvanas with concern, not reproach.

"Keep her away from me, Lor'themar," Sylvanas called. "Keep her *away*."

Keep her away, for now. Perhaps forever.

For Vereesa's sake, and her own.

Lirath was buried alongside their parents in the family plot. Both the king and the prince had offered to organize a formal funeral for him, but Sylvanas declined. Her parents had been national figures, so there had been little choice but for their funerals to be public. Lirath had been a royal musician; his burial would consist of family and dear friends only. Sylvanas did not think she could bear so soon to repeat the torment she had been through in burying their parents.

It was a small gathering; her, a handful of the Farstriders and, strangely, Lord Saltheril. Sylvanas had instinctively wanted to forbid his attendance, but whatever his flaws—and they were myriad and flagrant—Saltheril had cared about the boy and had helped him on his way. A letter came, marked with the royal seal, from either Kael'thas or Anasterian. Sylvanas did not care, nor did she open the envelope.

Later, Sylvanas would remember very little about it. All she could think about was how bare the three graves still were. Lirath had been killed so shortly after their parents that very little grass or flowers had had time to cover the mounded earth.

Sylvanas knew she could not have prevented the deaths of her mother and father. They were doing their duty; they had gone prepared for a fight. No one had understood the true nature of the threat.

Lirath was different. Lirath had not been duty-bound to battle, nor was he trained or even suitable to be trained, despite what her sisters had said.

As the mourners thinned, a familiar voice called her name from behind.

Vereesa looked like a ghost, her pale face gaunt, eyes shadowed, white hair no longer gleaming like the moon but stringy with neglect. Sylvanas imagined she looked much the same. Her sister came before her quietly, head bowed.

Nathanos moved between them.

"Nathanos," Sylvanas said. "It's all right. Let her speak with me."

"My hand is still cramped from the last time you two spoke," he said.

"There are things I must understand," she said.

Was it really her own sister of whom she spoke? It seemed so strange, and yet she could see no other way things could unfold. Nathanos left them, and the two sisters were alone at the graveside.

"*Why?*" Sylvanas had thought she would say a thousand things, all at once, but the single word was all that left her lips.

"Because he needed us, and we weren't there," Vereesa said softly. "He had always felt different. That he didn't quite fit with us. That what we did was more important, and in a way . . . what it meant to be a Windrunner."

Sylvanas did not speak. She simply listened.

"Alleria said it so casually, so confidently . . . Sylvanas, when you said you would consider it, I . . ."

Sylvanas ground her teeth. She had indeed said this, but she had never expected either sister to take it as consent. At last, the words found their way out. "You *knew* I feared for him. You *knew* how badly I wanted—I *needed*—to know he was safe."

"I . . . don't think I did," Vereesa said. "I don't think you let others see how deeply you cared. I wanted him to be safe, too, in his heart as well as in body. You didn't see him light up when he began to improve."

But, Lady Moon, you are sometimes too single-minded. People will end up getting hurt.

Lirath knew it, too. And in the end, he was the one to pay the price.

Alleria, with her certainty about people who had grown past the siblings she knew. Vereesa, the peacemaker, who only wanted harmony, and had brought death. And she, Sylvanas. She knew in her heart that she was perhaps even more guilty than they.

She could not bear that knowing, not now, if ever. One day, perhaps, she and Little Moon could talk again, with no shadow between them—as Lirath would want.

But not yet.

"As your ranger-general, I can tell you that it is your choice to stay and serve. I will not deprive our people of anyone who can defend them. But as your sister . . . I ask that you leave me be."

"I will," Vereesa said, her voice soft and sad. Defeated. "I will not come to you again. I see now it is of no use. It would seem neither you nor I have any more of our hearts left to wound—or to give."

From that hour, Sylvanas channeled all her emotions into her work. She took small groups of two or three Farstriders on incursions into troll territory, where they surprised and slaughtered whomever they found. She sent them into the wilderness barefoot with no food, water, navigation tools, or weapons, and only shirts and breeches for clothing. She marched them till they almost dropped, then turned around and marched back with no rest. Once, she put a mild sedative in their ale halfway through the march and demoted any who were not able to complete the circuit.

"Sylvanas," Lor'themar said, upon learning of the incident, "you need to stop."

"Stop what?"

"Stop punishing everyone, including yourself, for what happened with—"

"*Don't.*" Sylvanas's voice was sharp.

"These are your people. Your soldiers. They are here because they are loyal to you and to your kingdom. You must not treat them this way."

"Yet somehow, the best of the best and the *Alliance who aided us* managed to let orcs enter deep into the heart of our nation and kill hundreds of people. Including Lirath. I demand nothing from them that I do not ask of myself, and you know this. They are tough. They can fight. And they *will* fight, Lor'themar, they will, and some of them will die."

She ground her teeth as she thought back to her brother's blood, the ash-covered fields of her home. "But it won't be because I failed to train them properly. It won't be because they didn't learn to expect the unexpected, to push themselves past what they thought they could do. To excel in every area. And in the end, if only a handful can see this and understand it, I will take those few over the thousand who do not."

Sylvanas paused, then continued. "Including you, old friend."

The silence stretched out, tense and unhappy, and finally Lor'themar nodded. "I will do as my ranger-general commands."

So be it. Let them drop out. Let them talk behind her back. Sylvanas did not care. She was their leader, not their friend. The ones who stayed, the ones who followed her direction, her orders—they would become legendary. Unstoppable. Unkillable.

There was no sound behind her, but she sensed Nathanos. "Go back to the fire," Sylvanas said.

"I don't want to."

"I don't need you."

"You damn well do."

Neither of them moved. Then, wordlessly, Sylvanas turned and began to run. He followed, keeping up with her as she wove between tree trunks, leaped up into branches, sprang from tree to tree until she had exhausted her muscles so deeply they quivered in protest. Even then she did not stop, nor did he, this odd human who seemed to understand her better than her own blood.

Finally, in that moment that was no longer night but not yet dawn, Sylvanas dropped to the ground, looking up to realize that her blind flight had brought her feet back to the family's special place. Only there was no family, not anymore. No mother, or father; no Little Moon, or Lady Sun, or Little Lord Sun. She was all that was left, and she would not dance here again.

A sound startled her, and for a moment, Sylvanas did not realize that she was the one who had made it.

It was a short, sharp sob, of utter loss and pain, wrenched from deep inside, and Sylvanas doubled over as the agony she had striven so hard to repress refused to be denied any longer. Another sob, then another, and her face was suddenly drenched with tears and her throat was raw.

She felt strong arms slide around her and she clung to Nathanos. He was suddenly the only solid thing in a whirl of chaos and emotion. He held her tightly, silently, not offering words or soothing, asking nothing save to be there for her as long as she wished.

Sylvanas knew she was skirting madness. Part of her longed to surrender to it, for perhaps in that vortex there would be no such thing as memory, or love, or anything bright and good and true that seemed to exist only to be destroyed. But Nathanos, with his simple, flesh-and-blood solidity, gave her something to either hold on to, or release.

She clung to the lifeline that he offered.

Sylvanas lifted her tear-streaked face to him, and he brushed the dampness away. But she did not want gentleness. She wanted something greater than grief and deeper than despair. She wanted to replace the awful ache of numbness with a rush of sensation, to lose herself in something, someone, who reminded her that she was alive. Sylvanas kissed him fiercely, and Nathanos responded, pulling her roughly to him. And so Sylvanas Windrunner allowed herself the gift of forgetfulness, at least for a time, while the moons looked down and the world was still.

INTERLUDE

Anduin was quiet for a long while after Sylvanas finished speaking.

"War is a terrible thing," he began. "I take no joy in what you have endured. No matter what is gained, or for what cause, something is always lost. And sometimes, war takes the best of us. I am sorry for the pain you and your family endured."

No, Sylvanas thought. He would not gloat. Not Anduin. Even here, in this place of unthinkable cruelty, where one could not ever quite escape the screams of suffering, he would not harden himself sufficiently to find glee in another's anguish, even if it was that of one who had caused so much anguish herself.

"They seemed like kind people," he said, more to himself than her. Then his gaze darted back to her, and his face hardened slightly, even though he gave a small smile. "Even you, Sylvanas. How is that for something strange?"

She looked away. She had not told him everything, of course. Some of the darkest, most bitter moments would remain hers, and hers alone.

And she would never tell him how far from strange his words were.

Now the young king rose, stiff from sitting, and moved about in a circle, stretching his arms and rolling his head.

"What I find most interesting," he said, pausing and regarding her, "is Nathanos."

She stiffened. "What about him?"

"I don't think any of us ever thought you cared so deeply for him."

"He was useful to me."

Anduin smiled, almost slyly, and nodded. "Oh, certainly, that was it." More seriously, he added, "Perhaps later, after . . ." He paused. ". . . Later, that became true. But you are not as inscrutable as you think yourself to be." Then, almost kindly, "I saw it on your face."

She had forgotten how good he was at reading people.

"And if after all that's happened . . . you feel something when you speak about him, then that tells me your mortality is still with you, still connecting with—"

"You make my case for me," Sylvanas said, also rising to her feet. "Pray tell me, then, what the value of life and joy and love is, if we are forever severed from those connections in death? They are worth nothing at all! Indeed, they only serve to cause pain in the very act of remembering."

"So you and the Jailer are going to fix that," Anduin said. His tone was a mixture of scorn and pity, and she liked neither.

"We are." The strength of her conviction was audible even in her own ears. Zovaal had the knowledge and, once he reached the Sepulcher, the power to reshape reality. A vast concept, for mortal minds, but Sylvanas had understood it. That was why he reached out to her. She could grasp the enormity of it, weigh the benefits of their plan against its equally enormous cost.

"Your life has been cruel," she said. "What has kept you going? The Light? Hope? The Shadowlands rewards your service and faith by erasing your memory, twisting who you are! Everyone has the right to choose how—"

An incredulous laugh cut her off. "I don't think you can even see it, Sylvanas. You've been blinded."

"See what?"

"The depth of your hypocrisy. How many souls have you stripped of their choices by cutting their lives short? How can you stand in front of me somehow finding righteousness in these acts, as if you are no better than any other butcher? After all you've done, you're not even better than Arthas!"

There it was.

He had been turning it around in his mind, as Sylvanas suspected. Waiting for the right moment to trot it out for maximum effect. Her father would have approved of the young king's tactics. But in retreading such painful ground—all in an effort to show how deep the iniquity of life and death went—Sylvanas was armoring herself. The king had miscalculated. Now the hated name slid off her, as a blade might off gleaming steel plate.

"Arthas was, I see now, simply another step in the journey I had to take. The journey that now brings me to the precipice of justice."

PART
III

What are we if not slaves to this torment?

—SYLVANAS WINDRUNNER

CHAPTER TWELVE

Darkness, warm and comforting.

Like good, rich loam, where seedlings could grow again. Like the welcome brush of slumber to an exhausted mind and body. There was nothing to fear, only to welcome. Stillness. Quiet joy. Letting go.

I am content. I will be with—

Agony—ripping, tearing, *no, no no—*

Fragments of memories, broken images, pieces of sentences spoken by those suddenly unknown to her.

—A stern, elegant face. Long white hair. The smell of smoke clinging to the air. A title: king. *"The Alliance has retreated to Lordaeron to chase the Horde, leaving us to fight the Amani alone. And Zul'jin is taking out his rage at his own abandonment on us. I will not forget this."*

Amani. Troll . . . Horde . . . yes . . . these were remembered. After fire, fire, and something—

Pain. This was not to be remembered, not yet.

More flashes.

—A second elegant man, pale hair . . . calm, diplomatic . . . Father? No, no, but friend. Lor'themar. *Taken by the Amani, and tortured.*

—"We lost him." The elf was furious. Long, untidy hair, all the more

untidy for the battle they had endured. "We took Zul'jin . . . chained him . . . bastard cut off his own arm to escape."

The . . . elf . . . looked wrong, somehow. Then a name came back and an understanding: Halduron was almost always smiling.

—*Sisters. Two? Names. Where were they?*

—*Alleria. Lady Sun. Older sister, but not here, gone now. To the Alliance. No, no—dead? No, not to the land of death, no, through a gate, a portal, to another world, but still lost, lost forever, oh sister—*

Alleria would be seen no more; not her or her golden-haired human lover. But there had been a child born to them . . . a boy. Where was he, was he well?

—*Little Moon, peacemaker. She was sad. She had done something, something that could never be undone—*

Fighting. Trolls, Blood. Only this. Training . . . Farstriders. Rangers. Pushing them. The world will see, they are the finest in the world, they will become legendary, these people.

My people . . .

Identity came to her at last, at least partially. Ranger-general, quel'dorei—high elf.

Windrunner. I am Sylvanas Windrunner.

As if this realization had burst a dam, the fragments of recollection started to pour into her mind, flooding it. Bombarding, overwhelming.

—*The dead turned into something else, unliving things. A prince, a king, a knight of Death.*

—*Arthas Menethil.*

The name brought with it its own set of memories, and a tide of red-hot hatred that made them even more clear to her than the previous glimpses into her past.

—*Her scout had confirmed the rumors were true. A prince had made a dark pact, and his army that now swarmed her beautiful land were dead . . . and yet walked.* "Our land is impregnable. He will not enter. Do not fear. Have faith, my friend, in the Sunwell's strength . . . and in the strength and will of our people."

—*He rode a horse of bone and desiccated flesh. A massive runeblade was strapped to his back, and the dead . . . the Scourge . . . obeyed his every whim.*

Frostmourne. The name of the hated sword came to her with cruel ease . . .

Her Farstriders had fought with courage beyond what she had expected; even as they were overcome, even as their bodies were broken and raised into puppeted corpses, nothing but mindless soldiers in the very army that had slain them.

—*"You are not welcome here."*

The blood of nearly every ranger-general who had ever lifted bow or sword flowed through her, and Sylvanas had been filled with a sudden certainty that this was the moment she had been born for. She would take the courage and pride and fierceness of her forebears and use it to defend her homeland from this, the most horrific attack it had ever known.

"I advise you to turn back now," she cried.

—*"Death itself has come to your land."* A smile, gray lips in a white, white face—

—*"Do your worst!"*

And oh, he had.

The darkest, most despairing moment was not watching her rangers fall, or her eternally beautiful land being corrupted. It was the realization that the quel'dorei had been betrayed, as Arthas kept advancing, kept storming past gates that should have stopped him.

All that was left of Alleria were memories, and soon, that would be all that Sylvanas would leave behind, as well. Vereesa, the one among them who always sought harmony and togetherness in her family, would have lost them all.

—*They are breaking through*—

This song, why do I know this song . . .

—*The master of the undead lifted Frostmourne to her, a perverse gesture of respect. "I salute your bravery, elf, but the chase is over."*

"Then I'll make my stand here, butcher. Anar'alah belore."

By the light of the sun, with perfect equanimity, Ranger-General Sylvanas Windrunner died a hero on the battlefield, shouting defiance to the pale prince whose subjects were dead things as Frost-mourne cut into her with the coldness of ice and death.

Death. An ending, as comes to all living things.

Then . . . *No, no, I do not want to remember!*

—Pain, pain—peace falling away, out of reach, ripped away by a hunger unceasing. The hunger of a runeblade, pulling, ripping her soul from her body, from where it had been meant to go—

—*Where I deserve to go . . . !*

And with the death of the ranger-general, something else was born.

The past and present collided with a scream, a parody of a child's first cry, but this was a birth of something dark and angry and broken, incomplete, terrified and terrorizing.

Arthas was grinning at her. "Banshee," he said. "Thus I have made you. You can give voice to your pain, Sylvanas. I will give you that much. It is more than the others get. And in so doing, you shall cause pain to others. So now you, troublesome ranger, shall serve."

"No," Sylvanas replied, hovering over her sprawling, lifeless body. "I will never serve you."

He crooked a finger, and, helpless, she followed, floating alongside Arthas Menethil as if a physical rope bound them together. She drifted as a leaf on the wind, but even still, something inside her fought to keep remembering. To not forget who she was.

Sylvanas saw her land now only in hues of black, white, and gray; suitable to a world crowded with rot and bile and ichor. She struggled to remember the colors, to not forget the blue, red, and green gems on the necklaces Alleria had crafted from their mother's. The azure sky, the honey hue of the leaves.

No substance, no color, no breath, no life. Only a floating shadow of torment.

How little valor was worth, in the end.

How little love and courage mattered.

Bleakly she trailed after him, forcing herself to organize and name her thoughts and memories, although part of her sought to hide from this knowledge as she knew only pain lay there. The battle continued; her people fell, trampled or turned or both, ground into the dead soil or walking upon it. *Fairbreeze,* she thought. *Remember that name. East Sanctum.* The names of places she had loved, soon to be as dead and forsaken as she.

The army came to a halt in front of a great gate. Where was this?

Silvermoon. Made from the power of the Sunwell, crafted for beauty, and purpose, and comfort. A vision popped into her mind: An elegant, kind man, with eyes that most often held amusement. Verath Windrunner. Father. Here, he had advised their king—

—Anasterian—

—as a member of the council, the convocation, of Silvermoon.

Father—

Arthas's gleeful voice broke the flow of memories, and she felt a tug to rise, to look over the gate into the shining city itself.

"Behold your vaunted ranger-general!" he shouted. "Look at your rangers, culled from your army to feed my own. This is the fate that awaits you all—or allow me entrance, and live."

She was unable to resist. She darted and dived, all by his will, none by her own. It was not of her doing, yet shame filled her nonetheless. Shame, and rage, and grief.

She could see the elven king on the gates, clad in his bright armor of colors she could no longer distinguish. His voice did not carry, but she heard, though she had no ears.

"That is not our ranger-general. Sylvanas Windrunner fell in battle—a quel'dorei hero. We will never yield. We will die before you pollute the sanctity of this place."

"You have forced my hand," Arthas said, with a sigh of mock resignation. Almost absently, he twitched his fingers in their metal gloves.

Sylvanas rose higher, soaring like a bird above the gates, then floating over them. Below her she saw faces she knew she should recognize, but did not.

Arthas's voice whispered, for her alone to hear: "Kill the innocents, first. The others will yield more swiftly when hope is dead."

No.

I will not.

Oh, the hated voice whispered in her mind, *but you will.*

And she did.

Her spectral mouth opened wide, as the howling song of slaughter issued forth. How was Arthas doing it? He seemed to know how to reach deep, so deep, into her, and pull out the ghostly equivalent of a broken, beating heart.

Horrible, lethal, ghastly though it was, it was still a song. A song of pain, and fear, and grief; a song of love poisoned and betrayed and destroyed, of weeping that was a never-ending river. As she sang, helpless to remain silent or to alter the melody, Sylvanas thought of the sound of pipes, sweet and pure. Who had played them? No name, but a face, smiling and bright, and the songs he would sing, so deep as to make even the most stoic weep. Of love and courage, of hope and loss, poignant and powerful.

The children died first, those who had never known war and now would never know anything again. They grew limp in the arms of their shrieking, pleading mothers, as if the sound was nothing more dangerous than a lullaby. The older ones slumped silently to the ground, faces forever pale and still.

Others, too, proved vulnerable to the deathly music. The healers and the priests. The artists. The musicians. The innocent, the ones who could perceive grace and softness and grant that to others through their art or the skill of tender, mending hands. Her song was killing them. *She* was killing them, killing hope, the reasons that waited for a day beyond fighting, the people she had fought for.

Pipes.

Songs.

Lirath.

Her baby brother, who had captured her heart the day he was born. He had seemed to summon music as the magi did the power of the Sunwell, warming and soothing all who heard it. His voice, his laughter. All came flooding back.

I will never forget you, my Little Lord Sun.

But she had, hadn't she? This, then, was the memory she had kept suppressing. The one she would not allow to take hold, because even in that moment of chaos and despair, Sylvanas had known it would hurt worse than any other memory ever could.

That pain escaped her through the terrible song as, once acknowledged, the memories poured forth. Sylvanas had a sudden, dreadful comprehension that, no matter what she did, Lirath would have died by her hand. She had refused to train him, so he had been unable to defend himself against the orcs. Now, had he lived and been here, "safe" in Silvermoon, this song, *her* song, would have taken him.

He was destined to be lost to her. The knowledge only made her song the darker.

For a long moment, Sylvanas Windrunner, too, was lost. She became caught in the maelstrom of torture she herself was weaving. It was as if she stood outside time, outside even this specter she had become, and beheld someone, something, else performing the slaughter.

It made it easier, to think of herself as such. To surrender her own hope, to believe herself helpless. To acknowledge how broken she was, and to remove the pain of even thinking she could be otherwise. To accept her weakness, to know she was the victim; even to think of freedom was a lie.

But as soon as the self-pitying thought struck her, Sylvanas recoiled from it with greater strength. She could not stop what he was forcing her to do, but she seized on the power to say to herself:

He will not break me. I will be his doom.

As Frostmourne's chill froze the channel between the mainland and the Isle of Quel'Danas, she followed him. He slew her king. He polluted the Sunwell. He restored to ghastly unlife the remains of a once human mage, Kel'Thuzad.

All this destruction, all this horror, for this single act, Sylvanas thought.

An act that had been possible only by treachery. She—indeed, all her people—had been so comfortable in their certainty that the Sunwell would always protect them. They had never considered betrayal. Certainly not from one who had been held in such esteem by so many—including Lor'themar Theron. The mage Dar'Khan Drathir, the one Sylvanas had never trusted, had delivered the slaughter to Arthas, the death of not just the people of the shining city, but the kingdom—the land—itself.

It was with a lightening of her own agony that Sylvanas watched the traitor die, himself betrayed; Arthas, it would seem, did not wish to share any of the glory.

Time stretched by in a manner uncountable to Sylvanas. Forced to follow the pale prince, she learned of his true plan behind the making of the monstrous undead: to usher in the domination of demons.

Between battles, Arthas delighted in tormenting her. Not content with the slaughter in Quel'Thalas, or simply his hold over Sylvanas, he had seen fit to raise some of her rangers as banshees as well. "You were so used to ordering them around in life, I thought you might miss doing so in death."

There was a slight difference between her and these spectral rangers. Was it because Arthas had taken her soul? Had she somehow been fiercer at the moment of death? She did not know, but even as she grieved for what had been done to them, she commanded them.

Some of her people, though, he raised with bodies intact. Their once lustrous skin was now pale and lifeless, the blue glow of their eyes displaced by, he told her, a seething rage of crimson. These Darkfallen served the Scourge using perversions of the powers they wielded in life; former Farstriders stalked the land as dark rangers, while fallen mages turned to blood magic. Each of them bound to the will of the malignant prince and the master he served far away on his throne of ice.

Through it all Sylvanas waited, and watched. She would need them to be ready when an opportunity—for what, she did not know—presented itself.

Always Arthas controlled her movements, but sometimes, he let her speak. He was usually in good spirits at these times, and the "freedom" he allowed her was more for his own amusement than anything else. He would wax poetic about her death, and her help-lessness in the face of his utter conquest and nigh extermination of her people. Now and then he also taunted her with hints about what had happened to her corpse. She had last seen it thrown atop one of the meat wagons of his army, seemingly of no more importance than any other body.

"You were beautiful, once," he would say, as she floated along be-side him while he rode the dead, mummified horse he had named Invincible.

"So were you, I imagine. Sickly white does not flatter you."

"Intangible and transparent does not flatter you," he replied. "Do you miss being able to touch, Sylvanas? To feel? To taste and smell?"

"Not here," she said, "not near you and the stench that is surely present."

"And what do you think happened to your corpse?"

She had fallen silent, then, "Death is part of life. My body will return to the earth." *As my family has . . .*

"Oh no. No peace for you, banshee, not even the peace of sleeping in the dirt."

That had startled and wounded her, and the words escaped her before she could stop herself. "What did you do to me?"

"Perhaps the next time I am bored, I will show you. Did you dance when you were young, Sylvanas? With friends or family or perhaps someone special? I shall make your corpse dance for you. Perhaps you can cheer it on, and remember when once you felt the sun on your face, and held a bow, and blood flowed through your veins."

Look, Lady Moon! Even the stars have come out to dance!

Her formless throat somehow ached, craving the release of the banshee wail of rage and heartbreak. She would not let him know, for then he would command it of her, and she would be forced to obey.

"You sleep on stone, fair maiden, inside an impenetrable tower. Encased forever in a prison of iron, your body preserved and as lovely as you were in life—if perhaps in slightly different hues. It's like a fairy tale."

He laughed, and she hated him, and still she listened.

"Wherever the spirits of your family went . . . yours will never join them, for it is the Lich King's now. Your form will not even molder to dust alongside theirs in whatever sort of place they lie, for I have chosen to deny you that. No one will find you. And soon they will forget . . . what few of your people remain. Or perhaps they will remember, and curse you for failing in your duty."

Arthas was mistaken if he thought Sylvanas felt shame. She did not. Sylvanas knew she had done all she could, and the faint brush of peace that touched her before he snatched her soul confirmed that. Her king, who had served his people for so long only to die in vain, who had spat his defiance at Arthas and praised her even as she floated helplessly at Arthas's side. *Sylvanas Windrunner fell in battle— a quel'dorei hero.*

And then . . . Arthas had whispered, *Kill the innocents first.*

"Poor Sylvanas Windrunner, all alone in the darkness and the cold, where she cannot be with anyone . . . even the things of nature she loved. And if only you knew who was minding your corpse on my behalf."

The words did not strike as he intended, though Sylvanas pretended that they had. What the arrogant fool did not realize was that everything he said to her was a clue. But how would she pursue it? She had tried often enough to break free. But not even a finger moved without his will.

He had not broken her *own* will, though. Sylvanas wondered if he even could. She would let him rant, and laugh, and feel strong and smug. He would reveal one word too many. She would somehow discover where her body was hidden, and she would make sure it was brought to lie beside her parents. Beside Lirath.

Until then, she could wait, honing her anger and her hatred into an ever sharper blade.

CHAPTER THIRTEEN

Arthas, the Lich King he served, and the terrifying Burning Legion with whom they had allied were far from finished with their glorious conquest of Azeroth. The Legion was, Sylvanas was told, a vast army of demons and corrupted races. Their goal was nothing less than the destruction of all life, everywhere. There were more continents and cities to vanquish. More living things to turn into the mindless undead Scourge, and more demons to work with in bringing about those goals.

Sylvanas was an involuntary cog in this grand machine. Arthas commanded, she obeyed, and she, who was once a thorn in his side, became one of his top generals. She accompanied him as he spoke with Archimonde, one of the most powerful of the demonic dreadlords, and she stood beside Arthas as the demon destroyed the mighty city of Dalaran. The only pleasure she took from any of this was the chance to needle her master, sensing a hint of regret in the death knight at Dalaran's fall.

When Arthas, obeying his own master, traveled to the continent of Kalimdor, Sylvanas and Kel'Thuzad were ordered to stay behind to protect the capital city. The Legion had its own representatives, too, a trio of dreadlord brothers—Balnazzar, Detheroc, and Varimathras. Sylvanas did not fill the months that her tormentor was away from Lordaeron with brooding or fruitless anger. The Lich King only rarely spoke in her mind now; his attention was elsewhere, and she was glad of the respite.

Arthas unwittingly had given her a purpose, one she seized upon eagerly, and she turned her mind to the idea of discovering where her physical body lay, undecaying, alone, and preserved. Even as a banshee, Sylvanas loved a good hunt.

Sylvanas had been correct in her assumption of Arthas's inability to keep silent when it would serve him. He was like a drunkard in his cups, Arthas; intoxicated by the idea of his own cleverness. And like drunkards with too much wine, he let slip more than he knew.

The days unfolded and she continued to analyze what she knew, and the tangle began to unravel as she patiently pulled it apart thread by thread. Arthas would not have had much time to dispose of her body. It was likely somewhere in Quel'Thalas. *Cold stone* could mean anything, really. A box of iron . . . a sarcophagus? He had said, too, that she would despise the one . . . ones? . . . who guarded her.

Had he given her body to the trolls?

The thought infuriated her so utterly that for a moment, her mind was blank, filled with nothing but hate and vengeance. Then reason slowly reasserted itself. No, it could not be the trolls. They would have taken too much delight in ripping her to pieces, and Sylvanas felt certain that was not the case.

She let the puzzle go for now, discouraged and more shaken than she cared to admit at the thought of her lifeless body being given into the care of those who had hated and slain her people for millennia.

Her corpse lying alone in darkness, locked in an iron coffin atop cold stone in a tower . . . guarded by one she would find loathsome.

Her other amusement was watching—and listening to—the dreadlords. Hideous things, they were vaguely human-like . . . except for their cloven feet, horns, and batlike wings. She had overheard their conversations a few times, but she did not understand much of what they said. There were references like "sire," and "home," and "guests," but despite their courtesy to Arthas, Sylvanas had never trusted them.

Apparently, neither did those who commanded them. Arthas had gone to Kalimdor to aid Archimonde, but Kel'Thuzad told Sylvanas that "our king" had turned on the demon, and the Legion had been soundly defeated. Yet many months later, listening from a small hill above the three conversing demons, Sylvanas overheard them wondering why Archimonde had not sent orders for them.

They were to find that out scant moments later, as Arthas himself returned after so long away to inform the three of the Legion's defeat—and his intent to kill them.

"This isn't over, human!" Detheroc cried. The sickly glow of fel magic wrapped about their forms, and they vanished.

Kel'Thuzad hastened to greet his beloved master, Sylvanas trailing reluctantly after him. Arthas had not changed, she noted. He was still as confident and egotistical as ever—demanding to know if they had "missed" him, reminding them to call him king now that he had driven out the dreadlords. All was as it had been, and for a moment Sylvanas bleakly wondered if anything would ever change.

And then it happened.

Arthas grimaced and contracted in pain, hunching over his undead steed, unable to bite back a cry of pure agony.

"King Arthas!" Kel'Thuzad exclaimed. "Do you need assistance?"

Sylvanas did not think she had ever heard a sweeter sound. She had known the pain of Arthas's suffering would be gratifying to behold, but this was more satisfying than she had expected, even if she was not the one causing the torment. Indeed, she had no idea what was happening to the death knight. All she knew was that she hoped it would go on for a very, very long time.

But too soon, he recovered. To Kel'Thuzad, he said, "The pain has passed, but . . . my powers . . . are *diminished*."

Sylvanas was stunned. Could this be? Could he truly be weakening? Why? What did it mean? For him . . . and for *her*?

Arthas's pet lich helped him find a place to rest. She watched them go, pleasure and anticipation thrumming through her.

Her fingers, insubstantial, yet capable of great harm, twitched.
They curled into a fist.

Sylvanas smiled.

Sylvanas did not know how long this seeming freedom from Arthas's control would last. She needed to know more, and she had a hunch that the demons had not traveled far. She sent her banshees to look for them, and, as Sylvanas had expected, the demons took the bait and extended an invitation for her to speak with them. She followed the directions her scout had given her, floating over the pine needles and moss that covered the earth of Silverpine, heading in the direction of the eerie, sickly light.

Balnazzar greeted her with the exaggerated politeness of a court newcomer, who knew what to do but not how to do it. "Lady Sylvanas. We are pleased that you came."

But Sylvanas had had enough of such frivolous courtesies in Silvermoon. She had no wish to banter with demons, so, as she had done in life, she quickly took control of the meeting.

"How could I not? For some reason, I no longer hear the Lich King's voice in my head. My will is my own once again. You dreadlords seem to know why."

Varimathras answered, with barely concealed delight, "We've discovered that the Lich King is losing his power! As it wanes, so too does his ability to command undead such as you."

I am the only one like me, she thought but did not say. "What of King Arthas? What about *his* powers?"

Balnazzar, the most elegant among them, said, "Though his runeblade, Frostmourne, carries powerful enchantments itself, Arthas's own powers will also fade in time. It is inevitable."

She liked the word, and thought of the blade that had taken her life. The twining runes etched into the sword, glowing with pale blue light. Sylvanas could not read the runes, but she had stared at the blade often enough, memorizing their shapes.

Now the reason for their extreme unction had become clear. "You seek to overthrow him, and want my help to do it," Sylvanas stated.

If Balnazzar was the most elegant, then Detheroc was the most oafish. His large belly looked soft compared with the powerful physiques of the other two, but his tiny eyes flashed with rage and the hatred for Arthas that poured off him seemed almost—almost—as strong as her own.

"The Legion may be defeated, but we are the nathrezim! We will not let some . . . upstart human get the best of us. *Arthas must fall!*"

Balnazzar stepped in, his voice soothing and reasonable. "The time to strike is now. The Lich King strays from the path of his master, and Arthas is too consumed by pride and ambition to be the instrument that is necessary. Confused and distracted, both will be easy to overcome. But we must make sure we do not waste this rare opportunity. The lich Kel'Thuzad is far too loyal to betray his master. *You*, on the other hand . . ." He paused, as if the bluntness of the sentiment were too indelicate for him.

Sylvanas had no such concern. "Hate him," she spat. It felt good to speak the words after thinking them in silence for so long. She had her reasons to feel thus. He had murdered her people, she told them, and turned her into this monstrosity.

The closer she seemed to come to her vengeance, the more she did not wish to think on that awful day . . . and her song, at the gates of Silvermoon. "I might take part in your bloody coup," she said, hoping that it would, in fact, be bloody, "but I will do so in my own way."

She left without another word. She did not have time for it. Time was a precious and unpredictable commodity now, and she would not squander it.

Sylvanas would gather her troops . . . all of them. Not the banshees Arthas had mockingly given her, but the ones he kept from her. She'd led the rangers in life. Now she would lead them again in this unlife.

She found some of them wandering the forests, drawn even in death to the woods and growing things. Some had been sent on missions, and had returned to the capital city searching for answers. A few had simply stayed put, reasoning that others would return to scour the city for their sisters.

There had been horns Sylvanas and others had sounded, to call a retreat or signal an attack. Now Sylvanas had only her voice, and she used it as a clarion call. It echoed through the night, laced with pain and longing and rage.

Come back to me, she thought as she sang. *Return. Follow me, and I will lead you. Together we shall strike terror into this world.*

And they answered with action, strong legs racing, yet making no sound, quivers of arrows at their backs and bows in their hands. Sylvanas hovered over them.

"Our minds are our own again," she told them. "I have reached out to you, and you have chosen to answer. We will halt the creature who did this to us, and we will be free. And I . . . I shall hunt beside you again, my sisters . . . shoulder-to-shoulder. But before that moment, there is a hunt that calls to *me.* A hunt for vengeance and reward. Will you join me?"

Their shouts of affirmation almost shook the trees down to their roots.

Victory and freedom were at hand.

Sylvanas had solved the puzzle. She remembered the last two clues. Arthas had told her the corpse had been preserved—still beautiful, but a different hue.

The words perfectly described the dark rangers gathered before her. They, too, were dead, their skin gray, their eyes glowing. Surely whatever dark spell Arthas had used to transform them had also been cast upon her corpse. The only difference might be that her essence, this horrible banshee form, had not merged with it.

And if Arthas had not given her body to the trolls—and Sylvanas was certain he had not—there was only one other she could think of: the great betrayer of Quel'Thalas, Dar'Khan Drathir, whom she would find . . . in his tower.

Although for so long Sylvanas could not act, she had always listened. Often Arthas would speak freely in her presence, and why not? Neither of them expected his powers would wane. She had learned that Arthas had raised Dar'Khan into undeath, after the prince himself, having achieved what he wanted by taking the Sunwell, had slain the traitor. Now the former magister governed the undead in a place Arthas named Deatholme, ruling from the Tower of the Damned, ready to act whenever Arthas would have need of this unit of his army.

Sylvanas and her followers went boldly past the spectral guardians who served as the eyes of Dar'Khan. That she was Arthas's general was widely known. That she was no longer controlled by the death knight was not. Because banshee and dark ranger alike were undead, they too went unchallenged as they entered. It took some time, but at last Sylvanas found where Arthas had tucked her corpse away, exactly as described: in the darkness, locked in a coffin of iron that rested on cold stone, with none to mourn her.

Her sisters destroyed the iron prison, and Sylvanas beheld herself, composed, still. He had not lied: She was as preserved as her sisters were.

"You have taken so much, Menethil. But this day, I am taking something back."

And it would not be by magic, but by sheer will and pure hatred, that she would do so. Sylvanas focused on her still form and encouraged the memories that had stung so much a moment ago to return to her now, with all their pleasure and sorrow.

The softness of little Lirath's baby curls, and his smooth cheeks. The welcome coolness of water against her skin on a warm day. The taste of food, the sensation of her body moving swiftly and surely through branches or on the ground, leaping, striking, rolling.

The wind in my hair, she thought. *I can almost feel it. What it felt like to laugh. My hands holding my bow. The texture of tree bark and the softness of leaves.*

The reassurance of an embrace . . . the brush of a kiss.

Dancing in the twilight, grass beneath her bare feet, her hands warm and holding those of her sisters as they whirled and laughed while their bright sun of a brother played.

Sylvanas now seemed to feel the pain in her chest, the sore ache of a throat turned raw with grief.

I will hold to my pain. I will grip it tight. It's mine, and mine only, to feel, and I shall have it.

She clenched her insubstantial fists, the first act of independence from her vicious former master.

And her fingertips pressed on her palms.

She felt . . . she *felt!* . . . the lethargy in her body, as if she had been dosed with all the woundwood in the world. She was paralyzed and, for a moment, thought her efforts had been for naught. She doubled down on her determination, and at last, though with tremendous effort, Sylvanas opened her eyes.

Color, such as it was, had returned. Sickly yellows and browns, but she welcomed them nonetheless, for soon she would behold others: blue skies, green grass, yellow sun. When she lived, it had been nothing at all to blink, to breathe, to speak. Now it was as if she were encased in mud, moving slowly, so slowly.

But she was *moving.*

Her body was again hers to command.

She forced herself to sit upright, to turn her head this way and that, to make her lungs expand so that she might have air rushing over vocal cords to speak. There were no reflexes to aid her. Her flesh, as she had expected, was the same gray as those of the dark rangers, and Sylvanas knew that her eyes glowed red, as theirs did. A lock of pale yellow hair, almost white, fell forward into her face. She lifted a clumsy hand to brush it back.

She had beaten Arthas on this. She would do it again.

"I will be his doom," Sylvanas declared, moving lips and tongue and cheeks, learning to speak again as if she were a child. Her voice had an odd sound to it—echoing, hollow. But it was a sound she had made, and she heard it in physical ears. Beside her lay her bow and quiver, with a few arrows still in it.

"Oh, Arthas. You even left me my weapons."

She got clumsily to her feet. Her knees buckled, and she caught the edge of the stone table with fumbling fingers. Again she tried, and this time she stood, wavering slightly but upright.

Sylvanas moved her lips in a slow, satisfied smile.

Oh, Arthas Menethil. You glorious fool.

I name you prey.

Sylvanas had further questions to ask the demon trio before she would make her move against Arthas. But in the meantime, she had decided on a particularly cruel way of exacting her vengeance.

A thought had been growing, ever since the moment Sylvanas struggled with and almost failed in achieving the simple action of opening her eyes. The helplessness of not being able to move. The options it gave one's enemy.

It was sometimes painful to think of what—and who—she had been. She remembered kindness, and love, but seemed unable to feel them anymore. Yet, hidden in her memories were things worth digging for, and she remembered Saltheril's party; fighting trolls.

Those memories would now serve her very well.

It did not take her long to create the poison and anoint the arrow with it. Woundwood was a topical numbing agent. But what if it were to penetrate deep into the body? No one, of course, knew. That was not its purpose.

The trolls had crafted tarlike substances that the quel'dorei had studied in the hope of creating an antidote. The thought never crossed their minds to replicate the substance. No, in their days of glory, such a brief span of time past, the elves would have seen such appropriation as beneath them. One thing this wretched existence had taught the former ranger-general was that such morality—or perhaps simple superiority—was an impediment, not a virtue. Any scrap of information, any tool, any rumor—she would seize it and twist it to serve her own end: defeating Arthas Menethil in as brutal a manner as possible.

So she took the woundwood, used to help and heal those she

cared for, and mixed it with the poison used by their ancient enemy to slay her new one. Arthas would be paralyzed. Helpless before her, as she had been. And he would suffer even more exquisitely than she had—because for him, her suffering had been an amusement. For Sylvanas, Arthas's agony was the only target she could find in her vast sea of loss.

She practiced with the new substance on various healthy animals, and then some affected by the plague, observing the amount needed to bring them down quickly and keep them alive and immobile as long as possible. Sylvanas carefully adjusted the mixture until she was satisfied with the ingredient proportions, and tested it on a charging bear.

The beast bellowed, coming toward her, but it collapsed in only three strides after the arrow struck its shoulder. Sylvanas watched and waited. It continued to breathe, and even grunt, but its limbs and torso were otherwise still.

Sylvanas squatted down beside it, for a moment vaguely uneasy. Once, she would have shot to kill instantly. She would not have wanted any creature to suffer needlessly, and she certainly would not have done what she was about to do.

But . . . I do need it to suffer. *I need to learn, so that I will not fail when my chance finally comes. Its death and torment will not be in vain, but instead serve a greater purpose—eliminating Arthas.*

The bear's body continued to heave with labored breaths. And as Sylvanas began to cut into its flesh, slowly and carefully, it moaned in deep agony.

It did so for a very long time.

At last Sylvanas rose, looking down at the bloody mess.

She was ready for Arthas Menethil.

The trap to catch the king was not among Sylvanas's most elaborate or even most clever, but she had precious few resources at her disposal. She instructed her rangers to shadow the death knight closely without revealing themselves, and to seize their chance when it came time to lure him to their mistress.

Clumsy. He ought to be able to see right through it. Yet somehow Arthas did not suspect the banshee rangers of anything when he came under attack and they came to his "rescue," promising to lead him to Sylvanas. How? Was he so blinded by ego that he thought she'd forgotten all he had done to her? Truly, the world would be better off rid of his narcissistic, bloodthirsty presence.

The openness of the field into which the banshees guided the king, dotted with only the occasional tree, further allayed any suspicions of a trap. Sylvanas had been a superior hunter in life: agile, silent, deadly. But death had only augmented that aspect of her. She did not need to get close to him to shoot—

—*a fleeting memory of life, of Nathanos, of her splitting all but one of his arrows*—

Sylvanas banished the thought. It would only distract. She wanted to get close to the death knight, to sooner begin the second part of her entertainment. She knew he did not see her, did not hear her, yet something startled him and he cried out, clapping a mailed hand to his chest as the undead horse pranced, agitated, beneath him.

The Lich King. He had warned Arthas—but it was too late.

He seemed faint, blinking, trying to focus. Sylvanas stepped out from behind a slender tree and let him behold her in her old, yet new, body. He stared, disbelieving. Sylvanas smiled as she lifted her bow. It was already fitted with an arrow fletched with the feathers of the Dark Eagle; one of the precious few Sylvanas had taken from the quiver of her fallen mother. She had coated its point with poison, and spoke in a voice dripping scorn and satisfaction.

"You walked right into this one, Arthas."

Her second and third fingers opened, and the liberated arrow raced toward its target, impaling itself precisely where she wished it: in the death knight's shoulder. His further confusion was sweet to her, almost but not quite banishing the leaden, barely acknowledged ache of a deep, resigned pain.

He tried to lift his hand, to pull it out, but the poison was already working its dark, beautiful, sadistic magic. Rapidly numbing fingers could not grasp the shaft, only paw at it, like a pathetic dog. Arthas gasped, leaning forward on the horse's neck, trying to not slide to the ground and certain death.

"What have you done to me?"

For the first time since word came of marching undead, Sylvanas felt something close to joy. Angry, cruel, yes—but joy, still.

"It's a special poisoned arrow I made just for you," she said, almost purring, transferring the bow to her back and removing the dagger with which she would slice the pale king to ribbons.

They exchanged words, unimportant now, in this time before she began her torment. Except for when he demanded, "Finish me, then."

Oh no. Not when he had done to her the things he had. She thought she'd start with the face, that face that had once been handsome and even now had some hint of beauty to it. "You're going to suffer, as I did. Thanks to my arrow, you can't even run."

His eyes widened, and for the first time, she saw true fear in them. Had she lived, her heart would have leaped in excitement.

Sylvanas drew back the dagger—and then stared in horror as gray mist somehow grasped her hand and twisted it, forcing her fingers to open and release the blade. The mist shifted, its lines growing clearer, and Sylvanas realized it was the ghost of a young woman, really a girl still, when Arthas had killed her and everyone else at Lordaeron.

The little shade was smiling. She was happy to be helping her king.

Sylvanas had not thought it possible, but her hatred for Arthas burned even hotter.

The misguided spirit was not alone. Kel'Thuzad had arrived, shouting encouragement to his king in his loathed, sepulchral voice as reinforcements descended en masse. Waves of rotting undead, their eyes glowing, creatures of only slaughter and chaos, converged on Arthas, as if freshly conjured by magic. Sylvanas cursed even as she shook off the little ghost and began firing into dead flesh. She had made a terrible mistake. She had been so focused on Arthas, so certain of her victory, she had not paid attention.

For a few seconds, she fought on, desperate to murder the monster who had made her this way, until she realized that she and her followers were greatly outnumbered. Sylvanas glanced at him one last time, furious. "This isn't over, Arthas! I'll never stop hunting you!"

She fled, slipping away along with her banshees, easily outpacing the Scourge creatures even though she still felt at odds with her body. It continued to feel like something she manipulated and controlled, rather than a true part of her. More like a glove than skin. Perhaps it would feel right when she slew Arthas. She thought about the demon lords. Should she join with them? Arthas was protected by the Lich King, Kel'Thuzad, the Scourge. Sylvanas would need allies, but not them. Not unless she had to.

I will never be truly free until I have killed the wretch who murdered me. There will always be a chain between us, and I intend to break it.

A thought came to her abruptly, at once daring and centering and certain. There was a flicker of fear, too, but she brushed it away. She was different, yes. But she was still Sylvanas.

Wasn't she?

CHAPTER FOURTEEN

Sylvanas had always disliked failure, but never more than now, when she'd had Arthas right where she wanted him only to have victory plucked from her fingers. It was unlikely she would ever have such a clean opportunity again. Arthas, and perhaps even the Lich King who commanded him, was her pledged target, yet this was a hunt she could not complete alone. Her banshees—her rangers—had done what they could, but they were not enough.

Hard, and perhaps fruitless, as it would be, Sylvanas needed allies she could trust. Allies who also hated the death knight and wished to put an end to him. She realized she could not find them among the dead. Somehow, some way . . . she needed to convince the living.

A daunting task, to be sure. But so was keeping her own mind. So was breaking away from the fierce grasp of the former pale king . . . and finding and claiming her own body again.

Sylvanas had friendships, once. Tight, seemingly unbreakable bonds. Had Arthas destroyed these, too, as he had destroyed so much of her world? She had to believe he had not. Because to think otherwise would be to let go of the last remaining, shining thread of hope, and Sylvanas refused to do so.

Still stinging from the failure, Sylvanas once again found herself heading toward Quel'Thalas, this time to recover not her body but, hopefully, her friendships. There were two whom she believed would listen long enough for her to prove that despite everything, even death, she was still the Sylvanas they knew.

They would doubt at first, of course. What she had done while under the control of Arthas and the king who commanded him could not be dismissed. Sylvanas did not like to recall that dreadful moment, floating with no choice, unable to look away let alone stop her actions, as her voice had been used as a weapon of mass slaughter. But she could explain. They would see how she had struggled, and of course they would need little urging to destroy the true monster who had left a scar on the brightest place in Azeroth. A scar that would likely never fully heal. Once they understood, perhaps they would let her rejoin the unit she once commanded. Maybe even lead it again. Perhaps it was reckless of her to hope for so much, but then again, Sylvanas had never been known to think small.

She made it to the cover of the trees surrounding Farstrider Retreat, moving silent as a shadow in the familiar boughs once silvered by moonslight. Now, though, a haze of smoke hid the radiant orbs, and there seemed to be fine dust over every leaf. The thick air had a lingering reek of burned flesh. Sylvanas had almost convinced herself that the task would be an easy one. It made sense, everyone benefited, and they knew her better than anyone. There was no stirring from anything other than the night's creatures, so she settled herself and, still as a stone, simply waited.

Dawn came, but no sign of those she was expecting. She was patient, though. Finally, in the late afternoon, they came, just the two of them, as Sylvanas had hoped. She prepared to drop from the trees at once, but something held her back. She would control how and when she revealed her new form and wait for the right moment.

She watched them carefully through the spaces in the gently moving leaves, observing that their bodies moved stiffly, like those of aged men. When Lor'themar turned his head in her direction, Sylvanas saw that one eye was covered with a patch. Arthas had wounded them all, in so many different and painful ways. Halduron, so lively and cheerful, looked to have aged a thousand years.

As Lirath had looked, when he had pleaded with her—

Sylvanas ruthlessly shoved the memory aside and listened.

At first, there was nothing but the deeply familiar creak of leather, the song of the arrow, the faint *thunk* as it struck the distant targets. At last, Halduron lowered his bow.

"It feels so strange," he said quietly. His normally warm baritone, with an almost constant undercurrent of amusement, was flat and cold. "Here in Eversong, it is as if nothing has changed. But ... *everything's* changed. A few miles to the west and south ..." He fell silent but still didn't reach for another arrow. "It feels ... wrong to be here. Practicing. As if it were any ordinary day."

"With eight for every ten of us dead?" It was Lor'themar, his voice quiet and heavy. Sylvanas had thought that little would shock her, but this news did. She was aware a massive number of her people had been slaughtered, but the number was almost impossible to comprehend.

"This is the first day we have had half a moment to do anything resembling *ordinary*, my friend," Lor'themar continued. "For what seems like an eternity, our days have been spent gathering and burning the—"

"—The bodies. I know."

So the fine dust Sylvanas had noticed earlier was the ashes of Arthas's victims. The quel'dorei had been burning the corpses to prevent them from rising.

Lor'themar sat another arrow to the bow, aimed, shot. "I dream of them," he said. "The bodies."

"Which ones?" Halduron asked. Humor was in his voice now, but it was grim and cruel and cutting. "The ones we burned, the ones we buried, or the ones we had to cut down twice?"

"The ones still in the Scar," Lor'themar said, his voice as haunted as the lands through which she'd traveled to reach the retreat.

From her perch in the highest branches, Sylvanas could glimpse the twisting of the land that Lor'themar had appropriately called the

Scar. She had not wanted to think about it, but Halduron's words forced her to see, to remember. Arthas had not taken all his undead with him when he left. Scores of them still shuffled about, their single purpose to attack the living. She saw other dead in the Scar, too: corpses that had not been reanimated, yet could not safely be retrieved by the living. They would decompose, returning to the soil, but were exiled from the cycle of life, death, and renewal. Their bones would lie there until all memory of whom they had been had faded, their names lost to the wind.

A fresh wave of hatred swept through Sylvanas, threatening to carry her away with its intensity. Even now the shadow of Arthas Menethil loomed over her homeland. She wondered if it would ever recede, from the land and from the hearts and spirit of her people. But one thing was for certain: The two men below her, going through the motions of normalcy hollow-voiced and dull-eyed, would be more than ready to join her in the hunt to slay him.

The perfect moment had come. Sylvanas was about to jump from her perch and begin her well-rehearsed speech, to reassure them that they could trust and ally with her and so take down the hated Arthas together. But before she could do so, Halduron's words made her freeze.

"Sylvanas is the one who comes in my nightmares. That ghostly *thing* obeying the butcher's commands." His voice grew ragged. "All those innocents, Lor'themar. And that terrible cry. As if the obscenity was pained by what it was doing, yet unable to disobey."

Lor'themar went to him and placed a hand on his shoulder. "And that, my old friend, is how we know Sylvanas truly is no more. She would have found a way to resist. Even if it destroyed her. I will never claim to be able to dispel nightmares; if I could, I would start with my own. But I will tell you this. The monster that murdered so many was nothing of our old friend, and I believe with my whole heart she would be horrified to know that her image was used to turn harm upon those she died defending."

"Do you . . . do you think she has found some kind of peace?" Halduron sounded hopeful, wanting to be assured.

"I do. I must. She is gone, and truth be told, I am glad of it. She would weep to see what has befallen our people. Of that, you may be certain. Those whom the butcher raised . . . It will take time, but eventually, we will send them as well to the eternal rest that was denied them."

Had she lived, had she still had lungs she did not need to command, Sylvanas would have stopped breathing.

Monster.

So they had named her. So they saw her now; so they would see her were she to reveal herself and try to speak to them. There was nothing she could say or do to convince them that she had been used against her will. These two old friends would not believe that she had wrested that will back. That she was herself. And maybe . . . maybe they were right.

Another memory flashed, fully formed though it had been lost to her till just this instant: a young woman showing off a bow to two notable Farstriders.

I bet you will be telling stories about me when I join the Farstriders, she had told Lor'themar. And so he would . . . but they would be dark and bitter tales.

That's a way off. Halduron had been so flippant and light then.

Not that far. You're hardly ancient.

She has you there, Lor'themar had said. Playful teasing, dreams of glory.

There was a sharp, stifled sob. When he spoke, Halduron's voice was shaking and broken. "I miss her, Lor'themar."

"As do I. But she would not want us to grieve. Let us remember her as she would wish us to. As our friend: sharp-tongued, brilliant, so full of life and passion. That will always be *our* Sylvanas, not the monster who bears her face."

There was no point in lingering. Sylvanas had her answer. How foolish she had been in life, thinking it was noble for the Farstriders to shelter her people from the cruelty and darkness of the world. And even now, in this unlife of hers, this was what came of such naïveté—an inability to comprehend and accept anything but absolutes. Sylvanas was dead, and yet not, and therefore even to those who knew her down to her bones, she was no different from the mindless wretches who prowled the Scar.

This time, when the thought of her brother crept into her mind, Sylvanas was unable to shut it out. She could not help but wonder if Lirath would have felt the same way as Lor'themar and Halduron. Would he have been able to see his Lady Moon inside a corpse? If anyone would have been willing to listen, to believe in her, surely it would have been him.

The world is different now, Lirath had said. *That was a world of soft-ness, of privilege, of wine and song and laughter and* family. *That world's gone now. And it's never coming back.*

Of all of us, I thought you would believe in me. But you don't.

Words, and the memories of them, were the blades that cut the deepest. Regardless, he was dead, and she had been responsible for that. His grave was nearby, but Sylvanas could not bring herself to visit it.

She left her friends to their shattered idealism and their narrow minds, departing as silently as she had arrived, barely disturbing the dust of the dead that lay like a mortcloth over the land she had once loved.

Sylvanas tried, but she could not conceal her feelings from her loyal rangers. They floated about their mistress, concerned.

"You seem troubled, mistress."

Sylvanas could not bear to tell them how they were now per-ceived by their fellow Farstriders, so she turned to a different subject: the curse of undeath.

"Aren't you, sister?" Sylvanas replied. "Only days ago, we were the Lich King's slaves. We existed solely to slaughter in his name."

She could hear the sorrow and frustration in her own echoing voice. The banshees regarded one another. "I don't understand, mis-tress. Our wills are our own now. Is that not what we fought for? I thought you'd be overjoyed."

The words irritated her further. How could she be overjoyed with their freedom when all it meant, in the end, was that they were free to fully understand their own suffering? How could she find joy in anything anymore?

"What joy is there in this curse? We are still undead, sister. Still . . . monstrosities." She looked down at her arms, blue-gray. Dead. She had fought so hard to recover her body, reconnect with that lost part of herself, and yet she could find nothing of delight in it. "What are we if not slaves to this torment?"

Her brooding was interrupted by a familiar sound—the odd, echoing whirring of a demonic portal. She watched, wary but curious, as Varimathras appeared.

Sylvanas listened with half an ear as he lavished praise upon her and her efforts to "overthrow Arthas," paying true attention only when he said, "I've come to offer you a formal invitation to our new order."

No. Though the words of her erstwhile friends had cut her deeply, they had not robbed her of her wits. Sylvanas had labored mightily to rid herself of the bonds Arthas had placed upon her. She would not throw that away only to become another lackey. The clearly artificial formality irritated her, and her voice was harsh as she replied.

"Varimathras," she said, speaking coldly and clearly as if to a disobedient child, "my only interest was in seeing Arthas dead." It was *still* her only goal, made all the more urgent by the fact that she could no longer rely upon those who had readily obeyed her orders in life. "I have no time for your petty politics or power-mongering."

Sylvanas made no effort to hide her disdain, and Varimathras did not like it. He strode forward, oddly graceful on his long goat legs, and the sophisticated veneer vanished.

"Careful, my lady," he said, his voice low and heavy with threat. "It would be unwise to incur our wrath. We are the future of . . ." He hesitated, then continued, "these Plaguelands. You can either join us and rule, or be cast aside."

The dreadlords thought themselves so superior, and she knew they were indeed without conscience and very powerful. Even so, she marveled at how similarly the power-hungry types all behaved, be they quel'dorei lesser lords, or deathknights, or demons.

Her tongue was sharp and perhaps a bit too unbridled as she shot back, "I lived as a slave long enough, dreadlord. I won't relinquish my freedom by shackling myself to you fools!"

Varimathras was furious. He could barely control himself as he ground out, "So be it. Our reply will come soon." He was scowling as the magic of the demonic portal bore him back to his brothers. Sylvanas could make a guess as to what that *reply* might be.

"Would it not have been prudent to accept his offer?" Sharlindra asked.

"Another might call it wisdom," Sylvanas agreed. "But I call it folly."

She refused to serve, ever again. From this moment on, Sylvanas would do as she had in life—command. Find those who would follow. The living had scorned her, the demons were untrustworthy. Who, then, would be her new army, one suited to her new existence?

Only the dead and the dark. The reference to the Plaguelands was clear—they wanted to control the undead, as Arthas had. Sylvanas refused to allow them to do so.

There was an entire city inhabited by those who, like her, had once lived, loved, drawn breath. They had been under Arthas's control, too, those unfortunates of Lordaeron.

Another unwanted memory flashed through her mind.

You know . . . it's said in Lordaeron that high elves are the finest archers in the world, Nathanos Marris had said.

Oh, we are.

It's also said in Lordaeron that they are the most stuck-up, arrogant, self-centered, and vain people in the world.

Both descriptions are quite true.

Nathanos would not have been in the capital when Arthas arrived and released chaos and cruelty upon the populace. His family's farm, Marris Stead, was located in the Eastweald—now dubbed Eastern Plaguelands, as if it had never had a name before Arthas. Old names, old lives—they didn't matter, not anymore.

She had visited him there, lain with him in the little bed, woken to the sound of birdcalls, blinking sleepily as she lay in his arms. It was a simple, sweet, cruel memory, and it hurt so greatly her body cringed when she recalled it. She had loved him, though the word had not been shared between them, and now it was too late.

She could remember the sights and smells and sensations, but not how she *felt*. Her emotions seemed to be limited, if nuanced in their compactness.

Had he fallen, her Nathanos? And if he had fallen . . . had he, like her, been able to claw his way back to sentience? Or had he beaten them? Was he one of the few who managed to escape, through their love of the Light or their own cleverness or luck?

That thought gave her no pleasure, either. If Nathanos still lived, he would likely think of her the way her friends did—that she was an abomination. The words from Lor'themar and Halduron had been sufficiently cruel that she had no wish to invite the same scorn from one who had been so close to her. Even from her own sister, Vereesa, whom she heard still lived.

Sylvanas realized that at this moment, it did not matter. She did not need a lover, or friends, or family. Arthas had taken them all from her the moment he took her life. One day, perhaps, once she had settled the score with Arthas, she could think again on such things.

Her people had once been graceful, bright lovers of the sun and beauty. Some of them had been led by her—the sharp ones, who tasted the harshness of fear and danger.

She looked again at her rangers. Her banshees. She thought of the little shade, so happily saving her king's life. That child had been murdered by Arthas, no matter if he had dealt the killing blow or if one of his Scourge had done so. Her ghost should not be serving him.

And the answers came, easily, calmly, almost kindly.

Her old friends thought her a monster? Sylvanas would show everyone what a true monster was—she would conquer and lead them.

The demons sought to use her? She would use them. With a

strong enough army, manipulated and controlled by her banshees, she could take them down, one by one. Perhaps in the end, they would serve *her*.

Her people now awaited her arrival, though they did not yet know it. They were lost, confused, like the little shade. No longer Scourge, but not yet something else. Something more, as she was. Abandoned by not only the living, but also by the real monster who had made them. She would start her army with them, the ones with whom she shared a unique hatred.

They had been forsaken.

Soon they would be wanted, and then they would be hers.

CHAPTER FIFTEEN

S ylvanas stood in the throne room of what had once been the capital city of Lordaeron. Sallow illumination seeped in from the grimy skylight above, casting a faint glow on the great seal at her feet.

In life, she had learned all about the Alliance kingdoms and their seals, sigils, and colors. Her father, with his affection for the wide world, had seen to that. Lordaeron's enormous sigil was familiar. But her world, and the world itself, had changed since those days when Verath Windrunner quizzed his daughter on colors and symbols. The Horde had come, and then Arthas, and everything had been broken. Sylvanas had fought tooth and nail to take over the city that had once been his, and since that time, as more former Scourge found themselves again—as much as any of them could—Sylvanas had learned what had happened in these chambers. Arthas had committed double sins with a single sword blow—those of regicide and patricide. The seal of the fallen Lordaeron now had a twisted irony to it that faintly amused Sylvanas.

The blood of King Terenas still stained the floor. One of the Forsaken, who had witnessed the act, said there had been blood on the crown. There had been no crown present when Sylvanas defeated

Balnazzar and strode into the throne room at the head of a victorious army, the cowed demon Varimathras in tow. She did not care. She had not come for a dead human's crown, or his throne, in which she had yet to sit.

She had not even come for the city, at least not as it had been. The only thing of Arthas that Sylvanas had willingly accepted was his idea of building a city beneath the ruins. An Undercity, for those who had been citizens of the one above, but who had reclaimed it in a manner that suited them.

We will find our own path in this world, dreadlord, she had told Varimathras, *and slaughter anyone who stands in our way.*

In life, Nathanos had teased her that she would not enjoy human cities, and he had been right. For all her aversion to the formalities and beauties of her birthplace, she had still been a child of that world, that way of life. How twisted was it that she yet existed, but as an inversion of her old self.

The girl she had once been had paled in horror when Lirath told her that the victims of her prank at Saltheril's thought they were poisoned. Now Sylvanas had taken a medicine meant for healing, and turned it to one of killing. She had once fought to save lives, to protect the living, and now had sent so many into the darkness of death—without even a second thought, really.

Betrayal, demonic allies, denying beings their free will. She wondered if the path upon which she now trod had been inevitable from birth; this allyship with the dead, the rejected, against the living. One might not have thought so, but Sylvanas had seen both sides now, and was not so sure.

Her mother had never wanted her to be ranger-general. It had always been the Lady Sun Alleria; Alleria, who was now gone, who had left only memories and a locket with a blue stone to her sister. Even that trinket had been lost, along with Sylvanas's life, when she fell at the hands of a butcher.

Now with bitter clarity, she saw how Alleria herself had failed Sylvanas, ignoring her familial duties and leaving her little sister to pick up the slack and bear the full force of her mother's resentment and disappointment. Lirath . . . he had died rejecting the life of safety Sylvanas wanted for him, and her friends—the Trio—today saw her as nothing more than a monster.

Sylvanas had never been close with her extended family, had assumed that most if not all of them were victims of the slaughter that occurred on that terrible day of the Horde attack on Windrunner Village. Vereesa and she—they were the only ones who remained. There had been a thawing of the coldness between them surrounding Little Moon's role in the death of their brother in the years since that awful day, but they had never fully mended the rift. And now they never would.

Or would they?

Her melancholy was abruptly slashed by a rush of anger. No, Sylvanas was convinced that even Vereesa would recoil at the sight of her sister now, and Sylvanas shied from inviting that black-red pain of abandonment as a horse shied from a snake.

She was no longer ranger-general, or Lady Moon, or sister, or daughter. These identities had been ripped from her along with her soul. There was another title that had sprung up as if with a life of its own: the Banshee Queen.

She had saved the Forsaken. Made and shaped them. Returned their city and their pride to them and encouraged their wills. They had responded with gratitude and a near-religious worship of her. It was somewhat of a balm to Sylvanas, but even that did not ease the ache of knowing that there was no one to whom she could confide any of these thoughts. She did not trust Varimathras, and the Forsaken needed to see her as a strong, confident leader. She would be that for them.

But there was one who had kept haunting her thoughts since her failure to kill Arthas—and if she was being honest, even before. One who was not kin and had been more than friend. Sylvanas kept pushing thoughts of Nathanos Marris away, but they returned, stubbornly resisting her efforts.

If there was any possibility he would return to her, she needed him by her side. One who would never leave, one who had a sharp wit and a masterful sense of strategy. One who could—almost—match her shot for shot. In truth, Nathanos was the only one who had not disappointed her, one way or another, her entire life. Surely, he would be that same powerful, steadfast force in undeath.

"Once, I told you to take me here," Sylvanas said aloud. "Now it seems it is I who must bring you to Lordaeron."

"This was where it all began," came a voice, pleasant, deep, and resonant. "A king died. A people were born. I, too, like to come here, and think on this."

Sylvanas turned, annoyed that she had gotten so lost in her thoughts she had not heard her visitor approach. She did not recognize the Forsaken who stood before her. Indeed, there was not much left to distinguish him from any other corpse; undeath had not been as kind to him as to some others. He barely even had the remnants of a face. For the sake of that faint echo of pity this roused in her, Sylvanas tamped down her irritation at the disruption.

"Who are you?" she asked.

"You may call me Putress, Your Majesty."

Sylvanas did not think twice about the odd name. Many of the Forsaken wished to distance themselves utterly from their old lives, taking unique names and new identities for themselves. This was clearly one such.

"Putress, you have come to me with some purpose," Sylvanas continued.

He nodded. "Varimathras forbade me to see you, but he refused to hear me out, so I followed you."

At another moment, this might have infuriated her. Now Sylvanas found herself slightly impressed. This Forsaken certainly had confidence. Sylvanas thought, but did not say, that Varimathras was not likely to hear anyone out, or allow them access to her, unless he believed it would be worth his time. Most often, he was correct, but although Sylvanas only distantly remembered what it was like to feel compassion, she knew that not only was it kind, it was useful.

"Bold of you," she said.

"My conviction makes me bold," Putress answered.

"I am listening."

He tried to straighten as best he could with his twisted spine. "There is much that has been lost to my mind, but I remember my great passion. Experimentation. Creation. Discovery." He pointed to a partially opened skull. "There may be worms here, but there are also thoughts and a great deal of knowledge."

"About what?"

He paused. "Death. And pain."

Sylvanas frowned. "Have you come to remind me of my own?"

"Death and pain to our *enemies*, my queen. How best to destroy them all and make them suffer!"

The thought of Arthas, of the chance she had missed, flashed in Sylvanas's mind. This was more to her liking. She nodded for him to continue.

"In life, I . . . was not much at all. I do not need to waste time missing a beloved face. No shadow of remembered appreciation darkens my skills, for there was nothing worth remembering. For good or ill."

I envy you, Sylvanas thought. She had been so vain about her beauty, so proud of her skills, so arrogant and confident in her choices. She was still these things, too, to an extent. But would it not have been good to have forgotten them?

"This new existence has given me another chance. *You*, my queen, have given me another chance. What flesh I have left is rotting and putrid, yes, but my hunger for vengeance and knowledge blazes brightly. I am grateful and would serve. Grant me the tools to pursue my passion, which I will turn toward serving you and the Forsaken."

"Should I do this, what is it you seek to create? To do?"

"An eye for an eye, my queen. I will take the blight that made us and tame it for our own uses."

"Do you speak of . . . a cure?"

Is such a thing even possible? For a moment, Sylvanas allowed her imagination to run rampant. She thought about making true peace with Vereesa, being united with the rest of the trio. With Nathanos. Of her banshees, restored to their bodies. Of those who had been forced into becoming mindless Scourge . . . made whole again.

"I would never be so ungrateful!" Putress managed to look offended, which was no small feat considering how little remained of his face.

The words shattered her moment of hopeful foolishness. Sylvanas did not want to be "acceptable" to those who did not have enough faith in her to trust her as an undead. They did not deserve her, be she undead or restored to the living. Sylvanas would not allow herself to hope for such a thing. She was who, and what, she was . . . and what she would yet make of herself.

"Quite right," she said. "A weapon, then?"

He nodded. "Yes. It would have to be handled very carefully, of course. And much testing would have to be done. I would need to . . . experiment, on the living."

Sylvanas thought of the charging bear she had shot with the poisoned arrow. How she had needed to test it, to get the correct balance of woundwood and other, darker toxins. She, too, had experimented on the living in order to sate the feeling that seemed the most vital and, ironically, most *alive* of her emotions: the ceaseless need for vengeance. It was a truth that she could not deny, but nonetheless it did not always sit well with her.

But this Forsaken, with the deep voice, wormy brain, and enjoyment of his "passion," was correct. In many ways, Forsaken were hardier than their living counterparts, but in other ways, they were still vulnerable, especially the ordinary citizens among them.

Arthas was seldom far from her thoughts, and his pale, grinning visage floated back to her now. Varimathras had informed her that after her failed attack with Lireesa's poisoned arrow, the death knight had fled to Northrend's Icecrown Citadel. There, he had merged with the Lich King and was now seated on the throne, encased in the translucent substance from which the site drew its name.

All Sylvanas had to do was to reach him—with an army strong enough to destroy him.

Sylvanas made the decision. She would embrace and protect her charges fiercely, care for them as much as her stunted emotions allowed, and hurl them at their common enemy to take their revenge both on the one who did this to them, and on the ones who shunned them for something they had been helpless to prevent.

"Granted," Sylvanas said, "the living loathe us. Some would even think it a mercy to send us to a more permanent death. But Arthas Menethil and the Scourge are perhaps even greater foes."

"But . . . undeath is a boon," he began.

She cut him off. "Boon or curse, it simply *is*. And becoming Scourge is no boon at all. Whatever your plans are, they must also include a way to stop the Scourge and that monster who made them."

Sylvanas knew that the sort of weapon she was allowing Putress to experiment with would not be well received by many. Something that killed the Scourge and the living was also a threat to the Forsaken. "From this moment forward, do not speak of this task to which I have set you. Not everyone is as wise or foresighted as we. They will fear what they do not understand."

His head bobbed up and down.

"We may very well have only one chance to deploy this weapon at its single true target. And if that chance comes, we must not squander it. Arthas must die . . . and the Forsaken will be the ones who bring him down."

"It is as you wish, my lady."

So be it.

"Seek out Varimathras. Tell him of this conversation, and that I authorize him to give you whatever—and whomever—you might need to make this . . . weapon. You shall be my grand apothecary."

"From nothing, you have raised me to a rank I could never have dreamed of. I shall go at once. Thank you."

Putress, the mad, would-be savior of the Forsaken, bowed deeply, then left her.

The conversation had both stirred and calmed Sylvanas. She

would emulate him and refuse to entertain any more shame at her state—or fruitless desires to be other than who she was.

But the conversation, and her musing on this place—which was once the seat of so much power and now was nothing, really; nothing at all—had settled something in her mind.

There would be no comfort, no forgiveness, no compassion from the living. Her only allies were her own kind, the Forsaken. But she did not wish to be alone any longer, and she needed her champion by her side if she was to take down Arthas.

She would have to hope, then, she did not find Nathanos Marris alive.

When Sylvanas returned a week later, having scoured the Eastern Plaguelands, she was angry and frustrated. The area appeared as much of the region did—stripped, ransacked. There had been no evidence of Nathanos at his homestead—not alive, or dead, or anything in between. Either he had never reclaimed his mind, and was something both the living and the undead abhorred, or he had been elsewhere fighting with the Alliance and escaped the plague.

Lost in thought, she was striding toward the Royal Quarter when a voice called out to her.

"My lady! I come with news." It was Ranger Clea. Sylvanas paused and turned so that Clea might catch up with her. The dark ranger did not look like the news she bore was good.

"Speak, Clea."

"Nathanos has been located near his homestead. I regret to inform you . . . he is Scourge."

A sudden flood of memories washed over Sylvanas: Their archery challenge. Their first kiss. Their teasing, and most of all, how the two of them had shut out a world full of pain and made their own world, just the two of them, for a time.

The emotions these memories roused were intense. Horror, that he was mindless now, he of the quick wit and unique wisdom. Hatred for Arthas, who yet again had managed to corrupt something that had been precious to her in life.

Only belatedly did Sylvanas realize what emotions were absent. Longing. Passion. Grief at the loss of something that mattered.

Love.

Her feelings had been confused in life, so it should come as no surprise to her that in this undeath that she endured, such a tender sentiment was absent. But the others ... Sylvanas remembered feeling them, but they did not reach her now. Only echoes of what had once been.

She had a decision to make.

Had Nathanos been truly dead, there would have been nothing she could have done but let him go. Had he lived, he would be just as surely lost to her. Undead ... Scourge ...

Betrayal, disappointment, and hurt had been constant threads in her new un-life. Wisdom dictated that she avoid needlessly inviting them. Nathanos was not Forsaken. If she sought him out, it would only be to end him.

It was obvious, of course. She should ignore this news. It did not serve her to seek out someone only to put him down like a rabid beast.

But what if I can reach him?

Such a thing had never happened to the best of her knowledge. The Forsaken either regained their will and sense, as she and her rangers had, or they were simply things that walked and slaughtered. Nothing more.

What if I can bring him back?

Sylvanas was suddenly irritated with herself. It was foolish to hope for what wasn't possible. Nathanos was gone, just like everyone else she had cared for was gone, each lost to her in their own uniquely painful way.

But pushing back with surprising strength was something else: a need for connection that went deeper than any she had now ... and the desire to, despite the pain and vulnerability, truly *feel* again.

Nathanos was stubborn, too. Almost as stubborn as she was. If anyone could be brought back it would be him, and if anyone could achieve this impossible task, it was Sylvanas Windrunner.

"Thank you for the news, Clea."

"I understand it was not the outcome you had hoped for."

Hope. The most illogical, deceptive, and dangerous thing in the world. Sylvanas rejected the idea that her plan was one of "hope." It was simple logic. In life, she had always been at her best with Nathanos at her side. Surely it would be the same in undeath. He would stand, loyal beyond any other, as together they destroyed the monster who had destroyed them.

And maybe, just maybe, she would discover that Arthas had not destroyed what they once had.

"It matters not," she told Clea.

"Do you wish—we can take care—"

"No. Find Anya, and meet me at the flight master's. We will go to the Marris Stead, and do what needs to be done."

And I will return with my champion.

CHAPTER SIXTEEN

Some of those who had groomed and stabled animals in life had begun training the large bats in the area to obey them. As Sylvanas mounted its back, the beast chittered and flapped energetically, the beat of his membranous wings reminding her of those of a dragonhawk. She stopped her thoughts from wandering too far down that path; there were only painful memories at the end of it.

She, Anya, and Clea traveled through the Undercity sewers until they emerged into the dim light of Tirisfal, heading west toward the Plaguelands. While a constant pall hung over the land now inhabited largely by the undead, at least there were still some green things. The ground that gradually appeared below them was desiccated and dead, the grass and trees and most of the beasts victims of the blight. Those who survived had been changed; plaguebats and doglike creatures moved about below her, but no sign of anything that had once been human. A memory flickered, determined to be recalled despite Sylvanas's desire to forget it, of Nathanos on a dragonhawk, with she behind him. They had been investigating the deaths of Lireesa and Verath Windrunner, and Nathanos thought perhaps more evidence could be found deeper into the Eastweald, as it was called. The place had been verdant at the time; homey, pleasant. Fields of green and gold spread out in neat little squares, some hosting small white dots of woolly white sheep. All this was gone; Arthas's reach was so very long.

Sylvanas wondered if she would even recognize her champion. But no. Clea had known him; certainly his lady would.

And . . . there it was.

Once, the Marris Stead's isolation had been a welcome one. It had been peaceful and green, its wide fields stretching out and surrounding the house. They could meet here, she and Nathanos, without worrying about the rumors and the whispers. His younger cousin—what was his name . . . Stephon, that was it—had lived here for a while, but only once had intruded upon her time with Nathanos. Bright-eyed, lively little Stephon, who bubbled over with enthusiasm and talked about becoming a paladin.

Had Stephon survived? Achieved his dream? Become Scourge? It did not matter. The only thing Sylvanas cared about was Nathanos.

She and the two rangers landed a slight distance away and approached. The once cozy farmhouse had fared as poorly as the surrounding area: dark, damaged, seemingly abandoned, with no evidence of habitation of any sort. Senses alert, they walked inside. All the furniture was gone, and the windows were broken or boarded up. Her boots left tracks in thick dust. If Nathanos was in the area, he had not come home in some time . . . if at all.

"Clea," Sylvanas said, "Are you certain it was—"

She heard the scraping of claws on the floorboards, a deep growl, and turned just in time to see a giant hound launch itself at her, toxic slaver dripping from its jaws. Sylvanas dodged, deflecting the attack with her bow. The hound landed awkwardly and clambered to its feet, slightly dazed and shaking its head. It was too close for her to shoot it, so she simply seized an arrow and shoved it forward into the beast's throat, instantly silencing a growl.

Anya and Clea, too, were being attacked, easily dispatching the plaguehounds. But more were coming, baying in a strange, echoing tone, and Sylvanas was annoyed and impatient, and took the fight to them.

It was over in a few moments, and the three retrieved their arrows from the still-twitching corpses. "To answer your question, my lady," Clea said, "yes. I am certain it was Nathanos."

"Then let us be about finding him. And," Sylvanas cautioned them, "I will not easily forgive if you select the wrong arrows."

A quick glance at the former farmlands that spread out below the rise revealed pockets of Scourge, lurching and stumbling to no real purpose. From here, it would be impossible even for her to distinguish a face—especially a rotted one. *So we take them one by one,* Sylvanas thought. *Killing Scourge is never a wasted act.*

Sylvanas pointed to a cluster of the things and they descended. As they approached in utter silence, they drew no notice from the once human creatures. Nathanos was not among them. She shook her head, and her rangers nodded, nocking their bows and firing.

Sylvanas tasted doubt as group after group revealed themselves to be nothing but shambling undead. *No,* she told herself. *I will find him. No matter how long it takes.*

She had lost count of the number the three of them had killed when a woman's screams of anguish and terror caught her attention. One of the Scourge was making a kill, and in short order the screaming ceased and the Scourge began to feast on the warm flesh. After but a moment, though, it—he—rose and stood still as stone, offering Sylvanas a clear view of his face.

Nathanos.

It was far, far worse than she had feared. It was no surprise Clea had thought him irretrievably lost. For the briefest of moments, Sylvanas wondered if she should let him go. Perhaps the hand that had touched him with love in life should be the hand that dealt him the mercy of death.

But no. *No.* She needed him. He was her champion, and she, his lady. What with the Horde, Arthas Menethil, and the Lich King, everything Sylvanas had cared for, that had held meaning, had been ripped from her. She would not add Nathanos to that list.

I will bring you back.

Stealthily she, Clea, and Anya moved forward as the murdered woman rose a Scourge and looked at Nathanos.

Sylvanas seized this moment of distraction. She brought her fist down, and the other two fired until the newly made Scourge dropped, her unlife having lasted mere seconds. Nathanos, hunched, bloody, his never-handsome face a hideous wreckage, whirled toward them and started to charge.

"Aim for the legs!" Sylvanas shouted.

Nathanos went down, a barrage of arrows slamming into his thighs and shins; arrows that ended in small metal orbs made specifically for this task. It would keep him from attacking but would not harm him.

"Nathanos!" Sylvanas screamed his name, infusing it with all the dark banshee power that had slain so many at Silvermoon, the young, the kind, the artists. She could hear that power reverberating in the very air.

He lay still. Hope rose in her . . . could it be this easy?

And then he struggled again to rise, growling in frustration.

Again Sylvanas shouted his name. *Remember. Remember yourself. Remember* me. A third time she called to him, letting her pain bleed into the echoing tones until her voice sounded as broken as he.

She pulled off her hood. Perhaps if he could see her . . .

Yellow flickered in his eyes. He made an awful, guttural sound, but then something seemed to click into place, and he found a way to speak.

"S-Sylvanas?"

Their eyes met, then he lowered them, and put an arm up to hide his face, as if he did not want her to look at him. There came a soft, low moan that should have broken her heart but only infuriated Sylvanas more.

Oh, butcher, you will pay dearly. And I will not be quick.

Later, Sylvanas would find she could not remember what else was said. But she cut through his shame. Reminded him of who he had been, and still could be. Not even death could stop them. Finally, he rose and made his way to her.

"I am yours, Dark Lady. For all my days."

But as they walked toward where their mounts awaited them, Nathanos froze. He growled—not the feral, mindless sound of the Scourge, but a growl of annoyance. He looked about, seeming to not know who he was even though his farmstead was but a few yards away.

Anya and Clea exchanged glances. "Return," Sylvanas told them. "I will follow. Go."

She had hoped for a searingly painful, but quick, solution. That once Nathanos understood he had . . . *survived*? No, that was no longer the correct word: *endured* . . . he would be ready to accompany her triumphant return to her people.

But he was not.

Sylvanas steeled herself. He had returned to her before. She would bring him back again.

In a way, what Arthas had done to Nathanos was more damaging to Sylvanas than all the torture the death knight had put her through. She was strong. She had fought, clawed, *willed* her way to a knowledge of self that eluded so many thousands of others. Sylvanas knew that she would always have found a way back to herself, by herself. But in life her strength had, at times, been supported by strength other than her own, though those who knew Nathanos would never have suspected the man could be kind in any way. And now, Arthas had cut that support out from beneath her. But Nathanos had been there for her, in her moments of darkest despair, so Sylvanas determined she would be there for him.

Time passed. Fragments of him returned in his choices of words, the tone of voice. Then, like a tide receding, memory would leave him.

She walked him through everything they had done together, everything they had been to each other.

The periods of clarity began to last longer. While that was an encouraging sign, her furious frustration was also greater, as was the strange hollowness inside she no longer understood how to manage.

One day—the third, or thirteenth, or thirtieth—they were talking of shooting, of hunting, of arrows in flight, and his glowing gaze went to her bow.

"Do you want this?" Sylvanas asked.

Nathanos nodded. She took his left hand and folded it around the grip. Bones poked through the leather of his tattered gloves, and Sylvanas watched as his fingers first did nothing, then slowly closed. He got to his feet, hunched and unsteady, and lifted the bow into the proper position. His right hand came up to touch the string, rolling it between his fingers, then drawing it back, anchoring at what remained of his jaw. He did not release it, but eased it back, then turned to her and held out his hand.

She gave him the quiver, which he slipped over his hunched back. Nathanos was clumsy yet with his bony fingers, but he nocked the arrow correctly. He glanced over at her, his eyes glowing yellow, but seeing her. Sylvanas steeled herself for the madness that was surely hard on the heels of her most successful attempt yet.

Then he turned his head, aimed at the side of his old house, and let fly.

The arrow thunked into the old wood.

A sense of triumph filled her as she watched him shoot. The first few arrows were haphazard, but his aim grew truer with each one released from the bow. Finally, he grouped all of them together so closely one could barely insert a finger between them.

He slowly lowered the bow, then looked at her for a long moment. His eyes flickered.

"Is that the best you can do?" she asked, keeping her voice light even as she dared to hope that this time, he would stay with her.

"Only a select few see me at my very best," he said.

How odd, that with so many memories gone, this one remained. It was an unexpected gift, and Sylvanas would take it.

Nathanos remembered nothing about what had happened, only that there had been shambling corpses attacking him until he had emptied his quiver and they had fallen upon him.

"Those creatures were the Scourge," Sylvanas said. "And for a time, you were, too. But no longer."

"Only because of you," he said, quietly. "Scourge. Yes . . . I remember. We were told about them . . . but it seemed unbelievable. But . . . you, and I—"

"We are strong of will. Our minds are our own. We are the Forsaken."

"Did—did it take you long? To bring me back?"

Sylvanas thought of the endless times he had seemed to rally, only to fall back into the pit of oblivion. How she had argued with herself, almost left, only to return and continue to try.

"No," she said, the lie coming easily, and smiled. "It did not. You are my champion, after all."

"I would hate to think I failed you," he said, sounding relieved.

"Nathanos . . . tell me what you remember of us," she said. And he did. They sorted through the pieces of themselves that were left, after Arthas. Nathanos recalled how fierce, and passionate, and occasionally stormy their relationship had been. Sylvanas told him he was rough with everyone else, but gentle with her. They talked of climbing Sungraze Peak, and Sylvanas's opinions on beauty.

"Well," Nathanos said, drily, "as I am uglier than ever, I imagine I appeal to you even more." It was sarcasm, at which he excelled, and Sylvanas was glad to see he had recovered it. But then Nathanos's hand went to his chin, and he fell silent. That moment atop Sungraze was only a memory now, and it could never be re-created.

For a moment, the loss was more than Sylvanas could bear. She could remember love for Nathanos, but could not feel it. She remembered joy, but could not experience it. Then sudden anger and resolve chased away the melancholy.

"You are still my champion," Sylvanas said intensely. "You are strong—stronger than ever. Maybe even more so. I will *not* let our state dictate who we are. We *will* be what we once were to each other. I *will* make it happen."

"If anyone can," said Nathanos, "it is you, my lady."

She had done what she had set out to do. She had recovered Nathanos, and her champion now stood at her side. All things felt possible.

Arthas and his minions did not stand a chance.

INTERLUDE

"I have heard the stories of Arthas Menethil, of course," Anduin said when she had finished. "I even met him, I am told. My father knew him when he was young, and he came to Stormwind when I was a baby. Father told me he was shaken when . . . everything happened. This Arthas, this death knight—that was not the little boy he'd befriended, whose father had taken in refugees from Stormwind."

Sylvanas raised an eyebrow and said flatly, "People change."

"Yes," the youth said. "They do." His blue eyes looked steadily into hers.

"Some of us had change forced upon us," she said. "I never wanted to be as I am. I believe I made that clear."

"Abundantly. And you're quite right. I can think of little change in my own life that I would have desired. But Sylvanas . . . we can learn to adapt. To accept."

Anger flared in her. "What would you have me do? Remain content as an incorporeal banshee, flitting about in absolute acceptance of what a madman demanded of me?"

"Of course not! But some of us manage to acknowledge injustice without going on killing sprees. You speak eloquently of free will, Sylvanas, so therefore I must assume that you are in control of your actions. That you choose violence and cruelty and war."

"*How many times must I tell you?*" she spat. "*We have never* had *free will!*"

He laughed without humor, angrily, his brows drawn together in an uncharacteristic scowl that made him look so very much like his father. "*At least take responsibility for what you've done!*"

"*Did you not hear what happened at the gates of Quel'Thalas?*"

She was almost shouting. She had rarely spoken of that day, and certainly not to anyone she did not trust deeply—which, in the end, meant only Nathanos. Part of her felt rebuffed, that she had so made herself vulnerable only to be chastened for an evil act she would never have willingly performed.

Except . . . that isn't true, is it? *she thought.*

Something in her voice, or her face, reached him, and his brow unfurrowed. "I did listen," the king said quietly, almost kindly. "You have told me much I have never known. And I could hear your pain as you spoke. But . . ." He rubbed his face, searching for words. "I could also hear Arthas in your words."

Sylvanas stiffened. For a moment, she was unable to form words. "Everyone underestimates you, Little Lion. Even me. Or is it that we overestimate you? For I would never have expected such vicious words to come from one so devoted to Holy Light."

"Though they were not meant to wound, I know they were cruel," he said. "But for every incident you share with me, for every raw emotion I see on your face, whether you realize it or no—I see you are unaware of how you carry his legacy forward, now more than ever. Did you learn nothing from him, Sylvanas? You are bound again, this time eagerly, to someone who is using you to cause pain and suffering for his own ends!"

How dare he, so young, so certain. How dare he judge her.

"Of course I learned," she said, "when it was happening—and later. The Jailer explained to me what Arthas was. A failure. Arthas was small-minded, and petty, and if he had not been so terrifying in what he could do, he would have been laughable. He did not see what the Jailer and I saw. He could not, and, more important, he did not desire to. But his failure has paved the way for our success. The Jailer and I share a vision, one that you, I would have thought, could embrace. I am *his partner. We work together. Arthas?" She scoffed. "Nothing but a useful instrument."*

"Like me," Anduin said. His voice was soft, but dangerous, almost like the warning rumble a true lion would make.

She had said that, hadn't she? Or close enough. You are a weapon we will use to achieve our ends.

Very well. She had said it; she would not deny it. But she could continue to show him what it had taken her time to learn. If he would listen.

"You do not have to be," she said quietly. "You can stand with us. You can help us bring about justice, not only for us . . . but for all. Is that not what you wish?"

Anduin shook his head, exasperated, angry, disbelieving. "When you speak to me of these things, these aspects of you—I start to think that maybe there is a chance you truly aren't what your actions proclaim you to be. And then, every single time, I discover who you really are."

"I promised that I would speak truth to you, and I have," she said. "I do not shy from what I have done. I want your understanding, not your pity."

Your understanding about why I did what I did . . . and what I have been longing for without even realizing.

"I want you to see what I saw," she said, leaning forward intently, "that you may embrace the Jailer's plan, as I do."

CHAPTER SEVENTEEN

Sylvanas walked along the glowing, green river that flowed through the canals of the Undercity. Early on she had claimed one area for herself as the Royal Quarter, embracing the soubriquet of Banshee Queen. Others—notably the apothecaries and alchemists—had set up their labs in the sector. But there were yet long stretches where it was quiet and isolated, and Sylvanas and Nathanos strode alongside the sludgy liquid as they had once done in the meadows of Eversong.

"You are silent, my champion," Sylvanas said when Nathanos did not reply to her last comment.

He shrugged. "I do not wish to see you further hurt, my lady."

Sylvanas scowled. "Pain is a part of this existence. In life, I could run from it, but there is nowhere to run here, nor anywhere in Azeroth, where I might find balm or distraction. If the Farstriders will not have us, perhaps the Alliance will. We are, after all . . . them. Many here have living relatives. Perhaps the desire to see their families reunited will pressure their leaders to accept us into their ranks."

It was with an effort that she kept her voice casual. Her own family would never be together again, not after that final night, where her parents danced in each other's arms and her father toasted them all, telling her things that she tried to shut out but somehow always returned. Nothing ever seemed to last.

"Extraordinarily *tolerant* families, if your 'visit' to Farstrider Retreat was any indication."

Sylvanas gritted her teeth. "Time can heal wounds. Ease memories. Perhaps the humans will find even a changed loved one is better than no loved one."

"I would suggest," Nathanos said, drily, "that if you wish to speak with them, you avoid calling them human. No need to remind them that our people are not."

"It is the truth," she snapped. "What would you have me do, then? Turn to the Horde? The brutes that massacred my family?" Her voice rose in outrage fueled by pain. Her mother. Her father. Her little brother. And Alleria, entering through a portal into an unknown world in an effort to save it from the Horde's destruction. The orcs had so much to answer for. "Our people need protection! We can offer our allies untiring soldiers who are physically powerful and difficult to truly kill."

"You sound like you are justifying it to yourself."

She sighed. "I should have left you to rot at your homestead."

Nathanos made a grunt that sounded dangerously close to a chuckle. "I know you, Sylvanas. That's exactly what you are doing. And," he said, grudgingly, "perhaps you are right."

"I should have left you to rot?"

"Reaching out to the humans. It is worth a try. But do not hope too much, my lady."

"Ah, my champion," she said, "I do not hope at all, anymore."

She did a careful evaluation of possible emissaries and eventually sent a small group of four, selecting only the most intact, those who could almost pass for the living but for the faint sickly eye glow that betrayed the magic animating their cold flesh. They were all former soldiers, one from Southshore, two from the capital city, and one from Stormwind, Sarias Colton, who had a relative there. All of them had been noteworthy and admirable in life; hopefully their living reputations would give the humans pause. It was a delicate and dangerous mission, and Sylvanas knew they would need every advantage going in. She did have some shred of hope that these courageous individuals could at least open the door for discussion . . . provided they were even granted a chance to speak.

"Your challenges are myriad," Sylvanas warned them. They stood at attention, their spines as straight as they could make them, and she walked back and forth in front of them as she spoke. "The Alliance, especially humans, are quite right to fear and hate the Scourge. So do we. Everything hinges upon your convincing King Varian that the Forsaken are *different.* We have suffered, terribly. Despite our appearances, we are more like the inhabitants of Stormwind than we are Scourge, and anyone in Stormwind could have suffered the same fate as we."

She paused, looking at each of them in turn. "You are the finest emissaries I could find among our people. I know you will represent us well and truthfully. Do not shy away from who and what we are— but make them understand we are more than that, that we will be powerful allies."

They saluted her. Sarias said, "My lady, it is an honor. But the greatest gift of this charge you have laid upon us is the chance for me to see my sister again."

Sarias spoke earnestly, and Sylvanas hoped he would not regret the words. It was a reckless thing, to put one's hope in the living. But it was her only option.

They never returned.

A few weeks later, Sylvanas sent a scout to the outskirts of the city. He returned with a single item: the pouch Sarias had been carrying, which bore a letter, a locket with the face of a young woman enclosed in it, and a family ring.

Sylvanas suspected they had been murdered the instant they had been glimpsed. She thought it unlikely that Varian had even known of their presence.

The Farstriders thought her a monster. The Alliance wouldn't let them come close enough even to parley.

That left Sylvanas with only one solution: Ally with the Horde.

Losing one's parents was at least in the natural order of things, although not in such a brutal manner. Their murders had ripped away any comfortable illusion of hiding from the darkness of what life dealt. But she had also lost Lirath, who had only begun to discover what life had to offer, and with him, her complete faith in Vereesa.

The orcs had taken it all.

"How can I ever forget what they did to me? How can I entrust governance of the Forsaken to those with so much blood on their hands?"

"You don't need to do any of those things," Nathanos pointed out.

Everything crystallized then. Nathanos, in his detachment, saw what Sylvanas, lost in her hatred and anger, could not.

"You are correct, my champion. I need surrender nothing."

She would say the right things, of course. Make some gestures of seemingly genuine goodwill. Listen carefully, the better to exploit the advantages her people would have. What was it her father said?

What do you think politics is? You can't accomplish anything unless people come to the table.

Even he had believed in making the other party malleable to negotiation. If her true goal was defending and protecting the Forsaken, who represented her only chance to thrive in this cursed existence, Sylvanas needed to do whatever she had to.

She thought about the Horde. Orcs, of course. The great, green monsters who had raced through the Dark Portal from another world into Azeroth, having despoiled their own. Sylvanas had been unable to get the full story, but she heard they had allied with demons. Well, she had, too; she could not judge. Their young leader, who had the odd name of Thrall, had been raised by a human, but turned on him and liberated the orcs from the internment camps the Alliance had consigned them to after the war.

He, and most of his new Horde, were now on the far continent of Kalimdor, where they had allied with the ancient enemy of the elves—trolls—and befriended the tauren.

Instead of sending an emissary, Sylvanas did what she should have done with the Alliance: She sent spies. They reported back that this Horde did seem to be greatly different from the one that had burned Eversong. Even the trolls were not the ones the quel'dorei had fought, the bloodthirsty Amani. These new trolls were of the Darkspear tribe—one that had turned its back on the brutality of other troll races. And oddly enough, the most bestial of all of the Horde races appeared to be the most open-minded: the tauren. "They do not have a history with elves and humans," they told her. "We believe approaching them first would yield the best chance of success."

Sylvanas did so. And this time, all those she sent returned. They bore a letter from the leader of the tauren, a placid-tempered bull who had reached his elder years by being one of the finest warriors the race had ever seen: Chieftain Cairne Bloodhoof. Sylvanas's smile grew as she read.

> To the Lady Sylvanas Windrunner, Leader of the
> people called the Forsaken, High Chieftain
> Cairne Bloodhoof sends greetings.
>
> Your emissaries have told us of the tragedy you faced from the dreadful plague of undeath. It pains me to learn that your own people have rejected you, which seems to me a double sorrow you have not earned. How bitter it must be, to have endured so much, only to be turned away.
>
> We tauren celebrate life and honor the Earth Mother. We are uneasy around things that at first glance appear to go against the natural cycle of life and death. But even she has her time of death, followed by rebirth. Perhaps your own people have a place within that sacred cycle as well, and have lessons to teach us.
>
> I invite you to come to Thunder Bluff, to speak with me and my advisers, including my son, Baine, and our chief druid, Hamuul Runetotem. Let us meet in the Barrens, and from there, I pledge safe passage.

Sylvanas left Nathanos in the Undercity, to continue training her dark rangers and to keep an eye on Varimathras. "There is only so far one can trust a demon," she said. Sylvanas did not anticipate being away for any great length of time, but she would leave nothing to chance.

After dwelling so long in the Undercity, with its miasma of odors and dankness, the vast plains and rolling hills of Mulgore were unsettling. The sky seemed too wide, the place too open, the light too bright—even the light of the two moons and the stars. It screamed of *life* in a way that the Undercity did not. It also tugged on something Sylvanas had banished into a corner of her mind and did not wish to rouse.

But of course, such ignorant peace did not last. Her guide, the Longwalker Perith Stormhoof, noticed her shift in attitude and, concerned, inquired as to what was troubling her, and if he could do anything about it.

"My people live in a place beneath a city," Sylvanas said. "It has been long since I have traveled from it, let alone in a place so vast, that is all."

It was not all.

The meeting was to be held in the capital of the tauren land, the "city," if such it could be called, of Thunder Bluff. Sylvanas was taken to the highest rise, where Caine Bloodhoof, Archdruid Hamuul Runetotem, and other significant tauren awaited them.

Two guards stood on either side of the door that marked the high chieftain's long house. "We welcome you, Lady Sylvanas," one of them said, his voice deep and booming. "But we must ask that you lay down your weapons, and that your rangers wait outside."

"They are my sisters in suffering," Sylvanas said.

"We understand. Yet those are the rules of my high chieftain, and I would die rather than fail him."

Sylvanas narrowed her eyes. The arrogance of these . . . cows. She nodded to her dark rangers, Loralen and Vorel, to wait, then reluctantly removed her quiver and set down her bow. The hide covering the door of the large dwelling was lifted, and Sylvanas entered.

Wood and a fire that cast dancing shadows made the room feel warm. Beautiful woven rugs and banners adorned the floor and walls. Pillows were arranged upon the floor in a circle. Seated inside one circle was an older-looking tauren. His braided beard and hair fell across his chest. Beside him was a carved log painted with symbols, which could have been either a ritual item or a weapon or both, and—

"An *orc!*"

"My apologies, Lady Sylvanas," said Cairne, "but Warchief Thrall arrived on other business this morning, and I have asked him to stay."

Her eyes darted about, but she detected none of the telltale signs of feigned inactivity. Everyone seemed relaxed—and they could have killed her at any point on the journey. Still, Sylvanas had not anticipated this, and her mind began turning in a variety of directions as she nodded.

"Eventually we would need to meet regardless, Warchief," Sylvanas said, inclining her head. "I simply did not anticipate it being now."

"I know I have taken you by surprise, Lady Sylvanas," Thrall said. He was much younger than those around him, and for a moment she regarded him intently. He seemed . . . very earnest, and she had to remind herself that he had gained the title because he had fought battles against not just the Alliance, but mighty demons themselves. The Burning Legion had been defeated not by any one army, or even an Alliance or Horde, but by many factions working together. Horde and Alliance had done so too, largely because of the unusual friendship that had developed between Lady Jaina Proudmoore and the young orc. And in Kalimdor, the ancestors of the quel'dorei—the kaldorei—whom the humans called night elves, had made a reappearance. It had been the kaldorei dead, the wisps, souls that had not passed on in order to continue to protect their people, who had dealt the final blow to the mighty Archimonde. No, Thrall was obviously someone to whom there was more than met the eye.

"I have had worse surprises," she said, and sank down gracefully on one of the cushions.

"Please," Cairne said, "you are indeed unique. Tell us your story."

She did, reframing it all in her mind, spinning a tale that showcased both the suffering she and her people had endured, and their strength. Sylvanas omitted any mention of the Horde attacks, or her family, indeed skirted her living years almost entirely, focusing on the horror and evil that was Arthas Menethil. Of her will to break free from him, and what a struggle it had been even for her, let alone common folk of an ordinary city. She cited the cruelty of the humans she had met, dwelling on the sad discovery of a pouch that contained Sarias's belongings.

"A hope for unity, sought in peace, destroyed." Sylvanas shook her head sadly. "No. Do not fear that we will stray toward the Alliance. They have shown clearly enough how they view us. It is my great hope that the Horde can look past our appearances, to what we have to offer. Currently, the Horde only has support in Kalimdor. But we all know this world is wide, and danger can come from anywhere, at any time. It would greatly benefit you to have eyes and ears—and weapons and warriors—in the Eastern Kingdoms. Allying with us will instantly give you a secure territory—and friends—on a different continent."

"We are not the old Horde," Thrall said. "Conquest and domination are not our goals. But you are correct. I intend to keep our people safe and thriving. The Horde must not become insular or complacent. It seems the Forsaken do have much to offer us."

Cairne nodded solemnly. "My friends," he said, "we owe what debate we may have performed in front of her who has appealed to us. Tell me your thoughts."

Hamuul peered at her from over the flickering flames. "You were in the Lich King's army," he said. "In that service, you took many lives."

"*Service?*" Sylvanas laughed scornfully. "No. *Enslavement.* I could protest nothing he made me do. I was forced to use the power he bestowed on me to slaughter a city full of innocents—many of whom

I had loved in life." An exaggeration, but the pain in her voice was genuine. "Most of the Scourge were not sufficiently aware of themselves or their actions to understand what they did. Some of them, upon recovering their wits, lost them again in horror when memory returned."

Hamuul nodded and turned to Cairne and Thrall. "We have heard a story like this one before, have we not, Warchief? Of a subjugated people who did terrible things, and once freed from that power were filled with remorse. So strong was that remorse that their leader, as an act of penance, moved from a fertile home to the sere lands of Orgrimmar."

Thrall nodded. "I have seen what the taint of demonic blood did to those who drank from that cruel cup. I do have some sympathy for you and your people."

"Their numbers are finite," Cairne said. "If we do not aid them, we doom them to extinction. Through no fault of their own, they will be targeted, hated, and despised by every living thing."

"Is death not natural?" Thrall continued. "Is this type of existence . . . right?"

"Who are we to judge?" Hamuul said. "You pray to the ancestors. We speak with spirits. Death is not the end. Perhaps the Forsaken are merely another aspect, created in order to teach the world's children empathy. They have their own minds. Can make their own choices. How can we say we have compassion if we reject them?"

Sylvanas could barely contain her fury. How arrogant the living were. Of *course* the Forsaken existed only to enlighten *them,* allow *them* to feel good about themselves. They could go to sleep tonight with a clear conscience, knowing they were "showing compassion" and "helping others."

Pride told her to leave. Sheer will kept her sitting, quietly, giving no clue as to the rage boiling inside her. Despite her feelings, she recognized that the conversation had left her an opening, and she would take it.

"The archdruid is right. Death is not the end. And you, too, are correct, Warchief. What was done to us is not natural. The keenest minds in our new Undercity labor tirelessly to learn more about our . . . situation."

It was true, although her earnest delivery of the words made it sound as if the Forsaken were searching for a cure. She would let them draw their own conclusion.

Thrall searched her eyes for a moment. She wondered what, if anything, he saw in their glowing red depths. At last, he sighed. "Lady Sylvanas, I am still reluctant to bring your people into the Horde. But I am willing to give them—and you—a chance to prove yourself."

Oh, how terribly kind of you. "Thank you, Warchief."

"I trust the tauren people, my two friends Cairne and Hamuul most of all. They are closer to life, to nature, than any among the Horde. If they see something in you so clearly that they have made such a sincere argument to admit you, I will do so.

"I am also well aware of the failures of the orcs," he added. "The blood of a demon drove us mad, and the withdrawal from such a potent poison sapped our wills. But the orcs are themselves again, and it sounds as if your Forsaken are as well."

"We do hope so, Warchief," she said, and almost bit her tongue, the words were so sweet. "You will not regret your choice."

They talked long into the hours of the night, the fire continuing to burn, the shadows flickering like mad ghosts in the corners and on the walls. Finally, an agreement was reached. Sylvanas stepped out into the predawn, looking up at the lightening sky. The earth was damp with dew and smelled clean.

"We are now proud members of the Horde, my sisters," she said, making sure any listening ears heard clearly. "Today is truly a new day for the Forsaken. We have much to do."

As they embarked for home, Sylvanas kept her thoughts to herself, not even confiding to her rangers. Not yet.

The Forsaken would be loyal to the Horde . . . as needed. They would receive aid and protection in return. Her reign as the "Banshee Queen" would continue, and soon enough, she would convince the Horde that Arthas Menethil posed so dreadful a threat, they needed to destroy him and his evil once and for all.

Everyone, *everything*, was a weapon, now, to be aimed and released wherever she so chose. Certainly the Horde and its leaders, but even the Forsaken themselves, for Sylvanas Windrunner knew three things: They loved her, and that love was as pure and true as creatures such as they could offer. And the last truth, one she could never reveal, was that any semblance of compassion she felt for them depended entirely on their continued usefulness to her ambitions.

CHAPTER EIGHTEEN

"Fate does love a twist," Sylvanas said, almost purring as she listened to the latest report from her spies. It had not been so long ago, only a handful of years, that Sylvanas had returned to her homeland, still awkward in her new body, full of foolish hope that somehow her old friends could see past what she had endured to the Sylvanas they remembered. She had gone to them for aid, although they were unaware; and they had, equally unwittingly, refused.

Her former people had not fared well in the intervening time. By the start of the Third War their late king, Anasterian, had somewhat distanced his kingdom from the Alliance. Later, Kael'thas, smarting from abusive treatment and imprisonment at the hands of one particularly abhorrent human—Garithos, whom Sylvanas had used for her own ends before ordering his death—had renounced any union between the Alliance and the quel'dorei. The blood elves, as Kael had named them, were barely recovering from what Arthas had done, to them, to the Sunwell, and to their entire world of beauty and grace.

A thought found its way to her, something she had told Nathanos once, a lifetime ago—that she fought to keep her people from having to see the ugliness that was out there in the world. Well, now they had seen ugliness and horror aplenty, and they were alone. Because they had turned their back on the Alliance, they now had enemies on virtually the entire continent.

She had hidden her pride, though not swallowed it, to approach the Farstriders, Alliance, and Horde. While not feeling any particular kinship to the Horde, she was glad for a place that, albeit grudgingly, welcomed her people. They were all simply arrows to Sylvanas, arrows with which to bring down the hated foe in Northrend.

But what hunter did not leap at the chance to procure more arrows?

Anasterian had been universally loved, and that love had been well earned. Like Sylvanas, he had died standing in the way of Arthas Menethil, though Arthas had allowed the king to lie where he fell. The prince had not been so benevolent with Anasterian's ranger-general.

And where had Kael'thas been? Idling in Dalaran, wearing purple robes and protected by his books and magic, while Sylvanas and her rangers fell, and his people were reduced to death and decay. He had not been welcomed with open arms, either, so her spies had said, though he did try to lead. She had heard that Kael had refused to accept the mantle as king. Anasterian was king, not he, Kael'thas had said so at his father's service. He made a vow to Anasterian's long-fled spirit that there would never be another quel'dorei king. Now Kael'thas was gone again, this time from the very face of Azeroth. He had gone through the Dark Portal, as Alleria had, and was searching for a way to cure his people's addiction to magic, a particularly cruel result of the Sunwell's contamination.

So many repercussions from the arrogance and weakness of a single mortal man. Sylvanas wondered where the shock waves would finally stop—if indeed they ever would. She suspected not. Some things changed the world, for good or ill, and those that did not change with them did not survive.

Without aid, those she had once called her people would perish, picked off by the lumbering Scourge, or emboldened trolls, or something less dramatic such as famine or disease. They had already been reduced to siphoning energy off the naaru, the mysterious, crystalline creatures who were of the Light in some way she did not yet understand. The rest would succumb, eventually.

Unless she helped them.

"Bring me pen and parchment," Sylvanas ordered one of her guards.

Unto Lor'themar Theron, Regent Lord of Quel'Thalas,
Lady Sylvanas Windrunner of the Forsaken sends greetings.

You may believe me when I say you and those you lead have my deepest sympathies for what was done by Arthas Menethil to the kingdom of Quel'Thalas. I was among those casualties, as were far too many others. But as I have adapted and changed, taking command of my own destiny and shepherding the Forsaken to a rightful place in this new world, I know the quel'dorei can as well.

The Scourge continue to erode the once beautiful land and attack its people. Our old enemies the Amani have taken advantage of your weakened state. You are nothing if not a practical strategist, Lor'themar, and I know you understand that your kingdom will truly be erased and your people extinct if you cannot push back your twin adversaries.

I also understand that you harbor a deep reluctance when it comes to accepting the undead as allies. I assure you, the Forsaken are not the Scourge. Arthas's monsters are animated corpses, nothing less—and nothing more. We are people, like you, with our own minds and goals and dreams. Allow us to prove this to you.

If you are reading this you, hopefully, have not executed my envoys on sight, as I believe King Varian did. Please give them safe passage with your reply, whatever it may be.

I offer you, my former right hand, this: I will send some of my finest Forsaken fighters to assist you in driving back the Scourge from the gates of Silvermoon. I am certain you will find them impressive.

If you still feel you cannot trust me, trust the hatred I and every Forsaken harbor for Arthas and the Scourge. No one loathes them as the Forsaken do, which you will see.

I await your response.

She signed it simply "Sylvanas," scrawled boldly in black ink. It felt right. As she watched the envoys bow and depart the royal chambers, Sylvanas frowned.

"Something wrong, my lady?" Varimathras inquired.

"No," Sylvanas lied. "Merely calculating the odds on my subjects returning with their heads attached."

There was indeed something wrong, but she would never admit it to her demonic servant. Part of her . . . was anxious. Not about the envoys, but about how the letter would be received. Would Lor'themar tear it up? Refuse? Send a scathing letter of reproach for what she did at the gates of Quel'Thalas?

Why did it matter? This should be nothing to her. They and their once too-pretty world should be nothing to her. The only thing that should be troubling her was if they would agree, so that when the time was right, she could use them in the final battle to bring Arthas to his knees, so she could strike the killing blow. Instead, unbidden, thoughts came into her mind. Images of hunts and battles, of blades clashing and arrows singing, of laughter and meals and sleeping under the night sky, hearing the rhythmic breathing of friends on either side of her.

She no longer breathed, and they were no longer friends.

A dull ache settled on her chest, as if something heavy lay there.

"Fetch Putress," Sylvanas ordered. "I would have him update me on the status of the blight."

Surely that would be sufficient distraction. Sylvanas would focus on anticipating each step in bringing down the enemy, and forget that once, she'd needed friends, and had them.

Sylvanas had been prepared to wait weeks for a response. But it came in less than a fortnight.

Lady Sylvanas—

I am in receipt of your missive, and shall ease your mind by informing you your envoys are being well treated. We are grateful for your generous offer, and I am yet more grateful to learn that you have liberated yourself and other victims of the Lich King's cruelty from his control. It is no small comfort to learn that one who had led us so well and courageously had not willingly performed such atrocities. We had heard rumors that you were no longer with Arthas, but I believe you can understand that we mistrusted this word after what we had witnessed firsthand in Silvermoon.

Know that I, and many others who have been forced to shoulder the mantle of day-to-day leadership since the death of our king and the absence of our prince, do understand that your Forsaken are in your own way as much victims of Menethil's atrocities as we are.

I hope that in the very near future, I shall be able to report that your soldiers and ours have succeeded in driving the Scourge out of Quel'Thalas due to working alongside each other for the greater good of all.

　　　　　　—LOR'THEMAR THERON, *regent lord of Quel'Thalas*

Thrall sat on his throne in Orgrimmar, resting his chin on one hand as he listened, blue eyes narrowed in concentration.

"Between the trolls and the Scourge, Quel'Thalas faces multiple challenges if it is to survive," Sylvanas said. "While I have others who depend on me now, I can attest quel'dorei skills, weaponry, and knowledge of magic can benefit the Horde greatly. They must have aid, or they will perish."

"The Horde has come to the Forsaken's aid in response to your request," Thrall said at last. "Your people have proven useful to the Horde, and I'm happy to reward that service. It seems odd to me that you would ask for this, though, a favor to those for whom you clearly had little love. You were more than ready to take the Forsaken to them before turning to the Horde."

"That is true," she said, "and who could blame me for hoping? I once was one of them. But the Alliance has better things to do, it would seem, than try to rekindle relationships with a race that has rebuffed them."

"But you do not," the warchief persisted, leaning forward. "You are not known for having a soft heart, Sylvanas. Why them?"

There were several reasons for her actions, the main one being strengthening her position in the Horde by bringing them another useful ally. But there were other reasons, too, feelings that she couldn't quite access, but that bound her to her former people nonetheless.

"Warchief," she said, "When Arthas invaded Quel'Thalas, not only did he nearly slaughter indiscriminately, but he took from those who remained their best hope for recovery: the Sunwell. It nourished and protected the quel'dorei for millennia. They became dependent on it, without even realizing it. When this magical source of energy was first befouled and later destroyed, they experienced, and continue to experience, severe withdrawal."

Thrall's strong brow furrowed. He nodded quietly; such a grim situation was familiar to him.

Sylvanas pressed the point. "Where would the orcs be, had you not escaped your enslavement and liberated the encampments? Reminded them of who they were, and the glory they would be capable of? The quel'dorei need someone to aid them and believe in them as well."

"Do *you* believe in them?" he asked, quietly, and she knew that though Thrall's heart was great and surprisingly kind for one with so much power, he was laying a trap for her.

Unexpectedly, she heard in her head her father's last words: *Believe in yourself, dear girl, as I have always believed in you.*

She spoke a partial truth. "Everyone needs someone who believes in them. I believe that once their pride is restored to them, they will repay the Horde's investment a thousandfold. They will rise to the level you think them capable of. And so, Warchief, I believe it is best for all involved, including the Horde, to think them capable of the greatest feats you can imagine. They will not disappoint."

She thought of Rommath's skills, of Lor'themar and Halduron and the Farstriders; of the craftsmanship of the quel'dorei artisans, and their passion in whatever they turned their hand to, and allowed herself a smile. When she spoke again, it was with the complete truth.

"They will not disappoint you at all."

Lor'themar Theron, however, was not as easy to convince as Thrall had been regarding the mutual benefits of the elves joining the Horde. Thrall's letter, which had a few conditions attached to it, was politely but firmly rejected. Sylvanas's request was received no better. While they were grateful for her aid, Lor'themar said, the Horde had done too much harm for the elves to see them as allies.

Sylvanas let time do what persistence could not. After a few more months, Lor'themar agreed to allow a small group of Horde representatives to enter Silvermoon. They were permitted an audience with the regent lord, but no promises were made. Still, she waited. The hour was not dire, at least not yet. Putress was making progress, growing more arrogant and self-centered with every successful experiment, but he was a long way from making something that was usable. The Lich King was not stirring, and so the Dark Lady cultivated patience.

Finally, an emissary was sent to Thrall. Lor'themar had agreed to Thrall's conditions, but the regent lord had a few of his own. One such was that they meet in Quel'Thalas, not Orgrimmar. Another stipulated the maximum number of attendees from any race.

And so it was that Sylvanas Windrunner found herself astride a skeletal steed—one of the few beasts that would consent to bear her—standing at the entrance to the land of her birth.

The last time she had been here, her body was still clumsy. Yet she had made it all the way from Deatholme to the Farstrider Retreat, only to be met with disappointment bitter as gall. Before that, she had murdered so many here, merely with her voice. Now she would use that voice to bring them to the table.

She, Thrall, Cairne, and Vol'jin of the Darkspear trolls rode through the arching gates. Once resplendent in their white and gold and red glory, the great gates now looked as sad and dark as the surrounding gloom. There was despair on either side of the gate, now: Eversong had become the Ghostlands, and verdant farmlands were turned to Plaguelands.

A group of Farstriders had gathered to escort them the rest of the way to the enclave. Sylvanas recognized none of them—save one.

"Halduron Brightwing," Thrall said. "I am Thrall, warchief of the Horde. This is the tauren high chieftain, Cairne Bloodhoof. And—"

"Oh, we've met," Sylvanas said. "I trust you are well, ranger-general."

"I am," he said. His dark blond hair was still unkempt, and as ever, she wondered that it didn't get in his eyes. But his voice was deeper, cautious, and his visage so stern that Sylvanas found it hard to believe he had once laughed at the slightest provocation. *How many dark days has it been, my old friend,* she thought, *since any of us truly laughed?*

"Please, follow me," Halduron said, turning his gaze to Thrall, Vol'jin, and Cairne. "Your retinue will wait here. We will tend to their needs during the proceedings."

Cairne narrowed his eyes, seemingly unhappy with the announcement. Thrall started to speak, but Sylvanas interrupted him.

"Halduron is honorable," she said, tactfully withholding the memories where he had not been above duplicity if it would win the battle.

Halduron's head whipped around. Some of the guardedness fell from his face, and Sylvanas saw in the familiar features surprise, sorrow, and repugnance.

"If Lor'themar Theron wanted us dead," she continued, "we would be so, and never even know what had felled us. There is no ambush lying in wait, High Chieftain."

Cairne grunted and inclined his head. It was a gesture of respect among the tauren, but it always looked to Sylvanas as if the old bull was about to charge.

"I know it be hard for the elves, trustin' a troll," Vol'jin said. "For my part, I an' my people be takin' no offense."

Halduron's brow knit. Sylvanas knew him so well, she could almost read his mind. He, who had captured the dreadful Zul'jin only to lose him, was analyzing Vol'jin as he had analyzed her, weighing the benefits of trust.

"Trust is indeed earned, not given," he said to Vol'jin, "but many things have changed. Most for the worst. But . . . perhaps some for the better."

They followed the new ranger-general along the Thalassian Way, a route Sylvanas could have walked in her sleep . . . had she still slept. Everything was at once so familiar, and yet so strange. In recent years, she had become unused to dappled sunlight filtered through gold leaves; to birdsong and the smell of green, living things.

We named you for the beautiful woods of our homeland.

Farstrider Enclave, once the southernmost home of Farstriders stationed to patrol the area, was now almost deserted. Its open-air design and winding walkways made the place feel enormous and looming. But the fire in the center blazed, as it always had, and Sylvanas felt an odd sense of comfort. She glanced out at Lake Elrendar, remembering the bright blue mirror reflecting the cloudless skies. Now it looked murky and sick, like the rest of the land, and Sylvanas felt an odd pang.

Lor'themar, Jirri, and Salissa awaited them. Compared with Lor'themar's patrician composure, Halduron appeared a lively chatterbox. Theron spoke with perfect courtesy, but as if to a stranger; formal, polite, and distant.

His demeanor set the tone for the negotiations. Having brought Thrall and Lor'themar to the table, Sylvanas had little interest in the particulars and listened with only half an ear to the conversation, chiming in when necessary and retreating into herself when not. Thoughts came and went, like clouds on one of the afternoons when she and her three siblings would lie on the soft grass, pointing out shapes in the puffy whiteness, finding significance in nothing at all.

Was this the nature of things, in the end? That one was born, and then one died, and one needed to find meaning in the journey? Were they nothing without some sense of purpose?

The thoughts disturbed her. She had a purpose, clear and simple, and fulfilling that purpose was meaning enough.

Food was brought and consumed by those whose bodies still needed nourishment. Sylvanas noticed the springpaw appetizers, and her mind went back to that day that seemed like centuries ago, when Alleria had been running flat-out and the Mauler was close behind. How young they had been. But there was another memory, too, specifically regarding the delicacy itself. Someone had been very fond of it—

"Lord Saltheril," she said, suddenly. Lor'themar stopped mid-chew and looked at her sharply.

"What about him?" Halduron asked.

"Did he survive?"

"He did," Lor'themar said. "Not even Arthas Menethil could halt his parties for long. He still holds forth, pouring—and drinking— Suntouched with reckless abandon. I wonder if that is his way of clinging to sanity—or, perhaps, avoiding it."

"Well," Sylvanas said, "I suppose it is good that some things never change."

For a moment, just a moment, a tiny splinter of time, there was warmth among the three of them; shared memories of music, wine, and soft summer days sweet as spun sugar, and as fragile.

Then the moment was gone, and it did not come again.

The negotiations did not take long. Everyone knew that the biggest hurdle—that of the blood elves agreeing to even speak with the Horde representatives—had already been cleared. The rest were details. Parchments were brought, signatures and seals were affixed, and it was done.

The formalities continued, though. Lor'themar politely offered the warchief and all who had accompanied him lodging in Silvermoon for the evening. Thrall declined with equal courtesy, yet agreed to a tour of the famed city. As he and Cairne rose and began to walk to their waiting mounts, though, Sylvanas paused, then turned to Lor'themar.

"Tell me, Regent Lord," she said, "you now call this place the Ghostlands."

"Yes," he said, adding, "for the dead now outnumber the living." He was clearly trying to keep a hard edge out of his voice. He failed.

Sylvanas only nodded. "Since I have come all this way, I should like to see my home again. I hope you have no objection."

Even if he did object, he could not say so. Not when he had just agreed to join the Horde, with her as a leader of one of those Horde races—just as the blood elves were now.

"Of course not, Lady Sylvanas. I trust you do not need an escort."

"I know the way."

CHAPTER NINETEEN

hosts.

How many of them were there, here in her homeland? How many had Sylvanas herself birthed with her song of torment and death?

Sylvanas did not go directly to Windrunner Spire. She instead traveled up the road for a long time, nodding to the Forsaken she had sent to Tranquillien, noting the unnaturally aggressive, and sometimes horribly transformed, wildlife in the area—as well as the Scourge who prowled near the Scar.

She passed the road branching to the east and continued on to Goldenmist Village. She'd had friends there, once. Before the orcs, before Arthas. Before . . . everything.

The skeletal horse obediently bore her toward the village, but then Sylvanas halted it. She could see the curves of the buildings, the same graceful curves that were utilized throughout the kingdom. In the pallid, sickly light, she could make out figures moving. Figures who had an odd light of their own, who were translucent, but bore the form of elves.

Sylvanas almost turned back to the road, but something stopped her. Anger, never far, always hot, flared in her like a torch. This was *his* doing—he whom she hated with all that was in her. Just as *she* was his doing, now. She could not change that. But she could do something about the spectral beings who had once been quel'dorei.

Sylvanas uttered a war cry as she charged, releasing the reins and reaching for her bow with one hand and an arrow with the other. She aimed and let fly, a smooth motion, perfect in its accuracy and grace; one she had made so many times she could not count them all. It was as natural to her as running, as drawing breath when she lived, as hate in her undeath. She looked for those she knew, to whom she might whisper a parting word, but their features were a blur. They were solid enough to destroy, however, in their bizarre semi-present existence, and she cut them all down, not knowing if they would return or if she had perhaps sent them to a better fate than this half-life they endured.

Sylvanas dismounted and regathered her arrows, which appeared almost exaggeratedly solid in nigh-transparent bodies. There was nothing on the tip to indicate a kill.

There were not many of them, and for that Sylvanas was grateful. But there were enough. The horse's hooves clattered on stone as she rode the creature down every street, checking every home, taking down every specter she could find, until she had searched the entire village.

She remounted and turned south.

A sense of dread seeped into her. How was that even possible? She, the Dark Lady, the Banshee Queen. Doubtless children were frightened into good behavior by the very mention of her name. She commanded the dead, she feared nothing.

Except it would seem she did.

The outskirts of Windrunner Village came into view. The ruination Arthas had brought with him had claimed this place, too. Her memories of it were grim and painful. For a moment her mind's eye saw it littered with corpses, some elven, some orcish. But then, the grass had been green, the sky blue. Now there seemed to be nothing other than silence.

Sylvanas steadied herself and rode forward.

The still air broke into sound, and gray figures began winging their way toward her. Gargoyles; Arthas's pets that he had left behind to guard the area. Guard it from who? The quel'dorei were all but extinct.

A memory flashed into her mind: Standing to face Arthas atop his undead horse. *I am Sylvanas Windrunner, ranger-general of Silvermoon. I advise you to turn back now.*

Death itself, as he had gloated, had come to her land, and she was powerless to stop it. She aimed and fired—and Arthas, wielding Frostmourne, the blade that was to take her life and so much more, sliced the arrow in two.

Death in the form of animated gray stone, dropping from the sky to seize Vor'athil, snarling, snatching him up with sharp fingers. The elf had survived so many battles, including the legendary Battle of the Seven Arrows, but a carved monster would be his end. His blood dripped like warm, wet, coppery rain on her face. Her arrow failed her again, this time shattering against stone.

The gargoyle dropped its plaything, but not before slashing Vor'athil's throat.

How terrifying they had been, to the woman who had been ranger-general. Now she brought them down easily, almost casually. She was so much stronger than they; so much stronger than the woman she had been on that dark day.

But once the threat was ended, Sylvanas did not feel so strong. Other memories, older but still painful, were surfacing powerfully. Here was where the girl in the wine-red dress had fallen. Over there, she had discovered Belaria Salonar. Closer into the main part of the village, Aravan and Rendris had died.

And there . . .

She dismounted and walked to the place where the great hurt, the wound that had dogged her feet with its weight of grief and guilt, had been inflicted.

Sylvanas stood where she had found his body. Where the Little Lord Sun, so glorious and bright and warm, had been slain. A setting sun, but there was no dawn for those he left behind. He was gone.

At least, she hoped he was gone. Or did she?

She had seen no ghosts, not here. Now, in the silence and the unnatural twilight, she spoke his name.

"...Lirath?"

Sylvanas waited, tense, hoping to see his face, even translucent and spectral, but also dreading to see it.

Silence. Slowly, she relaxed. Exhaustion settled upon her, and she realized just how much his death continued to affect her.

It seemed as though her baby brother was truly resting, in the peace he so deserved after the tragedy he did not.

Calmer now, Sylvanas rode to where his grave was. It was still in Eversong, and wilting grass covered it, all but hiding the slight swell in the earth. Arthas had not raised him, and she was profoundly glad for his one unknowing act of mercy.

Sylvanas sank down at his graveside on the sun-warmed grass, drawing her knees to her chest and resting her arms on them.

"I am so sorry," she said, quietly. "I thought I was doing the right thing. I've thought that every time, every step. And it *has* been. I died protecting my people. I fought for my freedom. I reached out to friends, who I thought would—"

She bit her lip for a moment, then continued.

"I did what I needed to do to ensure my survival and that of others like me. Sometimes, there are no good choices, and yet one must still choose." She shook her head. "Is it even a choice then? I wonder. I cannot trust the living to understand. Perhaps . . . you will."

That there was something after life, something good, and comforting, she knew. It had almost been hers. If there was any justice, anywhere, that place, that feeling, that softness was now Lirath's.

"I wish we had gone there together, my Little Lord Sun," Sylvanas whispered. "I accomplished nothing, in the end. I died, and I did not stop Arthas, and I existed only to harm at his whim for too long. I am no hero, I am but a fool,"

Her own ears could hear the pain and self-pity in her words, and that angered her suddenly. What was the use in pathetic wistfulness? The gentleness of that place she had glimpsed was gone, and softness would do her no good. There was no place for it now, in her world. She needed to be strong and focused, and to hew to her purpose no matter the cost. The Lich King slumbered for the moment, deep in his ice, but not forever. Not forever. And the world could not bear what he would wreak upon it a second time. Anyone who could not see that was a fool.

She had come to see if her brother was a spirit, and to send him to peace if so. But he appeared to have gone before her, in all ways, and there was no need. It was both a comfort and an ache, and as she mounted her steed and turned its skull to the south, Sylvanas vowed to cease prodding this old wound and, like the ranger she had been and still was, return to the hunt.

Sylvanas was heading toward the Apothecarium, to demand an update from Putress, from whom she had heard little recently, when one of her rangers stopped her.

"My lady," she said, "You have a visitor in the royal chambers, seeking an audience with you."

"Someone I know?"

"I am uncertain, my lady, but I assured them you would meet with them. They bear a gift for you, I believe."

Sylvanas had little patience for the less consequential, more polite aspects of running a city and a government, and scowled. She barely had time for her lieutenants and advisers let alone some adventurer or peasant bearing a gift, but she was mindful of courtesies.

Still, she was curt, even when they pulled out a piece of jewelry that looked somehow familiar. Sylvanas plucked the necklace from their grasp and was stunned.

It was beautiful, and terrible, and ignited a cascade of chaotic emotions. Memories she thought locked behind a solid wall burst forth, almost overwhelming her.

To Sylvanas. Love always, Alleria.

Crafted to their mother's wishes, based on the colors her daughters had worn one night. Given to Alleria by both father and mother as she left for the wider world that called to her, so Alleria would not forget her family. Broken down by the eldest daughter and gifted to each of them.

"It can't be," she whispered. "After all this time . . . I had thought it was lost . . . forever."

She had worn it the day she had fallen to Frostmourne.

She was already far too raw from her visit to Quel'Thalas, from stilted conversations with old friends, to fighting the ghosts of people she had known, to the graveside confession. This sent her reeling, and she turned her full fury upon the hapless traveler, who had thought only to do something kind.

"You thought this would *amuse* me?" she fairly spat. "Do you think I long for a time before I was the queen of the Forsaken?" She took a step forward, gazing haughtily down at the one who had given her this jeweled torture. "Like *you*, it means nothing to me, and Alleria Windrunner is a long-dead memory!"

She opened her hand, and the pendant dropped to the stone floor.

"You may now remove yourself from my presence," she told them. And they did.

She watched them go, both her hands now clenched into fists. Who was she ready to fight? The adventurer? Alleria? Fate?

Sylvanas stood for a long time. Then, slowly, stiffly, she knelt and picked it up, closing her fingers over it gently, so gently, as if it would shatter.

Nothing, she realized, was a long-dead memory. Everything simply lurked in wait, to remind her of what she had lost and those who had abandoned her at the worst possible moment.

Sylvanas closed her eyes, brought her fisted hand to where her unbeating heart was.

She had to hear it, one last time.

As she opened her mouth to sing, the softer voices of her banshees joined and a haunting, achingly beautiful sound came forth. It wandered like mist through the empty, echoing chamber, like something half glimpsed out of the corner of the eye. She could hear the harp as Lirath played, his pure tenor carrying the old song to listening ears.

They were children when they sang it, really; children who had no idea of the true depth of horror behind the words. Children who were so ignorant of what was out there in the world, and beyond it. Ignorant of the terror and grief that would soon shatter and scatter them. A song that was for Sylvanas fixed in time, sung when the world held beauty and was kind. It was, as its name stated, a lament of the Highborne, those who were gone and replaced by spirits, and corpses, and children of the blood.

Sylvanas listened for a moment, eyes closed, head bowed, then she, too, sang softly.

> Shindu Sin'dorei
> Shindu fallah na
> Sin'dorei
> Anar'alah belore
> Belore . . .

The last note hung in the air and then faded. Sylvanas paid no attention to the singers, who drifted off when they realized they were no longer needed—or wanted.

The last time she had sung it, the bright boy of sunshine lay cold and dead in her arms, his voice forever stilled.

Sylvanas found herself on her knees, trying and failing to stem all that she was feeling.

Why can't I let it go?

CHAPTER TWENTY

Arthas haunted Sylvanas's thoughts with almost pristine constancy. There were moments when she could shift her knife-blade-keen focus to other things, of course. Nothing important suffered from inattention. And there were other times when she surrendered to it; sinking into it, as if into a sludgy pool, feeling the murky waters close about her and envelop her with hatred-fueled righteousness.

She had taken some time to compose herself after the adventurer's surprising and upsetting gift, then again had headed to see the grand apothecary. Instead, she had spoken with Putress's subordinate, Master Apothecary Faranell. Putress himself was engrossed in an active experiment at the moment, Faranell explained, but had not forgotten that Lady Sylvanas wished to be notified the instant said experiments were successful, and so he had sent Faranell to demonstrate to the Dark Lady. Putress had given his word that once it had been completed, he would report immediately to her in the Royal Quarter.

Sylvanas was not pleased that *anything* had come before her in what remained of Putress's mind. She vented her irritation on the hapless Faranell as he led her through the main workstation, where bodies were dismembered and reassembled, and ingredients for some potions were ground while other concoctions bubbled away on small burners. They passed corpses, some really just a collection of a few body parts, hanging from hooks, and turned into a side room.

Cages hung from the ceiling, swaying gently, their occupants moaning softly, stirring faintly, or very still. Other cages were on the floor, some empty and open, others not. The captives were human, and Forsaken, but they were all test subjects.

She had initially objected to the idea of using Forsaken in such a manner, but Putress had made the persuasive argument that it was difficult, and dangerous, to attempt to catch an active Scourge.

"Why," he had exclaimed, "think how many Forsaken might be lost obtaining a single subject!"

Sylvanas had agreed, provided that the Forsaken in question were criminals and the disloyal who deserved such a fate. Putress promised, and she had not investigated further. The need was great. Soldiers went to war knowing they might die, but they would be dying for a reason. These Forsaken she now regarded would also die for the best reason possible—to rid the world of Arthas Menethil.

The one before her looked as if he was ready to die, anyway. No protesting, no anger or wheedling, or defiance. He just sat, quietly, his head lowered, waiting for death. Not quite a willing sacrifice, but at least a quiescent one.

Odd, that he would be, in his own way, as much a hero as anyone wearing gleaming plate and brandishing swords.

As for the weeping human female in another cage, Sylvanas didn't spare her a second glance.

A potion was administered to the living woman and the dead man. Sylvanas folded her arms and waited. The fragile human died first, of course. And for a long moment, Sylvanas thought the woman would greet death alone. But then . . .

Ah, but then.

Putress had done it. He had created something that could kill both the living *and* the Scourge. As Sylvanas strode back to the royal quarters, she could not help but gloat to herself. Arthas, and the humans who had birthed him, would be destroyed. He could no longer hide behind his armies of non-sentient, unfeeling corpses.

It is time for the great machine of preparation to grind to life, Sylvanas thought as she stepped beside the hulking form of Varimathras. Modifications had to be made to the formula, of course. A different, more universal, faster method of dispersion to discover. Armies to be gathered and sent to—

The sensation crashed down on her with such intensity it felt almost physical.

She felt in her body what her mind knew was not real; the cold slice of a bitter, wintry wind, howling like a child in pain.

Sylvanas did not know how she knew, but she did. Arthas—now the Lich King—was awakened.

She almost stumbled with the inner knowing, then caught herself. Her gloved hands clenched and unclenched, a gesture of rage and defiance. The first gesture she had been able to make when she was once again a creature of free will. She cast a quick look around, but it did not seem that any of the other Forsaken had experienced what she had.

"My lady?" Varimathras actually sounded concerned, though of course he was not. "What is it?"

"Something has happened," she growled. "Something to do with the Lich King. We need to step up our plans. I believe that time has suddenly become a precious commodity."

It began, as it had before, in a deceptive and cruelly simple manner—with sacks of poisoned grain. After so many years of once fertile farmland yielding nothing, hungry peasants were hardly ones to question food, even when it arrived in a mysterious manner, and before long the tainted grain had worked its dark magic. Those who fed upon it died, returning as ghastly undead creatures fit only to be slaughtered.

Chaos erupted, and the Lich King capitalized on it by sending necropoli across the world, spewing more and more Scourge into the terrified populaces.

Now, at last, the hour of the Forsaken had arrived. Sylvanas felt vindicated by how quickly the Horde reached out to them—them, the Forsaken, the ones accepted only reluctantly, the ones no one ever quite trusted or liked at the start. Now all the work the half-mad Putress had logged for years was receiving the appreciation it was due.

"Is it ready?" Sylvanas demanded.

"Not quite yet, but soon," Putress reassured her. "Do not worry, Sylvanas. Soon our dream of watching our living enemies, the Scourge, and the Lich King himself writhing in agony as a painful end consumes them—soon, it will be coming true."

"Do not forget yourself in your enthusiasm, Grand Apothecary. You will address me by my title."

He bowed. "Of course, my lady. I apologize."

"We do not know when fortune might smile upon us. We must be ready as soon as possible. And remember—you must not, under any circumstances, hesitate to deploy the blight if you have a chance at destroying the Lich King."

She rarely glimpsed his eyes, hidden as they were behind the long mask he wore, but she saw a sudden flicker, as if he had heard something of particular interest.

"Never fear, Dark Lady," he said, with a deep bow. "I will not forget."

Unity that had not been seen since Horde and Alliance worked together to defeat the Burning Legion when it swept across the lands of Azeroth. Old and new grudges were put aside. Plans were made and shared, and Sylvanas watched, amused, as both factions now welcomed the undead death knights who broke away from the Lich King into their ranks as valued assets. Nothing, it would seem, was more important than stopping Arthas, the rest of the world tasting a hint of the obsession that had all but consumed Sylvanas since the moment he yanked her back into what he expected to be eternal servitude.

When Arthas launched attacks on both Stormwind and Orgrimmar, it was the final straw. The Horde sent ships to Northrend, where they gained footholds at what they dubbed Warsong Hold, named for the Warsong offensive, and the Alliance followed suit with bases at Valiance Keep and Valgarde.

Meanwhile, the Forsaken sent their own contingent. Zeppelin after zeppelin was loaded with soldiers eager to at last have the chance at striking back at Arthas, and with barrels of extremely well-packed containers of the latest version of Putress's blight. Sylvanas was there to see them off. Like a general riding his mount up and down the lines of waiting warriors, the Dark Lady of the Forsaken sat atop a bat that winged its way between the vessels awaiting departure. When she addressed them, she used a faint amount of her banshee voice so that all could hear her.

"My loyal subjects," she said, and they roared their approval. "It is impossible to tell you how very proud I am of each one of you—and, I admit, not a little envious. For today, you embark on the greatest war that this world has ever known: a war to bring down Arthas Menethil, the Lich King, and forever destroy his abominable handiwork. You shall at last have the revenge so long denied you!"

More cheers filled the air, ragged though they were coming from so many damaged throats. Sylvanas steered her bat around for another pass over the crowded zeppelins, allowing herself a moment to savor the knowledge that all because of her, so many doomed beings had been rescued, had been given a home—and a purpose.

"Others say they despise the Scourge. I am certain they do, but their loathing is but a tiny candle to the scorching fire of our hatred!" More cheering. "And so I name this contingent of Forsaken . . . the *Hand of Vengeance!*"

She found herself smiling as she regarded them. This was the closest thing to true joy she had experienced since the day when Arthas had come to Quel'Thalas. He had destroyed their culture, their people. Now they would do the same to him. And they would do so with wonderfully vicious glee. If only she could be there with them throughout this adventure . . . but that was impractical.

Icecrown Citadel, where Arthas, now himself the Lich King, had amassed his forces, was made from saronite—an incredibly strong metal formed from the hardened blood of an Old God. Angrathar the Wrath Gate was also made of this evil substance. It would take a lengthy, and costly, siege to breach. Sylvanas would stay in the Undercity until the way to Icecrown was clear. But then . . . ah, then. She had nursed her all-consuming need for revenge for too long not to be part of the kill.

"The Hand of Vengeance shall *strike*!" she cried. "The Hand of Vengeance shall *crush*! The Hand of Vengeance shall wipe Arthas and his vile army from the face of our world! And all shall look upon the Forsaken with eyes of gratitude, eyes full of wonder at our might, our conviction, and our will. Go then, with fair winds, to Vengeance Landing, and begin the work that will doom our enemy!"

In the Howling Fjord, at Vengeance Landing, the Forsaken continued the work Putress had begun, enlisting the help of Horde members eager to assist in destroying the Lich King. Buoyed by their successes, the Horde and the Alliance pressed ever deeper into the icy continent, finally ready to assault the Lich King at the base of his own citadel of Icecrown.

At long last, the time had come. Horde and Alliance armies gathered at the base of the Wrath Gate, standing side by side with one single objective: to challenge the Lich King with their combined might, and to finally put an end to him and the Scourge. Both armies had sent famed warriors to lead the assault. The Alliance offered Bolvar Fordragon, a highly respected paladin who had served Stormwind in capacities as varied as regent lord (when King Varian had gone missing and young Anduin was, for a time, the youngest king in Stormwind history), and now as high general of the Valiance Expedition. Not to be outdone, Dranosh Saurfang, the son of the lauded warrior Varok Saurfang who also still served the Horde, was chosen to lead the assault for the Horde.

Sylvanas, normally so poised and still, now paced like a caged cat in the royal chambers, heedless of Varimathras's amusement.

"I have seen you on the eve of battle before, Dark Lady," he said. "And have never seen you so agitated."

"That was when I was to be on the battlefield—or at least commanding the units," she snapped. "And there have never been higher stakes."

"Indeed, your hatred for Arthas has always been unmatched, even by myself and my brothers."

Sylvanas did not bother to reply. Of course it was. They had not been twisted by the Lich King as she had been.

She decided to walk off her agitation, telling Varimathras she would be back shortly. As she strode along the canals and through the various quarters, she could sense a heightened level of anxiety. It was to be expected. Everyone knew the battle was coming or, had begun. Perhaps already been won—or lost . . .

Sylvanas shook her head, angry with herself. No. The Horde and the Alliance had come so far together. There was the odd attack, of course; things did not change overnight. But the leadership on all sides had been grounded, even about their shared goals. Word had reached her that a friendship of sorts had developed between Saurfang the Younger and the paladin Bolvar; they coordinated attacks to the benefit of all. Sylvanas did not think any armies had been stronger, with so clear and so personal a cause. Surely they would destroy the Wrath Gate. And once they did . . . she would travel to Northrend, and take her vengeance.

Somewhat calmer, she returned to the Royal Quarter, frowning to see that Varimathras was not there. She had told him she would not be long, and she hadn't been. He should have been there waiting in case anyone had arrived with news from the battle. Even as she had the thought, he entered, fairly racing up the ramp toward the dais, his long goat legs covering yards with every leaping stride.

"My lady," he said, "I have been trying to find you. Putress has returned with a report!"

"What?" She was furious. "Why didn't you simply have him wait while you sent for me? Where is he?"

"He was wounded," the demon said earnestly. "He is being tended to in the Apothecarium. Come, we should hurry."

This made no sense, but the dreadlord was already moving and she had to hasten to keep up. Why would he report to the front, only to then leave? Why would he not stay on the battlefield and be tended to by the priests whose job it was to do precisely that? She remembered her reaction to him when they had first met. Even *he* had said his brain was riddled with worms. She could only hope that the news was at least good.

She and Varimathras hastened out of the Royal Quarter, her dreadguards falling in behind her. People watched in surprise as she passed, and again, Sylvanas picked up on a strange sense of anxiety. Many, many times, her senses and her instincts had saved her life or those of her comrades, and she understood that this was more than simple worries about the outcome of a battle. *Something is wrong. Varimathras is too concerned. Putress is in the Apothecarium and not the Royal Quarter where he knows I want him.*

She glanced surreptitiously to the right and slightly behind her. The dreadguards were dressed in their usual livery, carried their usual weapons. Wore the usual hoods . . .

. . . with the bottom part pulled up to cover most of their faces. *Dreadguards who are trying to hide their identities.*

"Oh!" came a gasp, and a woman collided with her right outside the entrance to the Apothecarium. Sylvanas was initially angry, then realized that the "accident" had been nothing of the sort, and was unsurprised when a small vial was pressed into her palm as she reached to help the fallen woman to her feet. As she bent down, their faces came close together, and the woman whispered, "Hurry, it won't last too long, my lady," then pulled back.

"My apologies, Dark Lady, I'm a bit clumsy today," she said, more loudly. "New feet, you see." She raised her skirts, shyly, as if she were a living young woman teasing a suitor with a scandalous glimpse of ankle.

"Leave Her Majesty be," Varimathras said with unnecessary gruffness, shoving the Forsaken to the side. This time, the woman's stumble was genuine, and for an instant all attention was on her. Sylvanas thumbed off the cork, swallowed a bitter liquid, and slipped the vial into her belt.

"We are in a hurry," Sylvanas said, sounding appropriately annoyed, and pressed forward briskly.

She gave nothing away, not by a misstep, or expression, or word. She was surrounded by enemies—one of which was a nathrezim—but in the small corridor, she dared not try to bolt now. From what she knew of both Putress and Varimathras, they would not do the expedient and intelligent thing—kill her quickly—but they would have something they wanted to show her, or tell her. That would buy her a few precious seconds to act. Up ahead was the cavernous Apothecarium proper, with its bloodstained slabs, cages for experimental subjects, bubbling potions, and pieces of bodies impaled on hooks that dangled from the ceiling.

Except there were no apothecaries.

There was no one in the room at all.

Except her dreadguards, hanging from the meat hooks, quite permanently dead.

Hollow laughter, far too familiar, echoed in the stone rooms. "Ah, Dark Lady," Putress said in a gleeful voice, "my blight was quite successful—and you did insist that I use it when I had the chance."

There it was. "Then you have done well. Why all the theatrics, though? If Arthas is slain by your blight, then we should celebrate. You will be a hero of the Horde."

As she spoke, her gaze flickered about the room in which she stood, and as much as she could see of the following chamber. The cages were empty. Was one of them intended for her?

"I fear that will be . . . problematic," Putress continued. "You see . . . I'm afraid there was some . . . spillage. Dranosh had a nasty accident with a runeblade, Bolvar developed a bit of a cough—as did a few hundred others. And Arthas left the party early."

Cold horror seeped through her, despite the danger of her present situation. "Putress . . . what have you—"

"What have *we* done," Varimathras interjected. "The Undercity is *ours* now. I will be the one to herald the master's victory, not you!"

There was no time to wonder what the demon meant. Sylvanas

had spied the cask, dark so as to be camouflaged in the shadows of the high ceiling. She was standing directly under it.

She sprang into action, leaping as far away as she could, twisting in midair to land behind the false dreadguards. They whirled just as she landed and attacked, their swords descending on her.

Their blades bounced off her shoulders, arms, and torso as if they had struck stone. Her skin was unmarred.

Sylvanas smiled, lowered her head, and slammed into the false dreadguards with all her strength. Varimathras snarled and leaped up, his batlike wings carrying him to safety as the dreadguards went flying. The casket crashed to the ground. Sickly green gas began to spread, quickly enveloping the guards, who struggled, and failed, to rise.

Sylvanas did not know if the potion would protect her from the blight as well as swords, but she took no chances. She raced up the corridor, hearing the screams before emerging to a scene of horror.

Clouds of blight were everywhere. Citizens of the Undercity were running frantically, trying to escape it and, Sylvanas realized, more mobile foes. Chaos was everywhere—and so were demons.

Something large and heavy clamped down on her shoulder: a terrorfiend. The winged demon's huge claws contracted, trying to dig in, but it snarled in surprise as its claws slipped, unable to get a grip on her smooth, impenetrable skin.

She had to get out. Sylvanas did not want to abandon her city, her people, but she was outnumbered. Her first thought was to head toward the Trade Quarter, but the stairs were already crowded with fleeing Forsaken, all jostling one another, shoving, desperate to escape.

Through the sewers, then. Could she get to them in time?

No. Sylvanas was on the wrong side of the city.

Something flew past Sylvanas and she struck out instinctively with her knife, only to yank her arm back in the nick of time. It was no flying demon, but simply a panicked bat who, like her, was trying to find its way out. When it came by for another pass, Sylvanas sprang atop its back and clung tightly.

As Sylvanas guided it northward, over the canals, she saw that the violence was spreading. Abominations, usually obedient servants, were attacking the citizens. Demons plucked up her people and dropped them in the canal for sport.

Putress and Varimathras had executed a coup and started a war with a single horrifying, grand gesture. Sylvanas was reeling. In the span of a few moments, it seemed that everything she had accomplished or had hoped to accomplish had been snatched away, like a toy from an unsuspecting child.

Arthas had escaped.

What should have been her greatest, most satisfying moment was instead stolen—twisted and used against her, against the Horde, and against the Alliance. In this one act, Putress had, instead of destroying Arthas—with quite possibly the only thing that could have killed him—slain those of the Horde and the Alliance who had chosen to fight together.

Sylvanas knew that, had Putress indeed been successful in killing Arthas, she would have counted the lives lost at the Wrath Gate worth it. Sacrifices must be made if Arthas was to be stopped. She allowed herself to believe that those who died this day would have deemed it worthy, too. Every single soldier in both armies was ready to die to stop the Lich King.

The blight had been squandered, missing its perfect target. Instead, it had killed the Lich King's enemies and rekindled a conflict that had been too briefly put to rest. Putress had defied her; she, who had taken that broken corpse with no memory and elevated him to one of the highest positions within the ranks of the Forsaken. She thought back on some of the last meetings they had, and realized she'd been foolish not to see the signs. His growing impertinence, his smug certainty. And if Varimathras's treachery was less of a surprise— she had never fully trusted the demon—it was nonetheless devastating to her cause.

Foolish of them, though, to have let her escape. If they had simply barricaded her in the royal chambers, she would easily have succumbed to the blight. Their vainglory, their arrogant need for her to see how clever and dangerous they were, would be their undoing.

Sylvanas would go to Orgrimmar, make an appeal to Thrall, and use the Horde to take her city back.

Varian blamed her, of course, though Sylvanas denied responsibility, and, as she had expected, he seized this opportunity to declare war. Even some in the Horde were deeply skeptical of both her and the Forsaken. This was certainly not the outcome she had worked so hard to achieve.

Fortunately, Thrall believed her. *Strange,* Sylvanas thought, *that standing beside me, believing in me, helping me—are the leaders of the same races who murdered my family.*

Over the years, she had come to accept that her parents had died in a war. That happened to soldiers. But even now, Sylvanas could not truly forgive Lirath's death. Thrall knew of it, of course, though she had never revealed the horrible details of it. That her Little Lord Sun had been barely more than a boy, only playing at being a soldier, when an orc had embedded an axe in his back.

No, she and the Forsaken—they would never truly feel they were part of a family, as the trolls, tauren, and orcs did. They were outsiders and always would be. She had thought otherwise, for a time, but she had been deluding herself.

Vol'jin was on her right, Thrall on her left. The warchief was issuing a battle cry. "Soon we march upon our fallen city and reclaim it for the Horde!" he shouted.

No. Not for the Horde.

For the Forsaken . . . and for her.

Sylvanas was not yet done with this war—or with Arthas.

With the Undercity restored to her, Sylvanas made her own way to Icecrown Citadel, refusing to deny herself the personal victory of slaying Arthas. But she had not encountered him since that day when the wretched Kel'Thuzad had snatched Arthas—and victory—from her at the last possible moment. Since then, he had become the Lich King, and when Sylvanas finally stood before him, snarling angrily up at his eyes glowing from inside the Helm of Domination, it was brought home to her just how powerful he really was.

She was forced to retreat, vowing to return.

And then the chance was gone. Something had destroyed the weapon—and the Lich King, too. Others had gone before her and stolen her kill.

Sylvanas Windrunner had been denied the moment she had held in perfect anticipation—to be the one to slay Arthas.

She felt it when the vile sword shattered. She should have been there. But she had not been, and for a long time she chose not to come.

In that time, the world had shattered, too, in many ways. Physically, the dragon known as Deathwing erupted from his rest deep in his earthen realm, bursting forth to fracture the world and reshape both it and its people. Prior to his monstrous rebirth, Azeroth's elementals had been in great distress, sensing what was to come. Thrall, a shaman as well as a warrior, traveled to his homeworld of Draenor to study the elementals there. They had survived a broken world; perhaps they could aid Azeroth during what came to be called the Cataclysm.

He passed the mantle of warchief to one of the heroes of the war against the Lich King, Garrosh Hellscream.

It had proven a grave mistake. A superlative warrior does not always make a good leader, and the Horde was beginning to suffer for Thrall's decision.

The Alliance, too, was shaken. The relationship between it and the king of Gilneas, Genn Greymane, tepid at best, had dissolved utterly after the Second War. Gilneas turned inward, even to the extent of literally erecting the Greymane Wall to keep out everything that could harm the kingdom, from wars to Scourge to any other humans. But the terrified elementals were no respecter of fee-

ble human walls, and the Gilneans, with all their secrets and vulner-
abilities, were thrust back into the world by a series of violent quakes.
Garrosh saw an opportunity, and, with the Forsaken under scrutiny
for Putress's attack, charged Sylvanas with taking Genn's kingdom,
to provide the Horde with a port in the region.

The message was clear: Sylvanas and the Forsaken were to obey.

The world was moving on to the next conflict, the next challenge.
But Sylvanas was mired in a past that she could not escape: that the
Lich King was dead, but she was still not truly free.

Before the invasion of Genn Greymane's kingdom began in
earnest, Sylvanas decided to make the journey—or, perhaps, the
pilgrimage—to where her adversary had finally perished.

She stood alone in the frozen snow, looking at the fragments,
now all that remained of the terrible runeblade, Frostmourne. All the
moments she had seen its cold blue gleam rushed back. In Arthas's
hand, slaying her people. Claiming her life, too, and binding her to
the Death Knight. Seeing it once again in the Lich King's grasp as
they confronted each other in the Halls of Reflection.

She dropped to her knees in the snow, crying out unashamedly as
pain far greater than anything physical bombarded her. Sylvanas had
thought her feelings dampened; all that had been left was rage. Now,
though, she felt everything all over again, and this time there was no
welcome filter of numbness. Nor was there, as there had been in life,
joy and kindness to soften the blows. All that existed for her now
were emotions painted in dark and violent shades. Madness danced
at the corner of her mind, and she wanted to surrender to it.

She gritted her teeth, made a fist, and got to her feet. No. She had
come too far to falter now. Perhaps there was still a flicker inside the
monster, a tiny flame she could yet extinguish.

Again, disappointment. Frozen pieces of armor. Blood in the
snow. But no Arthas, no Lich King, only the knowledge that she had
been too late to claim the triumph for which she had fought so hard.

Arthas was dead, and there was not even a victory by proxy. Another Lich King now sat upon the Frozen Throne.

She had achieved none of what she had so fiercely set out to do.

She had achieved nothing at all, save continuing to exist out of, perhaps, pure stubbornness. Now there was no reason to continue that existence, that failed attempt to hold back eternal night long enough for revenge.

Sylvanas knew she had been destined for peace, upon her death. For rest. A reward for sacrificing her life freely and courageously to save others.

But that had been the ranger-general's destiny, not the Banshee Queen's, and now, too late, Sylvanas understood.

Nine Val'kyr hovered, silent, as Sylvanas stood atop the peak of Icecrown Citadel, pulling memories out of her head to torment her, but she had one last act of defiance left in her.

Stay back. And stay out of my head!

The leap, freely taken, to perhaps the only place in this or any world that could mean certain death to the nigh-indestructible Sylvanas Windrunner—a long fall, to impale herself upon jutting spikes made from the blood of a god.

INTERLUDE

Sylvanas paused in her conversation, deciding to end it there for now. She had things to do other than tell stories to Anduin. The revisiting of this part of her unlife had proven, strangely, more difficult than anything else she had revealed to the young king. Besides, it amused her to leave him there, wondering how she had managed to escape with her life . . . such as it was.

Anduin looked stunned. "I . . . I had no idea that you had attempted to kill yourself," he said. He had doubtless picked up on the difficulty she had in relating the events, and looked more open than she had yet seen him. Perhaps she was actually beginning to persuade him.

"Not attempted," she corrected. "Succeeded. I succeeded."

He tried to hide it, but that bold statement shook him. However, instead of asking for more of the story—which Sylvanas was not going to reveal just yet—he said something that surprised her, though it should not have.

"But . . . you were wrong."

Her eyes narrowed. "Careful what you say, young lion," she warned. "You have no right to judge me."

"You misunderstand. You said that you had nothing left. But that *wasn't true. Even if you did not kill Arthas himself—he was gone. Dead. He would hurt no one, ever again. Was that not what you wanted?"*

"I am a hunter, Anduin, and someone had stolen my kill."

"So you didn't want him dead. You just wanted to cause him suffering."

The boy was baiting her. Being deliberately obtuse. Either that, or he was a shockingly brilliant advocate. But before Sylvanas could speak, he plowed on.

"You had a city filled with people who owed everything to you. They were yours. They would follow you anywhere. Don't you think every leader in Azeroth envied you that kind of devotion?"

Was he lying? He certainly seemed to believe what he was saying. "You had Nathanos. Your champion. From all you have told me, he loved you with all he had in him. And you—you could have easily given up on him, but you didn't. Very few ever know a love like that, Sylvanas. He was still there for you. Even death hadn't changed that. Do you understand how rare that is? And did you even spare him a thought?"

Damn the boy. "You speak of things you do not understand."

"I think it is you who doesn't understand what you had. Even your sisters. If you had reached out to them—"

"Silence!" *she shouted.* "None of that mattered, can you not see? All I had, truly had, the only thing that was uniquely mine, was my hatred. It was my anchor since the moment I became a banshee, the only thing that kept me from surrendering to despair and madness. It was the driving force behind all I did, thought, became. My revenge was everything. So much that had happened to me—my family, my people, my kingdom . . . my life . . . all came to an end in terrible ways. Being the one to kill Arthas would be the one small shred of justice I would ever wrest from a world that had wronged me. I was owed that moment of victory, and I was denied it. I was owed a clean death, an eternal rest, befitting what I had given the world in life. And I thought—This, this ending at least I can have on my own terms. I had tasted it, just once. I knew it was there, waiting. So I took it."*

He had been silent, focused with his whole being on every word.

Sylvanas could not walk away, not now. He had to know what she had experienced.

"But when I died . . . I was given nothing. And then . . . the Jailer gave me . . ."

What? Something greater than her deepest need or want. More than she had ever thought to hope for, or dream of. The last thread of pain, for her, for all that ever had and ever would exist, would be woven into a tapestry of joy and rightness that had never before been possible.

Anduin hung on her words, and when she fell silent, trying to find them, he said, quietly, "What, Sylvanas? What could he possibly give you that would justify so high a cost?"

She turned her face to his.

"Everything."

PART
IV

We are the same, Sylvanas Windrunner. We fought for something greater than ourselves and were made to suffer for it. Each of us twisted into an effigy of our own damnation.

—THE JAILER

Even in death, the Val'kyr would not leave Sylvanas. They held her, showing her a premonition: the end of the Forsaken. There was a great battle, and her people were pouring through the breach in staggering numbers only to be greeted by artillery and musketfire, falling, toppling down, seemingly by the dozen. Wave after wave fell, and Sylvanas saw the adversary. Not human, no, but the half-wolf, half-human beasts known as worgen. She was seeing the invasion of Gilneas. The sounds were muted, distorted, as if in a dream, but somehow Sylvanas knew this was nothing so harmless. Still, she told herself that it wasn't real.

The visions kept coming. Her people, in every scenario, were used by the Horde, sacrificed to win victory for the more "worthy" living members. Without her there to safeguard them, the Forsaken would die, down to the last one, used up like the finite resources they had been.

Let them perish! I am finished with them!

The Val'kyr granted her the oblivion she sought—but it was nothing like what she had briefly tasted before.

How foolish she had been her whole life. Naïve, to think that her death could have helped anyone. Stupid, to believe that revenge would bring satisfaction. And above all arrogant, to think that her deeds would not have consequences.

She saw only darkness, but it was not empty, and it was not oblivion. This was brutal cognizance; painful, agonizing presence, even though she lacked a body with which to physically feel. Emotions ripped her apart from inside her own awareness: agony, fear, regret.

These were the weapons the *things* around her used to torture a soul, as a mortal torturer used pincers, racks, and shears to physically torture the body. But the body had its blessed, welcome limitations: Unconsciousness. Death. An ending.

This did not. The gleeful, targeted torment would have no end, ever. No becoming numb to the pain, no disassociation from the physical—nothing between her and the agony, each twist or revelation more painful than the next.

Sylvanas would have screamed, but she had no mouth.

The single word came, thundering through the cacophony of silent excruciation.

ENOUGH.

And the torment ceased, though the memory, the horrible memory, continued.

How could she see, with no eyes? Move, with no body?

You perceive this place because I will it to be so.

Could she speak?

Yes.

"Show yourself, then!"

The darkness lightened slightly, shifting from utter blackness to a shadowy, gray-green gloom. Before her loomed an enormous shape not merely large, but *vast*. Powerfully built, he was human-like, but on a gargantuan scale. Around him were manacles and broken chains with links larger than she was tall scattered on the stone floor. The being was swathed in shadow, save for the hazy glow of blurry runes running along his spread arms, around his waist, and on his lowered face. He was barefoot and bare-chested, remnants of what must once have been armor on his lower arms, waist, and neck. He still wore pieces of chains, their ends glowing brightly with magic. Sylvanas sensed eternity weaving around and through him.

"This is the Maw. Only those utterly beyond redemption are banished here. And here, they will be tortured for all time."

Sylvanas regarded the figure. Now that the pain had receded, she could at least attempt control of her seething emotions, and chose to focus on the being.

"You were a prisoner," she said.

"I still am."

"Then who rules this . . . Maw?"

"I am the Jailer here."

His words were riddles. She decided to press him. "You claim to be both prisoner and jailer. What a curious fate you have chosen."

The deep voice grew bitter. "No one is here by choice, Sylvanas Windrunner."

He knew her.

"If my decisions brought me here, didn't yours as well?" Sylvanas asked.

"Your mortal mind does not yet understand," he replied, his voice weary but patient. "The greatest deception that the makers ever perpetrated was to fool us into believing that we have a choice in any facet of our existence."

The words struck her. She sensed the truth in them. "And what do you know of my choices?" She moved closer and saw that his skin was a hue of gray similar to her own, though she still could not make out the runes scribed onto his flesh.

"You have fought so hard for freedom, Sylvanas Windrunner, for control. It is a battle that I have fought as well, and one that I have witnessed play out across the eons more times than there are numbers to count. And all those battles, courageous and foolhardy alike, were for naught."

"I fought for and *won* free will, Jailer," Sylvanas shot back. "The instant I could, I wrested control back from my tormentor. I killed *when* I wished, *who* I wished. And when the vengeance I sought was denied me, I ended my life *as* I wished."

He sighed, and his next words were tinged with what could almost be compassion. "I am Zovaal. Before I was the Jailer of this place, I reigned over the realms of Death from the precipice of eternity itself. I stood as Arbiter over every mortal soul whose brief flicker of life had sputtered out. In an instant I knew the entirety of their existence. And time after time, do you know what I saw? Fragile beings left to the fickle whims of fate. Their world, their kin; whether they were wise or simple, hale or sickly; these things were forced upon them. From the moment they drew their first breath until they exhaled their last, the choice was never theirs. And when their lives ended, it was my duty to decide their soul's fate for all eternity."

Anger flared as she thought of her own life. The decisions made for her. "No. I refuse to believe this nonsense."

"Most deny it. A few eventually accept it. But no one can escape it, because escape has never been a part of the makers' grand design. *No one* escapes the Maw or any of the infinite afterlives forged to bind mortal souls. From its conception to execution and throughout all that has been, and is, the design is gravely, cruelly, and worst of all *indifferently* flawed."

When Arthas struck her down, Sylvanas had felt, just for a moment, the peace that had awaited her. Had that been part of this . . . flawed design? How could her situation, her death at the hands of Arthas, from the blade of Frostmourne—how could that have been inevitable? Her mind, still reeling from the cacophony she'd endured earlier, could not wrap itself around such a thing, not yet, and so she focused on something else.

"Why are you here?" she asked him. She did not care, but as long as he was speaking to her, the torment had ceased. And she did care about that, deeply. "What was your crime?"

"I dared to defy the will of the makers. I sought to break their flawed design, to replace it with a better one. And for this, my own kin condemned me to this unjust fate. A fate I must share with the damned, broken souls I oversee."

Again Sylvanas thought of all she had endured in life, and in undeath. Resentment, drowned out by blind agony, crept in again.

"In many ways, your story echoes my own," the Jailer continued. "We were both betrayed . . . and broken. I, too, was torn asunder, and I understand well what it is like to feel achingly, eternally incomplete."

He lifted his gray, hairless head. His eyes glowed the same hue as the blur of runes that led from either side of his nose down his face, one in the center of his forehead. Her gaze drifted down to the gaping chasm in the center of his chest.

Something in Sylvanas was terrified by that sight—a fear deep and primal. Had she hands of flesh, they would have clutched at her own lifeless heart. How often had it seemed to her that her chest was simply devoid of one?

Sylvanas thought of her death, of how Arthas's hatred and petulance had ripped bliss away from her when it was almost hers. How the world she gazed upon with unliving eyes seemed a shadow of the one that haunted her memories.

"They ripped out your heart," she murmured.

"Far more than that," the Jailer said. "I sought to change the fate of all. And for *that*, I was torn in two. They took the essence of my power and fashioned a new Arbiter, one without a will to defy the grand design. Then my own brother carved into my flesh the runes that were meant to bind me for eternity."

Her eyes focused on the glowing symbols, and for the first time the hazy shapes hardened into crystal clarity. And in that instant, she summoned forth the banshee's wail to shatter the darkness with her rage.

"*Frostmourne!* You bear the mark of the blade that ended me!"

The Jailer's voice remained cold, dispassionate. "A blade designed by the vengeful mind of my brother. The same brother who used his words of Domination to bind me."

Her mind raced. Could what he said be true? Could all the destruction and torment inflicted upon her world by Arthas Menethil be architected by the same cruel beings that created this Jailer? Her soul blazed like fire at the thought of it.

"You see it now, do you not?" His words were thick with bitterness. "We are the same, Sylvanas Windrunner. We fought for something greater than ourselves and were made to suffer for it. Each of us twisted into an effigy of our own damnation."

An effigy of my own damnation. Oh, how this piece of it gripped her. Arthas had done this to her. Snatched her away, siphoned her soul into the coldest of blades, forced her to use her voice, raised in the darkest way possible, to kill the innocents. And for that, she was doomed.

Even as she had the thought, she felt a faint stirring, a slight brush at the back of her mind.

He was here. Somewhere in the Maw. Of course he was. Arthas Menethil, the brightest of lights seduced into becoming the darkest of shadows. But it was not the grinning, sadistic master. It was a little boy, lost and alone and confused.

"I knew you would sense him," the Jailer said.

"How could I not?" she replied. "His voice was inside my head long enough."

"Does it please you to know he is trapped here, in the inescapable darkness?"

Sylvanas thought of all the long hours when she had rapaciously plotted Arthas's demise. She was a hunter, and knew how to remove skin and organs from the fallen prey. She wanted him to suffer—and he was.

And yet.

"Not even this gives me joy," she said quietly.

"Nothing will give you joy," he said. "This is the Maw."

The words struck her almost physically. He was right. There could be only suffering in such a place.

A thought struck her. "Jailer," she said. "Why did you pluck me from my torment, if it was fated that I endure it?"

"Because nothing escapes the Maw . . . *until it does.*"

The impact of his statement settled on her, so heavy and full of portent Sylvanas could almost feel it.

"You know a way to escape."

"It took countless eons for me to summon the strength to break my chains. Countless more for me to turn the runes used to bind me into a weapon I could wield. And though I could not leave the Maw, I found the means to extend my will beyond this prison, and sought allies who shared my vision for what must be done."

"What do you mean?"

"It needs to end. Life. Death. All of it. I know how to break it. And the place I must go to rebuild it."

"And the success of your plan, constructed and honed over untold millennia, depends upon the aid of allies like me?" she scoffed. "I doubt that very much."

"You are wise to be skeptical," the Jailer replied. "But a thing is no less true simply because you do not believe it. As Arbiter, I judged countless mortal souls from worlds beyond your imagining. And in all that time, none surpassed the potential of those that came from your world of Azeroth. Your wills are fierce, and yours is the fiercest I have yet encountered."

"Flattery," she retorted, growing inexplicably angry with the giant being. "You think I would be swayed by that?"

His voice took on a new tone. Not pleading, or wheedling—this one would never beg, she could tell—but sincere. And surprised. "You fail to see the greatness you are capable of. You have been underestimated. Unappreciated. But you failed no one."

Lirath, she thought, but did not say.

"You saved so many, some who did not even want your help, who did not deserve your help—but you saved their lives regardless."

She thought of her keening at the gates of Quel'Thalas, the sight of so many simply dropping down into death. If only the Jailer were right.

"The false Arbiter of the Shadowlands saw that, and *still* sent you here. It is not Arthas you need to be free of. It is your own mortality. Our path will have no place for the compassion, the regrets, the guilt of the living. It will have no place for their morality, because it, just like the machine of death, is at its heart flawed. And that flaw . . . is believing that anything is fair."

She was silent. So much *was* unjust, that was a painful truth. But predestination on such a scale?

"*I* believe . . . you spin a fantasy of lies to tell me what you think I most wish to hear. For all I know, Arthas and his blade were forged by your hand."

"I do not expect blind trust, and to that end, I offer two gifts. The first is knowledge, and the second, choice."

"Why?" Her tone was defiant, brazen. "Why offer gifts when you could just as easily compel me to carry out your will?"

"I do not desire a slave, Sylvanas Windrunner. I need an ally. Someone whose mind is keen enough to understand my goal, and who is strong enough to see it through, no matter the cost. Because nothing worth having comes without a price. I want you to choose to aid me willingly, with full knowledge of what I have done, for your own sake, and for those of everything that has or will live and die."

"I thought you said all our choices were made for us," Sylvanas replied.

"In life . . . and in death," he agreed. "But now, Sylvanas, in this moment, in this place, with me—you are neither. This is the first choice that is truly your own."

Had she a form, it would have trembled. It was a ludicrous thought, this idea of a lack of free will—and yet, as she thought back, she wondered.

"You have been studying me indeed, to tempt me with the one thing you know I value the most," Sylvanas replied. "Give me this knowledge you promise, then. And I . . . will choose."

The Jailer gazed at her unblinkingly for a long moment, then spoke.

"The mourneblade my brother designed was an object of immense power. Frostmourne was a harvester of souls, imbued with an insatiable hunger. A hunger I sought to use for my own ends."

"Wh-what . . . how?"

"Though I did not design the blade, the runes forged into its metal could be made to answer to my will." His words continued to hammer at her, striking her psyche with agonizing blows. "I used secret allies to guide the sword and the helm it was forged with along a path of my choosing. First into the inept hands of the Burning Legion, convincing the demons that it was a weapon they could wield. The instruments of Domination were to anchor the power of Death to your world of Azeroth. But the blade and helm found their way to Ner'zhul, a weak-willed orc whose mind was as broken as the world he shattered. He sought to bind himself to the body of his pupil, Arthas Menethil, yet it was the young prince who won that battle. So I sought to use this new Lich King to herald my coming, but his selfish desire for conquest made him defiant."

"You," she spat, her face contorted in a snarl of pure rage. "*You!* Not the Lich King, not Arthas—*you.* Do you know. Do you know *what you did to me?*"

"Arthas used Frostmourne to end your mortal life, but not by my command. He was too weak to truly master the mourneblade's potential. In the end, he used the tools of Domination to pursue his own selfish desire for power. He betrayed everything. His vows, his family, his friends, even himself, and that is why you can sense him here, powerless, frightened. Weak.

"But something survived the ashes of his failure. *You* did. Through the blade, I grew to know and understand you. You were strong when you lived, Sylvanas, and you are even stronger now. And you have the intelligence to understand, and the vision to see what can be done."

"I will listen to nothing you have to say," Sylvanas snarled. "Your words stink of lies! I am dead, I am *this,* because of you! Why would I ever aid you?"

"Arthas cut you down. I would have lifted you up. By my will, the torments that assailed you are held at bay. If my words are lies, then only more torment awaits you," he said. "If you distrust my words, then let your own perceptions reveal the truth of them. The Shadowlands are infinite. Though they would seem to be as varied as the souls who inhabit them, they all suffer under the yoke of the makers' oppression. My Val'kyr can show that everything I am telling you is true."

They appeared as the Jailer spoke of them, hovering, great wings beating steadily, their proud faces beautiful, strong, and resolute.

"Before you refuse me, remember what I am offering you. We will remake . . . everything. Life. Death. You will be by my side at each step. Together we will show every soul that both their lives, and the eternity that awaits them, are prisons. And we will bring them true freedom."

CHAPTER TWENTY-TWO

Sylvanas gazed at the mighty women, the steady beating of their wings creating the only breeze in the stillness of the Maw, and up, up, into the face of the Jailer.

Despite her searing anger, she had nothing to lose if she took advantage of his offer. As long as this mammoth being thought she was considering allying with him, she would be spared torment. She realized with only the tiniest brush of shame that at this moment, she shared a desire with every prey she had ever hunted, perhaps the simplest and most primal: a desire to exist without pain.

Sylvanas did not believe him, of course. She had learned to be instantly wary of anyone who assured her she would have her desires granted. It was one reason she had learned to drop her guard only with Nathanos, as he never played those games—even if he knew he could escape suffering with a lie. This Jailer—his explanation was so grandiose, so fanciful, it could not possibly be true. *No one* could do what he said he could.

But she was in a prison—an inescapable one—if he was even telling the truth about that. Exploring the boundaries and the limits of her captors would do no harm and be a wise idea.

"Lady Sylvanas," said Agatha, "we await your command."

Sylvanas hesitated. The Jailer's lips curved into a smile. He lifted a huge hand slightly and the Val'kyr flew upward, listening intently as he said something to them. He turned his gaze to Sylvanas once more, inclined his head, pivoted, and walked away, the ground trembling slightly with his heavy footfalls. He would leave her alone with the Val'kyr.

She returned her gaze to them. "The Jailer assures me you can prove that all he has told me is true."

"We can try, my lady, but only you can decide if what you see is the truth."

Fair enough. "How much of the Shadowlands are open to you? How many afterlives could I experience?"

"My lady, they are unending, and new ones appear at the speed of the Arbiter's judgment," Aradne said. "And we must be cautious. The covenants of the Shadowlands believe the Jailer to be a helpless prisoner. Should they perceive us moving among the realms of Death, it could imperil the master's plans. It is only because of his faith in you, and his unyielding will, that we dare show you anything at all."

This made sense to Sylvanas, though it was also terribly convenient. She wondered what the mighty being had whispered to them.

"What do you wish to see?"

That was not the question Agatha should have been asking.

It was not what, but *who.*

She wanted to see Lirath. Wanted to speak to him, to embrace him, if she could, look into his glorious, kind eyes and hear him say, *It's all right, Lady Moon. I'm fine. I promise.*

Could she possibly find her father, who had held such faith in her? Would he understand the dreadful choices she had to make? Would he believe she belonged in the Maw? Would her mother?

Part of her shied away from that thought, returning to the safe haven that her baby brother's love had always been for her. Sylvanas opened her mouth to ask, then closed it.

She would give the Jailer nothing to use against her. Lirath's name would remain unspoken, the status of his spirit still a mystery to her.

For now.

Still, it would be good to know if the possibility of seeing some-one in particular even existed.

"If there was some individual I wished to see—could you take me to them?"

"Indeed, my lady, if visiting that realm lies within our power, you have but to name this person."

That caught Sylvanas off guard. She had no doubt her request could be turned against her as a weapon, if the Jailer knew how much Lirath meant to her. Who would she like to see that would not give herself away, but still be believable?

He who led the people who had slaughtered hers for thousands of years.

"Zul'jin," she said. She thought of Lor'themar, who had been tor-tured by the trolls; Halduron, who had caught the bloodthirsty, cun-ning leader. The troll had only turned the tables by cutting off his own arm like a rabid beast in a sprung trap. "Is Zul'jin of the Amani trolls here?"

"By your command, my lady. He is in a realm called Revendreth."

Sylvanas frowned slightly. Already she was starting to see what the Jailer meant. "If Zul'jin is not in the Maw," Sylvanas said, "then the Arbiter judged *me* past redemption . . . but not *him*."

How could that be just? In her life, she had done only good, no true harm. She had died protecting her people. She had not wanted to be brought back, to live an unlife, and since regaining her will, she had fought for others like her. Guarded and protected them. Even allying with the Horde, whose predecessors had taken so much from her. Had helped those who thought her monstrous when they were in need. How could Zul'jin, who massacred her people in the most gruesome manner possible, be judged more worthy than one who had literally sacrificed her life to save others?

"So," Sylvanas spat, "is Revendreth a place of endless bloodshed, violence, and victory, then? A pleasure palace, perhaps?"

"You shall see, my lady," Brynja said.

The wind of wings, the brush of feathers. Strong arms around her.

Light and heat pressed against closed eyes, and when she opened them, she was standing in a cold stone chamber lit only by the flicker of red candles, the licking flames of torches, and magic from demonic-looking beasts.

This was no pleasure palace. It was, if such a thing was possible, almost ghastlier than the Maw. Sylvanas reached for her arrows—only to realize she had neither bow nor quiver.

Agatha's hand fell on her shoulder. "Be still, Lady Sylvanas. We are merely observers here; we cannot be harmed, or change anything."

Sylvanas nodded, trying to comprehend exactly what she beheld. Something blood red floated in the air as what seemed to be hungry spirits dipped and dived about the figure. Great chains bound him, held him in place for the demons' amusement. The spirits flickered bright blue in their excited search for suffering.

"What are those crimson ribbons that whirl about him so?" Sylvanas asked. The figure was cloaked in a flowing, hazy shroud of red energy.

"Anima," Arthura said. "The power that fuels the Shadowlands. Mortal souls accumulate it in life, and it is given—or taken—to sustain the realms eternal. Here in Revendreth, it is drained from prideful souls seeking redemption. This is not a . . . pleasant process."

"Still a better fate than the Maw," Sylvanas said, her voice almost a growl. "He—"

Her words were cut off by an echoing roar of pain and rage. "I hate you!" he cried, straining against his bonds. "I hate you all! You will never break me! I will fight you for *eternity!*"

Sylvanas could make out his shape now. Bigger than most trolls, who were already large. Older, but powerful still.

And he was missing an arm . . . and an eye.

"It really is him," she said. "And you tell me that this . . . this thing that has made rivers of blood . . . he is to be given a chance at being redeemed?"

"Yes, my lady."

Sylvanas could not believe it. She watched the troll warlord continue to struggle, shouting out his defiance, and the crimson ribbons drank it all. True, it was definitely not pleasant. But even so ... the inequity of her situation and his was appalling.

"Are there other souls here in Revendreth from my world?" she asked.

"Oh, very many," they said, as if amused at a secret joke.

Sylvanas wondered who else was here who should have been sent to the Maw. "Take me to one of them," she said.

The wings whispered, soft against her face, and Sylvanas again opened her eyes.

A spectral figure, chained, while the anima was bled from him only to be refueled. Except ... that wasn't right. Something was different about the process.

The figure cried out in pain—no, in anger. A chill went through Sylvanas. She knew that voice, though she had never heard its owner use it so. The voice Sylvanas remembered was cultured, civilized ...

Your father says you are a budding diplomat.

"Kael'thas," Sylvanas said, her voice barely registering, even in her own ears. "Does he know that Zul'jin is here as well?"

"Not to our knowledge, my lady."

A pity. It would be an extra torment to both souls if each knew the leader of the race he loathed was in torment alongside him.

"His situation is not like Zul'jin's. What is going on?"

"The Sire of Revendreth has special plans." Agatha pointed with her spear. "Look carefully. His anima is growing, not diminishing. Instead of gaining absolution for his own sins, he is having the sins of others foisted upon him."

In the scarlet cocoon, Kael'thas Sunstrider, the Sun King, wept and raged and writhed, a massive carved slab of stone fixed to his bone-white body. Hair the hue of snow floated about him; his chest strained, trying to burst the chains.

Sylvanas had never cared for him, and from all she had heard, he had gone from being an arrogant royal to allying with demons to damning the quel'dorei to an existence of addiction and suffering.

But he had been kind to Lirath—

Even so, surely he had sins aplenty. "Whatever plans this 'Sire' has for Kael'thas, the fallen prince has earned his share of suffering," she said.

"Then his current status should please you," Daschla said.

"The true injustice, though, is that both he and Zul'jin were sent here, to be offered a chance that would have been denied to me."

"And you are correct. It would indeed have been denied to you, had not the Jailer snatched your soul from the Maw's grip."

Sylvanas wondered how long Zovaal would continue to offer her reprieve. It was a troubling thought.

Abruptly, she decided she had seen enough of the prince's torture. "I do not know what form other afterlives will take," she said to the Val'kyr, "but the Jailer insists that death is just as unfair as life. Show me the rewards and the punishment of one such place. And show me what is unfair, that I may see this injustice for myself."

The breeze, the brush, feathers and wind, and Sylvanas saw fierce light behind her closed lids. She opened them onto an inferno.

She and the others were—and yet, of course, were not—submerged in a sea of liquid fire and molten earth. This was an obvious place of punishment, so blatantly dangerous and agonizing that Sylvanas was surprised when a black shape, long and twining, slipped quickly through the thick liquid, like a snake swimming easily through water. As she watched, several small legs extended from the snake-like creature's body, causing it to dip and dive.

Was it, too, part of the torture? Did it choke the hapless souls even as they burned? But it seemed to be alone here, and it certainly did not look to be suffering. She was confused.

"What did this . . . entity do?" she asked.

"Devoured her mate alive," was the reply.

"That . . . would indeed merit punishment," Sylvanas said, slightly taken aback.

"Oh no," Agatha said. "She consumed her mate because he was suffering and close to death. This ritual is a supreme act of love among her people." She nodded at the eel-beast. "To the aells, this is a perfect paradise. They live inside fire."

Sylvanas watched the creature, able to see its beauty now that she understood it. A thought struck her.

"Was her mate waiting here for her?"

"No," Kyra answered. "The Arbiter did not deem this the perfect afterlife for him. He was sent elsewhere."

"But . . . if her reward for loving so deeply is this idyllic place," Sylvanas said, "how can it be truly perfect for her if her mate is not with her?"

This time, the Val'kyr were silent.

"This makes no sense," Sylvanas murmured, looking again at the sleek beast. "To reward love by denying a soul reunion with the beloved? Nothing could be more . . ." Her voice trailed off and she was silent as the impact hit her.

She had been about to say, *unfair,* but realized that word could not do this dreadful wrong justice. It was *beyond* unfair. It could not even be called vicious, as there was no malice in the judgment. It was the sentencing of a judge who did not understand love, or hate, or anything that made mortals what they were—even if, in this case, that late mortal was a sinuous creature who lived in fire. A judge that was *incapable* of understanding, as it had never lived, never loved, never hated.

The Jailer's words came back to her: *The design is gravely, cruelly, and worst of all* indifferently *flawed.*

Something inside Sylvanas grew cold. A question was forming, and she did not want to hear the answer to it. But she had to ask.

"Are any families whole . . . in any afterlife?"

"We cannot answer that with certainty, as there are so—"

"Yes, yes, I understand, they are infinite, and you cannot travel everywhere. But in your experience—in all you have seen—are any souls reunited with their loved ones?"

Agatha's strong, beautiful face was grave and etched with sorrow. "In our experience, Lady Sylvanas, no."

Sylvanas Windrunner had thought that by now, she was past

anything like the sudden sick shock of grief that attacked her out of nowhere. But she was not. Her mind was not here, watching the solitary aell, or with the Val'kyr, but an unspeakably long distance away, in a place known as Eversong Woods, years ago, as she leaned against a tree, smiling as she watched her parents, eyes only for each other, her sisters, laughing and dancing as well, and the bright Little Lord Sun around whom they all revolved, each in their own way.

No.

And, as was always the case for Sylvanas since she had breathed her last, grief was not followed by the sorrow and cleansing tears that eased the heart, but by the rage that only served to inflame it.

"Show me more," she demanded, and they did.

How long Sylvanas traveled with the Val'kyr, she could not even guess. With no day and night, nothing to mark time, nor even a physical body to move through space, she relied only upon her fury.

Show me more. Show me more. Show me more.

There were some happy moments, but too skewed by the knowledge of the Arbiter's lack of care for them to be truly satisfying. These were far outweighed by scene after scene, soul after soul, struggling with the complexity of the rewards and punishments of the afterlife, when all should be astonishingly simple and logical.

And at some point, after seeing place after place, fate after fate, Sylvanas came to a conclusion. She had thought—hoped—to find Lirath, because she had taken for granted that he had been given a peaceful eternity. Now she realized she was afraid to find out—afraid that the Arbiter, in its dreadful impartiality and indifference, had doomed her brother to a terrible fate. And strong and hardened as she was . . . she knew she could not bear that.

But if the Jailer was right . . . if, together, they could *make* justice happen . . . then she could search for her brother with the certainty that all would be well.

She asked to be returned to the Jailer.

She gazed up at him, craning her neck up, up to see the enormous head and glowing eyes gazing down on her. He waited for her to speak.

"I have asked your Val'kyr to show me many places," Sylvanas said. She could not control the shaking in her voice. She had been exposed too long, to too much, and the words spilled out. "I have seen what you said I would see. Misery and injustice. Imbalance and illogic at this, the one place where mortals have so long believed the justice that escapes them during their lives might be corrected."

"Now you understand," he said.

"I do. But I am . . . cautious. Careful. I do not give my trust easily, and I still do not trust you," she said.

"Trust between allies is earned," the Jailer agreed, "but if your own eyes do not convince you, I am not certain what will. While I know that in the end, you will grant it to me, because you will not be able to deny the truth of what you have borne witness to, there is a risk if you delay. Time passes differently in the Shadowlands than in mortal worlds. It can be unpredictable. You may return to your body and find that a mere moment has passed . . . or you may find only a skeleton."

Sylvanas did not like being pressured, but she could understand how greatly different time must be to a place with no true time at all. She recalled how fiercely she had fought to regain her body once. She could not allow herself to be denied it again by her own inaction.

"I say again: I want a partner. One who is able to see and understand the flaws in the design, and who burns, like I do, for justice. One who has the courage to stay the course at any cost, because she is not deceived by illusions and flattery."

That certainly had not been Arthas. He craved power, and enjoyed using it in petty ways on those who could not fight back. If she did join with the Jailer, she would not make the mistakes her tormentor had. Even so . . .

"If you truly know anything about me," she said softly, "then you know that I will never serve."

"The Maw is filled with countless souls I can force to serve me,

Sylvanas," the Jailer said. He sounded ... almost tired, as if he was utterly disconnected from the very idea of servitude. "They are worth next to nothing. I need someone who will ally with me, who will set her own shoulder to the stone to help me move it. Who can travel where I cannot, do what I cannot. And trust," he added, "must be on all sides. I, too, have been betrayed before, by my own kin and many others I trusted. You are not like them, Sylvanas. You are like me."

She remembered his earlier words. *Our path will have no place for the compassion, the regrets, the guilt of the living. It will have no place for their morality, because it, just like the machine of death, is at its heart flawed. And that flaw ... is believing that anything is fair.*

"There will be a time for kind thoughts, for compassion," the Jailer assured her. "Once the machine is remade. But until then, you must dedicate yourself to breaking the chains you brought with you. Remnants of your life that failed you then, and will fail you again if you allow them.

"The one thing I can promise is that you will find yourself time and again at a crossroads, where what is right—what we must do in order to achieve our goal—is in lethal conflict with what seems good. Only a hard heart will endure when asked to do things that seem atrocities. Only a cold heart will continue, step after step, when the world screams with one voice to stop. Only an uncaring heart will turn away from the trap baited with hope, for hope is the worst illusion of them all. Sometimes there are no good choices, and yet one must still choose. The end is worth the means, Sylvanas, because the end is truly the *end*—the end of every moment of suffering and loss and torment, forever."

Sylvanas thought of her parents, her sisters, the boy who was the brightest light in her whole world, lost to war and violence and cruelty. Of the glory of the Farstriders and the Silvermoon that once was. Of every fool who hoped and dreamed and wished on stars and loved by moonslight.

False, all of it. The only thing that was real was the pain caused by existing in a world where hope was nothing but a dream the helpless made up for themselves.

"I lost hope long ago," Sylvanas said, quietly. "I have laid aside kindness and love. And . . . I am prepared to learn how to let go of pain and rage."

"Then go," the Jailer said. "When you have made your choice, send a Val'kyr to me, and if it is yes, watch for a child of the blood. With your new insight, you will see injustice everywhere, and fairness not at all. Watch for these five signs, and know my words are true. A fiery darkness will return. You must step out of the shadows and lead. A blade will pierce the heart of the world, and you shall hold the blood from that wound and sense its power. And finally . . . you shall topple a king, and shatter the sky itself."

Her way back was through the Jailer's Val'kyr, but there was a bargain to be sealed first.

As she had been, all nine of them had been bound to the Lich King, destined to remain on Icecrown for, perhaps, eternity. But now their needs and those of Sylvanas were aligned . . . and served the great purpose of the Jailer.

"We need a vessel," Annhylde said. "One like us, a sister of war. Strong. Who understands life and death. Who has seen the light and the dark. Someone worthy—worthy of power over life and death. My sisters will be free, but their souls will be bound to yours. You may walk with the living again. As long as my sisters live, so too shall you. Freedom, life . . . and power over death. This is our pact. Do you accept our gift?"

For a moment, Sylvanas did not understand, then comprehension dawned. *As long as my sisters live.* The bargain was not for all the Val'kyr.

Sylvanas had been plucked from torment in the Maw. Balance had to be kept; the Jailer could not risk anyone detecting what he had done. Someone needed to take her place—to suffer in her stead, so Sylvanas could aid their master. And that would be Annhylde.

She would add another unfairly judged being to her unending list, then. When the Jailer and she were done, Annhylde, and everyone in the cosmos, would be free of a faulty system that delivered justice to no one.

"Yes," Sylvanas said. "We have a pact."

For much more than is spoken here. And I vow to you, I shall keep it.

CHAPTER TWENTY-THREE

S ylvanas returned to the world of the living—and unliving—
brimming with power tempered by the caution that had always been a counterbalance to her passion. She had seen the
injustices of the Arbiter's decrees firsthand, had felt the essence of a
frightened little boy who had once been a terrifying death knight.
This knowledge, she trusted in. And if the Jailer's prophecies and his
views of existence proved correct, then so much more was possible
than she had ever dreamed.

She had existed ere now with the sole goal of destroying Arthas.
Only now could she understand how small, how petty, that was.
How small *Arthas* was. She could not yet find it in herself to be
grateful for all that she had lost, and endured, but she had a newly
birthed appreciation for it. Now that she was beginning to visualize
the vastness of what could be at play—and at stake—she was filled
with three things that had been lacking in a burning quest for simple
vengeance.

Righteousness.

Vindication.

And, if her own observations corroborated the Jailer's words, the
power to change fate—not just hers. Everyone's.

She would begin this new stage of undeath as she had the first—with the Forsaken that Garrosh was calling "the point of my spear." She galloped up to the Bulwark with the Val'kyr pacing her, the hooves of her undead horse churning up mud while the rain beat down in cold gray sheets.

"*Charge!*" the orc bellowed.

"*Belay that order!*"

The Jailer had given her more than insight and perspective. He had bestowed some of his power upon her. Even in corporeal form, she had always been able to summon her banshee voice. But now there was something more to it. Something strong instead of simply painful. And she had not yet begun to explore other capabilities that were now hers.

The response was instant. Sylvanas commanded the attention of all present, and the Forsaken—her Forsaken—knelt and bowed their heads.

She had Garrosh's full attention, as well, but his expression was one of outrage as he approached. *How dare she,* he was doubtless thinking.

Oh, she dared. And would continue to.

"Hellscream. Gilneas *will* fall. And the Horde will have its prize. But if you wish to use my people, we will do this *my* way."

And they did.

All went as planned at the outset. The vision granted to Sylvanas by the Val'kyr ensured she was prepared to discover that behind the Greymane Wall, many Gilneans had transformed into the lupine beasts called worgen. What was a curse for them was a boon for the Horde. Worgen were clouded by their rage, and as likely to attack their fellow countrymen as they were the true enemy. In addition to the feral beast-men, there were quarreling factions among the humans. Sylvanas, the hunter, understood the weakness of a splintered group of prey.

Then, incredibly, everything began to shift.

Before she quite knew what was happening, the factions had begun to work together—and the worgen appeared to be able to control their bloodlust. Including their king—Genn Greymane himself.

Sylvanas found herself in the heart of the city, beset from three sides, and Greymane was right in the thick of the fighting.

They were so full of fire and swagger, these Gilneans, and none more so than their king. How fitting, that one who had scorned making alliances with others, who chose to build a wall, was now likely desperately regretting that decision. Now these oh-so-proud Gilneans would serve a dark lady instead of a grizzled monarch.

All the worgen posed more of a challenge than most humans, but Genn's transformation, as accompanied by rage as her own had been, presented Sylvanas with a formidable foe. The peppering of bullets fired by the militia disturbed her not at all, but Genn, all white pelt and white teeth and white-hot fury, launched himself at her without a care, a sword that an ordinary man would have struggled to lift in two hands gripped in a single clawed one.

Sylvanas carried two blades, barely exerting herself as she dodged, struck, parried. Greymane was not as deft with the weapon as he would have been in human form, but the blows were much stronger, jarring her shoulder slightly as his blade crashed into hers. He pressed in close to her, spittle dripping from his snarling jaws. She felt hot breath on her face, could see the gleam of pure loathing in his eyes.

Sylvanas had learned from Arthas the delight of watching one's prey lying helpless before her. In a way, though, Greymane was a kindred spirit. The realization took some of the pleasure out of toying with her huge, furry opponent. While she had no desire to waste time killing Genn painfully, Sylvanas needed to ensure he did not survive.

Even that thought amused her. As if she could possibly miss.

Sylvanas paused. The thought had given her an idea. There was another, faster way to toy with her prey. Nearly ebullient in her invincibility and newfound direction, she made a spontaneous decision to level the playing field. She would make it a fairer fight.

"Enough!" she shouted. She harnessed enough of her banshee power to propel the startled king backward several feet. He landed heavily, panting and growling as he got to his feet.

"Let's see how brave Gilneas gets on without its stubborn leader," Sylvanas said. She closed her eyes, drawing the correct arrow by feel, nocking it, and aiming it. All her senses were in play, save sight: scent, sound, the feel of wind on her face—

A shout, from somewhere to the right, the voice young, male, full of anguish: "Father!"

For the briefest of instants, Sylvanas Windrunner hesitated.

You acted out of love, and with courage.

They were whispers of the past, nothing more. Her father was gone. Sylvanas knew too much now to mourn the dead—or even lament that their lives had been cut short. If the Jailer was right, and could do what he promised . . . there would be no need for anyone to grieve or fear dying ever again. With a slight motion, she released death by simply opening the first two fingers of her right hand.

"No! *Liam!*"

Sylvanas's eyes snapped open. Her arrow protruded from the chest not of Genn Greymane, but of a young man, fit and strong, with red-brown hair. But even in the dim light, she could see him paling, crumpling. And cradling the youth in his arms was the mighty Genn Greymane, imposing, ferocious, uttering a sound of raw grief that soared into the brooding gray sky and ended in a broken howl.

Slowly, Sylvanas lowered the bow. She could not possibly have missed . . . yet she had.

This . . . cannot be.

Liam Greymane had thrown himself in front of his father, and Sylvanas had killed him. Snuffed out yet another bright, shining flame of young life. As she did at the gates of Silvermoon, with her cursed song.

As she did by denying Lirath.

She pushed the feeling out of the way with the reliable force of rage. Genn Greymane should be dead, not this foolish child. And she—stupid, to have squandered the chance on a whim about "fair play." Nothing was fair. Nothing.

Her hand clenched on her bow.

"Such a waste," she said, her voice dripping scorn even as emotions chased one another around like fighting tigers in her mind. "That arrow's poison was not meant to be wasted on your whelp."

Slowly, Genn lifted his white wolf's head. Tears were in his eyes; tears, and hatred. Good. She wanted to punish him for her error, so she had gathered the cruelest words she could find, to drive a knife into him if she could not impale him with an arrow. The tide of battle had turned; it was time to retreat. "We'll meet again, Greymane."

She yanked the reins of her horse, and it clattered off. But Sylvanas could not outrun her own thoughts.

Would she have done what Liam did for her own father? Given her life for his?

She did not want to know the answer to that question. One thing she was certain of: She would never do so now, not after what she had learned of the futility of the struggle for life. What had happened, she realized, was nothing more or less than a lesson. One she needed to see. It echoed what Zovaal had told her, and the injustices she had witnessed in the Maw.

Attachments to memories. Regret for the death of a youth. The idea that she could ever experience anything more than what burned in her heart now. These things were useless, perhaps worse than useless. They could be dangerous.

She should let them go. Perhaps the Jailer of the damned was indeed right about that.

Time, she thought, *will tell.*

She turned her attention to the next step. For all his posturing and aggression, Garrosh feared the blight that had come so close to felling Arthas at the Wrath Gate. Feared it so much that the warchief forbade its use. He even sent General Warhowl to remind Sylvanas of this, and attempt to bully her.

It was almost like a dance, with steps Sylvanas knew well and could execute with practiced ease even with so clumsy a partner as the orc. First, Warhowl scolded her for Sylvanas's "losing control" of

Gilneas, and implied that Garrosh would take the task away from her.

I should like to see him try, she thought.

The second step in the dance: Sylvanas, of course, spoke earnestly to the envoy, assuring him that the current situation was a minor setback, and that victory was certain.

As inevitable as day following night, Warhowl reminded Sylvanas that Garrosh had forbidden the use of the blight. Her response was a vigorous denial of the possibility, going so far as to say that the weapon was no longer even being created. And even if it was, it would never, *ever* be used without Garrosh's approval.

For a moment, Sylvanas wondered if she had overplayed her hand, as Warhowl regarded her closely, his beady eyes narrowing. Finally, he nodded and bade her farewell. As the dance came to its close, Sylvanas could not resist a flourish as she mentally took her bow: "Go with honor, General!"

Her performance must have been convincing, as High Executor Crenshaw looked at her with some confusion and inquired as to whether they should stop production or use the blight as planned.

A silly question. Of *course* they would use the blight. Anything that distressed Garrosh was something Sylvanas took glee in. And it would solve the Gilnean problem. "Let the Gilneans enjoy their small victory. Not even their bones will remain by tomorrow."

In a way, Greymane, she thought, *I am giving you a gift. You and your queen won't have to live with the pain of your son's death for much longer.*

With dawn would come the blight, and the end of the battle for Gilneas. Her Val'kyr would be pressed into service, raising the fallen human Gilneans into Forsaken—her people; becoming the very thing they most despised. The worgen corpses would lie where they fell, with no stone or monument raised to their sacrifice.

Sylvanas would watch it all with satisfaction. Whatever lay in store for her, this, at least, was something of a victory—and a demonstration that the Jailer was keeping at least one of his promises to her.

It would do—for now.

Garrosh's leadership did not improve with time.

More and more, he burrowed deeper into his arrogance and sense of power. He demonstrated an insatiable hunger for conquest, by fair means or foul. For a race so obsessed with honor, Garrosh Hellscream seemed to have no compunctions about cowardly acts so long as they achieved his desired results. It seemed to Sylvanas that he was all but daring the Horde to rebel against his atrocities, such as the destruction of Theramore.

It was Alliance territory, true, and Garrosh had contrived to draw some of the most powerful generals and admirals of the Alliance there. But the inhabitants of an entire city were turned into violet ash from a mana bomb, and the city was led by Jaina Proudmoore, who had worked with Thrall to help win the Third War, and who had aided Baine when Thunder Bluff had undergone a coup.

Sylvanas could almost feel the Jailer towering beside her when she learned of the incident. She imagined what he would say: *A woman of peace. Of kindness. Who supported those who needed help. Surely you cannot say what happened was fair by any measure.*

When Pandaria was discovered, the continent was contested by the Horde and Alliance. And of course, Garrosh only saw in Pandaria's beauty things to be seized and made his own. Corrupted, if need be, to his own power. It became clear to the Horde—even to the orcs, who loved him for his pride in his heritage—that Garrosh must be stopped. Once again, the two factions joined to stop a monster, and Garrosh Hellscream was captured, charged with war crimes, and brought to trial; the beings who served the pandaren as deities, the August Celestials, would be the judges. A surprised Vol'jin became warchief when Thrall declined to resume the mantle. Sylvanas thought it a wise decision on both sides, as far as it went, but Horde politics were no longer her priority.

It seemed all of Azeroth was interested in the outcome of the trial. Sylvanas certainly was. Would the Jailer's assertion that everything was unfair be challenged, or further supported? Would Garrosh be executed—as he should be—or be given a chance to "change himself and atone"? She was curious. The testimony of the witnesses was mildly interesting, especially when they had a twist or surprise. For instance, Varok Saurfang, the old orc who had lost his son at the Wrath Gate, who had fought in every war between Horde and Alliance, who once promised to kill Garrosh with his own hands if he felt the younger orc was heading down a dark path—he flatly stated he did not wish execution. Sylvanas was surprised—but when Saurfang explained that he wanted to challenge Garrosh to the orcish duel of honor, the mak'gora, she understood.

He wanted the chance to kill Garrosh himself, just as she had once wanted to see Arthas die by her own hand. An idea began to form. Though at first glance it seemed as if she and Saurfang were nothing alike, they both had hated someone who was devastatingly violent, and had lost someone they loved. Someone like him, who had seen so much, might be interested in the new reality the Jailer planned to craft.

This one is half in love with death since the loss of his son. Perhaps I can use that.

But in the end, the greatest surprise was one she had never expected. It came in the form of a scroll and a small box delivered to her by courier.

Sylvanas, curious and cautious, portaled from the Temple of the White Tiger to the Undercity to open the parcel in private in her quarters. There were few enough belongings. A bed, when she wished to lie down to think. A shelf for books, and a row of weapons lining the walls. A desk with candles and writing materials, and in a drawer of that desk, a few private items. Decades-old letters, a rolled painted canvas that depicted a family of six, the youngest a babe held in his mother's arms. A few sheets of music.

And a small box that held a necklace with a sapphire, with the inscription: *To Sylvanas. Love always, Alleria.*

Sister to the necklace that lay coiled in her hand, the only difference being it was adorned with a ruby and an inscription that read, *To Vereesa. With love, Alleria.*

Strange that after so long, it was hatred that brought the two sisters together.

By the time Sylvanas stood shouting her defiance at Arthas Menethil, the rift between them had not entirely healed. It had gotten better with time, but there was still a distance. They were no longer the Lady Moon and Little Moon. They were adult women, who had made choices, and sometimes those choices had devastating consequences.

But it was the little peacemaker who had approached the Dark Lady with a burning desire to murder Hellscream. The monster had made a widow of Vereesa. Her husband, the human mage Rhonin, had sacrificed his life to mitigate the damage the mana bomb had done to Theramore. The youngest Windrunner sister, whom Sylvanas remembered clamoring to see Alleria's test, who had wept at the thought of conflict between those she loved, was all but gone. Vereesa had aged, become harder. Her soft open heart had been too badly battered. Life had left its mark on her, as death had left its mark on her sister.

They conspired together, hunted together, and Sylvanas realized that perhaps after all, there was someone other than Nathanos whom she could trust and rely upon. Someone who had lost her ideals and dreams and hopes, like Sylvanas. Who could come to the Undercity and aid her sister as Sylvanas and Zovaal pushed for a better universe.

"This is dangerous, Sylvanas," Nathanos warned. "I will support you if you do this, you know I will, but I fear it will not work."

"Trust me, my champion," said Sylvanas, thinking about Vereesa's rage and pain. "She is more like us than you think."

"I understand she has suffered," he said, "but she does not think as we do, *feel* as we do. There is still some . . ." He struggled for the word. "Brightness to her. Hope. Laughter. Joy. Vereesa is still human. Still alive."

She does not have to be, Sylvanas thought.

In the end, though, it did not matter. When Lirath had died, it had been Sylvanas who had turned away from Vereesa. This time, it was Little Moon who had rejected Sylvanas.

Why do I continue to allow myself to care? It never works. She was *always* betrayed, either wittingly or unwittingly, by faith in something or someone false, or the vagaries of the world.

It was madness, to think she could be loved. Once, perhaps, but not now.

The Jailer was right. She needed to divest herself of these pathetic shreds of attachments. The so-called ties that bind were nothing more than chains. She would harden her heart, let it be stone, let it be nothing.

But first . . . rage.

"Vereesa . . . is not coming to the Undercity, then."

It was, of course, Nathanos who had finally found her, outside in Silverpine. Sylvanas said nothing, merely shook her head.

She had lost all sense of time. The only indications of the passage of hours were that the blood had dried on her hands and clothing, and the decapitated wolf corpse in front of her had bloated.

Nathanos sat down beside her, leaning up against the tree trunk. Flies buzzed about them. "That dreadful trial finally got interesting. Pity you missed the fun," Nathanos said, conversationally.

Sylvanas did not reply. She was sunk deep in the perfect stillness of her pain and hatred, as trapped by them now as she had been earlier, when she had tried to rid herself of the emotions by slaughter. She cared nothing for the steps or even the outcome of the trial.

"Garrosh, as you might imagine, regrets nothing. He's also gone, thanks to a pair of plotting dragons who spirited him away—some place in time, no one knows where or when. Oh, you will appreciate this. The entire thing was a charade. The August Celestials were hosting this trial not to judge Garrosh—they were judging *us* the whole time."

How dare they. A stirring of anger that did not involve her own heart shivered through Sylvanas. *The Arbiter decides. The celestials decide. Vereesa reaches out her hand to me, then snatches it back. There is not a whiff of anything truly free, anywhere.*

"The smug creatures had already made up their minds from the beginning to let him live. They are all about redemption, and apparently, one can't redeem oneself after death."

That almost got a bitter smile from her as she thought about Revendreth, and the similar expressions of anguish on the dissimilar visages of Zul'jin and Kael'thas. So either the very "August" Celestials were not as all-knowing as they wanted mortals to believe, or they were liars of the highest caliber.

The thought of the Jailer, with his bluntness and his detachment, felt soothing now, like a cold cloth placed on a forehead raging with fever.

Vereesa had failed her, cruelly. But . . . was this not for the best? Her old life, her old concerns, her old duties and joys—why did she keep circling back to them? Did she think, somehow, this time, this person, this moment, would be different?

Liberation lay in the destruction of all that is, not in trying to exist in it. *There is a price to pay for sharing this world,* she thought, *and I am weary of the toll.*

Nathanos had been so quiet she had all but forgotten he was there. Now she looked up at him. He had warned her. She had ignored him. But he would never chide her for that, and he always knew what troubled her. He was no duty, no chore. While she had not kept her promise about them becoming what they had once been to each other, something was still between them. If the Jailer wished her aid, he must know she could not do all she needed to without trusting someone. She *did* trust Nathanos.

And I am weary of bearing this burden alone.

She had thought—hoped, she now realized, almost with shame—that Vereesa would be the one she could rely on. But Nathanos was hers, completely, in a way no one else had ever been.

"You have never asked how I managed to acquire the Val'kyr," Sylvanas said.

"You would tell me if you wanted me to know."

"I will tell you now," she said. "And you may think me mad as I relate this story. But I promise it . . . and all I have learned . . . are the greatest truths that exist."

He listened without interruption as she spoke. Sylvanas held nothing back. She spoke of the devastating loss she had felt upon seeing the pieces of Frostmourne. Of disavowing the Forsaken and leaping to her death on toothy spikes of saronite. Of the Jailer and his plight. And as it always seemed, coming full circle with Arthas, and eternity, and the terrible injustice of life and death and all between.

For a long time, Nathanos said nothing. She waited. Finally, he spoke, and the words were the first hint of recrimination she had ever heard from him.

"My lady," he said, his voice a raspy whisper, "if I'd lost you, it would have meant the end of me."

"Would it?" Before he could respond, she said, "Can you—can I—even feel such things for another? Rage, anger, self-pity—these things, I believe, you can feel. But not true heartbreak."

She thought of Vereesa, and wondered if she was lying to both of them.

He didn't argue—but he didn't agree, either. "I am glad I do not have to find out. This Jailer . . . do you believe him?"

"I believe what I saw," she said. "Why would he lie after revealing that he was tacitly responsible for my suffering? He has nothing to gain from tricking me. He has kept his promise, and I have seen that his insights into this existence are true. I have my Val'kyr. I do not know yet if I am willing to take the final step and commit to this cause. But I wished you to know."

She touched his cold cheek, remembering a beard there. Remembering lips that had kissed hers, with the warm sun shining on them at the top of a mountain peak. "I sought you out. I fought beside you as you battled to retain your sanity. I will need my champion, if I go down this path."

"You will always have him."

Would she? She looked upon him now, seeing him with eyes she believed had seen the last of any kin; would have wept if they could have. Eyes the keener for what she had endured.

Nathanos was, as she was realizing now, wearing down.

Though the magic that animated their flesh had stalled death's decay, that did not mean they couldn't be damaged. A thousand small cuts could create a wound as deep as a sword strike, and while replacements could be found, that brought its own challenges. So much of him had already been replaced or mended . . .

She reached to touch his shoulder, the dried blood on her gloves cracking and flaking off.

His glowing eyes followed the movement, then met her gaze.

Through life, through death, and beyond, he had always been there for her. The oddest match in the world, Sylvanas often thought, yet, just as oddly, it had endured. She did not want to lose him to this slow whittling of what flesh yet remained. She needed someone she could trust always at her side. Her thoughts turned to her Val'kyr. They had returned her to unlife more than once. Could they use the Jailer's power to save her champion?

Part of her knew exactly what she was doing. Loyalties continued to fall, as leaves did in the mortal world; fall with no seeming justification or satisfaction. Her circle of things and people who moved her grew ever smaller; today only by one person, but what a wound Vereesa had left. That emptiness had to be filled. And so Sylvanas Windrunner clung to Nathanos, the last one who remained.

Much later, Sylvanas would remember times spent at the Marris Stead, with Nathanos and his young cousin Stephon. She would seek out the adult Stephon had become, and rest comfortably knowing that his sacrifice to prolong Nathanos's existence was for the worthiest of causes. Long or short, Stephon's life, like all life, was only a momentary flicker.

CHAPTER TWENTY-FOUR

Sylvanas stood in Grommash Hold, gazing speculatively at the white-haired human mage. His name was Khadgar, and he had arrived in the form of an oversized raven.

She knew the name. Years ago, he had traveled to the orcish homeworld through the Dark Portal with a group that included the paladin Turalyon . . . and Alleria Windrunner. Khadgar had returned, but he did not bring Alleria—or even news of her—with him.

This suited Sylvanas well. Let Alleria and the paladin she had chosen over her own people be lost to history and time. The infamous portal continued to be a problem on occasion, but for the most part, Sylvanas had allowed herself to almost forget about it, as well as the wizard who could shift to the form of a raven.

She, along with Lor'themar, Jastor Gallywix, Thrall, and Baine, who had become high chieftain after his father's death, had been summoned by Warchief Vol'jin regarding a matter of "utmost urgency and dire importance," and it seemed that the troll had not exaggerated.

"I fear I bring news that no one on this world wishes to hear," Khadgar said, looking at each of them in turn with steady blue eyes. "The Burning Legion has returned."

Outbursts of horror and anger filled the hold. The demonic Legion was that rare thing that was bane to both dead and living, bane even to the world itself. The Lich King might have overrun Azeroth with mindless monsters, but the Burning Legion, if victorious, would consume it.

Sylvanas was horrified, too, of course—but her primary response was shock.

Shock . . . and then a slow sense of surprised pleasure, and satisfaction.

A fiery darkness will return.

The first of the Jailer's prophecies. What was the Legion, if not a fiery darkness?

She had been watching and observing, as she told the Jailer she would, and saw injustice and unfairness in nearly every aspect of existence, and now . . . this. Bit by bit, he was proving true to his word.

Vol'jin waved them all to silence, then shook his head. "Just as soon as ya think ya can take a breath, trouble comes to greet ya."

"I do not think I need explain the peril we find ourselves in," said Khadgar. "I have spoken with King Varian Wrynn and other Alliance leaders. They have agreed to meet with Horde representatives in a council of war."

"I would be happy to offer my very own pleasure palace for the meeting site!" Gallywix said. "Everyone will be welcomed with open arms! I will even go so far as to offer *two* tasty beverages for each attendee on the house, and can give a group disco—"

"Gallywix," rumbled Baine. His deep, normally placid voice had an edge. "Hold your tongue."

Rather to Sylvanas's surprise, the goblin did, though he shot Baine a sullen look.

Khadgar continued. "Trade Prince Gallywix's, ah, pleasure palace is not the appropriate venue, but he is correct about one thing," Khadgar said. "All must feel welcome. This needs to be held in neutral territory. I propose we convene in Dalaran."

"Dalaran?" scoffed Gallywix, turning to appeal to Vol'jin. "Warchief! Prices are sky-high in that floating city."

"Many of our magi were murdered in Dalaran not so long ago," Lor'themar said. "This does not sound *neutral* to the blood elves."

"I understand your suspicion," Khadgar said, almost kindly. "But few places in Azeroth are innocent of a violent history, and a gathering of all the world's leaders is sure to be noticed by the Legion's spies. Dalaran has no shortage of defenses and is likely the safest place. I cannot force anyone to attend, but I will say this: As we have seen before, there is no defeating the Burning Legion without cooperation . . . and trust."

Vol'jin looked at Khadgar, choosing his words. "Ya speak the truth. An' so does Lor'themar. The Legion makes no distinction between Horde an' Alliance. An' if we gonna beat 'em . . . we cannot afford to, either. So we gonna trust you, Khadgar. The Horde will be there."

Vol'jin was a troll of his word. Within two days, every leader of the Horde and Alliance met in the floating city of Dalaran. Sylvanas had come alone, as had the other leaders. Her Val'kyr, of course, could be summoned at will in the unlikely event she had need of their services. Nathanos remained in the Undercity, on alert in case the Alliance planned an attack, thinking the Forsaken had been lulled into letting their guard down. She would trust Khadgar, as Vol'jin did, but only to an extent.

The late prince of the blood elves had spent much of his youth in this, the glittering violet home of Azeroth's most renowned magi. Sylvanas could easily understand why it appealed to Kael'thas. It was opulent, lavish, and had the sort of elitist feel to it that she associated with him. She did not care for the place much.

She stepped out of the portal in the large main area. A young blood elf mage bowed to her and indicated the broad stone staircase that led to the upper part of the citadel. As she ascended, she heard snatches of conversation. Others, apparently, had already arrived. That was fine. She disliked having to wait.

Two guards stood by the tall wooden doors. At her approach, each opened one. Inside was a large room, almost cavernous. The walls appeared to be painted to represent the sky, a lighter shade at their base, deepening to black. Instead of painted stars on the wall, however, tiny, three-dimensional stars winked as they formed constellations. Moons and suns floated above the assembled diplomats. She recognized none of these worlds save their own: Azeroth was there, turning slowly, its two moons keeping it company.

Maps lined the wall instead of art, though they were arguably works of art themselves. Sylvanas took this all in with the briefest of glances as she entered, then turned her gaze upon the room's occupants. Thrall, Vol'jin, and Baine, of course. Gallywix was ... somewhere, doubtless annoying someone. She caught sight of Lor'themar's white hair, but did not try to catch his gaze.

She instead found herself staring at Genn Greymane.

Sylvanas rarely saw Genn in his human form. It had been the worgen part she'd been battling, toying with, flush after emerging from the Maw with visions of the Shadowlands still fresh and clear in her mind. All kings were of historical import to one degree or another, but Genn ... he was something else again. The gruff leader who sealed his people off, thinking to stay in safe isolation but only dooming the kingdom he was attempting to protect and sire to a son he had clearly loved as a father, not as a king. He had been speaking to the leaders of the night elves, Malfurion Stormrage and Tyrande Whisperwind, but he clearly sensed—or smelled—her and looked up.

Ah, if looks could kill. Not that he could kill her. Not now, not anymore. She kept eye contact, knowing how beasts often interpreted it as a threat. It wasn't—not here, at least. But Sylvanas wanted him to know that she did not see *him* as a threat.

"Genn," came a voice, and her gaze flickered over to another human, another king: Varian Wrynn. The man whose orders—either directly or indirectly—sentenced her envoys to death on sight; who had come for her head in her own city after Varimathras and Putress had betrayed her.

Wrynn had been a gladiator at one point in his life and continued to be a formidable warrior. His black hair, which showed no strand of gray, was held in a topknot, and a scar from some long-ago fight crossed his face. Her spies told her that as the years had passed, Varian had grown more focused, less reactionary and violent. His lips tightened, but he managed a nod that was exactly enough to avoid offense, though nothing more.

Beside the king stood his whelp, the prince, Anduin Llane Wrynn.

She had forgotten how quickly children grew. Anduin had shot up like a weed since Sylvanas had last seen him in Pandaria. His hair had grown longer, now caught back in a ponytail that was a subtle echo of his father's. They had never spoken, but Sylvanas had seen him in Pandaria and heard his testimony at Garrosh's trial. He still looked like a boy then, but now he had a height approaching his father's, though he was thin.

Varian's cub sensed her and turned his head to meet her gaze.

He regarded her steadily, calmly, with no hint of fear or revulsion, and inclined his head slightly. She narrowed her eyes, gave the briefest of nods in acknowledgment, and returned her attention to the matter at hand.

"I am grateful that you have all agreed to meet under the banner of truce," Khadgar said. "This is not about lands, or resources, or old offenses. This is about our continued existence, and that of our world itself. Please, be seated, and I will tell you all I know."

It amused Sylvanas that no one moved. She understood the instinct. Standing, one could react much more quickly. To be seated was to be vulnerable, and for all Khadgar's pretty words, no one was willing to let down their guard. And then—the scraping sound of a chair pulling back.

Sylvanas turned to see that it was none other than young Anduin, seating himself with the casual grace of a nobleman, no line of his thin body indicating any discomfort or mistrust.

The big lion glowers, but the little lion is at home, she thought. She wondered if he understood the confidence that represented to the others. Perhaps. She doubted he was oblivious to the possibility of violence in these chambers, despite all the promises. He had almost certainly been taught such things. She recalled her own father trying to instill in her these lessons. Anduin looked to be a better pupil than she had been.

Sylvanas did not want to think of her father anymore. So, doubtless surprising everyone, she herself took a seat, raising an eyebrow at the others.

"Well?" she said. "Shall we stand about and posture until the Legion politely inquires if it may destroy us?"

Varian pressed his lips together as if biting back a retort, then tugged a chair out and dropped into it. Sylvanas looked back at his son and found him slightly smiling at her. Nathanos had told Sylvanas that before judgment could be pronounced at his trial, Garrosh Hellscream had escaped into another time and place. That time and place had been an alternate version of the orc homeworld of Draenor, right before the orcs drank the blood of the great demon Mannoroth. Sylvanas had sent various troops to this alternate Draenor to deal with the situation, the dark ranger Velonara chief among them. Garrosh had met his end at the hands of Thrall in a mak'gora. High time, Sylvanas had thought, but it seemed the troubles weren't over. Somehow, Garrosh Hellscream was managing to be trouble from beyond the grave while still being dead, for one of the worst orcs in all their sullied history, Gul'dan, had come from an alternate Draenor into an extremely non-alternate Azeroth, and had opened the way for an entire Legion of hooved, horned, and fel-smelling friends with him.

While the trust seemed universal, it became evident astonishingly quickly that everyone had a different plan on how to proceed. Everything from conscription to moving the city of Dalaran to directing resources to long-infested strongholds of demonic creatures to insults and slammed fists ensued.

At one point Greymane suggested, in a voice dripping with venom, "Why don't we dispatch the Forsaken to the most dangerous known position? They're dead already, after all." Sylvanas could not stand it.

"Let us send your worgen after sheep, as they are wolves already, after all!" She was about to follow it with *I'll fetch Liam's body and invite him to come along* when a young tenor voice somehow cut through the cacophony, if only because it was so unexpected.

"Stop this!" All fell silent and, surprised, turned to stare at Prince Anduin.

His blue eyes blazed brightly, and his gold brows were drawn in a scowl. "All of you! Do not allow yourselves to be baited into rash words. Who here has *not* been wronged?"

He turned to address a dwarven woman, her reddish-brown hair done up in two tidy rolls on either side of her head. "Moira, do you remember when you attempted to seize control of Ironforge? And you, Father, when you tried to kill her for it?"

Sylvanas glanced at Varian, who was scowling but not protesting, then back at Anduin. The youth's intense gaze fell on Sylvanas, and to her surprise, she saw it soften into sorrow as he briefly regarded her with compassion before continuing to speak to Varian.

"The Forsaken were once members of the Alliance. Friends and kin to so many in Stormwind. And yet, you rejected them when they sought help simply to survive. That was a grievous wrong."

Sylvanas had schooled her emotions since early adulthood, but she barely kept herself from revealing her shock. All she had ever seen from humans, or even from the high elves, was scorn and abhorrence, and a desire to wipe the "unnatural" creatures off the face of the world. And yet here was a mere child, scolding those much older than he. She was, reluctantly, impressed not just by the youth's passion—anyone could be passionate—but by his insight and willingness to acknowledge that the Alliance—even his own father— could be just as terrible as the Horde.

Anduin continued speaking, young face so earnest and sincere, hair like newly minted gold—and there was a certain warmth in his tone that reminded her of—

Comprehension slammed into her like something physical.

There's my Lady Moon!

And there's my Little Lord Sun!

How could she not have noticed this before? She had seen the prince many times in Pandaria, but at a distance. At this moment, though, there was no denying the connection.

It was not so much the physical resemblance, though that was not inconsiderable, but his voice. His inherent gentleness. A kindliness that had been lacking in nearly everyone else she had ever met.

Every time thoughts of Lirath sprang to her mind, Sylvanas had pushed them back; sometimes reluctantly, sometimes angrily, but always firmly. But she could not tear her thoughts from him, not now, not when it was as if the ghost she had longed to encounter in Eversong had taken a physical form right here, in the midst of a war council.

A war council. This boy was as unlike his father as could be imagined.

Just as Lirath was unlike our mother . . .

Sylvanas forced her face into impassivity, returning fully to the room as Anduin finished. "We will be the easiest prey yet for the Burning Legion if they discover us bickering instead of taking advantage of the wisdom, skill, experience, and knowledge that is around this table. We have always managed to defeat the Legion when we have worked together. *Always.* Countless other worlds have fallen, yet we prevailed. We must act, and act with sincerity, and trustworthiness, or soon there will be no one in this world left to argue with."

He was not particularly insightful, nor did his plea for cooperation say anything revelatory. But he did pay attention and knew how to use his observations and knowledge in a persuasive manner. Varian Wrynn was a warrior before all else, but his son was a fine diplomat.

As Father had been . . .

"Your Little Lion is correct, Varian." The words had been spoken before Sylvanas even realized she had uttered them. "There is indeed a wealth of weapons to brandish against the Legion. Let us be about honing them."

Out of the corner of her eye, she could see the youth was smiling at her.

Sylvanas had dwelled in the Undercity for too long. It felt good to return to action. Battle. Strategy and skill and blood and death and victory were tastes she had missed—even if these delicious things had to be bought with lives.

She worked in tandem with the Alliance king, right from the outset when she had saved his hide while airships crashed. Those she led were skilled, battle-hardened, and knew little fear, even as gargantuan creatures bellowed and struck. There were casualties, of course. There were always casualties. But despite wave after wave of the fel creatures, the combined Horde and Alliance forces were making progress. The tide was at last beginning to turn.

Varian led the charge to reach Gul'dan, whose hands in any universe, it seemed, were stained with so much blood it made her own look pristine. Gul'dan, who had delivered his people unto the demons. Who always seemed to escape, whether he hid in alternate timeways or was simply too slippery to catch.

Sylvanas had diverted the Horde to the ridge. The demons would send in more from the air, and her archers and warriors could ensure that many of the Alliance's foes were dead before they could harm a single hair of Varian's glossy topknot.

She had wished him luck, with sincerity. Despite their differences, they were a superlative team, and he had won her respect—no easy feat. Sylvanas hoped he survived to impress the prince, who was keeping his father's throne warm back in Stormwind.

The collaboration was working. Below, the Alliance was making tremendous strides. They slaughtered with the endurance of those who did not live, and Sylvanas's spirits rose with every dreadlord and fel reaver and pit lord that was sent back to its nightmarish homeworld. Varian had called for the gunship, which was moving steadily to the battlefield. The way would be clear, and Gul'dan's end—and that of the Legion—would follow.

And then it happened.

The portal, opening behind the Horde atop the ridge. The flood of demonic creatures pouring out of it. Thrall fallen, Baine aiding him, Vol'jin gravely wounded.

"Do not let the Horde die this day," the warchief had managed to say to her.

There was a choice, but in reality, it was no choice at all. If they chose to stay and cover the Alliance fighting below, they *all* would die. If they retreated, the Alliance would die, but the Horde, at least, might survive to fight another day.

We'll take the ridge and cover your flank, she had said.

Sylvanas . . . thank you, the doomed Alliance king had replied.

Good luck, Varian.

And you.

But there had been no luck. Not for the Horde, or the Alliance. There had never been luck, only the implacability that the Jailer had described.

Sylvanas blew the horn. Her Val'kyr swept down to aid the retreat. Oddly, her thoughts went to Anduin, likely to become an orphan. Varian had seemingly been lost and returned before, but Sylvanas had a feeling that this time, Anduin's title of king would become permanent.

The warchief had been brought home, clearly only in time to die. The unnatural gray hue of his normally blue skin, the black, spidery marks along his arms and torso, and the fatal wound, its sickly green not quite hidden by the bandages, told the story.

"In the end," Sylvanas had said, quietly, "death claims us all."

A single thrust from a spear. How had Vol'jin not seen it? He was a veteran of many wars, a shadow hunter—a master of the dark and light magic of the trolls. It was unthinkable, impossible.

Unjust.

Vol'jin was angry, and confused, and she could not blame him. "I have never trusted you," he rasped, "nor would I have ever imagined that in our darkest time, that you would be the one to save us."

She felt taut as a drawn bowstring, and motionless, still as a stone, straining for the next words.

The loa had granted the dying shadow hunter a vision, and a

name. "Many will not understand," he said, his voice getting softer. "But you . . . must step out of the shadows . . . an' lead."

The words. The very words. Unmistakable.

"You must be . . . warchief," Vol'jin said, and then did not speak again.

Now, standing in Grommash Hold, Sylvanas locked her legs into position and endured, through the growing heat of the day, the cool of the evening, and well into nightfall as the activities of tending to the fallen warchief and the process of the transfer of power hummed about her. At last the stream turned to a trickle, and she was alone, staring at the empty throne where Vol'jin had done two things that had this morning been unthinkable:

He had died, and he had named her warchief.

The second prophecy from Zovaal. The first, certainly, regarding the Burning Legion, could be considered a lucky guess by the skeptical. But this . . . it was word for word what Zovaal had told her he would use when he was ready.

It was easier now to stand motionless for hours than it had been when she drew breath. Sylvanas turned over everything she'd learned since Frostmourne cut her down. Everything she had seen in the Shadowlands, that Zovaal had told her, and that she had witnessed herself in this world.

It was time, for the first time, for Sylvanas Windrunner to truly make her own choice.

She unlocked her legs, feeling no discomfort. Indeed, the only thing she felt was calm certainty and a cautious . . . was it hope?

Sylvanas summoned her Val'kyr. "Tell your master I have received his message . . . and I accept. And together we will dismantle this broken system, exactly as he promised. Not just for us . . . but for the entire world. For all worlds. Tell him—I look forward to true justice."

Signe smiled. "He will be pleased, my lady. Greatness lies ahead."

More certain of her decision than she had ever been of anything, Sylvanas turned and left the chamber.

Vol'jin's body had been cleaned and prepared for the rite. She regarded him, thinking that he had deserved better. They all had. In time, thanks to her, they all would have better.

Sylvanas took the torch and lit the pyre. Flames leaped up into the night sky, a burst of heat and light. A call to action. She turned and looked upon the sea of gathered mourners, their numbers stretching well past the range of the firelight's illumination as they coalesced into one great, dark shape.

"Vol'jin is dead," she said, her voice strong. "Who here will help me avenge him?"

The roar was deafening. Only she understood the double meaning of her words. They heard only the obvious—attack the Legion with even greater ferocity. She knew that avenging Vol'jin would be a more complex, delicate, shattering task, and she was so very ready.

She would step out of the shadows, and lead.

INTERLUDE

"I understand," *Anduin said, quietly.*

"You do?" A sense of relief, disproportionate to the situation at hand, washed through Sylvanas. "I am pleased. I knew that once I had told you of the Jailer's plan, and showed you how he proved its truth to me, you would agree."

He smiled a little. It was a sad, kind smile, and Sylvanas felt her pleasure ebb. "What I mean is, I understand, after all you were shown, and told, experienced, and were led to believe was true, that you could want to join the Jailer's cause. You saw no home for yourself in death. If my option were eternal agony, I would certainly want to find an alternative that convinced me. Remaking this machine of death would be the only way you could ever have what you feel was owed you, so of course you wanted to believe it.

"He gave you hope, and that is not necessarily a bad thing. Hope is what you have when all other things have failed you. Where there is hope, you make room for healing, for all things that are possible . . . and some that are not."

The anger and offense began as a cold hard knot inside her, like a shard of ice. "You think I'm gullible," she said, the words dripping venom. "You think I'm a fool, like a terrified old woman grasping at folk remedies when Death hovers near."

"I do not think you a fool, Sylvanas. I might even have made the same choices you did."

She looked at him with withering skepticism. "It's true," Anduin said. "No one knows what they will choose when faced with something like this."

"There is calculation in your kindness, Little Lion," Sylvanas said.

"Would you blame me if there were?" he asked.

"No. I think I would be disappointed if there was not. So. If you do not think me a fool, at the very least you think me blinded by desire and fear."

"I think," Anduin said slowly, "that the Jailer has had eternity to perfect persuasion. That he is a shrewd observer. That he knows what people want, and how to convince them they can have it." He hesitated, then shook his head.

"Spit it out, or I will come in there and rip the words from you," Sylvanas said.

He did not reply. Sylvanas was half tempted to carry out the threat when he looked up at her. "You already know you were not the first he reached out to," he said.

"Of course I do. That was one of the first things he told me."

"Because he knew that if you thought he was responsible for what Arthas did to you, you would never join him."

Sylvanas did not answer at once. "I will not say you are not powerful," the king continued. "I will not say you are not intelligent—brilliant, in fact. But what you cannot see, because you are on the inside of this, is that he does not care about you. Or me. Once he has what he needs, what reason is there to keep either of us?"

Doubt crept into her mind softly, like a cat. Sylvanas banished it at once. The Jailer understood her in a way that this boy, with his scant two decades of life, never could.

"You see only part of the picture," she told him. "He will not be patient with me forever. I must make you understand and accept this plan, or you will suffer the same fate that I did, when Arthas struck me down."

His eyes narrowed in speculation as he regarded her. "Why is this so important? I am nothing to you, Sylvanas. Why must I be swayed?"

She knew. But she could not speak the words.

CHAPTER TWENTY-FIVE

In choosing to accept the mantle of warchief, Sylvanas Windrunner had also accepted Zovaal's offer . . . and, more important, his cause. She had always been a woman fueled by purpose, be it to protect her people, or win her freedom, or take her revenge. In retrospect, those "purposes" seemed laughably small. Even for those with long life spans, life was short and fraught with pain, fear, and desolation. And after life? Stagnation. Rigidity. Even the name Arbiter was cold and impersonal.

How strange, that her ultimate purpose had been revealed to her by one she had thought she would hate more than any other. Zovaal might have been inadvertently responsible for her death and enslavement, but she would not have grasped the depth of his truth when she yet breathed. Sylvanas's mind had been opened in the cruelest of ways, and, unencumbered by the softer feelings, she had both understanding and determination to drive her.

Everything she did, everything she thought, everything she felt was secondary to the great purpose that blazed in her now: seeing the Jailer's plan through and standing with him every step of the way. The imperfect engine of death would be remade. Once, smaller things had irritated her. She yearned for vengeance, or to make her enemies suffer, or to have utter and complete control. But she could no longer sacrifice her greater goals at the altar of personal vendettas, or troublesome second chances.

She made no move that was not intentional; saved or sacrificed no life out of amusement or pain. All had a reason. No matter who suffered, no matter what she found herself forced to do—the goal was ending torment for all, even those who had no idea, who were as blissfully ignorant as she had been in her safe, sheltered childhood enveloped by love. Even if the momentary flicker of their lives had to end in suffering, the goal of a more just eternity was worth any price. There had never been stakes so high, or reward so great, not in all the time that had passed or might ever be.

Sylvanas did not wish to waste a moment of her precious time leading the Horde as they fought a war that was, in the end, nothing more than a distraction.

Nonetheless, she had to manage them properly, so they would not become an obstruction or a distraction. Her thoughts turned to Varok Saurfang, the grizzled old soldier who had burned cities, lost both mate and child. She thought that at one point he, who had tasted so much of life's cruel lack of justice, might turn an ear to what the Jailer had to say. Not yet, certainly. But one day. At the Broken Shore, where Varian had indeed died, Saurfang had been wounded and was not ready to return to the front lines just yet. She had placed him in charge of the defense of Orgrimmar, and instructed Nathanos to send several ships in her fleet to Stormheim in search of a rare artifact that would help in the defeat of the Legion.

Meanwhile, Sylvanas had set out on her own to complete the first task Zovaal had assigned her since she had agreed to stand beside him on this journey to justice: to meet with another of his allies on Azeroth and procure a certain item.

It should have been a triumph.

It was, unfortunately, an unmitigated disaster.

Sylvanas and her champion had been apart for some time, and when they finally met up at Dreadwake's Landing in Ashild's Bay, Nathanos found her fuming in her private field tent. She turned angry eyes upon him, as if he were somehow the target of her ire.

"I hope your quest went better than mine," she said.

"Why yes, I did indeed survive the attack by Greymane and the 7th Legion, thank you for your concern."

She waved the comment away. "I would have been surprised had you not. I do not, however, appreciate you sending him in my direction."

Suddenly Nathanos was all business. "Tell me, if you can. What was your task?"

"Nothing more or less than to retrieve an artifact from Helya herself."

He blinked. "A titan-forged watcher is another one of the Jailer's allies? Friends in high—or should I say, low places," he said. Helya was an ancient being, nursing grudges just as ancient. She, like the Jailer, was sovereign of a dark realm—that of the dishonorable dead, sentenced to an eternity of fighting—and defeat. "What was the artifact?"

"The Jailer called it a Soulcage. Helya was reluctant to part with it, but I pointed out that it would benefit her as much as it would benefit him. I was instructed to use it to command the leader of the Val'kyr to deliver the mighty souls she commands to Helya, who in turn would turn them to our purpose."

Nathanos looked impressed. "The Val'kyr are indeed magnificent souls. Bright and glorious. All that anima flooding the Maw . . ."

Her angry look silenced him. "It would have been lovely had that wretched old wolf not interfered."

"I apologize, my lady. For not making a nice hat and cloak out of the king of Gilneas."

"I had found Eyir," Sylvanas said, ignoring the quip. "The Soulcage did not look like much, and I admit, I was wary that its power might not be sufficient. It appears to be a simple lantern, but it was clear that I was tormenting her as I raised it and demanded that she submit."

The memory was emblazoned on her mind: She, smaller, but with the Soulcage so much more powerful, watching the glow from the lantern form bonds of blue light about the gigantic figure.

"Trust the fool to ruin everything. A few more seconds and Eyir would have been mine," she said.

"He stole the Soulcage?"

"He *smashed* it."

The look on Greymane's face, of sly triumph. The cold satisfaction when he slammed the artifact on the cold stone. The shattering of the glass and the fading of the light.

You stole my son's future. Now I'm stealing yours.

Sylvanas had let Genn leave unchallenged, and he did not try to finish her off. Why either of these things happened, she did not know. It was as if there was something unspoken between them. But Sylvanas stood as if merged with the stone, watching Eyir, golden and glorious, rise and vanish to freedom. All her efforts were for naught.

And, she thought bitterly—anger rising to the rescue as it did so often when she teetered on the brink of those feelings the Jailer had warned against—though Genn did not know it, all his efforts had been for nothing, too.

If anyone's future had been stolen, it had been that of Genn himself.

Who knew where the Arbiter had sent Liam? Who knew where it would send Genn, or indeed, any of his family? The possibilities were, quite literally, limitless, but the chance of them all being together?

According to the Val'kyr, there was no chance at all.

"Fool," she whispered. "Old, sad, fool."

———

The battle continued, and both the Horde and Alliance found new allies to join them in the fight. The Legion had been defeated once again. And for some reason, at the celebratory feast in Grommash Hold, Sylvanas found herself thinking about how, in many respects, it had ended as it had started.

It had begun with ships in the sky, heading toward the Broken Shore. Varian on one, she on the other, ready to strike fast and hard and victoriously. They were allies, then, true allies. Respectful, intelligent, determined. And then she had had to make the choice that was no choice: Fight a losing battle alongside that ally, and sacrifice all of them—or betray an ally and save the Horde.

No free will. Not then, not ever.

And it was with a ship in the sky, hovering in the darkness among the stars and barely evading the desperate grasp of the Legion's creator and leader, the mad titan Sargeras, that the threat from the Burning Legion had ended. But not without a price. A price that would have given her chills to recall, had she had flesh that responded so any longer.

Sargeras had come so very close to achieving his desire to destroy Azeroth. Too close.

A blade will pierce the heart of the world.

Such had been Zovaal's third prophecy, and sure enough, Sargeras had manifested an unholy blade of gargantuan proportions and thrust it deep into Azeroth.

Her musings were interrupted by quite possibly her least favorite person, Jastor Gallywix.

"Oh, Warchief? A moment of your time?"

"*One* moment," she said.

He took more than that, of course, spinning a lengthy tale about discovering a substance that was "Truly phenomenal. Unique!" on the island of Kezan. Gallywix had liked it so much, he'd made it into a decoration for his cane. And now he'd run across more of this substance. A great deal more.

It was seeping up from the ground, at the base of Sargeras's sword.

And you shall hold the blood from that wound, and sense its power. Zovaal's fourth prophecy; so hard on the heels of his third.

Sylvanas took the cane and touched the golden orb at its top.

Later, she would try to tell Nathanos what she had experienced, but words failed her. Suddenly, everything was possible. Just as the Jailer had promised. Sylvanas felt as though she could raise and fell cities, cultures, perhaps worlds—could create and destroy and create again. Energy pulsed through her, and ideas, sharp, keen, brilliant ideas.

It would change everything.

The war against the Burning Legion had ended as it had started: but this time with not one, but two, of the Jailer's prophecies being fulfilled.

The letter was brief and to the point:

> Our favorite spot.
> Tomorrow.

It was signed simply: A.

It was so typical of Alleria, Sylvanas thought. Blunt and assuming compliance. The bluntness could have been attributed to the need to make sure the letter, if intercepted, was mysterious enough so that its author could not be identified. But the assumption that simply because Alleria had asked, Sylvanas would be there, proved that Alleria was still much the same despite a millennia spent fighting demons.

Sylvanas's first instinct was to march to the nearest sconce and feed the letter to the flame within. But her second . . .

There were many reasons to deny the request, all of them obvious.

She had no fear, of course. She was stronger now than she had ever been. Could she learn anything of value by meeting with her sisters? Could she convince them to join her? Such an attempt with Vereesa had failed, but beneath all of this, she realized there was something else she could gain by seeing them, even if it was only to test her resolve, her dedication to the Jailer's cause—

"My lady, you have a visitor who will not give his name, but insists on being introduced only as 'a child of the blood.'" Nathanos's newly handsome visage twisted into a scowl. "There is something not right about him. I do not trust him."

Sylvanas's eyes widened, and her mind flashed back, as it did so often, to her conversations with the Jailer.

When you have made your choice, send a Val'kyr to tell me. And I shall then send you a child of the blood.

She rolled up the letter and tucked it into her belt. "Send him to my quarters," she said. It was the most private place in the entire Undercity. She knew this for a fact; she had abandoned sleep long ago and used the time wisely.

At Nathanos's look of annoyance and utter confusion, she said, "I believe he has a very important message to deliver. Trust me, my champion."

Sylvanas waited in her quarters for the "child of the blood," leaving the door open. She had not been there in some time; these days, she was seldom even in the Undercity, let alone her private room.

"My lady," Nathanos said in a voice that dripped disdain, "your visitor." He bowed, eyed the "visitor" one last time, and left.

He was indeed no one Sylvanas had known, in life or in death. Most blood elves had perfect features, but his were even more perfect. His mane was thick and black with nary a hair out of place. Nathanos had good instincts; there was something off about this one.

"Ah, Lady Sylvanas," he said. "How good to finally meet you." He looked around at her quarters. "It's almost too small."

Sylvanas was baffled. "For what?"

The elf lowered his chin, looking up at her. A slow smile spread across the too-perfect features, wide, wider, *too wide*—

The stranger had been right.

Her quarters *were* almost too small.

How he had managed to hide the reek of fel, Sylvanas did not know. But then again, the "unseen guests" were masters of disguise.

In a flurry of smoke, a dreadlord now stood in place of the sin'dorei, cloven hooves planted firm on the cold stone, his horns scraping the ceiling, and his wings tightly folded in the now cramped place. He already had his hands in front of him, palms up in a placating gesture, as Sylvanas gathered herself to attack.

"He told you to watch for the child of the blood, did he not?" the deep voice rumbled.

Sylvanas blinked. "You?" she breathed, barely believing it.

"The Banished One has sent me to you," the demon continued. "I am Mal'Ganis." A thick, gray lip curled in cruel amusement. "I believe you know the name."

Oh, she did. Arthas had ranted about him at length whenever he was frustrated or angry.

"So it seems we have two acquaintances in common, then," she said.

"Our master, and his failed minion, yes."

"The Jailer is not my master, demon," she said. "Not if you are running errands from him to me." She smiled again.

This time he did not smile. His wings reflexively tried to open, only to be thwarted by the smallness of the room. "Perhaps we can converse in a more open space."

"This is the most secure place in my kingdom. We will speak here." Her strong sense of purpose, it seemed, did not overshadow the delight she had always felt in taking the arrogant down a peg.

He snarled impotently, then composed himself. "You have been told of the Banished One's goals. Now that you have proven worthy, it is time for you to learn the particulars of his plan."

"I, too, would withhold information until I was certain of my ally's trustworthiness," Sylvanas replied coolly.

Mal'Ganis did not like this, either, and her smugness grew. She was starting to enjoy this.

"You know of the Arbiter, and that she and the Jailer are two parts of a whole," the demon said. She nodded, and he continued. "And that anima, the essence of a mortal soul, is the fuel that feeds the Shadowlands. It is *everything*."

"Yes," Sylvanas replied. "And if you continue to treat me like a child needing a primer, I have better things to do."

"No, Lady Sylvanas, you do not," the dreadlord replied. "You must make your purpose his, and the first thing he requires is power and resources."

"Finally, something useful. I presume you are about to tell me how I can do this?"

"Anima is everything," he repeated, "and since we have eliminated the Arbiter, every soul that enters the Shadowlands is flowing into the Maw."

He looked very satisfied with himself, as well he might. Sylvanas was startled at the revelation. She ceased toying with the demon and instead demanded, "How?"

"Great souls, good or dark, kind or cruel, have more anima. Ordinary souls, less. Can you imagine, then, Sylvanas Windrunner, the power that a world's soul—a titan's soul—might have?"

"I asked how, demon. Spare me your endless musings."

The dreadlord clucked his tongue. "You are mortal, the binding of flesh with soul. But we are beings of magic, and the nature of magic can be altered . . . with enough effort and patience. You call me demon because that is what we wanted you to believe we were, a deception that took millennia to unfold. But in truth, the nathrezim were formed by the hand of Sire Denathrius of Revendreth, a true ally of the Jailer's cause for longer than you can comprehend."

Sylvanas could scarcely believe it. Except . . . she could. The powers Zovaal possessed even now continued to challenge her definition of *vast*. It was unnerving to think of how long he had been there, how patient he must have been, and how much foresight he possessed, to sow seeds that took millennia to grow.

"And just as my kind learned how to alter our own natures to infiltrate every plane of the cosmos, we stoked the mad titan's fear of the Void to blind him to our true purpose. When he raged at the time it took his fallen demons to wake in the Twisting Nether, we told him we could forge him a resurrection engine that would make his armies rise again in an instant. All it would require is the necessary fuel—the soul of a world infused with the power of Death."

Sylvanas's mind raced as she recalled their recent war against the Legion. The Broken Shore. The Tomb of Sargeras. And . . .

"Argus," she realized.

The dreadlord smiled as if at a clever pupil. "The Arbiter was made to judge mortal souls, not the mad, hate-filled essence of a broken world. Yet by infusing Argus with the magic of Death, we ensured that once he had been struck down by eager mortals empowered by the meddling titan pantheon, the soul of Argus would fire like an arrow into the heart of the false Arbiter. Now every mortal soul, along with every drop of anima wrung from their meaningless existences, brings the Banished One closer to reshaping reality."

For a moment, old patterns of thinking intruded upon her. Fury, at the thought that the Burning Legion, who had destroyed so many worlds, who had targeted and been rebuffed by Azeroth's denizens so many times, was the Jailer's instrument.

No, she reminded herself. *We are on the same side now. That is nothing compared with what we will achieve together.*

Sylvanas realized that even when she had accepted Zovaal's offer after being named warchief, part of her still harbored at least a few shreds of doubt. Those doubts were dwindling rapidly.

"Though it's clear you enjoy boasting of your cleverness, that cannot be the only reason you've traveled all this way, Mal'Ganis," she said. "I presume I have some part to play in what comes next."

The nathrezim sneered as he nodded. "Indeed. With all mortal souls now flowing to the Maw, the Jailer merely asks that you continue to do what you do best: *kill.* Unleash death upon your world on a scale never before witnessed. Every soul you send screaming into the afterlife makes the Banished One stronger. And when the time is right, Sire Denathrius will unleash the torrent of anima he has quietly been hoarding to feed the Maw with power. The covenants of the Shadowlands will continue to descend further into drought and disarray, and no one will be left to oppose us."

"And then the Jailer will be free to remake the engine of death."

Mal'Ganis held up a clawed forefinger in a chiding gesture. "Freedom is such a mortal desire. The Banished One seeks not merely to break free of his confinement in the Maw. He seeks a forbidden realm hidden even from the Eternal Ones who rule the Shadowlands. Within it lies the Sepulcher, which holds the secrets of those who shaped the cosmos itself. It is from that sacred place that he will remake all there is, into all that can be."

Sylvanas narrowed her eyes. "I know why I have sided with the Jailer's cause, Mal'Ganis. But what do you hope to gain from your allegiance?"

The demon smiled. "Death comes for the soul of this world, Banshee Queen. When the Jailer succeeds and all of reality is born anew, those who served faithfully will be rewarded in kind."

"Is there anything else?" Ally of Zovaal or no, Mal'Ganis was not someone with whom she wished to spend more time than was necessary.

The dreadlord laughed. "You have just been told to do what you like to do best, Lady Sylvanas. I can think of little to add to that."

"Then begone," she said, "and tell my *partner* I will do everything I can to manifest our plan with all speed."

The smile faded at her brusque dismissal and choice of words. Irritated, he merely nodded. Sickly yellow green fel magic swirled about his frame, and then he was gone.

Sylvanas did not leave immediately. Something about the demon's words stung. She should not rise to the bait; demons were masterful at manipulating others.

Was killing really what she liked to do best? It was an unpleasant thought. It reminded her of the Scourge, of Arthas. *I am no mindless killer,* she thought. She was born and raised a hunter. Of course she understood how to kill. She did it by necessity and, when she lived, for sustenance. If there was sometimes pleasure in the act, it was because the deed was satisfying in some way. She was not a monster.

Sylvanas removed the letter from her belt, reread it, then went to a sconce and set it aflame. Its message was simple and instantly memorized; but nothing good would come of this missive being discovered. Certainly the Jailer would not be pleased if he knew that a few of her old ties still bound her, one way or another.

She would go . . . but she would not go alone. Sylvanas would assess her sisters, challenge the softness that persisted inside her. She would put an end to it . . . and to her sisters as well.

In the meatime, Sylvanas wanted a distraction. She left to find Nathanos and begin the plan she and the dreadlord had discussed: How to send still more anima to the Maw. Perhaps they would start with Stormwind.

The Jailer wanted a river of souls flowing to him?

Sylvanas Windrunner would send him an *ocean*.

CHAPTER TWENTY-SIX

"I told myself I would not return," Sylvanas said, standing in Eversong Woods beneath a beautiful blue sky as golden leaves fluttered in a soft wind. She knew better than most that the dead did not hear things said by their graves, and yet she spoke. Perhaps she simply needed to hear her own voice reasoning things out after the confusing and, yes, painful reunion she'd had with her sisters.

Lirath's grave was completely covered by thick grass, its gently swelling mound softening, flattening with time. Had the flesh decayed yet? Could she raise her brother, bring him back? Could Lirath, after all, be the sibling who stayed with her in Vereesa's stead?

She removed her glove and reached to brush her fingers over the healthy grass, springy and soft, and remembered lying on such grass and gazing up at clouds passing by. A younger, more innocent world; a younger, more innocent self, untouched then by time and sorrow and death.

Even though this was a grave, with the corpse of a youth who had barely tasted life in its earthen embrace, there was less of sorrow here than on any given day in the Undercity. For all her championing of the Forsaken, Sylvanas realized that, in the end, she did not wish such a fate on anyone. Not on Alleria or Vereesa, and certainly not on Lirath.

"The fear and pain of your death should be the only pain you ever know, Little Lord Sun," Sylvanas said. "I won't inflict more."

She turned her face up to the sun, closing her eyes, remembering those bygone moments. "I met with our sisters today. We all wanted to see, I think, if we could salvage anything from the early days. I needed to know. In some ways, things felt the same. But in most, they did not. Alleria wields power now, as I do, in a way—hers is the power of the Void. Mine—" She lifted a gloved hand, opening her eyes and watching the purple-black smoke twine about it like an insubstantial snake. "—is death. Vereesa's only power is the one she has always had—that of the peacemaker. She is . . . harder, now, but she still wants the family to have some semblance of happiness." Sylvanas pressed her lips together for a moment. "It is no longer possible."

She reached to touch the base of her throat, where the sapphire had once lain. "We stood on the balcony above the ocean and gave our necklaces to the sea."

A memory, of love and terror crescendoing as Sylvanas swam out to what she thought was Lirath's corpse, only to have him laugh at the prank with bright eyes.

"I miss you," she whispered. "But you were with us today, in a way. Even with so much dividing us—life, death, centuries . . . you were the one thing that still mattered. We knew you wanted us to at least try, and I do know you would be glad of my restraint," Sylvanas said. She had taken some of her dark rangers with her. They had stayed hidden, waiting for the order to slaughter Alleria and Vereesa. Sylvanas never gave it. "Though . . . I cannot help but wonder, little brother, what you would think of other decisions I am making."

She surrendered to the impulse and stretched out fully on the sun-warmed grass. "If—*when*—the Jailer and I succeed, everything will be different. We could see Mother and Father again. We could see each other. I couldn't find you in the Shadowlands, I wanted to search for you . . ." Her voice trailed off.

Surely Lirath would want that, too. She wanted to think that he'd have understood her when no one else did, as he always had in life.

So many moments go to make up a life, she thought. *Sweet ones, ordinary ones . . . lethal ones.*

Sylvanas recalled seeing Alleria, her arrows spent, running at top speed toward the safety of the tree with Mauler's breath hot on her heels. The look in her parents' eyes as they danced; the moment when she had learned of their violent murder. The startling agony of Vereesa's refusal, shattering a heart that Sylvanas knew ought to be long past breaking. The feel of infant Lirath's soft hand, clasping her finger as she held him for the first time.

Love, and courage, her father had said to her. She had taken those words and pressed them deep into her fierce heart. They had been guideposts for her youth, and she had breathed her last still convinced that they meant something.

How distant those feelings seemed now. How empty the words were.

"I tell myself this, at least," she whispered, softly for imaginary ears alone. "But love and courage are not distant, or empty. Foolish as it is, baby brother, dangerous, even, if the Jailer learns of it . . . a stubborn, stupid piece of me cannot let go of them." But in the end, that was irrelevant. It was useless to attempt to hold back the tide she herself was helping set in motion. There was no hope in anything of the mortal world; not in family, or tradition.

"Not even in love, or courage."

Sylvanas sat up slowly, thinking of the undead things that wandered about her childhood home. She and her sisters had worked together to slay them. But by now, Sylvanas knew, more would have taken their place.

She could slay them a thousand times, but they would never stop coming. *What a futile exercise it was,* she thought. One could try to hold on to something, claim it for a while, but nothing lasted.

Sylvanas got to her feet. She did not need her sisters. She needed nothing, no one, save her purpose. What was to come—the reward, the glory, the peace of true justice—it would be because of her.

The Jailer had been clever, to let her wander the Shadowlands and learn this lesson with her own eyes. No matter what she did, what anyone did, nothing mattered except the end in her sight.

CHAPTER TWENTY-SEVEN

Sylvanas did not delude herself that her devotion to the For-saken was selfless. That she and they had a bond was undeni-ably true, and it was not a weak one. They had helped each other survive, after learning how to recover their minds and wrest back control of their bodies, corpses though those bodies might be. They had given one another purpose, as well. A reason to keep going. It was a role deeply familiar to a former ranger-general. Care, duty, and the protection of her people had been practically given to Sylva-nas in her mother's womb.

Her gift to them was more than protection. It was also free will and a sense of belonging—what the Lich King and the world had denied them. The bond was strong, and genuine . . . and had also been designed to serve Sylvanas.

They had bestowed a sort of royalty upon her, their beloved Ban-shee Queen, their revered Dark Lady of the Forsaken. There was yet a wound in Sylvanas caused by the rejection of those she had held dear in life, and the Forsaken's near worship of her helped to soothe that old ache.

But now, it seemed, both were changing. Sylvanas had emerged from a second death with knowledge never before brought into this world. She saw and observed with fresh eyes, and when everything she had been told had unfolded as the Jailer assured her it would, she allowed herself to believe in and embrace the escape he envisioned not just for himself, or her, but for everyone.

And so her world had shifted. All here was temporary, an acknowledged truth that was now glaring in its blazing brightness. It was greater than a simple correction of an error, restoring a balance. It was erasure of what was broken, feeble, cruel, and replacing it with an order that was just and all-encompassing. No soul would ever be forced to remain caught in an afterlife perhaps suitable to them, but with no room for another. No spirit would need to wonder for all eternity, *Where is he? Will I ever see her? Are they happy?*

She would have never gone searching for a ghost.

This was her goal now, not the well-being of the Horde she led and the people who loved her. And it would seem that, as their Dark Lady changed, so did they. Sylvanas returned from the war to find a group that wanted to reject her gift of sentient unlife, opting for the final death rather than being raised again.

And when the new Stormwind king approached her about a gathering with an emphasis on "family" and "reunion," it was a slap in the face to she who had lost them all, one way or another. This unexpected turn had revealed that the Forsaken were less unified than she believed, at a time when she needed every one of them to obey without questioning if she and the Jailer were to achieve their goal.

In the end, Sylvanas agreed to reunite the Forsaken with their living families. If there was anything Sylvanas Windrunner trusted, it was the inevitable rejection from the living. There was *always* rejection from the living—even within the Horde. The Forsaken would be hurt and angry—perhaps enraged—and she would be there to remind them that in the end, they could only trust their own to understand them.

Sylvanas would shortly regret the soft impulse. A handful of hours later, she stood on the gate watching Forsaken fleeing toward the Alliance stronghold, with Calia Menethil—

—a sudden shock of anger flashed through her at even thinking the name—

—calling for the Forsaken to abandon their Dark Lady, their heritage, all they had struggled for, and defect to the Alliance.

My lady! What are your orders?

The Jailer continued to be right. Once again, her hand had been forced. Once again, she had been betrayed. Been *forsaken.* Allowed her emotions to get the better of her.

How often must I witness this hateful pattern of helplessness before we can act?

But she could act now.

She lifted her bow.

"Word has started to reach the general populace," Nathanos told her. "They are gathering outside. They are demanding explanations." He did not add, *And you had best give them something quickly,* but he did not need to.

"Good," Sylvanas said. "Have the guards go through the city and bring everyone up to the surface. It's the only place large enough to contain them all. And Nathanos—bring me the ones who returned."

Nathanos obeyed her, the guards obeyed him, and the Forsaken obeyed the guards. This was as it should be, as it must be. Sylvanas knew that "free will" was an illusion, but it was one that needed to be maintained if she and the Jailer were to succeed. She could not risk an insurrection, not now. The fact was, whatever her reason, Sylvanas was the one who had killed the Forsaken on the battlefield, not Anduin Wrynn. People liked things simple, clean, easy to understand. Few appreciated the nuances of politics—especially among the Forsaken, whose rotting brains were often their worst enemies. But her father had taught her that sometimes, the fate of millions hung on the right—or wrong—words.

So she would give them something easy to parse. And it would have enough truth in it to ring true. Nathanos had managed to find those who had returned early from the Gathering, disillusioned with the living, but even they looked shaken by the sudden turn of events. Some of them even pulled away from Sylvanas.

But one didn't. Annie Lansing, who had brought a basket of sachets, fresh flowers, and scarves to lessen the horror the humans would experience upon seeing them. She had hoped her mother would truly see her—Annie, her daughter, taken too soon. But all the human could see was the broken, rotting body.

"We should have listened to you, Dark Lady. We were terribly wrong."

You were, Sylvanas thought. *Now you understand.*

Sylvanas was taken off guard for a moment by the tone of the crowd. Some were weeping, some were raging. Some even had weapons. Everyone wanted answers—and answers she would have for them.

She took a position atop the gate. Beside her stood Annie, and above the crowd floated her Val'kyr. Sylvanas spoke in a loud, clear voice, amplified by her banshee ability so it carried to every listening ear.

"Forsaken! My people! Listen to me!"

Many faces in various stages of decomposition turned to her. Most of the talking died down, but not all of it.

"I have come to tell you exactly what happened in Arathi today. Rumors have begun to spread, passed by these who are understandably alarmed. I understand that you are confused. You are hurting. You are my people, and you deserve answers."

Now she had their attention. Even the skeptical ones were watching. Her gaze flickered to the Val'kyr.

"You know that the Forsaken are precious to me. I found you, I brought you together, I gave you a home and a place in this world. I found allies to protect you. And recently"—Sylvanas gestured skyward—"I have sought and discovered Val'kyr in an effort that we not become extinct. I continue to look for anything that will safeguard you, my people. And that is why I viewed the young Alliance king's offer with deep concern."

The Val'kyr continued to fly over the crowd, circling, now and then dropping downward, as if promising to protect them. They understood exactly what their mistress was doing.

"I warned you that you might be disappointed. Annie ... please. Your brethren in undeath deserve to know how callously your own mother treated you."

Sylvanas stepped back, and Annie stepped forward. While she told the story of how she wore a bandanna to hide her deformity and brought a nosegay to conceal any scent that might trouble the living, the Banshee Queen's gaze scanned the crowd. There—that one. He was talking to two others. To Nathanos, Sylvanas murmured, "Those three. Take them for questioning when the crowd disperses."

Nathanos nodded, slipping away to obey his lady.

Sylvanas returned her attention to the crowd. "I feared in my heart that this was a plan to attack us under a flag of truce. And so it was. The king of the Alliance sent a priestess onto the field, allegedly to help heal if there were any wounded. That priestess was none other than Calia Menethil. *Menethil!*"

She allowed her own loathing to infuse her voice, and the hated name drew the desired response.

The crowd roared in anger, shaking bony fists, their ruins of faces contorted in loathing. She let it crest and die, then continued.

"She began to subvert our people! She wanted them to leave our home, our family—their true family—and go to the human lands, where they would be despised and attacked. Is that what a family should do? Take someone away from a place of acceptance and parade them around as a hideous *freak*?"

Her voice cracked slightly at the word. Sylvanas found she could still dip into the well of pain, of hurt, of loss, of betrayal, when it suited her. The break in her voice was genuine, and they heard it and responded.

Sylvanas is the one who comes in my nightmares, Halduron had said. *That ghostly* thing *obeying the butcher's commands.*

And that, my old friend, Lor'themar had replied, *is how we know Sylvanas truly is no more.*

Cries of *No! Never!* swelled up from the crowd. Once more, addressing the execution of the traitors, and she would be done.

"You killed those who tried to come back!"

The voice came from the front, and Sylvanas stilled. She looked for who had spoken. She could not drag him out, not in so public a space, but she had to find—ah, there he was.

"Those who accepted the empty promises of Calia Menethil could have put innocent Forsaken in jeopardy. As for those who appeared to be returning—I had no certainty of their loyalty. What if they had planned to flee, but lost courage at the last minute, or were simply waiting for a chance to swell their ranks by whispering promises of the impossible?"

Sylvanas looked down. "I made a decision I believe to have been in the best interests of protecting the Forsaken. I could not permit *anyone* who was not completely loyal to return to our home. I need to protect you, my people, my true loyalists, from that sickness born of an ultimately foolish hope. Sometimes one must lose a limb to save the body. The poison must be excised, and from this day forward, I will hear no more talk of reunions. I will defend the Forsaken, no matter the cost it might be to me personally. I will defend *you*—and I will fight for you. Do I have your loyalty?"

The cheer was louder this time, as loud as damaged throats could make it. The protester was silent. So be it. Sylvanas stood, the wind playing with her hair, the hand that clutched her bow raised to the sky as she accepted their homage.

She found herself grateful for the Gathering. It had enabled her to weed out those who could be trouble in the future. Sylvanas was past long-term plans for her people, though they did not know that. She measured time far differently now.

Those below, with a few exceptions who would be removed, were ready to follow her wherever she led them. They were the unwitting soldiers in her war, and like any good general, she would position them where they were most likely to advance the cause.

There were fleeting thoughts of regret, but Sylvanas banished them. She had led the Forsaken as best she could. There was no time for inner conflict.

From this moment on, the Forsaken would either be loyalists . . . or anima.

CHAPTER TWENTY-EIGHT

S ylvanas turned her attention away from the distractions of family and Forsaken, and toward her true purpose. She had already begun speaking with Nathanos. War could kill two birds with one stone. Of course, many of her own people would fall. War was never without cost. But in the end, every casualty would advance the ultimate goal of a new reality for everyone. They would all be soldiers dying for the best cause possible, although they would not have the comfort of knowing that.

It would give both sides something to focus on. Something to hate, to become reckless for. Peace would not speed the process to which Sylvanas now devoted herself.

She would reach out to High Overlord Varok Saurfang, a tactician with a mind as sharp as her own when it came to strategy, and devise a plan of attack.

Sylvanas knew her goals were far different from the story she wove for Saurfang, yet the strategy—shifting from a direct attack on Stormwind to taking Darnassus and holding it hostage—satisfied the orc's martial plan and her own, far more complex one.

They met daily, refining their tactics, and at one point Sylvanas found herself standing over a map of the world, a wave of something like weariness sweeping over her. She had been a master of strategy before her death, and a master of manipulation afterward. But brilliant as a plan might be, it was always possible that the unexpected could derail everything. She was tired of maintaining the façade that she cared about the Horde—or, if she was being honest, even the Forsaken. She wanted to finally leave this prison behind. Shed what trapped her. Tear it all down. Rebuild, with every step right and just.

Under Saurfang's plan, the road to Stormwind would take years to walk. Sylvanas was undead; she could wait for years. As for Zovaal—he had existed since . . . possibly before time, he could wait a little longer, too. It was so very mortal of her to be impatient, but she could not deny that she was.

The plan she and Saurfang had concocted was flawed, if freeing the Jailer was the ultimate goal. It would take too long. What Sylvanas had come to realize was that she wanted Saurfang to design a plan that helped her accomplish her *true* goal, and she could not do that without confiding in him. She tamped down the impatience and said nothing . . . for now.

"I fear our high overlord will not understand the goal as you and I do," Nathanos said later that day. They were riding together on their undead steeds in the Barrens, the night sky clear and spattered with stars. Their goal was conversation; their sport was killing. They had ventured into the thorny heart of Razorfen Kraul, where the fierce-appearing quilboar continued to attack them even though the bodies were starting to pile up. More anima for the Jailer's army.

"It's so clear," she protested. "So obvious. He has suffered grievous loss. He has been through wars and done terrible things. I would think he would be chief among those who would long to champion a just existence."

She paused, aimed, and brought down a snarling, bristling quilboar. "Putress killed Dranosh with the blight, and Arthas took the body with him and raised him to fight against the Horde he and Saurfang both loved. If we succeed ... Saurfang could be with his son and mate again."

"He believes that to be true regardless," Nathanos said. They heard the telltale sounds of the beasts, and Nathanos loosed his arrow. "The orcs believe the shaman speak with their ancestors, and there appears to be ample proof that this is indeed the case. No, we are not lucky enough to ever be completely rid of orcs."

"He believes, but he does not *know*," Sylvanas pointed out. "I do."

"Yes. Because you have met the Jailer. Because you have seen what lies beyond the veil." He turned to look at her, his eyes glowing in the darkness. "I have not, but I believe you because I know you. If you tell me you have seen this, I know you have."

"You think I would not lie to you if it served my purpose?"

"Oh yes. But my lady, you also know *me*. And you know that lying to me would never serve your purpose."

"Perhaps you are right at that," she replied. "On both counts," she added. "Saurfang does not like or trust me. He executes my orders, he prizes his honor, and he loves the Horde. I think whatever order I gave him as my high overlord, he would obey. But ... I do not know how to make him trust me."

Nathanos was diplomatically silent at that. He was, indeed, probably correct. Strategist though Varok Saurfang was, this was most likely far beyond the old orc's ken. And yet ... to have him by her side along with Nathanos, carrying forth her banner before those who perforce needed to be kept ignorant, to comprehend that she worked toward something that would benefit everyone—and bring him his family—that would ease things considerably.

She and the orc would meet again tomorrow. This time, Sylvanas would steer the conversation into other directions than usual. She would test Saurfang, to see if he was able to share her vision. And if he did ...

Sylvanas allowed herself a slight smile.

———

"Were you noticed?" Sylvanas asked as Saurfang entered the hold.

"Of course," he replied. "The spies are getting bolder."

"Let them feel bold while they may," Sylvanas said. Saurfang headed toward the table at the center of the war room. Sylvanas followed him.

"Before we begin," she said, "something has been on my mind."

He grunted, indicating she should continue.

"I find it odd that, as we two plan and strategize about a war to end all wars, you have never mentioned my recent actions which might well have started a war much, much sooner."

Saurfang sighed, turning from the table to regard her evenly. "You speak of the Gathering."

"Ah, you stand on courtesy. Some are calling it the Slaughter." No one was, actually. No one had dared. But she wanted to see the warrior's reaction.

"It concerned your people, took place near your lands, and, in the end, did not result in a war. There was no reason to mention it."

"I killed my own citizens. Doesn't that trouble you?"

"You had your reasons," he said. "Most were actively defecting."

"But others were not," she said. "Was that . . . honorable?"

"Warchief," he said. "The day passes. We should get to—"

She shook her head. "No. I have asked my high overlord for his opinion, and I shall have it."

He rumbled, soft and low, and there was an edge to his voice when he spoke. "It is over, Warchief. It does not matter what I think."

Sylvanas was on high alert now, moving slowly, gracefully, toward him. "Oh, but it does. Answer me."

"Since you have so ordered," Saurfang said. "It is appropriate to kill traitors, if that is the warchief's decision. I doubt that a former historian and some mercenaries hired to guard farm wagons posed much of a threat to Horde intelligence, but they should not have fled the field."

"Even if they wanted to be with their families?" Sylvanas did not care one way or another if Saurfang thought her "honorable." There was a tacit agreement that they were long past that—and that the unspoken acceptance on Saurfang's part did not sit well with him. Sylvanas was probing him in an effort to discover where he drew the line between honorable and dishonorable—and where he stood with regard to reunions with loved ones.

"Even then," Saurfang said. "Loyalty to you, to the Forsaken, the Horde . . ." He shook his head, the two white braids on either side of his head swinging slightly with the motion. "One cannot avoid making painful choices, if one lives long enough. They made theirs and paid for it."

"But not those who were returning," she pressed.

"You cannot execute people for what you *think* they will do, Warchief."

She didn't answer. Saurfang, his thoughts elsewhere for the moment, continued. "As for family . . . Dranosh died a warrior's death. He was not responsible for the evil things he did. The Lich King took his will. My son had no choice."

"Have you noticed how much of our history revolves around choices—and the lack thereof?" Sylvanas said. Her voice was soft, soothing, inviting conversation. "Fighting for free will . . . and being denied. Making choices and dying for them—dying even if you did not make the choice, or chose something different. There are times when it seems so terribly unfair. Unjust. Innocents die, while their murderers flourish. If you could change something, Varok—bring your son back, whole and healthy, or even remake existence—would you?"

Saurfang stared at the table. His gaze traveled to Stormwind, to Orgrimmar, to Darnassus. And to Northrend, where it lingered. Where his son had fallen and been turned by the Lich King.

"No one should have that power," Saurfang said. "Even if they wished to use it for good causes . . . who am I, who is *anyone*, to determine what is best, or right, or wrong? I cannot see all ends, nor can you, Sylvanas." He looked at her then, with his small, dark eyes. His lips curved around his tusks in a bitter chuckle. "Do not worry. I am not engaging in a secret coup, if that is what you are trying to get from me."

So, she hadn't quite deceived him. He'd figured out something was behind this conversation—though he could not possibly guess at the truth. *Fair enough.*

Sylvanas smiled self-deprecatingly. "I fear I was being too obvious. Thank you for answering my questions. It is only that so much is at stake now, I must be absolutely certain I can trust those with whom I share my secrets."

"The goal is a worthy one, Warchief."

Ah, Saurfang, you have no idea.

He failed her, as everyone did, sooner or later.

Saurfang had disobeyed a direct order to kill the night elf archdruid, Malfurion Stormrage. The blow would have been "dishonorable."

There was no such thing as honorable or dishonorable any longer in Sylvanas's mind. There was only that which advanced the ultimate cause, or that which hindered it. And Saurfang had done the latter. She would be watching him.

They had done it, as she knew they would: cut a dreadful swathe through Ashenvale, arriving at Teldrassil, which they would occupy and hold. She was issuing orders as flames crackled around her, and the screams of the wounded filled the smoky air.

Yet somehow in that cacophony, the soft voice of a dying kaldorei caught her attention. "Why?" the young huntress whispered, blood pumping from her body as she drew harsh, quick breaths. "Only innocents remain in the tree."

"This is war," Sylvanas said in a cool, clipped tone.

"No," the stubborn night elf persisted, struggling with every breath. "This is hatred . . . rage . . . Windrunner. You were . . . defender of your people!"

The reminder stung, unexpectedly. It was true. She had once been like this elf, dying, trying to defend the land she loved from an invader intent on destroying it.

"I remember a fool," she said. And she had been. How small the ranger-general seemed now, how tiny and insular her focus. Unaware of the trap that life was; always striving, never winning.

"Life is pain," Sylvanas told the elf. Bleak, purposeless, useless pain, the worst kind—without meaning or sense. "Hope fails." It did. It needed to. Hope clouded the judgment, the comprehension.

Only an uncaring heart will turn away from the trap baited with hope, for hope is the worst illusion of them all.

To her surprise, the kaldorei's eyes welled with tears, shimmering and radiant blue.

Impulsively Sylvanas wiped the tears away. "Don't grieve," she said. And then she revealed a promise; a secret that the night elf would not understand, not now, but would, one day. "You'll soon be with your loved ones."

All lives ended, eventually. All souls must go to some afterlife, unless something untoward happened to chain them to a mortal plane. And in a way, the lives the Jailer had asked Sylvanas to deliver were ending a threat. Righting the grievous wrong the makers had done to all that existed.

Wars were always fought for ideals, after all. No one fought a war simply to kill, and neither did Sylvanas. She was waging a war against an eternity of injustice and coldness. Soldiers signed up to battle and lost their lives for far lesser things: money, land, nations, birth order . . .

There would be pain. There would be grief, and loss, and blood, and death. So very much of it.

And for a while, after death, there would be terrible torment. This young hunter would taste that soon.

But all things ended, and in a very short time even the Maw would cease to be.

"You have made life your enemy," the kaldorei whispered. But she could not know that life was *everyone's* enemy. This elf simply did not understand that yet, but Sylvanas did, and knew it to be a foe—just like death—that had to be defied. And despite the ranger's words, both forces could and would be defeated.

"You cannot kill hope." The voice was fading now.

But Sylvanas could. It was better, and kinder, in a way, that she did. Better that she move boldly.

Arthas's voice floated back to her, still sharp and cruel as the sword with which he took her life. *Kill the innocent first.*

For the first time, Sylvanas did not balk at the recollection. It did not matter where a useful thing came from, only that it was useful. Arthas had been right. But he had also failed. He was a weak vessel in the end, but Sylvanas and Zovaal would succeed where he and the Lich King had not.

And so, certain in her knowledge that the suffering was finite and the joy that awaited them was infinite, Sylvanas Windrunner ordered the World Tree set aflame, and countless numbers of souls surged forward to the Maw, the Jailer, and true freedom.

The screams would fade, the fires die, but the goal was closer than ever. "In the end, it will have been worth it," she whispered, for her ears alone, then turned to face the anguished confusion and fury of Varok Saurfang, who did not, and would not, understand.

In the end, as she had told Vol'jin, death would claim them all.

And it would be she and Zovaal who would remake them.

CHAPTER TWENTY-NINE

The battle between Horde and Alliance raged, and Sylvanas was single-minded of purpose throughout all the events of the Fourth War. She had blighted her own city, though she found herself, perhaps foolishly, unwilling to kill its inhabitants and instead saw to their evacuation. She confronted the young king, so like Lirath, but the enemy nonetheless, in the Lordaeron throne room. Continents joined in the fray, the casualties adding to the swell of anima the Jailer received. And as Sylvanas had anticipated, Saurfang turned traitor and allied with Anduin and the Alliance.

Sylvanas appreciated the faith her loyalists had shown to her. They did not know her plans, but still they followed her, trusting in her actions even when what she did must have seemed like senseless carnage; casual cruelty for sheer sport.

She was fully aware the list of her sins was nearly endless. Teldrassil, of course. The spark that lit the gunpowder keg. Death for the sake of death, or for spite, or simply burning the Great Tree because she could. That was how it had to have seemed. Unleashing the blight Putress had created in his slaughterhouse and torture chamber of a laboratory upon her own people as well as the enemy—unthinkable hitherto. But still they followed her.

As her goal grew closer, Sylvanas grew bolder. Her deeds grew objectively darker, more filled with bloodlust and senseless cruelty. She understood the repugnance the rest of this world had for her. Had she stood where they did now, Sylvanas would likely hold the same opinion as they.

But she did not.

And now, it had come to this: The Alliance and the Horde rebels were marching, united, on Orgrimmar. The war had at last come to her door.

The numbers were not as impressive as they might have been, but Sylvanas had heard that the traitors also were not many. It did not matter. The object, after all, was not for the soldiers to fight. It was for the soldiers to die. That a comparative few remained only meant that Sylvanas had been keeping her side of the bargain with Zovaal for quite some time now. Each life lost, particularly of the greater souls, was more anima, more fuel, which meant they were that much closer to their goal. And there would be many great souls sent to the Maw today.

She could see them approaching now as she and Nathanos stood atop the gates. These were not the proud Horde warriors of the past, with mighty weapons and armor and skill and strength. These were the last, all that remained, of the bloody contest in which Sylvanas and Zovaal were the only winners. They were dusty, and clearly weary; the Horde and Alliance flags were tattered, and what armor she could see was dented and damaged. All around her Sylvanas could hear the happy murmuring of her loyalists anticipating easy kills.

"It will be interesting to see what's left at the end of all this," Nathanos mused.

"If all goes as planned, it will only be a little bit of a mess for you and the others to clean up."

They had discussed the plan many times. Sylvanas knew Nathanos was not appreciative of her instructions to stay behind, but it could not be helped. She had one final, great task to complete before departing for the Jailer's realm after toiling so long on Azeroth. And Nathanos was the only one she trusted; he was the only one who could help her here.

It was a good plan. A sound one. And yet . . . she felt uneasy. Hollow. This was not what victory should feel like.

"This would have been so much easier had Saurfang joined our cause," she said.

"I don't know about that," Nathanos said. "He's helped, in his own way, and is about to help even more." He gestured at the approaching army.

The pair could hear them now: the drums, the stamps of thousands of feet. He was right.

The wind blew, fluttering the flags of the Forsaken and the Horde. The heat beat down. They were silent.

"My lady," said Nathanos, his voice unusually soft, uncharacteristically tentative, "for all the Jailer's words to the contrary, we do have one, you know."

"What?"

"A choice." He turned toward her now, red eyes blazing, brow furrowed. "We do not have to stay here." Nathanos gestured impatiently at the approaching soldiers. "Let them fight it out among themselves. Let the Jailer have his dutiful souls. There will be enough to sate his needs for some time. Thrall, Saurfang, Baine, Jaina, Anduin, Greymane, and all their bravehearted, bright-eyed followers. Do this last thing he requires, and then . . . it could be *over*."

Sylvanas stared at him, unsure as to whether anger or confusion was the right reaction. She settled on both. "What do you mean? Of course we must stay here! Of course I must join Zovaal. This is everything we have worked toward! Have you not been listening? What is done here today, and the next day, and the next—this world, *all* worlds, will rejoice when we have achieved our goal!"

"My lady," he said, and his strong, proud, acerbic voice trembled slightly, "*you* . . . are my world."

She had not expected that, and stared, mute.

"I care not for life, or afterlife. I have all I need here. This little world that is ours and ours alone. We can walk away, disappear, be forgotten. Be together."

"And be happy?"

It was a cruel thing to say. They both knew that happiness was impossible for such as they. If there were moments when it seemed as though it was within their grasp, those moments turned to ash, washed away by the waves of anger and frustration or sometimes an utter lack of feeling at all.

Sylvanas thought of the warmth that living bodies could share in an embrace. The softness of a kiss, the giddiness of shared humor and secrets, and the bittersweet heaviness of grief being eased by the sound of a loved one's beating heart.

Strange, how these things did not feel as shatteringly important when she had them.

We . . . I . . . do not have a choice, she wanted to say, but could not bring herself to utter the words.

"Sylvanas Windrunner!"

The deep, rumbling bellow, full of anger and righteousness, sliced through the silence between them, and the moment, if there ever was one, was gone.

Sylvanas turned to see the old soldier Varok Saurfang standing in front of the gates of Orgrimmar. He looked so tiny, from so far away. And yet his voice was strong.

"I challenge!" he cried. *"Mak'gora!"*

There was no turning back now.

A few hours later, Sylvanas walked in deep snow, icy wind tugging at her hair, and reflected on how this chapter of her existence had ended.

She reached to touch the wound on her still-beautiful face. The mark of Shalamayne. The double-bladed sword of Varian Wrynn, who had once hurled such bitter, vicious words of hatred toward her. Who had come to a war council, and had agreed they could trust each other to defend their world.

She saw the king's weapon again, in the hand of a boy facing brutal realities who strode into Lordaeron clad in golden, glinting armor, the double blades dripping blood on a floor that had been painted in years past with that of yet another king whose bright-haired son had marched through those doors. A pattern of violent death and loss that repeated, unending. She felt again the strange outrage at seeing a gentle soul forced to shed blood. To put himself in danger.

Shalamayne's journey continued, gifted by the young lion to the old soldier. It was Saurfang who had demanded the mak'gora, whom Sylvanas beat handily, and yet somehow, *somehow*, though the sword never touched her till that last blow, when he had pulled the blades apart—one strike missed.

The other . . .

Sylvanas felt again the burst of fury, frustration, and resentment she had felt outside the gates of Orgrimmar. From almost every moment of her existence, she had been trying to help. To save. Alleria and the springpaw. Lirath, from naïveté and idealization that became lethal to him. The quel'dorei, the Forsaken. And now she was trying to save every last ignorant, pathetic creature that walked, swam, flew, or crawled on any world that ever existed.

They would have called her mad. Accused her of lying. At best, accused her of gullibility. But they had not seen what Sylvanas had, or knew what she knew.

The Horde, Saurfang had shouted at her, again and again. *The Horde.* As if it was anything of consequence. As if shouting wishes about something made them true.

It was nothing, nothing at all, and still seething from the hot pain of Shalamayne's bite, she told him so.

For a moment, watching Saurfang gloat, as if he had won, as if winning a foolish duel had saved anything worth saving, Sylvanas could have wished the words back. She was not quite ready for the next stage, but the old orc had forced her hand.

Sylvanas was done with it all. Done with pretending she cared about anything except a better fate than the one all of them would receive, with restraining her usage of the dark power the Jailer had given her. Done with Azeroth altogether.

She straightened and told them the bitter truth. *You are all nothing.*

And yet, Sylvanas thought now, as snow swirled around her, *even so, I will still save us all. So that you may, at last, become* something. *There is no cost too high when eternity is at stake, and once we are done, you will understand, and you will be grateful.*

She took some satisfaction unleashing her anger upon Saurfang in the form of blue-black, smoke-like darkness; the Jailer's gift. And there was release and a sense of justification in the scornful words she heaped upon them, Horde and Alliance alike in their small-mindedness, their ignorance. They stood together today, but that was just a blink. No one knew better than Sylvanas that everything—every person, every ideal, every mountain and river and sky—was finite. Only injustice lasted.

There was no unfinished business, not really. Dribs and drabs of worldly things, a few tendrils of concerns that wound their way into things greater than a sleeping titan.

Let the world be blind. Let it be unaware of, and hostile toward, what lay ahead—and what she had done, and would do, to avert it for every soul. Let the name Sylvanas be on their lips, uttered in tones of anger and hatred for as long as they lived . . . for that would be all too brief a span next to the eternity of justice for which she fought.

Her tasks on Azeroth were over, and now, she was back to the place where her journey to true justice had begun:

Icecrown.

The last time Sylvanas had been here, she was awash in a sea of despair and bleakness, devoid of purpose and unmoored and adrift. How different it was now.

The Jailer had sent her here to defeat the Lich King, take the dread Helm of Domination . . . and tear it apart. It was part of the plan, and it would open many more possibilities. She would be at his side from now on, and together, they would continue their work.

Sylvanas was eager to begin this next phase, but she was also quietly pleased on another level. She had not been able to kill Arthas, but she, Sylvanas Windrunner, would be the one to put an end to the Lich King once and for all. In a way, this was better. The lessons had been brutal, and she would not willingly endure them again, but she was glad to be here, knowing she was doing the right thing.

She thought about other things the Jailer had told her. He needed her aid to find a great but humble soul; one who served truly, selflessly, from the heart. Who put duty to others before anything else. There was a special task for this soul, and he entrusted the selection to her.

Who would it be? Tyrande Whisperwind, the fierce priestess of the night elves? Baine, who defied her? Thrall, the orc raised as human, uniting disparate races under a single banner? Jaina, who had endured much personal pain, but grew past it to become one of the most powerful magi in the world?

All of them would serve, one way or another.

She could see Icecrown up ahead, a dark, looming shape in the whirl of snow, and she smiled.

It was time to tear open the future's path.

INTERLUDE

"I know the rest of the story," Anduin said. She could not read his expression. "You sent the Val'kyr for us. Tested us to find the soul you needed to use as your weapon. And it was me."

Sylvanas nodded.

"And it's been me . . . all along, hasn't it? Except not *me*, really."

"What do you mean?"

"The war council to fight the Legion," he said. "The many chances you had to kill me. The words you used in the throne room. 'The boy's playing soldier,' you said. I thought you were just trying to get under my skin, make me lose focus. But that wasn't it."

Sylvanas suddenly felt as if she were the one in the prison. She did not want to hear what he had to say next.

"You were thinking of someone else. Someone who looked like me, who thought much like I do. Someone you didn't want playing soldier."

"No," she said. "No."

"It all makes sense, now. There was no real reason to not simply use Domination magic and turn me right away, if that was what the Jailer wanted. But instead . . . here you are, telling me things you have likely not shared with anyone . . . trying to save my life. You see him in me, Sylvanas. You see Lirath."

Sylvanas clenched a fist at her side. So this was it—all he had taken away from their time in this place—something he could twist to manipulate her into saving him.

"You wanted me to know you didn't betray my father," he continued, not letting her speak. He was pacing now, agitated, the plate armor clanking. "What was it you said? 'Varian Wrynn's destiny was set in stone, Little Lion.' Because you truly believed that it was. That there was no free will."

"You have no—"

He uttered a short bark of laughter. "Even what you call me, Sylvanas. Little Lion. Just like your Little Lord Sun."

Sylvanas did not want to believe it. She had laid her cards on the table, done all she could to lead him to the right choice. But Anduin was correct in one regard—she had given him something that she hadn't given Lirath. She'd been transparent with him, granted him the wisdom to walk the right path. She hadn't trained Lirath to prevent the atrocities he would face, but she'd hoped to at least spare Anduin the bitter fate that awaited him.

"I am not your brother, Sylvanas," Anduin said now, stepping as close to the barrier as he could. "But I can still help you. If you feel this strongly about him, about me—then your mortality is still with you. I once said that I thought you were lost. But I know better now."

She dragged her gaze up to his, still disbelieving.

"Let me go. We can leave this place. And I will help you. Your goal is worthy. But not the way the Jailer intends to achieve it. Never like that."

Something inside her shattered. "You are a fool, Anduin Wrynn. And you have made one of me as well. Have you been angling to get my sympathy this entire time, to trick me into releasing you? To make me think that I have lost my perspective? That I would turn on the Jailer just because your face resembles someone I once loved?"

She shook her head angrily. "I am done," she said. "I am done with all of this. I leave you to your fate, Anduin."

There's my Lady Moon!

And there's my Little Lord Sun!

Fury made her tremble, and fury gave her speed as she stalked out. He called after her, but she did not halt. Did not look back.

If she did, she was afraid that everything she was would come apart.

EPILOGUE

Sylvanas Windrunner stood in the heart of the Maw, and looked up from her latest kill.

How horribly familiar this place was. How many cruelties she had witnessed here—or performed. But the Maw's time as a place of torment had come to an end. Now no soul was deemed beyond redemption . . . not even hers, it seemed.

Sylvanas had turned to the night elf leader, Tyrande Whisperwind, for her judgment, because she knew no matter how cruel it was, Tyrande's punishment would be just. And so it was.

Tyrande, rigid with rage tightly leashed, had led Sylvanas to the edge of the Maw. It was in this place, Tyrande decreed, that her penance would begin. *Every soul lost in its depths, betrayed or condemned, you shall find and send forth to the Arbiter.*

Both women knew the task was all but impossible. Souls had been entering the Maw since the very creation of the machine of death. Tyrande smiled coldly as she saw the realization on Sylvanas's face.

You will toil there, the high priestess had said, savoring the words, *scouring every darkened reach, until the final soul is free, and you are all that remains. This is how you shall bring renewal to your victims, and my people.*

However long it takes, Sylvanas had replied, *it shall be done.*

Even in the somberness and the shame of her judgment, there had been moments that had moved Sylvanas deeply. She had been allowed to say farewell to Alleria and Vereesa. Now that she was, if not entirely whole, at least some of who she had once been, Sylvanas could see that there was love there, still; awkward and alien to her, but precious. Now that the Jailer was destroyed and the covenants of the Shadowlands were working together once more, there was a slim chance that, one day, she might be able to see her parents . . . and Lirath . . . as well.

Sylvanas had not quite understood how enduring a tether her brother's memory had been for her; binding her, despite all challenges, not just to her mortality, but to all that was good and true. Its tenacity had enabled her to cling to who she was without realizing it. In death, as in life, Lirath had supported and loved her. It had been the source of her greatest pain, this inability to let go, but now she was fiercely glad of every painful moment.

She could not see the Jailer's true face until the moment he chose to reveal it. She had convinced herself that she wanted justice for all beings who lived and died, when she knew in her heart of hearts that what she truly desired was base and small—to do anything to stave off the darkness that she believed awaited her, and to be with those she loved. But then . . . was not that a desire shared by everyone? That was not the sin. The sin, as Anduin had said, was in how she attempted to realize that desire.

Anduin. He had seen it long before she had. The unacknowledged abyssal depth of her pain, of her yearning for connection, had left her vulnerable. Zovaal had exploited that weakness, and to punish her for her refusal to serve him, he had given her back the missing piece of her soul.

She lifted a hand to her chest, where her heart, though not beating, still was.

This . . . *rejoined* Sylvanas she was now could taste remorse. And it was bitter.

The Jailer had taken Shalamayne, the blade that had cut her, the blade of Anduin's father, and forged it into a mourneblade greater even than Frostmourne. *Kingsmourne,* it had been named. And with the now corrupted blade of kings, Sylvanas had forced the same fate upon Anduin that Arthas had on her. Sylvanas had stolen his free will, and had watched it slip away, bit by bit. She had been too greatly in the Jailer's thrall to stop it; too mortal for it not to wound her. And somehow, foolishly, she had clung to the hope that his suffering and hers would truly be worth the dread cost.

So many regrets. Not just for the great injustices she had performed, but the lesser ones, though in their own way they were just as painful. The failure to recognize that what she and Nathanos had in life could have made them happy. Nathanos had seen it. With conscience and kindness restored to her, Sylvanas could, too. Her champion was here, somewhere in the seemingly infinite Maw, with all the other souls her bargain had doomed. Sylvanas would find him. She would always find him.

As for the Little Lion and the Little Lord Sun . . . Sylvanas had seen Anduin Wrynn not as himself, but who she had wished he could be, and so in a way had wronged both him and her brother. But no longer. Her illusions and excuses had been as stripped away as her armor, weapons, and titles had been. There was no ranger-general, no Banshee Queen or Dark Lady. Not here in the Maw. Just Sylvanas Windrunner . . . whoever she might be, now.

Her mind drifted back to the reality of her duty. How proudly she had announced to Arthas and the Jailer that she would never serve. And how right it felt to now be of *service,* and appreciate the difference.

She squared her shoulders. *No matter how long it takes,* she had said to Tyrande. *Let it begin now.*

But before Sylvanas could again stride forward into the vastness of the Maw, she heard a sound. One familiar—and utterly unexpected.

The distinctive *clank* of metal armor.

Hope, Anduin had told her, *is what you have when all other things have failed you. Where there is hope, you make room for healing, for all things that are possible . . . and some that are not.*

Sylvanas Windrunner felt hope rise within her, and for the first time in so very long, she invited it in.

ACKNOWLEDGMENTS

As one might imagine, the task of chronicling Sylvanas Windrunner through her long and complex history was daunting, and it's no surprise that during its writing, Life decided to throw a few extra challenges my way. This book owes a tremendous debt to those behind the scenes who helped me take *Sylvanas* from conception to fruition, offering professional and personal support and their own tremendous skills and experience along the journey. All books are collaborative to one degree or another, media tie-ins even more so, and I am so grateful for my colleagues on this one.

First, a huge thank you to the Warcraft community for supporting me and my work for over twenty years in this fantasy world we all love so much. It's deeply appreciated, and I hope I have done both the ranger-general and the Dark Lady justice.

At Del Rey, thanks goes to my superb editor and friend, Tom Hoeler, with whom I have worked on many projects and who was a steady rock during our collaboration on this one. And to the rest of the Del Rey team for their tireless efforts in bringing this book to life. To my brilliant cover artist Evyn Fong, all I can say is *wow*. A book *is* often judged by its cover, and no author could have had a better one.

I'm grateful to my Blizzard editor, Chloe Fraboni, and our fantastic publishing team. Chloe offered insight and a sharp eye to help bring what might have been a sprawling story into something tight and fast-paced that yet had the depth such an endeavor required. Longtime Blizzard employee Justin Parker made sure we stayed on the path and didn't wander too far from our lore, and our magnificent producer Brie Messina kept us heading in the right direction on another sort of path. Betsy Peterschmidt art-directed our wonderful cover, and Byron Parnell and Derek Rosenberg were powerful allies in aligning all the publishing and marketing details; the book could not have been in better hands.

On the *World of Warcraft* team, narrative lead Steve Danuser was an extraordinary partner. We were in harmony on our vision of the character, and he offered so many inspiring suggestions to make the book as strong as possible. Working with him is a joy. Longtime-friend-turned-co-worker Anne Stickney also brought a keen eye and a big heart to this project—both invaluable.

Truly, thanks goes to the entire team, who work so hard with such passion.

On a final note, over the last nearly five years working together, Terran Gregory and I have spent many happy, thought-provoking (and intense) hours discussing this fascinating character. I deeply appreciate his insights, observations, and inspirations. Thank you, friend.

For Azeroth!

ABOUT THE AUTHOR

CHRISTIE GOLDEN is the award-winning, *New York Times* bestselling author of fifty-six books and more than a dozen short stories in the fields of fantasy, science fiction, and horror. Her media tie-in works include her first novel, *Vampire of the Mists*, which launched TSR's game line; more than a dozen *Star Trek* novels; the Fate of the Jedi novels *Omen, Allies,* and *Ascension* as well as the standalone novels *Dark Disciple* and *Battlefront II: Inferno Squad*. For Blizzard Entertainment, she's contributed five StarCraft novels, including the Dark Templar trilogy, and the Warcraft/World of Warcraft books *Lord of the Clans, Rise of the Horde, Arthas: Rise of the Lich King, War Crimes, Before the Storm,* and *Exploring Azeroth: The Eastern Kingdoms*. In 2017, she was awarded the International Association of Media Tie-in Writers Faust Award and named a Grandmaster in recognition of thirty years of writing. She currently works full-time for Blizzard Entertainment, where she frequents Azeroth on a regular basis.

christiegolden.com
Twitter: @ChristieGolden

ABOUT THE TYPE

This book was set in Caslon, a typeface first designed in 1722 by William Caslon (1692–1766). Its widespread use by most English printers in the early eighteenth century soon supplanted the Dutch typefaces that had formerly prevailed. The roman is considered a "workhorse" typeface due to its pleasant, open appearance, while the italic is exceedingly decorative.

EXPLORE THE WORLDS OF DEL REY BOOKS

READ EXCERPTS
from hot new titles.

STAY UP-TO-DATE
on your favorite authors.

FIND OUT about exclusive
giveaways and sweepstakes.

CONNECT WITH US ONLINE!
⊙ ⨍ 𝕐 @DelReyBooks

DelReyBooks.com